ASSIGNMENT MILAN

A NICO ARGENTI NOVEL

KEN TENTARELLI

ISBN: 978-1-7331773-7-5 (ebook)

ISBN: 978-1-7331773-8-2 (paperback)

This one is for my editor.

1

PALAZZO STROZZI, FLORENCE

SEPTEMBER 1464

Agostino Mozzi, First Chair of The Ten of War, arrived early for the meeting, the one that he had convened. As the bell at nearby San Tommaso church tolled the hour, the door to the grand salon at Palazzo Strozzi swung open and Mozzi's invitees entered: Scala the Chancellor and Corsini the First Chair of The Eight of Guard, the agency responsible for the Guardia and the safety of Florentine citizens.

"These are indeed elegant surroundings," Corsini observed. Looking toward Mozzi, he added, "Certainly superior to your office, Agostino. It must be an urgent matter that brings us here."

Meetings organized by Mozzi were always efficient and without distraction. As soon as the three men were seated, he wasted no time stating its purpose. Looking to Corsini, he said, "You are correct. There is an important matter that needs our attention. As you know, the Chancery collects and analyzes dispatches from our embassies. Recently the Chancery received a disturbing account from our representatives in Milan." He turned his head to face Scala. "Bartolomeo, please tell us about the latest report."

Scala forward and rested his hands on the table. "Two of our embassy staffers in Milan were taking dinner at a restaurant when they overheard a conversation among the duke's advisors and his trade minister. The minister was expounding on a trade negotiation underway that would give the Duchy of Milan overwhelming advantages over Florence. When our staffers heard Florence mentioned they took notice. At first, they thought the claims were idle boasting, but the words took on a threatening tone as the discussion continued. Although our embassy workers heard only fragments of the conversation, they believed it was important, so they entered it in their latest report."

"Prior to 1460, Milan depended on Florence to fund its businesses and its huge army," Mozzi said. "But in the past five years the duchy has grown. Once it was an infant; now it is like a growing child ready to flex his muscles."

Corsini stiffened. With alarm in his voice, he interrupted, "Milan cannot be allowed to make unilateral trade agreements. Maritime treaties govern the international shipment of goods, and Milan is a signatory of those treaties that protect the rights of ships carrying goods to the seaports of all Italian states. My brother's woolen mills depend on fleece imported from England. Milan cannot be allowed to violate the treaties." Corsini's face reddened and his voice rose as he became increasingly agitated. "What if they levy exorbitant tariffs on products delivered to Florentine merchants?"

The others waited until Corsini ended his rant and slumped down in his seat; then, in a calm voice, Scala cited a broader concern. "Nearly half of our people work in the woolen trade. If Milan were to disrupt that industry, they would ruin our entire economy." He slapped a hand down onto the table. "Milan would not have dared to turn against us when Cosimo de Medici was alive, but now they are becoming brazen. We need to know what is happening in Milan and we need to know it now."

Mozzi leaned back in his chair. "We can't be certain the minister was referring to the wool trade. Milan maintains the best armorers on the Italian peninsula to supply its army with swords and mail. Perhaps the minister was referring to shipments of weapons. There have been other worrisome reports as well. What concerns me most is that we have no means to investigate the reports and remedy any potential threats. That is why I called this meeting. It's time for us to act to protect the security of our republic."

Antonio Corsini asked tentatively, "What do you propose, that we establish a network of spies?"

"Perhaps subterfuge will become necessary," Mozzi replied, "but I suggest we begin with diplomacy. Although we are already rich with commissions, I propose that a special commission be formed to investigate and resolve possible threats to our republic, and that it be directed to take immediate action."

The room fell silent as the men considered Mozzi's suggestion and waited for him to detail a plan derived from his experience dealing with foreign states. Before rising to his position as chief administrator of the Florentine military, Mozzi had served as an envoy to Genoa, a Florentine representative to the peace negotiations at Lodi, and the person responsible for security during the Holy Father's visit to Florence.

"My recommendation is to form a Florentine Security Commission composed initially of three members: an investigator skilled in gathering information, a lawyer to seek legal recourse when the evidence warrants, and someone to assess whether adversaries are contemplating military action."

Mozzi looked from one man to another. He judged their expressions as acceptance of his proposal, so he continued. "Antonio, as First Chair of the Eight, you oversee the Guardia, so you should be the one to designate an investigator. The Guardia regularly investigates crimes, so it must have many skilled investigators who could serve our purpose."

Corsini thought for only a moment before responding, "Yes, I can find someone to serve on the commission."

Next, Mozzi turned to Scala, "Chancellor, with your administrative and legal background, you are in the best position to name someone, a lawyer, to deal with legal issues."

Scala hesitated before nodding his agreement. While he willingly accepted the charge, he also recognized the complexity of the matter. Scala's reaction gave Mozzi pause because he too appreciated that finding members for a commission with a yet-to-be-defined purpose was problematic. Nonetheless, he continued, "As a member of the Ten of War, I will search out a military representative." Again, looking to Scala, he said, "To be effective, the commission must operate with the full authority of the Florentine government; therefore, we must bring our proposal to the Signoria since they alone can establish official commissions. As a participant in their meetings, can you bring forth our request that they authorize the formation of a Florentine Security Commission?"

Scala replied, "Yes, I can do that." Scala remained seated as the others rose to leave. His expression showed him to be deep in thought. Mozzi moved to where Scala was sitting and asked, "Are you troubled by my proposal, Bartolomeo?"

"Not at all. I fully agree that action is warranted, and your proposal of a three-man commission seems appropriate. I was pondering who might be the best lawyer to join the commission. I imagine the commissioners will find themselves in different jurisdictions. Perhaps one matter might take them to Milan, and another might have them in Rome."

"Yes, that could be," Mozzi agreed.

"So, ideally, the lawyer appointed to the commission should be familiar with the laws of all jurisdictions. If he were sent to Rome, he would be subject to the laws of the Papal States, and in Milan or Mantua he would need to operate within the laws of those duchies."

Mozzi pulled out a chair and sat beside Scala to listen as the Chancellor reasoned through the complexities. "It is not common for Florentine lawyers to practice outside the republic," Scala continued. "They are versed in our laws, but most have little knowledge of laws and procedures in other states. Very few have represented Florentine clients in foreign tribunals."

Mozzi laughed. "The few who have made their reputations practicing internationally are too wealthy, too old, and too fat for our purpose. I agree, the commission must have a lawyer who knows laws beyond those of our republic. He must understand and appreciate the sensibilities of other states. That may call for a young person with a flexible mind."

Scala sat up straight and brightened. "Nico Argenti."

"Argenti?" Mozzi repeated. "I have not heard that name."

"Did you hear of the village in the Papal States whose sovereignty was threatened by the Lord of Rimini?"

Mozzi spoke slowly as he reflected. "I recall the incident, but not the name Argenti."

"A Florentine relative of one of the villagers called upon Argenti for legal advice. He agreed to help and sought relief on behalf of the village in a Papal States tribunal. Argenti only recently graduated from the law school at Bologna, and he is still awaiting induction into the guild, so he cannot yet practice law, not even here in Florence. Despite that, he took an approach consistent with the laws of the Papal States; then he enlisted a lawyer accredited by the Vatican to prosecute the case."

"Impressive determination and initiative. Do you have personal knowledge of him?" Mozzi asked.

"I have known of him for many years. When he was a youth of about nine years, I attended a lecture that his father gave at the University of Florence. I spoke with Nico after the lecture and was impressed by his curiosity. Years later, I followed his progress when he attended the law school at Bologna. He consistently received high praise from his professors. I have no doubt that he will be a fine lawyer; what gives me pause is that he lacks experience."

Mozzi smiled and replied, "None of us were born with experience. When he first answered the call, even our beloved Pope Pius was an inexperienced novitiate."

"Ah, but His Holiness received guidance from the Holy Spirit."

Mozzi placed a hand on Scala's shoulder and laughed. "Unless Argenti has a connection to the Holy Spirit that is unknown to us, he will be looking to you, my friend, for guidance."

Mozzi's remark caused Scala to smile, but it did not remove his uncertainty.

2

TICINO RIVER, DUCHY OF MILAN

"It's coming. I can see it now." Tonio squinted to identify a horse and wagon through the swirling fog as the barge approached the wharf.

"I can't see a damned thing," Bruno protested. "I need to get closer."

"If we get closer, people on the wharf will see us. Here we're hidden by the trees. Just wait. If it's him, he'll have to come this way."

The barge, heavily laden with hewn timber as well as the horse and wagon, drifted slowly to the riverbank. A young deckhand jumped from the barge with the mooring line in hand. Unbalanced by the weight of the rope, he landed awkwardly on the wharf. His leather shoes slipped on wet slime and sent him skidding across the wooden decking. A worker who was waiting for the incoming craft grabbed the youngster by the collar only a moment before he slid into the cold, churning water. With the worker's help, the flustered deckhand stood and cautiously tested his footing. He moved warily to the edge of the deck and fastened the mooring line to a cleat. He then secured another line thrown to him from the barge to a second cleat.

"Can you see the horse? Is it the right one?" Bruno pressed.

"A black mare with a white diamond-shaped patch on its right flank. Yes, that's the one. The farmer is climbing onto the wagon seat; they'll be coming this way soon," Tonio replied.

"He broke the guild's rules. Now he will suffer," Bruno said aloud anticipating the punishment he would soon deliver.

Bruno stayed hidden in the shadow of the trees while Tonio moved to the side of the road and watched the wagon approach. Workers unloading timber from the barge were too busy to notice him standing in the road. There would be no witnesses. When the horse reached Tonio's position, he stepped into the road, grabbed the animal's bridle and yanked it hard, forcing the horse to stop.

The farmer managed only one word, "What?" before Bruno leaped from his hiding place, jumped up onto the wagon, and slammed his fist into the side of the farmer's head. Bruno grinned broadly, pleased that his single blow had rendered the farmer unconscious. He pushed the inert body aside and took hold of the reins. As soon as Tonio climbed into the wagon bed, Bruno loosened the reins and coaxed the horse forward.

The two thugs paired as night and day. Nothing pleased iron-fisted Bruno more than dispensing punishment and pain. Although his pleasure came with a price: the missing teeth, diminished hearing, and blurry vision that he sustained from blows inflicted by adversaries. Wiry Tonio was the thinker. He had determined how to identify the target and where to seize the wagon without being seen. It was his scrupulous planning that invariably kept the outlaws out of prison.

In a quarter mile they turned from the main road, the one that would have taken the farmer to Milan, onto a narrow dirt path that curved around to parallel the river. In a short distance, a clearing in the thick woodland opened out to the river. Previously, Bruno and Tonio had tied their horses to a bush in the clearing. Bruno turned the wagon into the clearing, then Tonio jumped from the wagon and guided the horse until the rear of the wagon was at the river's edge.

Bruno slapped the farmer and growled, "Wake up, stronzo." When the farmer only shifted slightly and groaned, Bruno laughed heartily. "Maybe I shouldn't have hit the bastard so hard." Bruno turned in his seat to view the wagon bed. "What is he carrying back there?"

"Some kind of melons," Tonio replied.

Bruno climbed down and walked to the rear of the wagon. He lifted one melon into the air and smashed it to the ground where it shattered, scattering chunks of pulp around his feet. He bent to pick up a small wedge and bit into the orange flesh. "It was a melon," he laughed. With the sleeve of his tunic, he wiped the juice dripping from his chin. Then he reached into the wagon for a second orb, lofted it high in the air, and watched it splash down in the river and drift away in the speedy current. "Help me with these," Bruno called. Tonio joined him and the two men worked together emptying the remaining melons into the river. As the last melon floated away, Tonio noticed the farmer had regained consciousness and was sitting, slumped forward and rubbing his head.

The two thugs climbed onto the wagon seat, one man on each side of the farmer who looked with a puzzled expression from one man to the other. "What do you want of me?" he murmured. "I'm just a poor farmer. I have nothing."

Bruno responded, "You broke the rules. You should not be here."

The farmer shrunk away from Bruno's foul breath. "Rules? What rules?"

"Many years past, merchants battled one another. They

destroyed each other's shipments. Some were killed. To stop
the fighting, the guild made rules. One rule says merchants
cannot cross the river to sell goods without permission," Tonio
explained. "Now, you and others like you are again coming to
the markets in Milan. That is not allowed."

"I'm a farmer, not a merchant. I don't belong to any guild. I
know nothing of your rules. I go to the market in Milan
because I get better prices than in Novara."

"No more, old man," Bruno taunted. "You're not welcome in
Milan. Stay on your side of the river and tell all the other
Novarese fools to stay there. Now get your ass back where you
belong."

Tonio said, "This is your only warning. This time we take
only the melons. Next time you cross the river, you will not
return." Bruno and Tonio climbed down and then watched
silently as the wagon headed back toward the boat landing.

Bruno spat on the ground and whined, "Half a day we
spend riding here and back just to throw melons into the river.
My life is turning to shit,"

"We got paid. It's a job," Tonio said, trying to console his
cohort.

"It's a shit job. The pay is not even enough coin for a turn
with the new Russian whore, the young *zoccola* with the blue
eyes."

Tonio could not disagree; the pay was meager. He walked
toward his horse, who stomped the ground, eager to be untied.
Tonio called back over his shoulder, "A message came from the
paymaster. He may have a job for us. He wants to meet at
Bierposto."

"He is an ass," Bruno complained. Then he brightened,
"But the bastard does have connections to wealthy clients who
pay in gold. The last job we did for him, the one where we

burned down the mill, it kept me in whores and beer for a month. What's the new job?"

"It didn't say in the note. It just said to meet him tonight after compline."

Bruno climbed onto his mount; his mind filled with a vision of the young Russian whore.

3

BIERPOSTO TAVERN, MILAN

Gunter, the proprietor of Bierposto, never imagined that he could live anywhere other than his beautiful Saxony, until a dark-haired angel from Milan captured his heart. To be with his Maria, he abandoned all connections to his homeland save one, the beers of Einbeck praised by many as the world's finest. For many months, Gunter struggled to find a way to transport beer from Einbeck to Milan with no loss of quality. When he finally succeeded, Gunter opened a tavern called the Bierposto, the beer place, in the Ticinese district of Milan. With Gunter pouring his prized Saxon beer, and Maria serving traditional Italian *spuntini*, snacks, Bierposto became a popular gathering spot for hard-working laborers in the city.

The bell at Basilica di Sant'Eustorgio was sounding the call to compline prayers, signaling the end of the workday when Tonio entered the warren of narrow streets of the Ticinese district. Long ago he had learned how to navigate through the maze of old streets. Every night young Tonio had been taken by his father to a tavern in the seedy district. By the time father had indulged to the extent of his coins, he was unable to retrace his path through the maze of alleys. It fell to the boy to reverse their route. Tonio swore he would never become a slave to drink. Although he avoided that curse, he found no honest opportunities open to boys of his status. Artisans with a choice of eager apprentices were unwilling to take the son of a habitual drunk. Petty crime was one of the few options open to him.

Tonio executed a series of turns until he saw the small sign marking his destination, the Bierposto tavern. Dirty, tired, sweaty men filled the Bierposto when Tonio entered. The pungent odor of spilled beer was not unusual. Most surprising, though, was the relative quiet in the room. Tonio followed the gaze of the others to discover the object of their rapt attention, a French jongleur who was finishing a raunchy story. "... so the bishop just slapped her on the ass," he joshed. The punchline brought forth an explosion of laughter powerful enough to create ripples in beer steins throughout the room. When the howling subsided, the entertainer picked up his lyre and began strumming the notes of a bawdy tune he learned in Capua.

At the rear of the room, Bruno sat alone at a table. His slouching posture, reddened face, and glassy eyes suggested that his beer stein had already been refilled several times. Tonio entered and scanned the crowd until he spotted his associate. He wended a path through the crush of tables and chairs to take a seat opposite Bruno.

Notes from the jongleur's lyre filled the room. The festive throng recognized the song, a well-known tune from Naples that ridiculed Pope John, who was said to have died while in bed with another man's wife. As the jongleur played the music, spirited revelers bellowed the words.

Tonio signaled to Gunter for a beer; then he motioned for Maria to bring antipasti, one plate for him, and one for Bruno. Tonio scanned the room searching for Pagatore, but the paymaster was not among the crowd. Perhaps Pagatore had found others to perform the task he had mentioned earlier. If so, other fortunate souls would claim the heavy purse. Tonio opted to wait until he finished his beer before concluding that the lucrative job was lost.

Tonio sipped his beer slowly and settled back to enjoy the performance. A server brought the plates of antipasti to the table. Maria prepared all the foods, but she remained in the kitchen because Gunter refused to have her subjected to patrons' groping hands. With Tonio's encouragement, Bruno pushed his beer stein aside and began devouring the tasty assortment of meats and cheeses.

The jongleur finished the Neapolitan song and followed with another well-known tune, one that belittled the King of France. He was amusing the crowd with yet another story when the door opened, and Pagatore entered. Tonio raised a hand to attract the paymaster's attention.

The three men sat within earshot of others, but no one listened to their conversation because the entertainer's fascinating story had captured everyone's attention. Pagatore shook his head in disgust upon noting Bruno's inebriated condition. Looking toward Tonio, Pagatore asked, "Has this bastard been sitting here drinking all afternoon? He looks like shit."

Tonio merely shrugged. He knew well Bruno's weaknesses for beer, whores, and gambling, but he also appreciated Bruno's strengths. Aside from his physical prowess, Bruno was reliable. He followed through on commitments and completed tasks despite severe obstacles. The trait most important to Tonio was Bruno's loyalty, a rare quality among thieves and thugs.

Pagatore opted to describe the job to Tonio in the hope that Tonio would be able to control his companion. "I have been approached by a new client, the agent of a wealthy and influential person. I cannot say his name. This client wants to have someone abducted."

Tonio nodded out of habit. Pagatore's assertion was nothing new. He prefaced every project with a claim that the client was wealthy and influential. Abductions were easy. Tonio and Bruno were experienced at making targets disappear. They had done it many times at the behest of Pagatore and others who hired them.

Without thinking, Pagatore kept moving his beer stein across the table, left to right, right to left, then to the right again. His agitated state suggested that there was more to the job than he had disclosed. Tonio did not have to wait long before hearing the complication. "The mark is a *superiore,* a member of the elite, and a foreigner," Pagatore said. "The client insists that the mark must not be harmed. He is to have no broken bones, scars or bruises."

Pagatore motioned to Bruno and asked, "Can this *somaro* abduct someone without having to beat the victim? You will need to control him. Can you do that?"

Tonio understood and shared Pagatore's concern. Bruno could act with calm and restraint when looting an elegant palazzo, but abductions always aroused his ire and Tonio understood the reason. Abduction targets were generally aristocrats who gained wealth through inheritance or chance. It was unfair, Bruno maintained, that the goddess Fortuna should smile upon them and not him. They deserved punishment, he reasoned. Tonio glanced at his partner; then to Pagatore he said, "I will find a way to constrain him."

"If you cannot and something goes wrong, my reputation will suffer, and should that happen, our business together will be finished. You will be forced back to stealing melons from farm wagons." Pagatore slapped his hand down onto the table to emphasize the threat.

Tonio reiterated, "I will find a way."

"The target must be hidden away somewhere and unharmed for two or three days, maybe longer. While he is being held, an agent of the client will come to speak with him. The mark must hear the message, but he must not see the messenger."

Tonio's neck muscles tightened. This job was more complicated than a simple killing or abduction. Pagatore saw Tonio's tension so he added, "The pay will be good, good enough so the horse's ass sitting next to you can bed a clean whore for a change, and you can do ... whatever it is that you do."

"Who is the target?" Tonio asked.

"His name is Portinari. He is the manager of the Medici bank here in Milan."

"Shit!" Tonio blurted, unable to contain his astonishment.

"Why are you surprised? I told you he is a foreign superiore. In two days, Portinari will attend a meeting with Filarete, the architect commissioned by Duke Sforza to design the new *Ospedale dei Poveri*, the hospital for the poor. Portinari always stays late at the bank. He will not leave to meet with the architect until all other employees have exited the bank. He will be the one who locks the door; then he will walk directly to the office of the architect. All the other bank employees will be gone, so if you follow him from the bank, you can be sure you have the right person. He will be walking alone. That is when you can take him."

Tonio wondered how Pagatore had learned Portinari's schedule, but he did not question the paymaster. "You said he must be held for two or three days. Where is he to be held?" Tonio asked.

"Finding a place to keep him is your problem, and remember, I said it could be more than a few days."

Bruno finally showed that he had been listening. He raised

his head, took a quick swig of beer, and said, "My cousin raises pigs on a small farm near Gaggiano. The stink is so bad that no one comes to his farm. We can hide the fool there." Then with contempt he added, "I will make sure that his fancy banker's shoes get filled with pig shit."

Pagatore reached into his pocket, withdrew a coin purse, and pushed it across the table. "This is the good faith money. The rest you will get when the job is done." As Bruno eyed the purse, he noticed the hand grasping it. Pagatore's middle finger was shorter than the adjacent fingers. Although he had worked for the paymaster on the many occasions, but he never before noticed the deformity. Pagatore saw Bruno staring, and in a rare moment of candor, Pagatore explained, "I was barely old enough to walk when my father sent me to work to support his drunken habits. While other boys were begging in the piazza, I drudged in a flour mill. The finger got clipped by a grinding wheel."

4

AGOSTINO MOZZI'S OFFICE, FLORENCE

Chancellor Scala was already seated in Mozzi's office when Corsini entered. As he moved to the conference table, Corsini scanned the room then spread his hands, palms up, and said "Stylish enough, but lacking the elegance of Palazzo Strozzi."

Mozzi smiled, "That is true. Signor Strozzi generously offered his residence as a venue for our initial meeting but I fear that repeatedly accepting his invitation might grow into imposition." When the others were seated, Mozzi began. "Before we begin to discuss candidates for a commission, we should hear whether the Signoria accepts our proposal."

"Members of the Signoria overwhelming agree that action in needed to combat foreign threats, and they are willing to authorize a new commission having that goal," Scala reported. "They are concerned, however, that unrestrained action by such a commission might provoke hostilities with a foreign state. To avoid that possibility, they require that the commission be under the guidance and supervision of a highly experienced administrator." Looking directly at Mozzi, Scala added, "And they asked that you bear that responsibility."

Mozzi's expression remained fixed as though he expected the request. "If it be the will of the Signoria, I accept the charge." Then glancing from one man to the other he said, "Know though, I intend to solicit your counsel and advice." After seeing nods from the others, he continued, "The Captain-general of the Florentine militia and I discussed military officers and qualifications appropriate to the commission. After reviewing several candidates, we concluded that Sergeant Massimo Leoni has the experience and character needed for this assignment.

"Leoni joined the Florentine militia in his seventeenth year to help oppose the incursion by Alfonso of Aragon at Maremma. The courage he displayed in that battle earned him the Citation for Valor for entering a burning building to rescue a fellow patriot. Since then, he has consistently advanced in skill and experience and now instructs other soldiers in battle-field tactics and leadership."

"Is the Captain-general willing to release Leoni from his existing duties to serve on the commission?" Corsini asked.

"We are at peace, so he is willing to have Leoni serve on the commission. If Florence were engaged in hostilities, he would undoubtedly take a different position."

Mozzi then turned to Corsini. "Have you identified an investigator to serve on the commission?"

Corsini replied, "Yes, Vittorio Colombo is an investigator in the Guardia with an impressive ability to discover evidence that others overlook. Everyone in the Guardia regards him highly. He is well-qualified to serve as the commission's investigator. However, it is important to realize that investigators like Colombo work in isolation, not in teams. Working closely with other commission members will be a different experience for him."

"Will he be able to adapt?" Scala asked.

Corsini shrugged. "A good question, and one I have pondered myself. Colombo is a talented investigator, so I believe he will see the need to cooperate with the other commission members." He lifted a hand palm up to signify his uncertainty and added, "But as we know, relationships are not easily predicted."

Mozzi then signaled for Scala to speak. "Florence is certainly rich with lawyers. Most have established careers making it unlikely that they would be willing to forego their existing practice for a commission appointment. Agostino and I believe that it is best to chose a young lawyer who is flexible and not caged by Florentine legal practices.

"Nico Argenti is a recent graduate of the University of Bologna law school. I followed his career during his time at the university. He received outstanding evaluations from all of his professors and at graduation his fellow students nominated him to the *lista dei migliori studenti*, the list of superior students."

Corsini said, "I know that name. The consul of the Magistrates Guild speaks highly of Argenti's father. It is sad that young Argenti's father and mother were both taken by the plague when he was just a boy." Corsini stroked his rough beard stubble while forming his words. "It troubles me that he lacks experience. I accept that he accredited himself well at the university, but this assignment will demand more. I am not certain..." Corsini's voice trailed off.

From the corner of his eye, Scala caught Mozzi's expression. Mozzi wanted Scala to mention Nico's exploits since he returned from the university. Taking Mozzi's cue, Scala said, "I am sure you recall the attempted assassination of the hospital directors in Siena. Nico Argenti was the one who uncovered the plot, identified the intended victims, and enlisted the support of Sienese officials to confront the assassin."

Corsini brightened. "Yes, of course. I remember that vicious scheme. His accomplishment is remarkable for one so young. While I agree his action was commendable, my doubts remain. Can we agree that Argenti be appointed—that all three men be appointed—on a conditional basis and that we will review their performance in the future?"

Mozzi glanced at Scala who all nodded his endorsement of Corsini's suggestion. "Are we agreed then with having Leoni, Colombo, and Argenti being the three Commission candidates?" Mozzi asked. He looked from Scala to Corsini as each one, in turn, signified his approval of the candidates.

After the slate was accepted, Corsini asked, "Agostino, will you meet with the nominees?"

The question caused Mozzi to chuckle. "I will leave the challenge of recruiting the men to Chancellor Scala. His tongue is cast from a much finer grade of silver than mine."

Times have changed, Scala thought. No longer do states rely on armies to steal their neighbors' lands. Instead of waging war, they conceive devious schemes to plunder wealth and undermine the prosperity of other nations. The men we appoint to the Florentine Security Commission will face difficult obstacles; I hope that these three men can overcome the challenges.

5

MILAN TO GAGGIANO

As a *banchi grossi*, a great bank, the Medici bank made loans and issued letters of credit to international merchants, wealthy aristocrats, and the Duchy of Milan itself. It did not host accounts for the average Milanese citizen, nor did it serve merchants or the owners of small businesses.

Long before the bank closed, Tonio positioned himself near the entrance to a pastry shop within sight of the bank where he could watch the trickle of clients entering and leaving the building. The bank had a small elite clientele, so he did not expect to see many customers. The few clients that he did see convinced him the bank was open and operating normally. The longer he remained standing in the cool autumn air, the more the aroma of fresh baked torte disrupted his concentration. To avoid the temptation of abandoning his post to make a purchase, he moved from the pastry shop to a narrow passage alongside the bank. He walked through the passage to the rear of the building where he could see whether other egresses might let the target slip away from the building unnoticed.

The two thieves owed their longstanding success to Tonio's careful planning, which eliminated as much uncertainty as possible. A criminal genius had brought Tonio into the profession and schooled him in skills that the master had honed over a lifetime. The master's abilities had earned the respect of the guardia as well as his contemporaries. He was a suspect in many high-profile thefts, but there was never enough evidence to indict him. By the time he retired to a grand villa on an island off the coast of Naples, the mentor had amassed considerable wealth and left Tonio to carry on as his legacy.

As Tonio suspected, the building had a rear exit, but a fence enclosed the area behind the bank so no one could leave from the rear of the premises. Anyone who used the rear door had to follow the path, the same one that Tonio had used, to the front of the building.

Next, heeding the teachings of his mentor, Tonio planned out each step of the abduction. First, he familiarized himself with the routes between the bank and the architect's office. There were three feasible routes that the target might choose. After walking each route, he concluded that all three were equally likely choices. Since he could not predict which path the target might select, he would have to follow the mark from the bank.

Tonio walked each route a second time, looking for the best places to stage the abduction. Ideally, it would be on a narrow stretch of road where shops had already closed for the day, and locals would not be likely to pass en route to restaurants, taverns, or evening church services. Each road offered at least one suitable location.

Later, at the bank's closing time, Tonio again stood at the entrance to the now-closed pastry shop. He watched bank employees funnel out into the street and scatter individually and in small groups. He remained at his post long after the employees disappeared. He recalled his mentor drilling him on the importance of patience. "There are times when patience will be your most valuable weapon."

The sun crept toward the horizon, and chilly fall air turned even colder. The lengthening shadow of a nearby building told Tonio he had been in position more than half an hour when the bank door opened, and a lone figure emerged.

Tonio stood fast until the target passed his position, then he pulled his cloak tight and stepped into the street. He glanced over his shoulder and waved his arm as a signal to his companion. A discreet distance away, Bruno threw off his blanket covering, sat up straight in the wagon master's seat, and picked up the reins of the horse harnessed to the wagon.

The target walked at a brisk pace, carrying a document folio under one arm. Where the roads split, he picked the one that would take him farthest from the center of the city. His choice pleased Tonio because that road was least likely to have walkabouts—witnesses—and it had two places suitable for an abduction.

When the target reached the first location that Tonio had selected, Tonio glanced around and spotted two men walking on a side street near the intersection with the target's route. Their slow, casual strides led Tonio to wonder if they might be members of the guardia on a routine patrol. Although they were moving away from the intersection, Tonio worried that they might be close enough to hear any cries for help from the target, so he opted to wait until the target reached the second of the two sites he had selected.

At the second site, Tonio again scanned the area. This time there was no one in sight. He waved to Bruno, signaling him to advance. Bruno loosened the reins and encouraged the horse to increase its gait. The animal responded at once, and the wagon lurched forward.

As soon as the wagon passed the target, Bruno pulled back on the reins. The horse jolted the wagon sideways before bringing it to a stop directly in front of the mark. Bruno jumped from the vehicle, grabbed the target by the arm, and delivered a powerful punch to his stomach. The man doubled over in pain, emitted a sickening low-pitched moan, and then sprayed Bruno's shoes with vomit. Tonio withdrew a length of rope from the wagon and used it to bind the man's hands and feet. Bruno pulled a sack down on the victim's head to block his vision. The stench of rotting onions permeating the sack added to the victim's distress and brought forth a second spray of vomit that soaked into his tunic. The two thugs lifted him by his arms and shoved him into the wagon bed. "Make a sound, and it will be your last," Bruno snarled.

Moonlight painted the ground when the wagon finally arrived at the pig farm. From Milan to the town of Gaggiano they followed the well-traveled road paralleling the Naviglio Grande canal. Finding the road that veered north toward the pig farm proved to be a challenge. Bruno's clue to the proper turnoff was a stone fortification built three centuries earlier by the army of Frederick Barbarossa as a prelude to its attack on Milan.

The dim light and a screen of scraggly bushes made identification of the structure nearly impossible. Twice Bruno thought he sighted the formation. He sent Tonio into the brush to verify the sighting. Bruno's third guess was correct. They made the turn and after several minutes they spotted the entrance to the farm. "That's it," Bruno said. "That's my cousin's farm."

Bruno approached the farmhouse and banged on the door. The man who opened the door had grease smeared across his face and held a half-eaten pork rib in one hand. "*Porcama*, pig lover," Bruno laughed. "I need to keep a package in your barn."

Guido, the one Bruno called *Porcama*, shifted his expression from surprise to puzzlement to indignation. "What in hell are you talking about, you thieving bastard?" Bruno ignored the insult and pushed a small coin purse into his cousin's hand— the hand not holding the pork rib.

Guido glanced down at the purse and then returned his focus to Bruno. "Surely you know I am an honorable man, dear cousin." Bruno laughed at his own cynicism. "You will need to feed the package every day. These coins are payment for your hospitality."

Bruno turned and walked to the wagon, trailed by the bewildered Guido. Tonio helped the abductee from the wagon and wrapped a blanket around the shivering man's shoulders.

"What is happening? Why are you doing this? I am not a rich man," he pleaded. The words barely escaped through the victim's chattering teeth.

"Someone will come and tell you the reason," Tonio explained. "You must wait. You will not be harmed."

Bruno shoved the victim toward the barn. Inside, he pushed the hapless man down onto a pile of hay. Bruno fastened one end of a chain brought from the wagon to a post and secured the other end tightly around the victim's waist. Tonio untied the captive's hands.

"You can't do this. You can't leave him here," Guido protested. He stepped in front of Bruno to block him from leaving.

With a thrust of his powerful arm, Bruno shoved Guido aside. "You have been paid to care for him. He had better be alive and well when we return. If he is not, you will share his fate, dear cousin," Bruno growled.

Sobs from the helpless banker drew a final glance from Tonio as he followed Bruno to the wagon. The abduction had gone flawlessly. Bruno salivated in anticipation of his purse being swelled by Pagatore's silver.

6

THE PALAZZO DELLA SIGNORIA, FLORENCE

Nico entered the Palazzo della Signoria to meet with Chancellor Scala. The meeting location specified in the invitation, a conference room, was puzzling because their prior meetings had all been in Scala's office. Nico arrived before the appointed time and found another man sitting alone in the room. He had a lean wiry build, a thin face, and black hair pulled back in a horse tail. His clothes were well made but lacking the styling details favored by the upper classes. Impatience or nervous energy had the man drumming his fingers on the table. Upon hearing footsteps entering the room, he looked up at the newcomer and nodded slightly but offered no verbal greeting.

"Are you waiting for the chancellor?" Nico asked as he stepped forward to introduce himself. But before he could state his name, Scala entered the room followed by a tall, broad shouldered man who strode with confidence and purpose. He wore no uniform but the mirror shine of his boots marked him as an army officer.

Scala gestured for the others to be seated, then he took a seat across from them. "Thank you for accepting my invitation," he began. "Before we discuss the purpose of this meeting, introductions are appropriate. Signor Colombo, would you begin?"

"Vittorio Colombo, an investigator with the guardia."

Scala waved a hand to Nico. "Nico Argenti, a lawyer recently inducted into the magistrate's guild."

All turned to the third man who said, "Massimo Leoni, sergeant in the Florentine army."

Scala brought his hands together, rested them on the table, and smiled. "One quality you all seem to share is modesty, so I must expand on your brief words. Signor Colombo is the guardia's most accomplished investigator. He has traveled throughout the republic to solve crimes that have baffled others. Signor Argenti attained top rankings at the University of Bologna law school. Shortly after graduation he helped uncover a plot to assassinate a member of the Signoria. And Sergeant Leoni has twice been decorated for exceptional bravery on the battlefield." Scala looked across the table from man to man. "You are here because you are all outstanding among your peers."

While Nico focused his attention on Scala, Vittorio studied the other two men. Massimo leaned back in his chair as though he were an uninvolved observer. "Now, to the purpose of this meeting," Scala continued. "Reports from our embassies contain increasing indications of plots by outsiders to undermine our republic. To counter those threats, the Signoria has approved the formation of a new commission, the Florentine Security Commission. It will operate with the full authority of the Signoria and its mission will be to investigate and eliminate threats by legal and other means. Initially, the commission is to have three members, an investigator, a lawyer, and a military officer, and you three men have been nominated to serve in those positions."

Vittorio spoke for the first time. "Serving on the commission would conflict with my duties in the guardia." Massimo nodded to express that he had a similar concern.

Scala looked first to Vittorio, "Signor Corsini, First Chair of the Eight of Guard, nominated you to the commission. Your status as a member of the guardia will remain unchanged. Your appointment to the commission is considered a temporary assignment. However, if the commission is successful, as we expect it to be, temporary could become indefinite."

Next Scala turned to Massimo. "Signor Mozzi, First Chair of the Ten of War, proposed your membership. Your service on the commission will also be considered as a temporary assignment. You will retain your army rank and advancement opportunities."

Finally, to Nico, Scala said, "As you might have surmised, I am the one who suggested your membership. We can discuss details of your position later, but I am confident you will find the arrangement to be more than satisfactory."

Scala spread his hands wide. "Of course, you are all free to decline these appointments, but before you reach a decision, let me explain how the commission will function. Indications of possible harm to the republic come from many sources: our embassies, foreign diplomats with loose tongues, and Florentine merchants with foreign contacts, among others.

"All reports are collected by the Chancery. Credible reports must be investigated to determine the severity of the threat. That is your specialty, Signor Colombo. Past experiences have shown that many difficulties can be remedied through negotiations and legal procedures. Those require your expertise, Signor Argenti. Other situations might demand a harder hand. It is not our intention to provoke our neighbors, but we must know if any are contemplating hostile action against our republic, and therein lies your expertise Signor Leoni.

"The Signoria has given Signor Mozzi overall responsibility for administering the activities of the commission, and he has requested that Messer Corsini and I provide him with our guidance. I will arrange to have copies made available to you of all reports submitted to the Chancery. Office space will be provided here in the Chancery for your use."

Scala shifted his gaze from man to man to gauge their response and to elicit their questions. Vittorio said, "Investigations cannot be conducted from the confines of an office."

"Yes, certainly," Scala agreed. "Travel arrangements and other resources will be made available as needed to support the activities of the commission." Hearing no other questions, he said, "The choice to accept or decline appointment to the commission is yours; however, I urge you to weigh carefully the import of this assignment to the security of our republic and I request that you inform me of your decision by the end of this day. If you wish further discussion, come to my office." And with that, Scala walked from the room leaving the three commission candidates to ponder their decisions.

Nico sat quietly and stared straight ahead to avoid the appearance of evaluating the men sitting beside him. He had lain awake many nights wondering about his first job as a lawyer. He had speculated with his cousin Donato on possible openings in Florence's many tribunals, but they had never considered the possibility that he might be chosen for a totally new commission. What had Scala called it, the Florentine Security Commission? His decision was easy: he would accept the appointment.

Vittorio also sat quietly looking straight ahead. He had already studied the other two men; his stern expression showed him to be deep in thought weighing the information that Scala had presented. He had no doubt that he could make a valuable contribution by serving on the commission. His concerns centered on the other candidates. Past encounters with the military had been both amicable and contentious. Is Sergeant Leoni one who respects members of the guardia, he wondered.

As soon as Scala left the room, Massimo rose to follow. When he reached the doorway, he turned back to face the others, and said, "I look forward to joining you, if you accept the appointment." As an army officer, he was accustomed to receiving orders and carrying out assignments. He had learned to team with good men and bad, and to avoid close relationships. For him, the character of the others on the commission was of little consequence.

7

PALAZZO CASTELLINI, FLORENCE

Once again, Agostino Mozzi called together the men who had created the Florentine Security Commission. This time they met in a salon at Palazzo Castellini, the private home of a venerable Florentine family. A jug of lemon water and a tray of dolce for their refreshment awaited the men when they arrived. When the Castellini clan held family gatherings in the salon, they enjoyed the comfort of soft couches clustered at one end of the room. The men opted instead to conference at the table generally used for family dinners.

"Again, we are meeting in luxurious surroundings," Corsini said. "I am wondering, Agostino, why we are meeting here rather than at your office. Are all the elegant palazzos in our city open to you?"

"I thought you might enjoy the pretense of being an aristocrat, Antonio," Mozzi teased. "Perhaps when I can no longer perform the duties of my office, I will recommend you as my successor."

When everyone settled into their seats, Mozzi began, "First, I am pleased that the Signoria has accepted the nominees we proposed for the *Commissione sicurezza speciale,* Florentine Security Commission.

Scala said, "After reviewing the qualifications of the nominees, all the members of the Signoria enthusiastically endorsed their appointment to the commission." He displayed a document bearing the official seal of the Signoria. "This authorization empowers the commission to act with the full authority of the Signoria."

Scala held out a sheet of paper. "I recorded a list of security concerns brought forth by members of the Signoria and I was told that similar concerns have been voiced at guild meetings by merchants who conduct business in other countries. I'll deliver this list to our new commissioners."

Mozzi said, "We must also recognize Bartolomeo's accomplishment in recruiting the three commissioners."

Scala demurred. "I claim no credit. The three appointees are dedicated patriots who understand the need to guard against foreign challenges. They understand the basic purpose of the commission, and fortunately, my inability to provide details of how the commission will operate did not dissuade them."

Corsini said, "It is my opinion that we should not restrict the commission initially. Rather than imposing limitations, I think it best for the men to be given latitude. Eventually, as we gain experience, suitable boundaries will become clear. No one spanks a child until it misbehaves."

Scala and Mozzi found Corsini's analogy perplexing, since they knew he had no children. Mozzi struggled to keep from laughing. He had heard from more than one source that Corsini's mistress enjoyed friendly spankings.

"We may learn how the commission should operate very soon," Scala said. "I received another report from Milan. This one does not involve hearsay. An employee of the Medici bank has disappeared." The others tensed upon hearing Scala's remark. "Our knowledge of the incident is from Signor Portinari, the manager of the Medici bank branch in Milan. He informed our embassy, and they sent a report to the chancery."

"Who is the missing person?" Corsini asked.

"The report only gives his name as Salito Salvetti," Scala replied. "The embassy notified the guardia, who were indifferent. They told our ambassador that people disappear for many reasons. They dismissed the report claiming that it is too soon to begin an investigation,"

"So, they are doing nothing?" asked Corsini.

Scala and Mozzi looked at each other and it was Mozzi who replied, "Yes, that is correct; the guardia is doing nothing."

"I can't imagine what would keep Milanese officials from investigating the disappearance of a foreign visitor," stated Corsini. "I assure you that such neglect would never happen here in Florence. We take great care to protect foreign dignitaries and make them feel welcome. Two years past, we even responded to a Venetian envoy's request to help locate his missing dog. Milan maintains a sizeable army. If the guardia are too busy to respond, they should ask the military for assistance."

"You are touching on an interesting point," Scala said. "When I was studying law in Milan, I saw several instances where matters involving foreigners were referred to the military. That is the usual protocol in Milan. It is unclear why that did not happen in this case."

"Perhaps it is time to involve one of our new commission members," Corsini said. "Since the Milanese are not investigating, we should send Signor Colombo to Milan to find out what happened."

Mozzi leaned forward, folded his hands, and rested them on the table. "I am delighted to hear your suggestion because

Signor Scala and I already told Signor Colombo to prepare to depart for Milan."

Corsini's brow furrowed. "I wonder if the Duchy of Milan will allow foreigners to investigate incidents in its territory?"

All eyes looked to Scala since he had knowledge of Milanese law. "Without the permission of local authorities, he cannot operate in an official capacity, but he can certainly ask questions; any private citizen can ask questions."

After a brief pause, Scala added, "Filippo Visconti was in power when I studied in Milan. The laws may have changed under Duke Sforza."

Scala's caution did not dissuade the men from adopting Corsini's proposal. "Should we send only Colombo, or should we send all three men to Milan?" Mozzi asked.

"Colombo is the investigator. I am not sure what purpose would be served by sending the others. Here in Florence, our investigators operate independently. Colombo is accustomed to working alone," replied Corsini.

Mozzi polled those at the table and found that all concurred with Corsini's suggestion. "We are agreed; the Florentine Security Commission has its first assignment."

8

THE COMMISSION OFFICE, FLORENCE

As word circulated among officials and administrators that a commission had been formed to investigate potential threats against the republic, reports began flowing to the Chancery. Most were sketchy tidbits derived from hearsay and rumors. Mozzi arranged for the commissioners to interview various government officials to obtain further details—no Florentine administrator dared refuse an interview request endorsed by Mozzi. As the commission's overseer, he also scheduled regular sessions with the commissioners to review their progress and share his insights. To supplement the interviews, Scala had copies of all relevant embassy reports sent to the commissioners and arranged for them to have full access to the documents cataloged at the Chancery Archives.

The three commissioners had intended to work together, conducting interviews and gathering information until the disappearance of a Florentine citizen in Milan disrupted their plans. Slaves, peasants, and criminals went missing with regularity even in Florence, but the missing person in Milan was not one of those. He was a *collaterale*, a bookkeeper, at the

Medici bank branch in Milan. More importantly, he was a distant cousin of Piero de Medici, the Medici family's new patriarch. There was no reason to believe the loss of a mid-level bank employee could impair Florentine security; however, the guardia in Milan refused to act, so Vittorio had been dispatched to Milan to investigate the incident. Nico and Massimo remained in Florence to conduct the interviews.

The Signoria allocated a compact room on an upper level of the Palazzo della Signoria as an office for the newly formed commission. Building custodians had cleared old paintings, rolled tapestries, and other disused items from the space. A handsome white oak table and padded chairs were available to the commissoners; however, the table alone would have filled the entire room, and the chairs were too broad to fit through the room's narrow doorway. Instead, the commissioners brought from storage straight-backed unpadded wooden chairs and a single low table that was barely larger than a writing desk.

Nico had suggested that they adopt the practice used by Chancellor Scala to organize information by affixing notecards to the walls of the office. Onto each notecard, they recorded a single fact or observation. Then, they arranged the cards in columns, with each column representing a topic of interest. That technique made it easy to find information quickly and eliminated the need for furniture or shelves to hold documents.

Nico's method for studying the accumulated information was to concentrate on one column at a time. After absorbing the data from all the note cards in that column, he shifted his chair to view the notes in the next column. Halfway down one of the columns, a piece of red yarn caught Nico's attention. The yarn extended from the item he was reading to a note on a different column. The colored yarn had been added at Vittorio's suggestion to enhance Scala's original method. Vittorio had suggested using yarn to connect facts in a column to related items in other columns. Vittorio's plan involved using different colors to identify the type of relationship that linked the two elements, but thus far, neither Nico nor Massimo had mastered Vittorio's color code.

Massimo found that Scala's method offered another advantage. Rather than sitting inanimate at a desk pouring through a stack of papers, Massimo studied the notes by moving around the room. When he first heard about Scala's method, he said, "That will be good for me. Soldiers need to move. If ever I am dispatched by the blade of a foe, I may become fixed in one place like a stone, but until then, I prefer to be in motion."

Massimo began at the first column, read the newest note in that column, then moved to the next column and did the same. He continued his advance until he came to a corner of the room where Nico had set an incense burner on a small table, hoping the incense would dispel the musty odor that the office had acquired when it served as a storage room. Three windows high on one wall let light into the office, but the fixed panes provided no ventilation.

Before Massimo reversed direction, he paused near the thin spindle of smoke rising from the incense and inhaled tentatively. The fragrance was unfamiliar, a hint of cinnamon certainly, and other scents that Massimo could not identify. "Where did you find this incense?" he asked. "It reminds me of Sicily."

"My sister made it," Nico replied and explained casually. "I believe she used a mixture of Tunisian oils and Middle Eastern spices. She has a collection of fragrances that she uses to make perfumes."

Massimo raised an eyebrow upon hearing Nico's unexpected answer. "That is an unusual practice for a woman. Is there an apothecary in your family who schooled her?"

"No, there is no apothecary in our family. She taught herself to make potions and ointments." Massimo watched Nico intently, expecting a further explanation. Thus far, work had kept the two men from having any informal conversations, so Nico took Massimo's curiosity as an opportunity to share personal information. "My father was a legate in the Florentine army. He was on assignment in Rome, and my mother had joined him when the plague struck that city. Both succumbed to the plague, so I went to live with my uncle Nunzio and his son Donato. Now, my sister Alessa and I live with Donato and his wife." Nico judiciously avoided delving into Alessa's complicated past.

Massimo pulled a chair next to Nico and sat facing him, his lips curled up in a thin smile. "I struggle to comprehend how the son of an army legate could forgo our venerated military to become a lawyer."

"My father and others like him—like you—have brought us peace. I see treaties and diplomacy as the way to retain it. We have not lifted swords against our neighbors for a decade. My hope is that this era of harmony will have no end."

"A noble aspiration, but one born of optimism that I do not share. My father was a soldier, I am a soldier, and I believe the day will come when my son must also wield a sword."

Nico registered surprise upon hearing Massimo's remark. "You have a son?" he asked.

Massimo rose, placed a hand on Nico's shoulder, laughed, and said, "Not one that I know of."

The two men resumed their study of the note cards. They worked quietly until they became aware of faint footsteps climbing the staircase at the far end of the hallway. There were no other occupied offices on the upper level; either someone was coming to fetch items from a storage area, or they were about to have a visitor.

Massimo listened attentively to the sound. When he had trained new army recruits, he taught them how to recognize distinctive footfalls. As the person advanced through the hallway, Massimo said, "He is wearing soft leather shoes, and he walks with the shuffle of one who has a shorter leg. It is one of the chancery clerks, the one with the boyish face and the crooked smile."

Massimo had honed keen observational skills in the military; in contrast, Nico had not distinguished any of the clerks as having one leg shorter than the other, much less a boyish face with a crooked smile. When the messenger stepped into the doorway, he was surprised to see Massimo and Nico looking directly at him. He did indeed have a boyish face. In halting words, the clerk said, "The chancellor asks that you come to his office."

"Both of us?" Nico asked.

"Yes," the clerk replied in a soft voice, almost a whisper. Having delivered his message, the timid lad exited the room and retreated down the hallway.

Compared to the cramped office of the commissioners, Chancellor Scala's office was expansive. The center of the room held a conference table surrounded by padded chairs to accommodate visitors. A modest desk was set against the wall in a corner. Bright light streamed in through large windows along one wall. One was open to let in the crisp autumn air.

As usual, Scala was standing so he could scan the array of notes filling the walls of his office. After brief greetings, Scala said, "I have received disturbing news. Our couriers have brought word that Milanese authorities have detained Signor Colombo."

Nico tensed. "Detained?" he asked.

"Has he been imprisoned?" Massimo questioned.

"No, they have not put him in prison, nor charged him with

a crime," Scala replied. "He is being confined in the Florentine embassy. The guardia says it will not file charges out of respect for the Florentine Republic."

"Why is he being confined?" Nico asked.

"The embassy dispatch says that Signor Colombo was inquiring about the disappearance of the Medici bank book-keeper. The Milanese guardia claims that the inquiry was inter-fering with his investigation, so he convinced authorities to have Signor Colombo detained."

Nico said, "Two weeks ago the embassy reported that Milan was not investigating the bookkeeper's disappearance. Has that changed? Did they finally begin an investigation?"

"The dispatch does not say what steps, if any, are being taken by the guardia in Milan. But in any case, Signor Colombo should not be detained for asking questions. Signor Mozzi and I have discussed the issue and considered possible courses of action. We agree that the confinement is an unjust overreaction by some Milanese officials, and we believe that they will relent if their misstep is exposed." Scala looked directly at Nico. "We request that you journey to Milan and use legal means to get the restriction rescinded."

Nico nodded to acknowledge Scala's request. He had never been to Milan and knew little about the city itself. He did know it was the principal city of the Duchy of Milan, a long-time ally of Florence. More importantly though, he knew nothing of the duchy's laws or legal system. "Doesn't the embassy in Milan already have lawyers?" Nico asked.

"There are notaries at the embassy, but not lawyers. We use Milanese lawyers to represent us in routine matters, but this is a more delicate issue." Scala then turned to face Massimo. "We request that you accompany Signor Argenti to Milan. If legal means fail and another approach is needed, your talents might be invaluable." Massimo squared his shoulders in anticipation.

Something real, he thought. Much better than sitting in an office staring at note cards on a wall.

To both men, Scala said, "The government of Milan is different from ours. You will need help from someone who knows its laws and rules of behavior. When I studied in Milan, I studied with another student, Piero Tollino. I still correspond with Piero; he is now an *uschiero*, a mid-level official, at the Judicial Chancery." Scala handed Nico a letter. "This is a personal letter from me to Piero asking for his help. Contact him when you arrive. I have instructed a chancery courier to arrange horses for your travel in the morning."

Scala gave Nico a second paper. "This is a letter of introduction issued by the Signoria. It names you three commissioners as envoys engaged in official business of the Republic of Florence."

Nico left Scala's office apprehensive about the mission. Massimo beamed with excitement, eager for adventure.

9

THE UCCELLO, FLORENCE

On the evening before their departure for Milan, Massimo joined Nico and his family for dinner at the Uccello, the restaurant owned by his cousin Donato. Loyal patrons praised the Uccello as the most elegant restaurant in the city. Massimo eagerly accepted Nico's invitation. In the military, Massimo had learned never to dismiss the opportunity for a meal, especially when one is a guest.

When Nico entered the Uccello, he found the tables throughout the dining area occupied by older men who adhered to early meal schedules. Along the periphery of the room, younger men wearing more stylish garb sat on couches clustered around low tables to enjoy drinks, snacks, and pleasant conversation. As they threaded their way toward the rear of the room, Massimo slowed to watch men at one table playing a game of cards. "Not the usual activity found in restaurants," Massimo observed.

"The Uccello is unique. It is a dining club," Nico explained. "Donato conceived the idea of making the Uccello a place where men can play cards or relax with a drink, as well as enjoy a delicious meal. As you can see, his concept proved to be very popular among the men of Florence."

Across the room, Donato stood at a table listening to one of the diners, who laughed and clapped his hands repeatedly while he regaled his friends with a story. Nico gestured in Donato's direction and told Massimo, "The one standing is Donato. He is my cousin, but ever since my parents died, many years ago, he has been like a brother to me. The men seated at the table are members of the *Arte della lana*, the wool guild. In the past, when they were active in their businesses, those men were fierce competitors, always attempting to lure customers from each other. Now their sons operate the shops and carry on the rivalries, while these men want nothing more than to share old stories with good friends."

Rather than interrupt Donato, Nico led Massimo to the kitchen, the restaurant's activity center. They entered the kitchen where the *capocuoco*, the head chef, and an assistant were tending a line of slowly simmering pots. As soon as Massimo inhaled the oily aroma, he beamed and exclaimed, "Pheasant! If I were not already hungry, I certainly would be now."

Massimo's outburst drew the attention of the head chef, who responded, "You are correct. This is the ideal season to serve pheasant. All the poult born in the spring have grown enough to be plump and tender at this time of year, but they are not yet old enough to be tough and stringy. Pheasant and other game birds fill the fields in the hills outside the city." Grinning, he added, "They are just waiting to be eaten."

"When I was young, my father and I would hunt pheasant," Massimo began. "Lazy hunters use snares because it takes no skill to hunt with snares. They merely set the traps and then come back later to collect the unlucky birds. Father taught me the art of hunting with a bow. The challenge is to target the head or neck because a strike to the body might pierce an organ and spoil the meat. During my first year, I landed more arrows in the brush than in pheasants, but by the second year, I had as much success as my father."

"Have you kept your skill with the bow?" Nico asked.

"No, my interest in hunting waned after my father died. However, his influence continued to guide me in other ways. Wars were unending during his career in the army. He fought against Milan and later against Venice. He even survived the brutal and foolish attacks against Lucca, only to be stricken years later by a malady that the physicians could not cure. While father shared with me many accounts of battles and conquest, I credit his stories of friendship and camaraderie for drawing me to a career in the military."

Massimo walked closer to the steaming pots and drew in another sample of the complex aroma. "We always roasted the birds on a spit. We never made a stew such as this."

Nico said, "This restaurant is named Uccello, bird, in honor of the chef's creativity in preparing game birds."

"Today, we are making pheasant in a mushroom and wine sauce," the chef explained. "Before we cook any birds, we hang them on a rack to let the oils develop. It is the oil that creates the aroma you noticed as soon as you walked into the kitchen. The oils help to make the meat tender. Today, we are preparing both pheasant stew, which you see here, and roasted pheasant with vegetables. Roasted pheasant is the most popular offering. For the roast, we begin by searing the meat to lock in the juices. We do that outside. Come, I'll show you."

The chef led Nico and Massimo through the rear door to the outdoor area behind the kitchen. He pointed to his right, where a cook was placing pheasant breasts on a fiery hot grill. "One or two minutes on the grill and then they go inside to bake in an oven," the chef explained.

To their left, two adolescent boys were removing birds from the hanging rack and plucking feathers. Standing alongside the boys, Donato's wife Joanna was selecting the most colorful plumes from the pile of plucked feathers. She waved her collection in the air as she approached Nico. "This evening there will be a birthday celebration for the daughter of Bernardo Bardi in one of the private rooms. I think the girl will delight in seeing the room decorated with these."

Nico introduced Joanna, then explained to Massimo, "The private rooms are for special events hosted by members. Women and non-members are not permitted in the Uccello's main dining room, but they are allowed in the private rooms as guests of members."

The men followed Joanna inside and through the kitchen to one of the private rooms. Moments later, Donato entered the room carrying two bottles of Chianti. As he poured the wine, he said, "There is nothing in Milan to compare with our outstanding Tuscan wines." He held out a glass to Massimo and said, "Drink heartily, Massimo, so you can carry the memory of this rich Chianti with you." He passed glasses to the others, then raised his and said, "May your visit to Milan be enjoyable and successful."

Nico had just raised a glass to his lips when an attractive woman with chestnut-brown skin entered the room. She approached him from behind and tousled his wavy hair. Without looking back to see her, Nico said to Massimo, who was seated across from him, "This is my sister Alessa."

Alessa slid into the seat next to Nico, looked across the table and said, "And you must be Massimo, the soldier." He nodded to confirm that her assumption was correct, but before he could respond verbally, she added, "You have the powerful aura of a soldier, one who has seen victory in battle."

Massimo recalled reading a biography of Julius Caesar that described the great Roman as having a warrior's aura. At the time, Massimo dismissed the claim as literary hyperbole. Many of his military comrades had superstitions, and some believed in the supernatural, but none had ever professed to seeing auras. Although Massimo was not a believer in the occult, he smiled broadly to acknowledge Alessa's compliment.

Alessa withdrew a thin leather strip from her pocket and fastened it around Nico's wrist; then she moved around the table and attached a similar band on Massimo's wrist. When he raised his arm to examine the strap, Massimo saw an oxblood red design in the shape of a hand engraved in the leather. He looked quizzically at Alessa, who explained, "Religions have found meaning in this symbol for millennia. Christians call it the Hand of Mary. In the religion of my tribe, it is the Hand of Fatima, the protector. May it protect you from evil and harm on your journey."

"Your tribe?" Massimo questioned, as confused as ever.

Nico explained, "Alessa was taken from her first family in Morocco at a young age. We are thankful that Donato rescued her from a life of slavery and brought her to join our family."

"Traditions, like the Hand of Fatima, are all I have to connect me with my heritage," Alessa said. Nico recognized her wistful tone whenever his adopted sister spoke of her child-hood. Discretion kept Massimo from pressing for details about her rescue from slavery. He assumed correctly that doing so might bring forth unpleasant memories. Similarly, discretion kept Alessa from inquiring about the scar that marked Massimo's cheek.

Alessa returned to her seat just as servers entered carrying bowls of soup and crusty artisan bread. They were followed by the head chef who helped to deliver the main course. As he set a heaping platter of roast pheasant onto the table, he said, "In recognition of the hunter with us today, it is my pleasure to offer samples of both of today's featured dinners, pheasant stew and roasted pheasant."

"*Eccellente*," Massimo declared after tasting his first mouthful of the stew. "Your delicious creation honors the life of this animal."

Conversation dwindled during dinner and resumed only when the platters of roasted and stewed pheasant had been emptied. Joanna turned to Massimo and said, "The Signoria tells us that we are at peace with our neighbors, yet Alessa senses you saw conflict during your time in the military." Her statement was intended to engender a response, but Massimo was not one who relished speaking about his military endeavors. Whenever he and his comrades gathered in taverns after missions, Massimo preferred to sit quietly while others boasted of their feats, real and imagined. He gave only a curt response to Joanna's statement, saying, "My unit saw time in the north, keeping roads safe for travelers." He made no mention of the citations for valor that he had earned by repelling enemies of the republic.

Massimo's curt reply told Joanna that he did not wish to dwell on his military career, so she switched to a less sensitive topic. "Have you ever visited Milan?"

"I have traveled to Pavia in the Duchy of Milan, but I have never visited the city of Milan itself. On that occasion, my military unit escorted a professor who was returning to the University of Pavia."

Joanna stiffened at the mention of a military escort. Her husband did not expose himself to precarious situations, so her protective instincts centered on Nico. She was not overly fearful, but in her mind, Nico seemed disposed to risky ventures. "Thank God I don't know of your escapades at the university," she had once told him.

"Why did the professor need an escort? Are the roads in the duchy unsafe?" she asked hesitantly.

"Two roads cross the mountains to link Tuscany with Lombardy, the Via Frangenica, which has been used by pilgrims since Roman times, and La via degli Abati, the way of the abbots. Both of those roads are well-traveled and safe." Massimo paused before adding, "However, I cannot speak about the byways in the duchy."

His answer did little to assuage her concern. "How long is the journey?" she asked.

This time it was Nico who answered. "The courier who will be traveling with us said we will spend several days en route. The chancery will arrange for new mounts at villages along the way, so we need not spend time resting the horses."

Joanna looked again to Massimo and said, "Nico said it is a legal matter that draws him to Milan. Is that also your purpose? Do you have legal training?"

Before Massimo could respond, Nico said, "If my legal efforts fail, Massimo will devise a more imaginative means to free Vittorio.... and keep me from becoming another unwilling occupant of our embassy in Milan

Worried that the journey might place Nico in danger, yet somewhat reassured knowing he would have a protector, Joanna smiled weakly. She scanned Massimo's muscular arms, rugged face, and well-toned body. "You certainly look capable of applying pressure whenever it is needed," she teased. Massimo, who by now had become accustomed to her light manner, returned her smile. Donato gave his wife a playful kick under the table while saying, "Joanna, you must let our guest enjoy his meal and not question him without pause lest he feel subjected to a Papal inquisition."

"My words are hardly adequate repayment for this outstanding meal. Nico is indeed fortunate to have such a fine and caring family," Massimo replied. After they enjoyed a cherry custard dessert, Massimo thanked everyone for their hospitality, promised Joanna that he would keep Nico from harm, and excused himself, saying he needed to prepare for an early departure the following morning.

After the others left, Donato and Nico lingered over glasses of grappa. Donato's brow furrowed as he considered the situation that Nico would be facing. "You said that your purpose in going to Milan is to gain the release of your colleague Vittorio. Since you are unfamiliar with the local customs and legal practices in Milan, how will you proceed when you arrive?"

"If Vittorio were being confined in Siena or Venice, I would know how to enter an appeal because those states are republics with legal practices like ours," Nico replied, "But every duchy has its own peculiar legal system. Some dukes and lords crave power, and they do so by meddling into all but the most insignificant matters. In their territories, justice comes at the whim of the ruler, so it could be impossible to overturn a ruling in one of those states. Fortunately, Duke Sforza is a just ruler who cares for the people of Milan, although even he exerts some influence over judicial procedures. Chancellor Scala has an acquaintance at the chancery in Milan who can provide me with guidance on how to issue an appeal, so my first move will be to visit the chancery to seek his assistance."

Donato studied Nico's expression, hoping to discern his level of confidence in the mission. "Massimo appears to be experienced and trustworthy," Donato opined, then said, "You have not spoken of the other commission member, Vittorio. Is he alone in Milan?"

"We had scant time to become acquainted before Vittorio was dispatched to Milan, and in our time together, he said little. Vittorio is a respected investigator and investigators prefer to work without assistance, so it is not surprising that he was sent to Milan alone. Whether he will be comfortable working with Massimo and me will not become clear until we reach Milan."

10

TRAVELING TO MILAN

Nico, Massimo, and a courier set out at daybreak. "We will go until dark," the courier said. The statement was of little concern to Massimo, who had spent many long days in the saddle during his military service. He enjoyed the exhilaration of patrolling the countryside atop a responsive steed.

Nico, in contrast, was not an equestrian; to him, the courier's words were a forewarning. Only two days into the journey, he lay awake at night for what seemed like hours, waiting for his muscles to relax enough to let him sleep. Whenever he felt such discomfort at home, Alessa would create an ointment to soothe the ache or a potion to drink for relief. Lacking her treatments, he could only wait for time to ease the soreness.

Near the border with the Republic of Lucca, they passed a Florentine military encampment. As he rode past, Massimo sighted two of his former comrades. Under other circumstances, he would have stopped to exchange greetings, but time was precious, so he settled for exchanging waves and shouts with them as he rode past.

On the relatively flat terrain between Florence and the town of Pontremoli, the travelers changed to fresh horses only once each day. Beyond Pontremoli, they began the steep ascent into the Apennine mountains. Horses tired more quickly in that rugged terrain, so each day saw the men using three mounts.

As they approached the highest elevation, the Cisa Pass, the road ahead disappeared into a featureless curtain of fog. "There is usually fog at this time of year," the courier announced. "We are fortunate today because only the highest part of the road is fogbound. Often the fog extends farther down the mountain." The courier cautioned, "The mist will be cold. You will see." At his direction, they dismounted so that each man could don a wool mantello and a hooded rain cloak.

His warning was proved true minutes after they entered the fog by an icy gust whipping through the narrow pass. Nico lowered his head to ward off the swirling mist while hoping they would soon descend into the warm Po River valley.

They reached the bottom of the valley and the Po River itself at Piacenza, a bustling town where heavily traveled trade routes converged. Merchants arriving from the west carried goods from ships in the port city of Genoa. Other traders were making their way across the Italian peninsula on the Via Aemelia with merchandise bound for the Adriatic seaport of Rimini.

At the river edge, they dismounted and walked the horses onto a flat-topped ferry to transit the wide river. Two heavily muscled oarsmen strained to move the craft through the fast-flowing water. Nico wisely positioned himself upwind of the sweaty boatmen. Massimo soon joined him. Eyeing the oarsmen, Nico said, "Hard work."

"They certainly have the smell of hard-working men," Massimo laughed.

Modest stone and log farmhouses dotted the countryside near Milan. Rows cut into fields where crops grown in summer had been turned into brown mud by autumn rains. Scrawny goats searched the croplands for any remaining clumps of grass. The city ahead showed neither defensive towers reaching skyward nor a cathedral dome comparable to Brunelleschi's magnificent creation in Florence. The few buildings that poked above the distant city wall were as gray as the dismal sky overhead. Nico sighed, anticipating that he was about to enter a distressed city filled with impoverished people.

His opinion changed when he passed through the Porta Romana gate into the heart of the walled city. The streets held buildings with shops on the lower level and residences on upper levels, just as in Florence. In the distance were palazzos akin to those of Florence's wealthy merchants, and at the center of the city was a prominent government building that resembled Florence's Palazzo dei Signori. Churches appeared everywhere.

One striking difference between the two cities was that buildings were spaced farther apart in Milan. A sign proclaimed the plaza in front of the cathedral as Piazza del Duomo. Every Italian city with a cathedral seemed to have a Piazza del Duomo. All other streets and piazzas had unfamiliar names making Milan feel both familiar and strange. On closer inspection, it was clear that Milan lacked Florence's affluence. While the major roads were paved with cobblestones, the minor streets had only dirt surfaces.

Nico dismounted for the final time at the Florentine embassy onto unsteady, rubbery legs. "Will I ever walk again with straight legs and my knees together?" he wondered aloud.

Massimo waited until the courier departed with the horses before he gave Nico a friendly slap on the back and said, "This was but a single journey. It may have been difficult for you, but you will recover. The couriers who sit astride horses every day;

they are the ones who turn themselves into giant wishbones. I have never met a courier who could touch his knees together."

As he joked with Nico, Massimo's military training had him surveying the embassy surroundings. He concentrated on the two sentries standing in a grassy clearing across from the embassy. Their conversation came in spurts: a brief exchange followed by a lengthy silence. In the quiet intervals, the beefier man pushed a stone along the ground aimlessly with the toe of his boot. Their behavior made Massimo recall the many long hours he had spent on boring assignments early in his military career. "Poor bastards," he said to himself. "But at least you have each other for company." Guards were not routinely assigned to protect foreign properties, so Massimo assumed that the purpose of these sentinels was to deter Vittorio from escaping his confinement.

Massimo studied the building, looking for ways to engineer an escape should that become necessary. The embassy was not large enough to contain spacious living quarters befitting an ambassador as well as diplomatic offices and staff housing, so Massimo concluded that the ambassador made his home in a fancy palazzo elsewhere in the city. In Massimo's experience, ambassadors always demanded elegant living arrangements and other perquisites. If this embassy is configured the same as others I have seen, he thought, it will have reception and meeting rooms on the first level, offices on the second level, and staff living quarters on the upper level. There will be two staircases, one near the front of the building for embassy officials and dignitaries, and one at the rear for workers.

From his position, Massimo could see the front door, the one used by official callers. The two sentries watched that door. On the side of the building near the rear was another door, a smaller one, where deliveries were received. That door was not visible from the officers' vantage point. Massimo laughed as he realized how easy it would be to free Vittorio, much easier than the prison breaks he had orchestrated to liberate drunken comrades from confinement when he was in the military. Milanese officials were relying on the integrity and good faith of their Florentine allies to keep Vittorio contained in the embassy. Massimo pointed to the door as he said to Nico, "These guards serve no real purpose; they are merely symbolic. Unless he is locked in a room, Vittorio could walk out the side door at any time without being seen. Those guards have no way to know whether Vittorio is still in the embassy." Laughing, he added, "If Vittorio were to leave, the guards might return faithfully to their post for many days to contain a phantom."

The image of men standing vigil over a spirit had Nico laughing as well. "However, we need Vittorio's help to locate the missing bookkeeper. If he were to leave the embassy and then be seen questioning witnesses throughout the city, the guardia would quickly realize he cannot be in two places. They would know that he had escaped."

They advanced to the building's entrance where Massimo pulled open the ornate front door. Inside, a receiving clerk welcomed Nico and Massimo to the embassy and led them to the spacious and well-appointed office of the ambassador on the second level. Florence's chief diplomat stood near a window with a book in hand when Nico and Massimo entered his office. A scowl signaled that he did not welcome the interruption. Nico withdrew two letters from a folio and presented them to the ambassador. The first letter identified him, Massimo, and Vittorio as members of the Florentine Security Commission. It stated that they were engaged in official business on behalf of the Florentine Republic, and it requested that the reader grant them courtesies and considerations. The letter bore the imprint of the Florentine Signoria and the signature of its secretary.

"Yet another commission," the disinterested ambassador mumbled as he scanned the page.

He returned the formal letter of introduction to Nico, who produced a second sheet. The second letter was addressed to the ambassador and signed by two Signoria members. It stipulated that the Commission was accountable only to the Signoria and that no one at the embassy should impede the commissioners from carrying out their mission, nor should commission members be expected to share their findings with any persons at the embassy. The diplomat stiffened and his ears reddened as he read the note. He was the Florentine Republic's highest-ranking representative in Milan. It was unthinkable for this fledgling commission to operate outside his authority. If these neophytes antagonize the Ducal Court, it will be my ass that suffers the consequences, he told himself. Without a word to his visitors, he turned to the clerk and said, "Take them to see their colleague."

As the three men stepped from his office, the ambassador crumpled the second paper into a tiny mass and called out to the clerk, "The embassy has limited space. We do not have extra rooms for two more ... transients. Tell someone to find them accommodations elsewhere."

In the hallway, Massimo commented, "Is the ambassador always inhospitable?" The clerk just shrugged.

11

FLORENTINE EMBASSY, MILAN

Vittorio sat with his arms folded across his chest, looking out a window of his sparse room when Nico and Massimo entered. "Look at him sitting there enjoying the scenery happier than a pig in mud, or maybe he has fallen asleep," Massimo quipped.

Startled by the sound of Massimo's voice, Vittorio sprang up with a force that propelled the chair backward and crashing into the far wall, and uttered only a single word, "What?"

"The Signoria expects our commission to serve a purpose. As much as you might enjoy the confines of this embassy, you were not sent to Milan to sit idle," Massimo jested.

"Much longer in this room and I will go mad. If you look up, you might see my footprints climbing the walls and criss-crossing the ceiling. Am I free to leave?"

"Not yet," Nico replied, "but we were sent to Milan to secure your release. Have you been mistreated?"

"No, the embassy staff tolerates my presence, but they keep me isolated. They refuse to share any news with me. Has the bookkeeper been found?"

"No, Signor Salvetti is still missing," Nico replied.

Vittorio slammed his fist against the wall. "The guardia in Milan must be fools. Damn them! They should be searching for Salvetti. Abductions have only two outcomes. Captives who are rescued quickly suffer only beatings; the others, those who are held longer, are never found alive."

Nico waited a moment for Vittorio's ire to subside; then he said, "Massimo and I were sent here to secure your release so you can resume your search for Salvetti. My main objective is to have a magistrate vacate the confinement order that restricts you to the embassy. To do that, I need to understand the circumstances that led to your confinement."

Vittorio righted the upturned chair and offered it to Nico. He sat on the bed, the only other furnishing in the room. Massimo remained standing and paced between the window and the doorway of the cramped space.

"The officer assigned to investigate this case is a disgrace to his dirty, sweat-stained uniform," Vittorio fumed. "Judging from his appearance, instead of investigating, he spends his time eating."

Vittorio took a few breaths and calmed himself before continuing. "When I arrived in Milan, I went to the guardia office to ask about progress in the investigation. That is when I met the cretin. He told me the guardia does not share information about official matters with anyone, especially foreigners. He said I should get my ass back to Florence.

"Since he was no help, I began my own investigation looking for evidence and witnesses. I started by speaking with a bank employee who told me that after the bank had closed for the day, Signor Salvetti went to deliver a proposal to the office of architect Filarete. Salvetti was making the delivery in the place of the bank manager who had taken ill. Filarete is the architect that Duke Sforza commissioned to design a new hospital that will care for the poor. When the hospital is completed, it will be the largest in Milan, possibly the largest on the Italian peninsula. The proposal that Salvetti carried described an arrangement for the Medici bank to fund the project. I walked the route from the bank to the architect's office, and from there to Salvetti's house, looking for clues."

Vittorio moved from the bed to the corner of the room, where his duffel rested on the floor. He withdrew a shoe from the duffel and held it out to Nico. "Along the way, between the bank and the architect's office, I found this under a bush."

Massimo took the shoe and studied it. "What are these two rows of holes?" he asked.

"Teeth marks. Canine teeth marks," Vittorio explained. "Notice also that the strap has come loose. The fastener that fixes the strap in place is missing. In the road wedged between two cobblestones, I found this." Vittorio held out his other hand to display a small silver clasp cradled in his palm. "I suspect that a dog found the shoe in the road and dragged it to the lilac bush where he chewed it. When the dog pulled on the shoe, the clasp broke free,"

"The shoe must have been under the bush for several days before you found it. Why didn't the guardia investigators find it?" Nico asked.

Vittorio grimaced to express his disdain for the Milanese investigator and raised his hands with open palms outward, signifying that he had no explanation for their oversight. "The shoe was in plain sight. If they had been looking, they would have seen it. I brought it to Salvetti's house to see whether his wife could recognize it as belonging to her husband. She was too distraught to meet with me, so I spoke with a servant, the same one who had reported Salvetti's disappearance to the guardia, and he identified the shoe as belonging to his employer."

Vittorio paused briefly to organize his thoughts before

continuing. "The servant told me that Salvetti is the *capocollaterale*, the head bookkeeper. He is not merely a clerk, which is how the guardia investigator had described him. I have the impression that the guardia is trying to hide the fact that Salvetti is a foreigner, and one of respectable standing."

"To what end?" Nico asked.

Vittorio shook his head to signify that he did not know the motive for secrecy, then he continued his explanation. "Knowing that the shoe belonged to Salvetti, I reasoned that he was abducted before he reached the architect's office. To validate my assumption, I went to the architect's office where an apprentice confirmed that the bookkeeper never met with architect Filarete. Next, I decided to visit houses in the area where I found the shoe, hoping someone might have witnessed the abduction. None of those I questioned admitted to having seen or heard anything." Vittorio's voice descended into mockery, "I swear, if Duke Sforza and the Holy Father had paraded through the street naked, those people would deny seeing the spectacle.

"Yet one of those unhelpful bastards rushed to the authorities to report that they were being interrogated by a foreigner. I was at the fifth house when the investigator and two young officers accosted me. They claimed it was not permitted for foreigners to roam the city asking suspicious questions. They alleged that I was interfering with their investigation, although I saw no indications that they were actually conducting an investigation." Vittorio's frustration was palpable.

"Asking questions about an incident does not rise to the level of interfering with an official investigation," Nico stated. "It would not surprise me if the people you spoke with are now asking each other similar questions. If all you did was ask questions, the guardia had no basis for ordering you to be confined." At least there would be no basis under Florentine law, Nico told himself.

Vittorio's voice hardened as he continued venting. "I urged the embassy to intercede on my behalf, but they refused to get involved. Their reluctance is inexcusable. One of the major reasons for their existence is to represent Florentine citizens."

Nico nodded to acknowledge that he understood and sympathized with Vittorio's plight. As he rose to leave, he said, "I am going to meet with a member of the chancery, an acquaintance of Chancellor Scala, to seek his advice on how to bring this matter before a magistrate." Summoning his bravado, Nico added, "I am confident the district confinement order will be rescinded."

Massimo followed Nico. When he reached the door, he turned back toward Vittorio, winked, and said, "You will be out of here sooner than you think. You have my word."

12

JUDICIAL CHANCERY, MILAN

Light rain fell from a dark sky when Nico and Massimo left the embassy. They donned hooded capes and stepped carefully on the slick wet cobblestones. Despite their raingear, a cold wind-driven spray lashed their faces. Fortunately, the Florentine embassy in Milan and the offices of the Judicial Chancery were in the same district of the city, separated by only a short distance.

In Milan, each ministry of the Ducal Council had its own chancery unit, unlike Florence, where a single chancery served all branches of the government. Piero Tollino, Scala's friend and Nico's contact in Milan, was an *uschiero*, a mid-level administrator, in the Judicial Chancery. He, along with the other *uschieri* and clerks of the Judicial Chancery, occupied a small suite of offices where they processed and stored legal records dealing with civil proceedings.

The office had few visitors, so none of the staff had been explicitly tasked with receiving callers. An alert page noticed Nico and Massimo when they entered. He greeted them warmly, in contrast with the frosty reception they had received at the embassy, and led them to a meeting room where they waited while the page sought Signor Tollino. The compact room held only six chairs set around a circular table. A painting of someone in fancy dress uniform hung on one wall. "He must be a *condottiero*, a mercenary," Massimo stated. "The uniform is not that of an army officer."

"It could be Duke Sforza," Nico speculated. "Francesco Sforza was a condottiero before the people of Milan welcomed him as their ruler and gave him the title of duke."

Nico had no training in the arts, but his friend Sandro Botticelli had taught Nico how to recognize paintings created by a master. The portrait he was viewing lacked the qualities of a master's work. "The face shows distinct color separations instead of smooth gradations. The shadows are unrealistic, and in some places, they are missing entirely. An apprentice probably painted it," Nico opined. "Perhaps they commissioned students to do the work so every government office can have a similar copy."

Massimo looked out through the open doorway to observe the activities of the chancery staff. "I suppose what they are doing has value, but they seem to be just moving papers from one stack to other stacks."

Nico explained, "The clerks are reviewing reports received from officials throughout the duchy. Most of the reports will be filed, but some require action by an administrator or the chancellor. The clerks are culling out the documents that need attention."

Tollino hummed a tune as he bounced into the room. He was Scala's age, with gray hair, a paunch, and a vivacious spirit. His happy face radiated perpetual cheer with a smile that drove all wrinkles from his brow. Tollino's willingness to help others made him beloved by everyone at the chancery. Before even asking his callers the reason for their visit, he dispatched the page to fetch refreshments.

Nico presented Tollino with two letters of introduction. One was a personal note from Bartolomeo Scala. The other was the official authorization of the Florentine Security Commission. Tollino barely glanced at the formal letter. The note from his friend, he cradled lightly while he read and re-read it slowly several times. He folded the paper with care, looked up, and said, "Welcome to Milan. I am happy to be of assistance. What do you require?"

After the three men took seats at the table, Nico described their two-fold mission. "My first goal is to free our colleague Vittorio Colombo from his confinement at the embassy. Then, after Vittorio is released, we will turn our attention to solving Signor Salvetti's disappearance. The guardia claims that Vittorio is being confined to prevent him from interfering with their investigation, but there is no indication that they are actually investigating the incident. For some reason, they are unwilling to consider the possibility that Signor Salvetti was abducted."

Tollino digested the information Nico provided and then said, "It may be that the investigator is incompetent, but there is also another possible explanation for his behavior. Our legal structure in Milan is different from yours. We have two distinct and often competing judicial systems. The local magistrates decide which cases the district guardia should investigate. When Signor Salvetti's disappearance was reported, the district magistrate examined the facts to determine whether an investigation was warranted."

"Yes," Nico confirmed, "that is similar to our system in Florence."

Tollino raised his hand to emphasize his next words. "Here is the difference. The authority of the local magistrates is limited. Within the Ducal Court is a Privy Council responsible for political and diplomatic issues plus judicial proceedings of great weight."

Massimo tilted back in his chair, folded his arms, and closed his eyes. He could fathom that there might be an overlap between local magistrates and the Privy Council, but understanding the full implications was for lawyers like Nico to comprehend.

Tollino waited for Nico to register the significance of his statement. A few moments passed before Nico asked, "What exactly is a judicial proceeding of great weight?"

The question brought a twinkle to Tollino's eye. "It is whatever the Privy Council declares it to be."

Massimo had learned the importance of power when he was in the military, and Tollino's remark told him that in Milan the Privy Council had the power. He opened his eyes and speculated, "So, if the Privy Council were to become aware of Salvetti's disappearance, they might push the district authority aside."

Tollino spread his hands and smiled broadly. "Very astute; that is a very real possibility. Drawing from past actions of the council, I believe they would assert that the disappearance of a bank official who is a foreigner and a relative of Piero de Medici is a politically sensitive matter. They would assume jurisdiction over the matter even if there were no crime."

Both Massimo and Nico had seen instances where the involvement of higher authorities resulted in unwanted complications. He wondered if that were also true in Milan or if attention from the Privy Council might help his cause. "Would our best course be to engage the Privy Council?" Nico asked warily.

"No, not at all," Tollino replied. "The military conducts all investigations that are ordered by the council. Milan has one of the largest and finest armies on the Italian peninsula. They are skilled in waging war, but very few are competent investigators. Asking soldiers to solve crimes is a failing of our judicial system. You might draw a skilled investigator, and there are some, but there is a greater likelihood of an incompetent being assigned."

The intricacies of Milan's complex judicial practices became clear to Nico. He stated his understanding so Tollino could point out any flaws in his reasoning. "Local magistrates wish to retain control, and they can only do so when incidents presented to them are minor infractions. The guardia takes its direction from the magistrates, so the investigator tried to minimize the importance of Salvetti's disappearance. He did that by calling Salvetti a clerk and denying that a crime might have been committed."

"Exactly," said Tollino. "While an investigation is underway, it must be made to appear as an insignificant matter to avoid the involvement of the Privy Council. Then, after the case is solved, its importance can be revealed to earn praise for the magistrate and the guardia."

"Your explanation suggests that Vittorio's fate rests with the local magistrate. To get him released from confinement, I should file an appeal with that magistrate."

Tollino nodded. "That is the place to start. You can enter the appeal at the office of the Podestà."

"Then there is the issue of uncovering the reason for Salvetti's disappearance," Nico mused. "Vittorio has a great deal of experience solving crimes that have perplexed other investigators. He would be a valuable participant in the investigation, but the guardia are unwilling to accept his assistance."

Tollino rubbed his chin, ran a hand through his silver hair, and shook his head. "If the guardia desired help, there would be no issue, but I am not surprised that they do not want to have foreigners involved in their business. There may be precedents or statutes that could benefit your cause; however, I cannot help you with those because I am not a lawyer. I am not familiar ..."

He stopped speaking abruptly. Moments later, he clapped his hands and resumed speaking in a confident tone. "Ordinarily, I would suggest that you seek advice at the law school of the University of Pavia. But the goddess Fortuna is smiling on you. Ciupo Beccaria, one of the most highly regarded professors at the law school, will be giving a lecture here in Milan tomorrow. I plan to attend his lecture. After the lecture, there will be an opportunity to speak with the professor. He may be able to cite statues that can help you make your case."

The prospect of obtaining guidance from a legal expert raised Nico's spirit. When their legal discussions ended, Tollino asked Nico and Massimo where they were staying while in Milan. Massimo replied, "A person at the embassy recommended the Two Angels Inn."

Tollino's face twisted in disgust. "That is not a suitable accommodation," he insisted.

The chancery clerk who had been listening to the conversation chuckled, "Two Angels has a reputation for its bugs outnumbering its guests."

"You must stay at the palazzo of Contessa Maddalena del Carretto," Tollino asserted. "When her husband Conte Pietro Torelli died, his estate, including the palazzo, passed to his young son. The boy is a minor, so the Contessa serves as custodian of the proprieties. She is delighted to have foreign dignitaries as her guests. Among them have been French princes and Austrian dukes."

Nico and Massimo looked to each other and shared the same thought: "Never in any dream have I considered myself to be dignitary akin to a prince or duke."

Tollino continued, "The Contessa believes that the only way

she and her children can learn about the outside world is to expose themselves to people who live there. I am certain she would like to hear news from Florence."

Nico and Massimo looked skeptical until Tollino added, "It is my honor to be the godfather of the Contessa's younger son Francesco. I will bring you to the palazzo and introduce you to the Contessa and her lovely family."

Nico remained at the chancery while Tollino finished the task he had been doing when his two visitors arrived. Massimo excused himself, saying he wanted to take a short walk to get familiar with the city.

13

PALAZZO TORELLI, MILAN

After leaving the chancery, Tollino escorted Nico to Palazzo Torelli. The Palazzo, named for the contessa's late husband, stood taller than the other dwellings in its district where large private residences were the norm. Palazzo Torelli had four levels, a spacious courtyard, and an elaborate guest house. Meticulously landscaped grounds surrounded the structure. A curved path wound through a garden on one side of the building with stone benches spaced along the path that allowed visitors to sit and enjoy the natural setting. Nico could only imagine how pleasant the space must be in spring, with blossoms and flowering trees in bloom.

Tollino led Nico to the palazzo's front entrance and raised the heavy door knocker engraved with the image of a bull. "The bull is a symbol of the Torelli family. It appears on their family crest," Tollino said.

A servant answered Tollino's knock and escorted him and Nico into the anteroom where they waited while the servant informed the contessa of their arrival. On one wall, a luxurious silk tapestry depicted ancient gods feasting in a lush garden. Two large gold-framed portraits of distinguished-looking men faced each other from opposite walls. With a quick glance, Nico discerned that the paintings were superior in quality to the portrait displayed in the chancery. Nico assumed the images to be notable members of the Torelli family, a lineage established in Milan for centuries.

Contessa Maddalena del Carretto flowed into the room wearing a pallande overdress with gold brocade and rows of pearls spiraling downward from its collar to its hemline. A cuffia, a close-fitting bonnet, decorated with pearls in a matching design, covered her head. The jewels would have violated sumptuary laws in Florence. Either Milan had no such laws, or it exempted its nobility from prosecution. The contessa went directly to Tollino and extended both of her hands. Tollino took her hands and bent to kiss the Contessa lightly on each cheek.

"Maddalena, please forgive this unannounced visit," Tollino began.

"Piero, your visits always brighten my days." Still holding Tollino's hands, she took a step back, shifted her gaze to Nico, and waited for Tollino to make introductions.

"Maddalena, may I present Messer Nico Argenti, an envoy of the Republic of Florence? He and two colleagues recently arrived in Milan."

In contrast with Tollino's formality, the contessa laughed as she said to Nico, "You arrived on horseback. Is that not so?"

Nico, who had not washed nor changed clothes since arriving in the city, flushed with guilt for reeking of animal odor in the magnificent home of this noblewoman. In a low voice, he replied, "Yes, Contessa."

"Do not feel distressed. My late husband was an avid equestrian. He often rode to hunt, and occasionally he took part in races. Having a horseman in the house brings back loving memories. But you must not address me as contessa. I use the title in public, but in my home, I prefer to be called Maddalena. I insist on informality."

She looked down at her own attire and laughed. "Do not be unsettled by my clothing. I have just returned from an event hosted by the duchess. I do not wear formal dress at home. As Piero can tell you, I delight in breaking the chains of society. I insisted on being the trustee of my son's inheritance, even though Francesco wanted to appoint one of his ministers as overseer."

Tollino chuckled, "When Maddalena says Francesco she is referring to Duke Sforza. She uses a familiar address with everyone. I remember a dinner that she gave in honor of the King of France when Maddalena kept calling him Charles."

The contessa laughed and added, "Charles did not warm to the familiarity, but his wife Marie adjusted easily. She suggested to Charles that they adopt the practice in France. I could not tell whether she was serious or merely teasing the king."

She looked to Tollino expectantly. He recognized her expression and nodded. Taking his cue, she turned back to Nico and said, "If you are not required to live at the Florentine embassy, I would be delighted to have you abide here as my guest. Piero knows how much it pleasures me to learn fresh perspectives from my foreign visitors. I am certain that is why he brought you here. He mentioned that others accompanied you from Florence. Will they be joining us?"

"One of them is out getting oriented to the city. He will be joining us. The other is ... well, his situation is more complex."

"Ah, Piero, you have outdone yourself bringing me three

Florentines who are on a mysterious mission. It will be a wonderful topic for our dinner conversation."

Maddalena turned to address a servant who stood silently in the vestibule at the entrance to the anteroom. "Please show Nico to the guest quarters and see that he and his associates have ample hot water to freshen after their arduous journey."

The servant hefted Nico's duffel and led him through a series of corridors to a covered walkway that connected the Palazzo to the guest house. While they were walking, the servant said, "The Duke of Saxony and his bride were the most recent occupants of the guest house. They were traveling across Europe as an extended marriage celebration. On their way to Rome, they stopped in Milan as a courtesy to Duke Sforza."

When they reached the guest house, they entered a large common room with a stone fireplace, a stairway to the second level, and a corridor leading to the first-level sleeping quarters. The servant explained, "There are six rooms with sleeping accommodations, three on this level and three on the upper level. You may select whichever ones you and your colleagues prefer. Water for bathing will be brought when it is heated. The contessa also instructed the chef to prepare supper for you and your colleagues. If there is anything else you desire, pull on this cord. It will ring a bell in the main house, and one of us will respond."

Fifteen minutes later, two burly servants carried buckets of warm water to the bathing room in the guest house where they filled the large metal tub. The room contained a selection of scented oils and the softest towels Nico had ever touched.

A lengthy soak had Nico feeling clean and odor-free for the first time since leaving Florence. He was closing the final clasp on his tunic when the guest house door swung open and Massimo entered with Vittorio close behind. Nico's surprise at seeing Vittorio lasted only an instant because Massimo had all but announced that he intended to liberate their team member. "I had a suspicion that you intended to revisit the embassy."

Massimo beamed as he recounted his escapade. "I entered the building with a swagger that dissuaded any of the pluggers from questioning my purpose, and I marched directly to Vittorio's room. As soon as our good investigator saw me, he hefted his duffel, ready to leave. He needed no persuading. We followed a corridor to the rear of the building, down the rear stairs, and out the door. No one made any attempt to stop us. To avoid being seen by the officers watching the front of the building, we cut through an alley to the street behind the embassy."

"Does the ambassador know the chicken has fled the coop?" Nico joked.

"Not yet, but when he learns the prey is missing, he can use his imagination to concoct an explanation for the local authorities," Massimo growled. "If he cannot squirm out of this situation, he is too pitiful to hold the title of ambassador."

Nico spoke his thoughts aloud, "If the ambassador protests to the Signoria, they might dissolve our commission before we even complete a single assignment."

"Vittorio is a handsome Florentine," Massimo responded. Still buoyed by his successful exploit, he added, "We can tell the Signoria that a throng of passionate Milanese women stormed the embassy and carried him away."

Vittorio shifted the conversation by asking, "Is there any hot water remaining?"

"There are ample buckets of hot water for both of you," Nico replied. "And the servants said they will bring more if necessary."

As Massimo and Vittorio walked past Nico on their way to the suite of guest rooms, Nico gave Vittorio a friendly tap on the shoulder. "Regardless of how the ambassador might react, I am happy that you are liberated."

Massimo could not resist joshing Nico one more time. "The next move is yours, lawyer. Our law-abiding investigator is now an outlaw. You need to use some legal magic to get him exonerated." While Vittorio enjoyed his freedom and Massimo perused the selection of wines, Nico contemplated his meeting in the morning with Professor Beccaria.

14

NAVIGLIO CANAL, GAGGIANO

A watery sun filtered through late afternoon clouds, and the raw chill of the air hinted that this might be the coldest night of the season. Bruno and Tonio had watched five boats pass by, hoping each would be the one carrying the client' representative.

Bruno paced impatiently as another barge approached. "He better be on this one," Bruno grumbled. "I'm starting to freeze my ass." Tonio stood calmly by the farm wagon, not complaining but agreeing that the cold was seeping through his lightweight tunic.

"What is he called, the one who is coming? Bruno asked.

Tonio replied, "We weren't told his name, only that he is called the Intermediary. According to Pagatore, he represents a wealthy client."

Bruno spit on the ground. "And like Pagatore he does not dirty his hands. He hires others to do the real work. The client hired him; he hired Pagatore, and Pagatore hired us. Maybe we should find people to hire." Tonio said nothing. His attention was on the approaching barge.

The oarsman guided the barge to the Gaggiano pier. He did not leave his position because the stop was brief, only long enough to discharge a passenger. The man who stepped from the boat had a predatory face with a pronounced hooked nose and bulging eyes. A twitch in one of his legs set his whole body vibrating with his every step.

A hopeful Bruno walked toward the hooked-nose man, but before drawing close, he called out, "Are you the Intermediary?"

The man scanned Bruno from head to toe, then waited until Bruno moved closer before responding. "Are you even more stupid than you look? Do you always shout your business loud enough that the whole town can hear?"

Taken aback by the insults, Bruno stood dumbfounded. The hooked-nose man continued, "I am the Intermediary. I am here to deliver a message to the captive from the client, the one who is paying you. Where is the captive?"

"At a farm not far from here. We can take you there in that wagon," Bruno answered, pointing to the farm wagon parked nearby.

"What kind of farm is it?"

"It's a pig farm. Why do you care what kind of farm it is?"

"I thought so. That explains why you smell like pig shit. I am not going to a stinking pig farm. Bring the captive here," the Intermediary demanded.

Bruno's hands clenched, and the muscles in his neck tightened. I should teach this insolent bastard a lesson, Bruno thought, but before he did anything foolish, Tonio came beside his associate and placed a hand on Bruno's shoulder to calm the building fury. Bruno's fists did not unclench, but nor did they lash out.

"We will fetch him. The farm is not far. We will return

soon," Tonio said as he ushered his fuming companion to the wagon.

The Intermediary did not watch them depart. Instead, he turned and headed to the nearest tavern. He ordered a beer and sat at a table that gave him a view of the road to the farm. He downed one beer and concluded that an advantage of late autumn was that beer could be kept cold, as it should be. He emptied one tankard; then ordered another.

From his vantage point, the Intermediary observed dust rising from the road in the distance as the first indication that the farm wagon was returning. He finished his drink unhurriedly before exiting the tavern and walking along the canal bank to the road. He arrived at the same time as the wagon and made sure to keep a discreet distance from the stench that was made more intense by Salvetti's presence.

Bruno propelled Salvetti from the wagon, sending him crashing to the ground. With his hands tied, Salvetti struggled to push himself to a standing position. Although his legs were not bound, the rope looped around his neck prevented him from fleeing.

With anger building in his voice, the Intermediary snarled, "Who is this miserable creature, and why have you brought him to me?"

"He is the person we took in Milan," Bruno explained

"Stupid fools. He is not the bank manager. He is not Portinari. You bungling asses took the wrong man. I was told that Pagatore employed competent people, not fools incapable of doing even a simple job. I wasted my time coming here."

The Intermediary did not wait to hear their excuses; he turned abruptly and limped along the path beside the canal toward the wharf where a barge was about to depart for Milan. He moved rapidly at a pace that accentuated his twitching to the extent that any onlookers might well have imagined he was having a seizure. At the wharf, he climbed aboard the boat, flipped a silver coin to the steerman, and settled down onto the wooden crate that would be his seat on the journey to Milan. As the barge departed, the Intermediary looked up. Heavy clouds hid the sun and darkened the western sky. Thank God I was able to board this craft, he thought; if the weather grows worse, this might be the last barge of the day traveling to Milan.

"He was coming from the bank exactly as Pagatore said he would," a perplexed Bruno said to himself as much as to his associate.

Tonio spun through possibilities, things he could say or do, that might remedy the situation, but none came to mind other than the truth. Their action needed defending. He sprinted after the barge and reached it just as it pushed away from the dock. He fell in step behind the horses towing the craft and called across the water to plead his case. "We were not given a description of the target. We were told that he would be walking alone from the Medici bank to the office of architect Filarete shortly after the bank closed. This man was the only one who did so."

The steerman scrunched his face in a puzzled expression, wondering if the strange commentary was meant for him. The Intermediary listened to Tonio's plea. He did not respond, but his scowl faded. With nothing more to add, Tonio ended his pursuit and gazed at the barge as it pulled away. He thought he detected a slight nod of the Intermediary's head as he turned back toward the road. Did the Intermediary accept his excuse? He looked up just as Bruno hoisted a boulder the size of a pallone ball and smashed it into the side of Salvetti's head. The sharp crack reached Tonio with a sound like a lumberman's ax cleaving a chestnut log. The bookkeeper's lifeless body slumped to the ground.

Bruno always had a penchant for violence. At age ten, he

beat a neighborhood boy so severely that the child landed in a hospital with two broken bones. But this impulse-driven killing represented a new level of violence. There were times when Tonio questioned how much longer he could tolerate Bruno's vindictive outbursts; this was one of those times. He and Bruno had been brought together in the past for good reason, but those motives no longer existed.

"He saw us, so I had to do it," Bruno rationalized. "What if he told about the farm, and about us?" Tonio said nothing.

Bruno grabbed a length of rope from the wagon. He secured it to the boulder and then around Salvetti, taking care to bind both arms tightly against his torso. "Help me move him."

At this point, there was no other choice, so Tonio lifted Salvetti's feet while Bruno grasped his shoulders. The two men carried the body to the canal and threw it into the murky water. Bubbles rose to the surface as the canal swallowed the weighted package. When the last bubble burst, Tonio looked down into the water. He saw only his reflection looking up at him.

"He's gone for good," Bruno announced. "He can never be traced to us."

15

PALAZZO DELLA RAGIONE, MILAN

The following morning the three commissioners enjoyed a lavish meal delivered to the guest house by a servant. The contessa had correctly assumed that the men preferred privacy while they considered the vital matter that had brought them to Milan. After breakfast, Massimo and Vittorio discussed ways to resume searching for the missing bookkeeper without Vittorio being seen by the guardia. Vittorio said, "Salvetti was taken for a reason, and finding that reason will help me know who took him and where he is. Nothing would be gained by speaking with his family. Families are the last ones to learn a man's secrets. If anyone has information, it is the people he works with at the bank. I can question them without being exposed to the guardia."

Massimo opted to accompany Vittorio, and Nico departed for the Palazzo della Ragione to meet with Professor Beccaria. On his way to the meeting, Nico stopped at the Office of the Podestà to file a petition for the release of Signor Vittorio Colombo. The clerk who accepted Nico's petition did so with indifference. In his opinion, processing filings from lawyers living in the duchy kept him busy enough. He considered submissions by foreigners as an unreasonable burden. However, the clerk's attitude changed when Nico presented him with the letter that formally introduced himself as an envoy representing the Florentine Florentine Security Commission. The letter was signed by five of the highest-ranking officials of the Florentine Republic.

While the clerk read the document, Nico stressed, "The Florentine Republic considers this an urgent matter since an envoy of the republic is being confined without due process." Nico chose not to reveal that the envoy had already violated the confinement order. The clerk became contrite upon hearing that the petition was not a personal affair, but an official request by a Florentine diplomat. He assured Nico that he would pass the filing to a magistrate who would deal with it expeditiously. Usually, magistrates dealt with filings in the order they were received, but they could change the sequence at their whim. Lawyers in the good graces of magistrates had their petitions acted upon promptly. Those in disfavor suffered interminable delays. Filing clerks also had the ability to alter the sequence of petitions, so Nico departed the office optimistic that his request would be acted upon quickly.

On his arrival at Palazzo della Ragione, Nico learned that Professor Beccaria had come to Milan not to deliver a lecture, as Piero Tollino had believed, but to consult with lawyers of the Privy Council. The council planned to issue new regulations, and they wanted to be sure that their revised rulings were consistent with existing statutes. Professor Beccaria was the duchy's expert on such matters. Nico felt as though he were invading a private gathering when he entered because the small group meeting was already underway. A large table surrounded by at least twenty chairs dominated the meeting room, with the lawyers and the professor occupying only six places at one end of the table.

Nico would have reversed course had he not seen Piero Tollino sitting alone on a bench against a wall. Nico joined Tollino, and the pair waited quietly while the lawyers conversed with the professor. When the lawyers had all their questions answered, they thanked Beccaria and rose to leave. Nico and Tollino moved to the table and asked the professor for his counsel.

Nico did not raise the matter of Vittorio's confinement. He felt sure that the petition he had filed earlier would gain Vittorio's freedom. What he needed from the professor was advice on how to get permission for Vittorio to take part in the investigation. Nico explained, "Signor Colombo has repeatedly demonstrated an extraordinary ability to solve crimes that have baffled others; yet the guardia has barred him from participating in the search for his countryman. I wish to find legal means for him to apply his skills here in Milan."

Although Beccaria became intrigued by the situation that Nico described, he was not optimistic. "No tribunal will give Signor Colombo the authority to investigate autonomously. Granting such power to any foreign entity would undermine the sovereignty of the duchy. The Ducal Court would never permit that."

Beccaria leaned back in his chair, folded his arms across his chest, and remained silent for several moments while he considered various possibilities. Just as disappointment started to grip Nico, the professor sat up, raised a hand, and said, "Sometimes Milan has granted rights and privileges to foreigners during the negotiation of treaties. In those cases, grants were proposed during difficult negotiations, often without careful thought, and subsequently recorded as part of written covenants. I do not recall a specific treaty that will serve your purpose, but my suggestion is to study the treaties that involve Florence and Milan. If there is any hope for your cause, it will be found in those documents."

Nico knew there were bilateral trade pacts between Florence and Milan; however, it seemed unlikely that a trade agreement would mention criminal investigations. Peace agreements to end the wars of earlier decades might be more promising. After prolonged hostilities, participants wanted swift ends to the conflicts. Negotiators were under pressure, which sometimes led to foolish settlements. Nico believed it unlikely that he would find a treaty with a helpful clause, but he was not one to dismiss even remote possibilities. He said, "In Florence, the chancery maintains all official records. Is that true in Milan as well?"

"In Milan, the Privy Council Chancery preserves all diplomatic documents," the professor replied. Beccaria paused again before continuing. "You will need to research all agreements and treaties where Milan is a signatory, not just bilateral pacts between Milan and Florence. Even when verbal agreements are stated precisely, careless wording of written transcripts has been known to expand the scope of pacts beyond their original intent. The most egregious example was a trade arrangement made with the Duchy of Savoy. For certain concessions, Milan agreed to sell grain to Savoy at a discounted price. The notary who prepared the final document made a grievous error by not stating explicitly that the discounted price applied only to Savoy. The minister who administered grain sales in Milan followed the written record and sold grain at the discounted price to everyone: Savoy, Modena, even to Florence. Grain stores in Milan would have been depleted if the mistake had not been discovered and rectified in time.

"Errors of this type are more common than you might expect, and I suspect it will be this kind of error, one that unintentionally broadens the scope of an agreement, that could give you the leverage you seek."

Nico realized that searching through every pact Milan had made with foreign states to find a useful flaw would be a daunting challenge, but he had no other recourse.

From his meeting with Beccaria, Nico went directly to the Privy Council Chancery. Unlike the bustling Judicial Chancery, where Nico had first met Tollino, only three men occupied the Privy Council Chancery. Nico presented his letter of introduction to a clerk who barely glanced at the page before returning it to Nico. Nico tensed, fearful that the indifference meant the clerk would be uncooperative. In his most authoritatively sounding voice, Nico declared, "I am here to examine the records of agreements with foreign states."

The clerk raised his arms and spread his hands. "As you can see," he said, "there are no documents here. They are not stored in this building because space here is too valuable. All records are kept in the annex." Just as in Florence, thought Nico.

The clerk's words seemed dismissive, so Nico was taken aback until the clerk added, "There are papers that need to be put into storage. I can take them to the annex now, and you may accompany me. It is not far."

The clerk hefted a stack of folios and handed them to Nico. "It will help if you can carry these." Then he lifted a second batch to carry himself. They headed away from the center of Milan, passed through one of the city gates, and made several turns onto increasingly narrow streets until they reached an isolated wooden structure set in the middle of a large clearing. The clerk nudged a latch on the door and eased it open with his foot.

"At one time, this building was a stable. When the owner was killed in turmoil following the death of Duke Filippo

Visconti, the duchy seized the building and made it available to the chancery."

The clerk set his stack of folios on the floor. Then he took the stack that Nico was holding and set those atop the pile. Raising his arm in a broad sweep, the clerk said, "As you can see, all these shelves are full. We have a desperate need for additional storage space."

The clerk made his way down an aisle by stepping over piles of papers placed haphazardly on the floor. He removed a window covering, and with the added daylight, Nico saw that the shelves were crammed with papers.

"How are the materials organized?" Nico asked.

The clerk chuckled. "At one time, we arranged documents chronologically, but the enormous quantity of materials makes that impossible now. We pile papers wherever there is space." Both men ran their eyes across the disorganized collection before the clerk added, "I must return to the chancery, but you may remain here to search for the materials you need. Please latch the door when you leave."

Surprised by the chaos, Nico gained a greater appreciation for the system used in the Florentine chancery, where everything was filed chronologically and indexed by subject. In Florence, he could quickly locate items dealing with pacts, treaties, agreements, accords, or any similar classification. In this room—this stable—disorganized piles of papers were everywhere. He looked to his left, then to his right, wondering where to begin. He started pulling documents from shelves randomly with no clear direction: first from a high shelf in one aisle, next from a low shelf in the next aisle. He noted the title and date of each record. Before long, he noticed that the dust film and the yellowing of the pages correlated with the age of the documents.

Nico decided that a magistrate could reasonably claim that

any agreements made in Milan's distant past were no longer relevant, so he bypassed the yellowest pages and the folios with the thickest dust coatings. After two hours of perusing papers, Nico came upon documents and letters pertaining to a peace treaty signed at Ferrara by Milan, Florence, and other states. It was a short-lived agreement since war resumed a few years later, but Duke Filippo Visconti was the signatory on behalf of the duchy. Visconti preceded the current duke. Nico felt he could argue before a tribunal that agreements made by Visconti still applied. Unfortunately, Nico found no helpful clauses in the treaty.

Nico moved on, and one hour later, he located a folio of notes from the Treaty of Lodi. Most major powers on the Italian peninsula were signatories to the agreement, so negotiations were complicated. Diplomats proposed and discarded many resolutions before settling on the final terms. After reading draft scripts and letters penned by various negotiators, Nico again discovered nothing to support his case.

Nico walked outside to clear his thoughts in the cool autumn air. His spirit as dark as the gray sky overhead. He wandered around to the rear of the building where a narrow stream passed over a bed of stones and stared down at the rippling water. Was this a hopeless pursuit? Would a veteran lawyer like Messer Pruso spend time sifting through an endless collection of documents, or would he take a different approach? At the university, all the problems given to students had solutions. Maybe this problem had no solution. Maybe Vittorio could not gain official standing as an investigator in Milan.

An animal scurrying through nearby brush pulled Nico from his reverie. He returned to the building where he focused on the papers describing the Italic League, an agreement that broadened the scope of the Treaty of Lodi. Finally, the ancient goddess Fortuna smiled. In an amendment to the treaty, the parties promised not to wage war with each other. The League called on them to join in a military defense alliance. It established a system of permanent embassies, and it required the signatories to employ all measures to protect their citizens.

Nico re-read the wording several times. "All measures to protect their citizens." That stipulation was added to an amendment upon request of the Papal States. Nico searched further until he found the original proposal submitted by the Papal States, which included precise criteria. In the interest of brevity, the negotiators shortened the wording, and in doing so, their vague language had broadened the document's scope significantly. The oversight resulted in precisely the kind of error that Professor Beccaria had predicted.

The wording of this amendment did not explicitly call for cooperation between investigating authorities, but Nico believed he could construe it to make his case. For a nation to protect its citizens, he reasoned, it must be allowed to investigate crimes against those citizens.

16

DINNER WITH THE CONTESSA, MILAN

Vesper bells sounding at churches near and far echoed through Milan's streets as Nico made his way to the guest house. The contessa's servants had told him that she valued punctuality. Dinner service would begin as soon as the final vesper's note faded. Nico splashed water on his face, then raced to the palazzo where Vittorio, Massimo, Contessa Maddalena, and her younger sister Benedetta were already seated when Nico arrived.

He hesitated upon seeing plates and utensils set before four still empty chairs. The contessa motioned to one of the chairs. As Nico seated himself, she explained, "Two places are for my sons, who are studying with a tutor in Pavia. A third place is in honor of my late husband. Maybe it is a foolish practice, but it lets me feel close to them. My memory allows me to visualize them sitting with us."

During dinner, the contessa quizzed her guests to learn news of Florence. Through his close interactions with Chancellor Scala, Nico knew more than Vittorio and Massimo about Florentine politics, so he became the target of her interest. She peppered him with questions: Has the death of Cosimo de Medici altered the mood in Florence? Will his son Piero gain the confidence of the people? Are the rumors true that Piero is ill? Will Cosimo's passing dampen the alliance between Florence and Milan? Have you met Cosimo's grandson, Leonardo? To the contessa's great delight, Nico also shared bits of Florentine news he had overheard at his cousin Donato's restaurant.

After dinner, they moved to a sitting room to enjoy a warm fire, soft couches, and glasses of potent grappa. To Massimo's dismay, the contessa's sister did not join them. In the comfortable surroundings, the contessa dispensed with the etiquette that had restricted their conversation during dinner. She, rather than a servant, filled the glasses and brought them to her three guests. She graciously began the conversation by telling of her heritage and proudly quoted a poem written by her father, a highly respected poet and former marchese in the Republic of Genoa.

She recounted her experiences in managing her husband's estate. "Someday, women may hold positions in the worlds of finance and business, but today those doors are closed. I would not be able to administer this estate, which now belongs to my son, were it not for the support of Duke Sforza."

Her words sent Nico's thoughts to Bianca, the woman who quickened his heart. Bianca's customers praised her innovative dress stylings, but the same social obstacles encountered by the contessa hampered Bianca's business success. Bianca wished to expand her business to include men's wear, but the guilds would not permit her to do so.

With eager anticipation, the contessa said, "In two years my son will be of age to control his inheritance."

"What will fill your days when that time comes?" Massimo asked.

Her face brightened. She lifted the flask of grappa and moved to refill the glasses of her guests—no more for her—as she said, "I am eager to travel. Kings, dukes, and foreign envoys have brought me news of wondrous places during their visits. I aspire to see those sights with my own eyes. Genoa will be my first destination. I hope to explore the city where my father lived."

With her story complete, the contessa paused as she refilled Massimo's glass to examine the scar crossing his cheek. "Is that the mark of a highwayman's blade?" she asked unabashedly.

Massimo, who rarely revealed himself, opened himself freely to the contessa. Perhaps the grappa had loosened his tongue. He ran a finger down the purple arc. "Ten years past, King Alfonso of Naples sent troops to invade Tuscany. One of the king's men struck this at the battle of Maremma. It was his last cut. I keep his blade as a reminder of my lapse in concentration that will never again be repeated." A brief silence ensued as everyone pictured the event.

Next, the contessa fixed on Nico's time at the University of Bologna. "My son has one more year with a tutor," she said. "We planned for him to attend the law school at Pavia, but you make a compelling case for Bologna. Perhaps we should broaden our thinking. I will speak with him when he returns to Milan."

Only Vittorio, the investigator, was reluctant to discuss his past. He offered nothing, and the contessa, recognizing his reticence, did not press him. When a servant brought a tray of dessert pastries, she used the interruption as an opportunity to take her leave so the three Florentines could discuss business matters.

As soon as the contessa exited, Nico pulled out a slip of paper and waved it in the air. With excitement in his voice, he said, "This was waiting for me when I returned to the palazzo.

My first call this morning was at the Office of the Podestà to file a petition to rescind Vittorio's confinement order. This notice says that a magistrate is prepared to act on my petition. I am to appear before him tomorrow morning. Such quick action on a filing is extraordinary. It is not unusual for petitions such as this to languish for many days before being acted upon."

"Whatever you put in the plea must have been persuasive," Massimo said.

"Although I would like to claim credit, more likely the letter of introduction from the Florentine Signoria prompted the rapid response. The clerk became very attentive after reading the letter. The judiciary would be disgraced if it became known that they had detained a foreign envoy unjustly."

"You had better be convincing tomorrow," Massimo joked, "or we will have to send Vittorio back to his little room at the embassy."

"I am optimistic that the magistrate will rescind the confinement order but getting permission for Vittorio to continue his investigation is a more difficult problem." Nico's speech slowed as he explained, "I spent four hours searching through hundreds of pages in the Privy Council archives, and I found only one document that might prove helpful."

"Regardless, I will find a way," Vittorio declared.

"Have your interviews with Salvetti's associates at the bank advanced any reasons for his abduction?" Nico asked.

"In my experience, two reasons account for nearly all abductions. I know of many instances where the children of wealthy men have been seized and then ransomed for gold. Salvetti is not the son of a wealthy man nor is he personally wealthy, so that reason does not fit his situation. The other situations are those where men create their own predicaments by amassing gambling debts or falling prey to the other vices that ensnare gullible men. Those men often suffer beatings as inducements for them to settle their debts. If Salvetti is one of those, he may have told an associate at the bank about his problem. I began interviewing Salvetti's colleagues today, but thus far, none have provided any useful information. I will continue interviewing other bank employees tomorrow."

Vittorio took another sip of the digestivo before continuing. "I spoke with Signor Portinari, who is the manager of the Medici bank. He had intended to deliver the finance proposal to the architect himself, but he took ill, so he asked Salvetti to make the delivery."

In a hesitant voice, Nico asked, "So...might Portinari, not Salvetti, have been the intended target? Could the abductors have taken the wrong man?"

"There are many possibilities; that is one," Vittorio replied. "It is unlikely that the abductors took the wrong man, but we cannot dismiss the possibility. If Portinari were the intended target, it raises the question of how the abductors learned about his meeting with the architect. Was an employee of the bank or the architect paid to reveal that information? I will also explore that question during my interviews with the bank employees tomorrow."

"If Portinari was the intended target, might he still be in danger?" Nico asked.

"Massimo and I discussed that possibility with Portinari," Vittorio replied. "He has agreed that whenever he is out in public, Massimo will accompany him."

"There are two taverns in the district where the abduction occurred," Massimo said. "Vittorio thought their customers might have seen the abductors, so I visited both taverns to ask questions. No one recalled seeing anything usual, but the incident happened seven days past, and most of those slackers do not even remember what happened yesterday. Maybe Vittorio's investigative skills could have pried something from them, but I had no success." Massimo paused for questions before continuing, but there were none. "I shepherded Portinari to his house this afternoon, and tomorrow morning I will escort him to the bank."

When neither Nico nor Vittorio spoke further, Massimo capped the discussion by asking, "Do either of you know whether the Contessa's sister is betrothed?"

17

DISTRICT GUARDIA HEADQUARTERS, MILAN

The district magistrate presided in a modest chamber on the second level of the building that housed the local guardia detachment. Nico arrived well in advance of the specified time, to familiarize himself with the setting. Upon entering the chamber, he found a clerk preparing for the tribunal by placing a jug of water, glass, and gavel on the magistrate's desk.

The clerk noted Nico's indecision. He pointed to one table and said, "prosecutors," then indicating the other position he added, "defendants. The chairs against the wall are for observers."

Although Nico had entered the petition, he was the defendant in this proceeding because the guardia had issued the original order of confinement which meant its representative were the prosecutors. Nico selected a chair at the defendant's table.

He had debated whether to wear his finest tunic, one with embroidery and silver buttons, to emphasize his stature as a foreign dignitary. Upon further consideration, he feared that a local magistrate might find it pretentious and react negatively.

Ordinarily, lawyers dressed in judicial robes when appearing before tribunals, but Nico had neglected to bring his robe from Florence. He hoped the magistrate would not take offense at that oversight. In the end, he opted to wear a conservative light gray tunic with black trim.

Nico placed his folio on the table and slid it to cover the initials TA that someone, most likely an accused criminal, had cut into the tabletop. The weight of the document caused the surface to tilt slightly. Using one finger, Nico rocked the table back and forth on its uneven legs. He took a sheet of paper, folded it repeatedly, then pushed it under the short leg to steady the table. Thankfully, his chair did not have the same defect.

He had just opened the folder to review his notes when the door behind him opened, and he heard the voices of four men entering the chamber. Three men were in uniform, and one wore a lawyer's robe. As soon as the newcomers spotted Nico, their conversation ceased.

The two younger men angled off to the observer seats at the rear of the chamber. The third man matched Vittorio's description of the investigator who initiated the confinement order. He sported a dress uniform embellished with silver trim, customarily reserved for celebrations, parades, and other important events. The fancy tunic contrasted with his otherwise unkempt appearance. On his moon-shaped face, two jowly cheeks squeezed against his flattened nose. His belly bounced with every step as he waddled to the prosecutor's table. When he passed by, Nico noticed that the fancy uniform had a sweat-stained collar. The lawyer stood a head taller than the investigator, his angular face serious and intelligent.

As the lawyer and the investigator moved toward the prosecution table, the lawyer looked in Nico's direction to assess his adversary. Before taking his seat, he flashed a brief smile. As

Nico puzzled over the friendly expression, a bell rang to announce the arrival of the magistrate, who entered the courtroom slowly with the aid of a cane. He walked with a pronounced limp. The clerk helped him into his chair.

Nico had dreamed that his first appearance in court might be before a tribunal of three or five high ranking magistrates in a bright, pristine setting. It was the grandiose dream of all law school students. An infirm jurist presiding over Nico's first court appearance in a dimly lit chamber was the reality that shattered his fiction.

The magistrate signaled the clerk to begin recording; then, in a raspy voice, he addressed Nico. "Are you the defendant?"

"I am his lawyer, Nico Argenti. The defendant is confined at the Florentine embassy."

"Ah, yes. You are the one who entered the petition. Is your client willing to let you proceed without him being present?"

When Nico confirmed that he was, the magistrate turned to the prosecution. "State the reason for the confinement order."

The lawyer rose to respond, but the magistrate motioned for him to sit. "You will have your time to speak, Messer Avocino. Right now, I want to hear from the investigator."

"He ... I mean the defendant," the investigator stammered.

"Stand up," the lawyer coaxed as he pushed on the investigator's arm.

The investigator rose and began parroting the words given to him by the lawyer. "The defendant was inciting people with his questions."

The magistrate interrupted. "State the name of the defendant for the record."

"I do not know his name."

"You do not know the name of the man whose confinement you ordered?"

The investigator's negative response only made the magistrate more irritable. He looked to Nico, who responded, "Signor Vittorio Colombo."

Looking back toward the prosecution, the magistrate twirled his hand impatiently and said, "Continue. Continue. Explain what you mean by inciting."

"The defendant...um...Signor Vittorio Colombo, went from house to house interrogating honest, law-abiding citizens of Milan, questioning them for no reason. He claimed that a crime had been committed, but there is no evidence of a crime. There are many reasons why people go missing. The clerk might be in a love nest pounding his mistress this very minute."

The mistress comment brought scowls to the magistrate and Messer Avocino, and a titter of laughter from the two observers at the rear of the chamber. Having nothing more to add, the investigator sank into his chair and wiped the sweat flowing down his chubby cheeks and enlarging the stain ringing his collar.

The magistrate, looking somewhat surprised, asked, "Is that all? Signor Colombo was asking questions?"

The investigator rose tentatively. "Yes," he replied.

"Messer Argenti," the magistrate summoned. "Present your defense."

"The Republic of Florence takes an interest in this case because both the missing person, Signor Salvetti, and Signor Colombo are Florentine citizens. Signor Salvetti is not a clerk, he is the head bookkeeper at the Medici bank, and the defendant is an envoy of the Florentine Republic."

The magistrate interrupted. "Florence's interests and Signor Salvetti's position at the bank are detailed in the petition you filed. Repeating them here misuses the court's time. Confine your statement to the reason you believe the confinement order should be withdrawn."

The magistrate's rebuke elicited a smirk from the investigator, but Messer Avocino's expression remained solemn, implying sympathy for his counterpart. Sympathy earned because Avocino himself had often been the target of the magistrate's impatience.

Nico set his notes down onto the table, then continued. "Signor Colombo is a highly skilled investigator who was dispatched to Milan specifically to look into the disappearance of Signor Salvetti. The people whom Signor Colombo questioned lived in the vicinity where the abduction occurred."

Avocino bolted up. "There is no evidence of an abduction," he exclaimed.

Nico swiveled to face Avocino. Professors at the University of Bologna consistently reprimanded students who shouted counter-arguments when another student was stating his position. Still, Nico was uncertain whether that decorum also prevailed in the tribunals of Milan. The answer came immediately when the magistrate's hand shot forward, his finger pointing to Avocino's chair. The gesture, coupled with a fierce scowl, prevented the embarrassed lawyer from uttering another word as he slunk down into his seat.

"Be patient, Messer Avocino. You will have an opportunity to challenge the defense," the jurist growled; then to Nico, he said, "Messer Avocino's remark was poorly timed, but it does have merit. Do you have a basis for claiming that Signor Salvetti was abducted?"

Nico opened the sack on the floor at his feet, withdrew a shoe, and held it aloft. "This shoe was identified by a servant as belonging to Signor Salvetti. Signor Salvetti disappeared while en route from the Medici bank to the office of architect Filarete. Signor Colombo found this shoe alongside the road that joins those two locations. He was questioning residents who live on the road where he found the shoe."

Everyone was eyeing the shoe with interest as Nico pulled a

second item from the sack. "This clasp was wedged between two cobblestones in the road. As you can see, it matches the clasp on the shoe. I submit that Signor Salvetti lost the shoe during his abduction and that the clasp tore free during the struggle with his captors. This evidence supports the likelihood that Salvetti was abducted. It is not reasonable that a man going to meet his mistress for an illicit encounter would leave his shoe in a public roadway." Mention of a mistress prompted laughter from the observers until the magistrate's glare silenced them.

Nico wanted to say that the investigator would have found the shoe had he been conducting a competent investigation, but for the sake of any future relationship with the guardia, he chose not to risk humiliating his opponents. He was delighted when the magistrate voiced his thought. "Why did the guardia not find the shoe?" the jurist asked.

The investigator blurted, "We did not perform a search." He might have said more had Messer Avocino not silenced him by driving an elbow into his side.

Avocino sprang to his feet. "Unfortunately, the criminal element has been very active of late in our city. Their behavior puts a great strain on the guardia's sparse resources. Investigators must use judgment in deciding where to focus their efforts. They deemed other cases to have higher priority."

Addressing Messer Avocino, the magistrate countered, "In this instance, it appears that their judgment was flawed. The petition claims that the defendant's actions did not impair the guardia's investigation and that the questioning of area residents was reasonable. It asks that the court lift the confinement order against Signor Colombo. You have just stated that no investigation was being conducted. Therefore, I fail to see how the defendant could have been interfering with a non-existent investigation. Further, you have presented no evidence to show that the defendant's questions caused harm to those being questioned. Having seen the evidence presented by the defense, does the prosecution wish to reconsider the confinement order?"

The magistrate waited patiently while the investigator and the lawyer conferred. Moments later, Avocino rose and declared, "The guardia will rescind the confinement order."

The magistrate was about to end the hearing when Nico asked that he be allowed to speak on a related matter. "Be brief," the magistrate insisted.

"As I stated earlier, the Florentine Republic has an interest in this matter because Signor Salvetti is a Florentine citizen. On behalf of the Republic, I request that Signor Colombo be permitted to investigate Signor Salvetti's disappearance in conjunction with the guardia."

Avocino's jaw dropped open. He rose to object but held his tongue until the magistrate indicated he should speak. "Messer Argenti's request is not within the scope of this hearing," Avocino began. "The Republic of Florence is not named as a defendant in the petition. The petition concerns only Signor Colombo's confinement, and the guardia has already agreed to rescind that order."

"You are correct, Messer Avocino," the jurist responded. "It is beyond the scope of this hearing to entertain a request on behalf of the Republic of Florence. However, I am confident that dismissing the request now will only result in Messer Argenti filing another petition, which would cause us to reconvene at a later time. Therefore, in the interest of efficiency, I am inclined to consider the request now unless the prosecution objects."

Avocino thought for only a moment. Not wanting to antagonize the magistrate, he agreed that the matter needed to be settled, if not now, then later. He nodded to signify his willingness to proceed. "We have heard Messer Argenti's request," the magistrate said. "What is the position of the guardia?"

Avocino replied, "The request is inappropriate and without precedent. Messer Argenti asks that the guardia and the Florentine envoy cooperate in an investigation. Cooperation would require that the guardia share confidential information with the representative of a foreign government. Doing so would violate the mandate of the guardia to protect the privacy of Milanese citizens, and it would violate the sovereignty of the duchy.

"Additionally, the guardia has consistently demonstrated that it is fully capable of conducting investigations without assistance. Any interference by a foreigner could impede or undermine its progress. Further, we submit that an independent investigation by a Florentine envoy could be detrimental to the citizens of Milan."

Looking to Nico, the magistrate said, "Messer Avocino's arguments are sound. While I recognize that finding Signor Salvetti is important to Florence, the sovereignty of the Duchy of Milan must be protected."

The magistrate was about to deny the request when Nico stood. In his hand, he held one sheet lifted from his portfolio. Seeing that Nico had additional material to present, the magistrate signaled for him to speak. "Nine years past, when all the powerful states on the Italian peninsula joined together to form the Italic League, they expanded the agreements signed at the Treaty of Lodi. Milan and Florence were signatories to both the Treaty and the amendments. We all know that the amendments created a system of permanent embassies as one measure to ensure the citizens of all states are afforded a measure of protection when in foreign territory. Another provision, one less well known, calls upon the signatory states to take all reasonable measures for the protection of all citizens. I submit that a cooperative investigation is within the scope of that provision." The tribunal clerk took the sheet from Nico and delivered it to the magistrate for his examination.

Neither the magistrate nor the prosecutors were aware of the amendment that Nico cited. The magistrate read the paper, stroked his chin, shifted in his chair, and thought for several long minutes before responding to Nico's plea. "Before rendering a final verdict, I need to understand the context of this document. In the interim, I must protect the sovereignty of the duchy, so I cannot approve a cooperative investigation that would have the guardia share its expertise and disclose its findings. However, I recognize the desire of the Florentine Republic to locate the missing bookkeeper quickly. Therefore, I will permit Florentine envoys to conduct an independent investigation with the stipulation that their efforts do not interfere with the activities of the guardia." For emphasis, the magistrate looked directly at Nico and added, "Any independent action taken by Signor Colombo must be done with restraint. If he in any way interferes with the investigation being conducted by the guardia he will be subject to serious charges."

The ruling was a perfect compromise. Both parties could be comforted by their partial win, and both could bemoan their partial loss. Everyone stood while the magistrate made his way to the exit, then the investigator stalked out of the chamber without a word to his lawyer. Before Avocino exited, he looked to Nico. He nodded as an expression of respect for his young adversary.

The guest house was empty when an elated Nico returned. He was eager to tell Vittorio that the guardia had ended the confinement order, but Vittorio had not returned from the bank, where he was trying to find a motive for the abduction. Nico did not even try to guess Massimo's whereabouts. The hearing had concluded much more quickly than Nico had expected, so there was time before he would join Massimo and Vittorio for lunch. He decided to use the time by sharing the joy of his first legal victory in letters to his cousin Donato and to Bianca.

Donato,

Today I pleaded my first case as a lawyer. I always expected my first victory would be in Florence, but I am pleased, nonetheless, even though the outcome was not a total victory. In truth, I was fortunate that the magistrate held an open mind because I am finding that legal rulings can depend as much on the attitude of the presiding magistrate as they do on the law itself. That fact was never mentioned in any of my classes at the university. I wonder whether more surprises await me here in Milan.

We are staying in the palazzo of a contessa. She is a most gracious woman who treats us like royalty. We are staying in her guest house adjacent to the main building. One week past, the duke of Saxony and his bride occupied the elegant guest house.

Vittorio is relentless in his investigation. At first, he held doubts that a lawyer could help his cause. Perhaps my youth and inexperience contributed to his sentiment, but gradually he is seeing that I add value to our team. He is so detached that we may never become friends, but slowly I am earning his respect.

Even though the contessa is treating us like visiting dignitaries, I am eager to return home. Milan is a fine city, but it is not Florence. Tell Alessa, Joanna, and Giorgio that I miss them.

Nico

The letter to Donato came easily. Nico had frequently

written letters to Donato and his sister Alessa when he was at the university. The message to Bianca took more thought. He had planned to travel to Siena so that he could share news of his guild induction and his appointment to an official government commission with Bianca in person, but that plan was interrupted by his assignment to Milan. Now, he felt that he could not wait to share with her the news of his first litigation. In the past, he had penned brief notes to Bianca to arrange meetings, but he had never written her a real letter. Several crumpled pages ended on the floor before he had a rendering that pleased him.

Dearest Bianca,

A whirlpool has captured my life since we were last together. I wanted to join you in Siena to tell you about my induction into the guild, but the stars had other plans for me. These words are coming to you from Milan. Yes, Milan.

No sooner did I gain membership in the guild than I was offered a position in a newly formed commission and sent on a mission to Milan. There is much to tell you, too much for a letter. At least I can tell the latest good news: today, I presented my first case before a magistrate, and I won a favorable verdict. I often mused about my first case as a lawyer and wondered in which of Florence's many tribunals I would begin my legal career. I never dreamed my first would be in a foreign country.

Sharing the details of these events is only one reason that I long to be with you. I miss you more each day and pray this mission will reach a favorable conclusion quickly so we can be together soon.

Your Nico

Since Nico was a Florentine envoy, his letters could be taken to the chancery in Florence by an official courier. A friend at the chancery would see that they were sent on to their final destinations. Nico sealed the letters, then he stared ahead at the blank wall to let his mind paint Bianca's image. Her eyes came into focus first, bright and intelligent. Then the curve of her nose, her oval chin, and her flowing honey-gold hair.

18

GAGGIANO

Traffic on the Naviglio Grande, grand canal, peaked in summer when barges carried grains and building stone from farms and quarries to the hub of the duchy, Milan. Late in the year, wood for heating and cooking fires was the only cargo, so very few boats traveled the waterway. Because the canal was barely wide enough for two barges to pass each other, steerman were attentive during the peak season when they applied all their skills to the task of maneuvering their unwieldy craft. In late season, they grew lax.

Antonio began piloting boats on Naviglio Grande in his teen years. As a young man, he paddled small craft carrying produce from outlying farms to the town of Gaggiano. In later years he advanced to ever-larger craft as his skills developed. Now he enjoyed the prestige of being a steerman on the largest barges permitted on the grand canal.

Steering big heavy boats required precise control. Their inertia kept them from turning quickly; every course change had to be planned and initiated well in advance.

As Antonio's barge, piled high with logs from a forest near

Lake Maggiore, floated by the town of Gaggiano, a pretty girl in a too-tight dress walking beside the canal caught Antonio's attention. It mattered not that she was decades younger than he, younger even than his own daughter. The steerman did not move his eyes until his ears sent him the crunching sound of the boat striking the sidewall of the waterway. The impact dislodged two giant logs from the stack; they swept across the deck and into the water, nearly taking Antonio with them.

The impact sent the boat veering across the water toward the opposite bank. In a panic, Antonio shouted, "Stop! Stop!" to the horseman. He grabbed the long guide pole and plunged one end down to the canal's muddy bottom. He braced a knee against the boat's low rail for leverage and strained his biceps until they nearly popped. With all the strength he could muster, he pulled on the pole in a frantic effort to stop the barge's wayward motion. Ever so slowly, the massive barge responded, finally becoming still in the water. Even though his hands were shaking and his heart was pounding, Antonio could not help but glance to the bank; the girl was no longer in sight.

"It is stuck on something," Antonio called to the horseman.

The hooked end of his steering pole had snagged on an underwater object. He wiggled the pole, hoping to free it, but without success. He retrieved a coil of rope from the equipment locker, lashed one end to the pole, and tossed the other end to the horseman who attached it to the team's harness. The powerful animals easily raised the pole, and with it the book-keeper's body, to the surface and up onto the bank.

The horseman had done a stint as a mercenary during the War of Succession, so the sight of Salvetti's bloated body did not upset him as it did Antonio. "We should leave him. We need to go, or we will be late to Milan," the horseman declared.

"We can't do that," Antonio protested. "If we leave the body, animals will feast on it. Whoever he is, he deserves a proper burial. I will go report him to the authorities in town. I will be quick." They secured the craft to the side of the canal, and Antonio headed into town.

A short time later, a sergeant and a young recruit, returned with Antonio. The recruit had never seen death before, at least not death that turned the skin blue and swelled it as though it were pumped full of air. A wave of nausea made him turn away.

The sergeant gave his young colleague time to regain his composure, then said, "You must look at him. Think of the body as not a man, just an object pulled from the water, and tell me what you see."

"He...I mean, the body is tied to a stone to hold it under the water. His death was not an accident."

"Good. What else?"

Gradually the recruit regained an analytic perspective. "The skull is crushed, again proving that the death was not a suicide." The young man shuddered as he added the obvious, "He was murdered."

The sergeant nodded his agreement and said, "I do not recognize him. Do you?" The young officer merely shrugged. The sergeant continued, "Someone in the town may know of a missing person. We can ask at the shops, taverns, and churches, although I doubt that he's a local. Many times, I have been called to disrupt heated disagreements and brawls, but I cannot believe that anyone in our town would commit murder. I suspect that he was thrown from a passing boat,"

Turning to Antonio, the sergeant said, "You may leave, but when you reach Milan, you must report this incident to the military. Tell them we are arranging to transport the body to Milan." The army assumed jurisdiction over all difficult cases occurring in towns and outlying areas because the local authorities did not have the training or experience to investigate murders or other complex crimes.

To the recruit, the sergeant said, "Fetch Grisaldi. Ask him to come for the body. Tell him that it cannot be buried soon, so he must embalm it and prepare it for transport to Milan."

A short time later, the doctor and two laborers returned with the young officer to the site where the body was stretched out on the ground, still bound to the heavy stone.

"The body was dragged out of the canal by a barge steerman. We did not move it while we waited for you," the sergeant informed the doctor.

The doctor untied the rope and slid the stone aside. "From his color, he could have been in the canal for several days. It is difficult to say." He leaned over to get a better look at the head. "This injury did not result from a fall into the canal. He was definitely struck with something. I agree with your conclusion that this was most likely a murder."

The doctor kneeled to examine the body closely, looking for any other clues. After several minutes he stood and said, "I cannot find any other marks on the body, but the tunic is interesting. It is fine silk of an unusual style. No one in Gaggiano and few even in Milan wear this style. Quite possibly he is a foreigner."

With his examination complete, the doctor instructed the laborers to transport the body to his office. He accompanied the sergeant to the town office to prepare the official report of the incident.

19

POLLO DA CIELO RESTAURANT, MILAN

Midday bells summoned the three commissioners to the Pollo da Cielo, chicken from heaven, restaurant where they had agreed to meet for lunch. Scala's friend Piero Tollino had recommended the restaurant, claiming, "Members of the Ducal Court all consider it a favorite."

Massimo was already seated and sampling a glass of local wine when Nico arrived. When Vittorio arrived a short time later, he was greeted by two smiling colleagues holding their glasses high in the air. "A toast to you, investigator," Massimo announced. "You are now a free man thanks to our talented lawyer." He laughed as he added, "I passed the Florentine embassy this morning, and the two pathetic officers were still standing guard over your ghost. They had no idea that you had left the embassy. Apparently, their colleagues have not informed them that the confinement order has been lifted."

Vittorio poured a measure of wine from the jug on the table, then raised his glass to acknowledge the greeting. "Now I no longer need to walk in the shadows."

Massimo noticed that Vittorio did not express gratitude for

Nico's efforts and success. Perhaps Vittorio does not yet appreciate the benefit of our working together as a team, he thought.

Nico, who did not weigh Vittorio's words, proceeded to describe the situation. "The magistrate not only ended your confinement; he also granted you the authority to conduct your own investigation, although that authority might be temporary. He intends to review the obscure document that I cited. If he disagrees with my interpretation, he may reverse his ruling, so work fast.

"I was fortunate to have drawn an unbiased magistrate, but there might also be another factor that influenced the magistrate's decision. In Milan, all diplomatic matters fall within the Privy Council's purview, so the magistrate was overstepping his jurisdiction by hearing the case. Perhaps he feared that if he ruled against me, I would appeal to the Privy Council and he would be reprimanded for overstepping his authority."

Massimo said, "I would venture that he was intimidated by your legal prowess." He grinned, then recounted his own morning activities. "I went to meet Portinari at his house to escort him to the bank. He lives on a farm outside the city. His wife was raised at a vineyard in Chianti, and she wants to carry on her family tradition by having her own vineyard. They rented a farmhouse surrounded by land where she has begun growing a variety of Oltrepò Pavese grapes.

"Portinari rides to work each day in a carriage, and fortunately for me, the carriage is kept at a stable just beyond the city wall. It is a short walk from our guesthouse to the stable, and from there, I ride with the carriage driver to meet Portinari."

"You had better hope the news does not reach Florence that you are using your status as a Florentine envoy to travel through the Duchy of Milan in a carriage," Nico quipped. Then in a serious tone, he asked, "Is Portinari concerned about his safety?"

"No, at least he says he is not," Massimo replied. "However, his wife became concerned when she heard of Salvetti's abduction. I had a chance to speak with her while Portinari was dressing. Her fear was heightened upon hearing the speculation that Salvetti might have been taken in error and that Portinari might have been the intended target. She is grateful that I am accompanying Portinari as a precaution but even that measure has not relieved her worry completely."

Nico leaned toward Vittorio and jested, "Should we warn Portinari not to let his wife alone with this handsome soldier?"

Massimo responded in kind, "Portinari need not worry about his wife because there is a kitchen wench in the house who is eager to pluck my codpiece. When word reached her that I am a Florentine envoy, she invited me into the kitchen to sample her dumplings. I used to think that the fancy dress uniform of an army captain was the ideal accessory for enticing women, but if this maid's behavior is typical, army uniforms don't impress women nearly as much as diplomatic titles."

Returning to a serious tone, Massimo continued. "Portinari wanted to arrive at the bank earlier than usual this morning. He gave no details except to say there is an opportunity to finance a new business venture. The project will be very profitable for its funders, and Portinari wants to be sure the Medici bank submits a winning proposal."

Vittorio said, "The bank employees I spoke with this morning were also excited about the new business ventures. It is commendable for employees to be so enthusiastic about their work, but their fervor detracted from my purpose. It took pressure to keep them focused on the issue of whether Salvetti had any personal problems that might be the motive for his abduction. None of them recalled Salvetti mentioning gambling, drinking, or having an affair with a married woman. To the contrary, they all gave the impression that Salvetti should be a candidate for sainthood. Either he had no vices, or he hid them well from all his colleagues."

Vittorio paused to refill his wine glass before continuing. "There are other employees I have not yet interviewed; however, if they also confirm that Salvetti did not have any personal problems, I will need to shift my attention to other possible reasons for the abduction."

"Perhaps that Portinari was the intended target?" Nico posited.

"That may be more difficult to discover," Vittorio responded. "Salvetti worked closely with others at the bank, men with whom he might share his feelings and problems. As the bank manager, Portinari is somewhat isolated from others, so he might keep his problems to himself."

Conversation ceased when their meals arrived. "These are thin slices of breast meat from our own farm-raised chickens," the server boasted as he set plates before each of the men.

After the dessert course, the server brought complimentary glasses of a digestivo. A few sips of the potent liquid drained the stresses of the day. Before he grew too relaxed, Nico decided to share an idea he had been mulling since he returned from the tribunal. "In his ruling this morning, the magistrate authorized us to conduct our investigation into the disappearance of Signor Salvetti, but he did not agree to have the guardia cooperate or share information with us. The guardia sees Vittorio's efforts as adversarial. I believe it could be advantageous for us to establish a more cordial relationship with the guardia and the prosecutors. It may be too late to help with this case, but a warm relationship could be beneficial in the future."

"What are you proposing exactly?" Massimo asked.

"If Vittorio agrees, I would like to approach Messer

Avocino, the prosecution lawyer who represented the guardia, and offer to share with him the information that Vittorio has uncovered."

Massimo asked, "Why would you contact the lawyer rather than the guardia?"

"Vittorio has a low opinion of the investigator, and after watching him this morning, I share that opinion."

Before Nico could continue, Vittorio interjected, "Saying that I have a low opinion of him does not accurately portray my feelings. He is an ass who has no right to call himself an investigator."

Nico continued, "My brief interaction with Messer Avocino leads me to believe he is a competent lawyer who believes in justice. The magistrate was harsh with him this morning, undeservedly so in my view. Since the guardia is unwilling to cooperate with us directly, Messer Avocino might be willing to be the conduit for exchanging information between us and the guardia. Of course, I will only pursue this path if Vittorio agrees."

Nico waited for Vittorio's reaction. Vittorio brushed a wayward lock of hair and took another sip of digestivo before responding. "My goal is to solve this crime as quickly as possible. If my findings help to motivate the local authorities, then I have no objection to sharing information with them."

"Will you join me when I meet with Avocino?" Nico asked. "You are the source of the information we have to share, so you should receive the credit for it."

"I do not seek credit. Chasing after accolades is counterproductive. My time is best spent interviewing bank employees." Upon seeing Nico's eagerness dissolve, Vittorio added, "However, I can spare a brief time to join you."

20

AVOCINO'S OFFICE, MILAN

Prosecutors for the Duchy of Milan had offices in the district guardia headquarters. Messer Avocino's office was on the building's third level, one level above the courtroom where Nico had appeared earlier in the day. The building had a stairway that allowed access to the upper levels without passing through the guardia offices. The arrangement pleased Vittorio, who wished to avoid any chance encounter with the incompetent investigator.

Avocino was surprised, but not displeased, to see Nico at his doorway. He gestured for Nico and Vittorio to enter and be seated.

Nico began, "Messer Avocino, allow me to introduce Vittorio Colombo. He was the absent defendant in the proceeding this morning, the one who had been confined in the Florentine embassy."

"I trust that you are enjoying your freedom," Avocino said. "Restricting you to the embassy was an unkind gesture. Milan is a vibrant city, and everyone should have the opportunity to cherish it. I am sorry you were deprived of that opportunity until now. I hope the experience did not tarnish your view irreparably and that you will make time to discover the many treasures of our city."

Vittorio responded dispassionately, "I am here to locate an abductee and to apprehend his abductors. Being able to move freely through the city will help me to achieve those objectives."

Avocino turned to Nico. "Does your presence here mean you are unhappy with the magistrate's ruling? I thought he was more than fair." Avocino chuckled, "And in what musty old archive did you find the document that you cited?"

"Yes, I agree that the magistrate's ruling was just. I spent hours in the chancery archive hunting through documents before finding the agreement that I referenced." Nico smiled, "And the archive is, as you said, in a musty old barn. I understand the need to protect the sovereignty of the duchy and its agencies, but I believe that the best way to solve Signor Salvetti's abduction is through cooperation. Even though the guardia is under no obligation to share information, Signor Colombo is prepared to disclose the findings of his investigation with the hope that they can be helpful to the guardia."

Avocino inhaled deeply and leaned back in his chair, relieved that Nico's purpose was not an adversarial confrontation. "That is a generous proposal." Avocino's brow furrowed as he decided how to proceed. "The investigator you encountered is not representative of the many fine members of the guardia. I have worked with the captain of this district for many years. He is astute and open-minded, and I am confident he will welcome your offer. May I invite him to join us?"

Avocino's question caused Vittorio to stiffen. He opened his mouth to voice a protest, then thought for a moment and nodded his agreement. He would not wish all members of the Florentine guardia to have their reputations tainted by a single inept member. Avocino summoned a clerk and directed him to request that the captain join them. Minutes later, the ranking guardia officer in the district entered the room, seated himself, and locked his eyes on the two Florentines sitting across from him. Streaks of gray in his hair evidenced his age and presumably his experience. His clean unwrinkled tunic signified pride in his profession.

The captain listened attentively as Avocino explained Nico's proposal. When Avocino finished, the captain addressed the two foreigners. "Signori, I welcome and accept your proposal." Then to Vittorio he added, "Signor Colombo, on behalf of the Duchy of Milan, I apologize for your confinement. That is not the way foreigners should be treated, especially not a diplomat from a valued ally of our duchy. I read the transcript of this morning's court proceeding. Truly unfortunate. I speak often with my counterparts in other districts, so I know that each of us is burdened with a smattering of inept subordinates. I regret the action taken by the investigator who ordered your confinement, and I assure you that he now regrets it as well."

The captain's frankness impressed Nico and Vittorio. "The condition you describe is certainly not unique to Milan," Vittorio said. "Before receiving my current appointment, I spent a decade as an investigator in Florence where I encountered similar men.

"As Messer Avocino said, our purpose here is to share information that may be helpful to you in conducting your investigation." Vittorio opened a sack he had carried, removed two items, and handed them to the captain. "This broken clasp was wedged between two cobblestones in Via Meravigilia along the route that Signor Salvetti walked from the bank to the architect's office. The shoe was under a nearby lilac bush. A servant at the Salvetti house identified both as belonging to Signor Salvetti."

He reached into the sack again to retrieve a collection of papers. "These are notes from my interviews of bank employees. Those I spoke with know of nothing in Salvetti's personal life that could account for his disappearance. Thus far, I have interviewed about half of the employees. I intend to interview the others and will notify you if those interviews reveal anything useful."

Nico added, "Signor Salvetti is the head bookkeeper of the bank. He reports directly to the bank manager, Signor Portinari. We have arranged for an escort to travel with Signor Portinari between his house and the bank. It is a precaution in case the abduction was done by someone with a grievance against the bank."

When the two visitors finished speaking, Avocino lifted a sheet from his desk. "Earlier, I received this notification from the Office of the Podestà. Whenever a major crime is committed anywhere in the duchy, the podestà sends reports to prosecutors and the guardia in every district of the city."

Avocino handed the page to the captain, saying, "This notice may not have reached you yet. It says that a body was pulled from the Naviglio Grande, the Grand Canal, near Gaggiano."

Vittorio asked, "Gaggiano? Is Gaggiano a town?"

"Yes, it is a town about an hour's ride from Milan. The body was not found in Milan, so I would not have mentioned the incident except two items gave me pause when I read the report. One fact that caught my attention was the description of the victim's clothes. It says that the victim was wearing a fine silk tunic. The doctor who examined the body noted that the tunic is an unusual style, one not commonly seen in the Duchy of Milan. The men of Gaggiano rarely wear silk tunics even on special occasions. The sergeant who filed the initial report believes that the was murdered, and the body dumped at Gaggiano from a passing boat."

"Why does he think the victim was murdered?" Vittorio asked.

"The report says that the victim's skull was crushed, and the damage was greater than that which would have been sustained by simply falling into the canal. The unusual silk tunic supports his belief that the body came from elsewhere. Milan is the only city in the duchy where businessmen wear silk."

"If the murder happened in Milan, why would the body be dumped in the canal at Gaggiano?" Nico wondered aloud.

"That I cannot answer," Avocino replied.

Vittorio asked, "Has the body been buried, or is it being preserved at Gaggiano?"

"The body is being preserved, but not at Gaggiano. Small towns do not have the resources to investigate major crimes. They refer murders and other major crimes to the judicial branch of the Milanese army. The body was sent to at an army base not far from Milan."

Vittorio said, "I would like to visit the camp to determine whether the body is that of Signor Salvetti." Looking toward the captain, he added, "unless that would interfere with your investigation."

The captain replied, "As Messer Avocino explained, the army has the responsibility to investigate this matter. Since the body was found in Gaggiano, and there is no solid evidence linking the crime to Milan, there is no reason for my men to be involved at this time. Should the army determine that body sent to them from Gaggiano is that of Signor Salvetti, the army may return jurisdiction to us, but until then we have no role in the matter."

At Vittorio's request, Avocino and the captain gave him

directions to the army base. As Vittorio rose to leave, Nico asked, "May I join you?"

Although Vittorio preferred to work alone, he recognized that this new information flowed from Nico's suggestion that they meet with Avocino. Earlier, Nico had success in court and now his idea had resulted in a possible lead. Vittorio's view of the young lawyer was softening. "Yes," Vittorio replied, "but first we must stop at Salvetti's house to fetch one of the servants who will be able to tell us whether the body is Salvetti."

At Salvetti's house, Gusto, the servant whom Vittorio had met previously, agreed to accompany them. When the three men reached the camp, Nico presented the introduction letter from the Florentine Signoria to the army physician. The officer barely glanced at the document before returning it. "Official papers are not needed here. We welcome anyone who can help identify the bodies in our crypt. Sadly, many of the bodies sent here are never claimed. Surely, they are missed by someone. I cannot understand why their loved ones do not come forward. The bodies awaiting identification and those waiting for burial are kept in a below-ground vault," the physician explained. "Come with me."

Nico wanted to be present when the body was identified, but he recalled his unpleasant experience seeing the disfigured corpse of a young man in Florence and said, "I would rather wait here."

The officer led Gusto and Vittorio to the entrance of the underground chamber, lit a lantern, and climbed down into the cold musty shaft lined with crypts set against each wall. The physician stopped beside one of the vaults. "This is the one. The body recovered at Gaggiano is in this coffin," he said.

Vittorio helped the physician slide the wooden cover aside, revealing the body. Gusto managed only one glance at the sunken cheeks of the gray corpse before being overcome by the sight and the odor. Color drained from his face, his knees buckled, and he dropped to the floor.

"This happens often," said the detached physician. "Death is never a pleasant sight."

The physician and Vittorio lifted Gusto's limp form and carried him out of the underground chamber into the fresh air. They set Gusto on the ground with his back leaning against a tree. Although he revived quickly, he battled waves of nausea for several minutes before he calmed enough to answer Vittorio's questions.

When the spasms ceased, Vittorio asked, "Are you able to tell whether that is Signor Salvetti?"

In a fragile voice, Gusto responded, "I think so, but I'm not sure. The body was gray. What happened to it?" Then, more forcefully, he protested, "The smell. It's terrible. I can't go back in there."

Nico sat next to the distraught servant, trying to comfort him. "I know it's difficult to see someone like that. Once I had to identify a young man named Jacopo. He was hardly more than a boy. It was not easy for me, so I know it is not easy for you, but we need to know whether this is Signor Salvetti."

The servant slumped with his head resting in his hands for a minute and then said, "Show me a button."

Nico thought Gusto was hallucinating until he added, "The buttons on the tunic. I can be certain if I see one of the buttons."

Vittorio took the lantern and descended the stone steps into the crypt. Thread nubs marked the locations where two buttons had already been torn from the garment. Vittorio cut one of the remaining red and white ceramic buttons from the frayed tunic and carried it outside to where the servant was sitting with his back propped against an oak tree. "This is one of the buttons. Do you recognize it?" Vittorio asked. He held the button where the servant could view it.

"That is one of Signor Salvetti's buttons," Gusto said. "I am certain. They were a present from his wife to remind him of Florence. She had them custom made by an artist. The red design is a lily, the symbol of Florence."

Angered by the situation, Vittorio pounded his fist against a tree. "It didn't have to end this way. He didn't have to die. If only those bastards at the guardia had searched for him rather than sitting on their asses. But they did nothing."

Vittorio paced for several minutes to calm his ire before returning to the crypt a third time. Now that he knew the body belonged to Salvetti, he wanted to look for any clues that might lead him to the killer. The physician followed Vittorio and held the lantern as Vittorio carefully examined the body. "I saw the bruising on his wrists," the physician said.

"Yes, his hands were bound," Vittorio replied. "His hose are torn at the ankles, so it is likely that his feet were bound as well. They are minor abrasions. The only serious injury is the head wound."

Vittorio cut away a small patch from the tunic. "There is no other evidence here that will help us find the killer, but the tunic has been abraded in several places. When I find where he was killed, I may find fibers that match the ones on this cloth."

As the two men climbed out of the underground chamber, the physician said, "We always have at least three unidentified cadavers in our crypts. Many never get identified. This one has been here only one day. I never remember having a corpse identified so quickly," he said, obviously pleased that the viewing had a decisive outcome.

"What will happen to Signor Salvetti ... to the body?" Gusto asked.

"Embalming slows deterioration, but it does not prevent

decay," The physician explained. "Bodies can only be kept here for a short time. The army judicial unit will decide when to dispose of the body, but generally, once a body is identified, the judiciary is quick to release it to the family of the deceased."

"I must be the one to tell Signora Salvetti," Gusto declared. "The news will be painful enough coming from me, one who has faithfully served the family. Her pain would be unbearable if the news came from a stranger." Without another word, Gusto walked away, his head down, his eyes filled with tears.

"I need to visit Gaggiano," Vittorio announced. Nico nodded and said that he would accompany the investigator. "You can travel there by horseback or canal boat," the physician explained. "Gaggiano is not far from Milan. Horses can take you there in less than two hours." Vittorio allowed Gusto to return to Milan while he and Nico departed for Gaggiano.

21

GAGGIANO

The town of Gaggiano was midway along the Naviglio Grande canal from Milan to the Ticino River. Barges traversed the canal frequently during summer months, and most also carried travelers for a small fee. But few boats passed through the canals late in the year, so Vittorio suggested that they travel to Gaggiano by horseback. Nico agreed, saying, "Since we are on official business, the embassy can provide the horses."

At the embassy, Ugo, a Milanese boy who was employed as a page, greeted them. Having Milanese citizens working in the embassy seemed problematic to Nico. Their loyalties had to be to the duchy, not to Florence. Nico wondered what policies prevented the locals from gaining access to confidential information.

Ugo had befriended Vittorio during his confinement. Upon seeing Vittorio, Ugo smiled and clasped the Florentine's hands. "I am happy that you are now free so you can see the treasures of my wonderful city. To shut you up in that small room—it was not right."

Vittorio pulled the boy close and tousled his hair. To Nico, he said, "This is the young man who brought me treats from the kitchen. Every night he would come to my room and tell me about all the beautiful sights in Milan I must see after I am released." To the page, Vittorio said, "And this is the lawyer who secured my freedom."

The awestruck page looked up at Nico. "I hope to be a notary one day. There is an excellent law school at the University of Pavia. The school accepts very few applicants. I am fortunate that one of the notaries here at the embassy is helping me to study. Perhaps in another year, I will be ready to apply."

Nico smiled at the boy and said, "Recently, I met one of the professors from Pavia. If he is representative of the quality of their teachers, then I agree that Pavia must have an excellent law school."

"Do you wish to see the ambassador?" the boy asked.

"No," Vittorio answered sharply, his dislike of the ambassador evident in his tone. "We need to borrow horses. Is there someone who can arrange mounts for us?"

"There is a stable that provides horses and carriages for the embassy staff. If you tell the stable owner that you are from the embassy, he will furnish mounts for you."

Nico and Vittorio followed the page's directions, which took them out of the city through the Porta Vercellina gate. When they reached the stable, the owner brought two sturdy horses and gave them directions to the Naviglio Grande, the canal that connected Milan with Gaggiano. "Mules and oxen pull barges through the canal, so there are towpaths for the animals along both banks of the canal. Gaggiano is on the southern bank, so take the path on that side because there are no bridges beyond Milan."

Nico and Vittorio encountered little traffic during their journey, passing only a few farm wagons and one barge coming toward them on its way to Milan. The barge was piled high with lumber, but the oxen had no difficulty pulling it through the slowly flowing water. The advantage of water transport was evident. Moving that much lumber by road would have taken many wagons pulled by teams of animals. Farms filled the expanse of the broad Po River valley on both sides of the canal for the entire distance from Milan to Gaggiano. Farmers had harvested their crops months ago, leaving only withered plants in the fields. In spring, the dry foliage would be plowed into the fertile soil. Nico felt as though he were riding across a brown carpet under a gray sky.

When Nico and Vittorio neared Gaggiano, a woman carrying an overflowing laundry basket directed them to the office of the local law enforcement authorities, a small single-story building in the town's central piazza. Inside, a young officer sitting behind a desk rose to greet them. Nico handed the letter of introduction to the officer and stated, "I am Messer Nico Argenti, and this is Envoy Vittorio Colombo."

Their titles and letter of introduction bearing the seal of the Florentine Republic startled the unworldly officer. He had never met anyone from Florence, much less a pair of dignitaries. He loosened his grip on the letter, fearing that he might deface the document with fingerprints.

After reading the paper, he returned it to Nico and accepted a second sheet; this one authorized the men to investigate the disappearance of Signor Salvetti and bore the signature and seal of a magistrate. The officer was so flummoxed by the official documents that he did not realize that the authorization of a district magistrate had no standing outside the city of Milan.

Because his sergeant was the person who dealt with unusual situations, the young officer's first words were, "The sergeant is not here."

When Nico and Vittorio did not respond, the young officer thought that aiding foreign dignitaries could be an opportunity for him to impress his lady friend Maria. He straightened his tunic, smiled, and said, "I am Ercole Vernaccia. How may I help you?"

Nico said, "There was a body found in the canal two days past."

"Yes, I was there. I saw him, but we do not know his name. The sergeant had him sent to the army camp in Milan."

"We identified the body in Milan," Vittorio explained. "It belonged to a Florentine citizen. That is why we are here. We want to see the place where you found the body."

"We believe someone threw the body from a boat as it passed through town. I can show you the place," Vernaccia said as he came from behind the desk. He beamed as he moved toward the door, thinking how impressed Maria would be when she learned that he had escorted two Florentine diplomats.

"Did anyone see a suspicious boat or anything unusual?" Nico asked.

"We asked at the market whether anyone knew of a person being missing. Gaggiano is a small town. If a local were to disappear, people at the market would know, but no one did. That is why we think he was thrown from a boat. No one reported seeing anything suspicious."

Vittorio believed there was a reason why the body was discarded near the town. If someone wanted to dispose of a body so it would not be found, he would dump it into the canal along a vacant stretch of farmland, not near a town. Vittorio wanted to know why the body was put into the canal at Gaggiano.

Nico and Vittorio followed the officer to the boat that served as a ferry. With a long wooden pole, Vernaccia maneuvered the craft to the opposite bank of the canal, and then along the bank for about one-half mile.

Vernaccia stopped the boat, drew it close to the bank, and pointed into the water. "Here. This is where they found him."

Vittorio scanned the area. Even this close to the center of town, there were no houses or other buildings nearby. Low scraggly bushes formed a border alongside the path, with farms and pastures extending from there into the distance. A single dirt road headed north through the farmland.

"Was the body floating in the water?" Vittorio asked.

"No, it was on the bottom, held down by a stone," Vernaccia replied. "The steerman of a passing boat snagged the body accidentally with his steering pole. When he tried to pull the pole free, he raised the body from the bottom of the canal."

"Where is the stone now? What happened to it?"

"The sergeant sent me to town to get the physician. In Gaggiano, the physician is also the mortician. He is the one who untied the stone. No one took the stone, so it is here somewhere. Maybe that one," Vernaccia said, pointing to one of many similar stones along the canal bank.

None of the stones had any distinguishing marks, so Vittorio disregarded Vernaccia's speculation and asked, "You said the stone was tied to the body. What happened to the rope?"

"The sergeant has it. He can show it to you."

Vittorio scanned the area then turned to Nico and said, "With all the animal traffic on this path, we aren't likely to find any useful footprints, but we should look for any other possible evidence."

Nico followed the path in the direction toward the town searching for any items that might have been dropped or discarded by the killers. Vittorio scoured the track in the opposite direction. Nico went only a short distance before he came to a patch of flattened grass. Tangled in the grass was a length of cord. Nico did not think the short length of cord could be significant, but he knew that Vittorio never discounted anything, no matter how unimportant it might seem. He called to Vittorio, "I found something."

Vittorio came to where Nico was holding the item. "Fishing line," Vittorio said, then he asked the officer, "Do you know who comes here to fish? From the way the grass is matted, it looks like someone comes here often."

Vernaccia's face brightened, pleased that he knew the answer to Vittorio's question. "Sozzo, the baker's son. He likes to fish here. He says this is the best place to fish. Maybe there is a deep hole at the bottom of the canal."

The men continued searching until Vittorio became convinced that there was nothing else to be found. Finally, Vittorio said, "I would like to speak with Sozzo."

Vernaccia said, "We can go to the bakery. Sozzo is probably there helping his father."

The three men walked back to the ferry and climbed aboard. Using the long wooden pole, Vernaccia pushed the boat away from the bank and across the canal to the town. A short walk beyond the main piazza brought them to the town bakery. In a clearing behind the shop, young Sozzo was cleaning ash from the fire pit of the clay oven. Sozzo's hands were covered with wood ash, and streaks of soot ran along his cheeks and dotted his hair. Working alongside the boy, the baker in a spotless white apron was obviously skilled in performing the daily cleaning without transferring ash from the oven to himself.

The officer introduced the two visitors from Florence; then he asked the boy, "Were you fishing in the canal two days ago?"

The appearance of the officer and two foreigners intimidated young Sozzo. He answered with a hesitant "Yes," worried that he had done something wrong.

For many years, the baker had served as a prior in the town.

He was not cowed by the visitors and asked boldly, "Why are you questioning my son?"

"Our interest is not with your son," Vittorio explained. "We are here about the body found in the canal."

The baker put a protective hand on Sozzo's shoulder to reassure the boy.

In a non-threating voice, Nico asked, "Did a boat stop near where you were fishing, or did you see anyone push an object from a boat?"

"No."

"Did you see anyone or anything unusual?"

"Nothing unusual, just two men standing near a wagon. They seemed to be waiting for someone."

"Do you know the men?" Vittorio asked.

"No. I have never seen them before."

"Can you describe them?"

"They were big. One of them just leaned against the wagon. The other one kept pacing back and forth and seemed to be talking to himself. He sounded angry, but I could not hear what he was saying."

Vernaccia said, "If Sozzo doesn't know them, they are not from Gaggiano. All the townspeople come to the bakery to buy bread, so Sozzo knows everyone who lives in Gaggiano."

Vittorio focused his questioning, "Can you describe the wagon? Did it have any distinctive markings? Did you see anything in the wagon?"

Sozzo paused for a few moments while he tried to recall images from memory. "There was nothing unusual about the wagon. A brown horse pulled it. There was something in the wagon, but I don't know what it was. It was covered, so I could not see it."

Vittorio had hoped that the journey to Gaggiano would have yielded more information than that two men stood near a wagon, possibly waiting for someone. The only useful bit was that the men were not locals. Vittorio found it intriguing that two strangers were lingering in the same place where the body was found. Unfortunately, there was no way to identify the men.

Just as Vittorio was about to thank everyone for their help and ready himself to return to Milan, Sozzo said, "I do know where the men were from."

All four men stared at the boy, puzzled by his statement. If he did not know who the strangers were, how could he know where they came from? The men waited for Sozzo to explain.

"They smelled bad, so bad that I couldn't keep fishing. I had to leave. They smelled like pigs, so they must have come from the pig farm." The boy pointed to the road, angling north through the farm fields. "I went to the pig farm when I was helping the butcher. The smell there was so bad my stomach got sick."

Although Vernaccia knew of the pig farm, he had never been there, and he did not know the owner. When the three men returned to the town office, the sergeant was sitting behind the desk. Vernaccia introduced the two visitors to his sergeant and explained their purpose in coming to Gaggiano.

"I have never been to the farm, and I don't know the owner. It is the only pig farm in this province, so it must be the place where Pasquale goes to get pork. Pasquale is our town butcher," the sergeant said. "My wife sometimes buys pork from Pasquale. It must come from that pig farm, so Pasquale can tell us who owns the farm and how to get there."

The sergeant led Nico and Vittorio to the macelleria, the butcher shop. A lamb carcass sat atop a block of hardwood in the center of the small shop. The butcher was cleaving the animal into sections when the three men entered. He wore a stained apron, and the coppery smell of blood hung in the air.

Pasquale put down the cleaver when he saw his visitors. "Preparing meat is messy work," he said. "I wait until the shop is empty after everyone has bought what they want for dinner before I start butchering. My customers don't like to see this side of the business."

He looked down at his hands covered in blood and his soiled apron and laughed. "Seeing me like this would scare many of them. What can I do for you, signori? The meat on this lamb is very tender, but I don't think you came here to buy lamb chops."

After introducing the two Florentines, the sergeant asked, "We were told you buy pork from a farm on the road to Vittuone. Is that so?"

"Yes. Is there a problem? Nardo's farm is not the cleanest, but he is the only one who raises pigs, and his pork has never made anyone sick before."

The sergeant ignored Pasquale's question. "What is Nardo's family name? Does he live alone?"

"I don't know his family name. He does live alone; of that I'm sure. No one else could tolerate the smell."

"When is the last time you went to the farm?" Vittorio asked.

"Four days past. Every three days, I go to a different farm. Yesterday I brought this lamb from a sheep farm. In two days, I will get beef, and then I will go back to Nardo's farm for pork three days after that."

"Was there anyone else at Nardo's farm when you were last there?"

"I did not see anyone else, but I did not actually visit the farm. Nardo brought the butchered hogs to the road in his wagon." Pasquale speculated on the reason he was being asked about Nardo. "Is Nardo connected to the body found in the canal?"

Again, Pasquale's question went unanswered. "Does he usually meet you at the road?" Vittorio asked.

"No, usually he has the carcasses hanging in his barn. I was happy he met me at the road because it spared me from having to smell the stench in his barn. As I said before, there has never been a problem with meat from the farm, but Nardo does not keep his animals as clean as he could."

Unusual events and circumstances always drew Vittorio's interest. "There must be a reason why Nardo met you at the road. I want to speak with him," Vittorio said. The sergeant nodded and got directions to the pig farm from the butcher. They left the butcher shop, and the sergeant led the two Florentines to the ferry. It took three trips on the small ferry to shuttle the men and their horses across the canal. Vittorio, Nico, and the sergeant rode to the pig farm while Vernaccia stayed in town, sitting behind the desk to protect the citizens of Gaggiano in the unlikely event that a crime occurred.

When they neared the farm, they no longer needed any directions; they simply followed the smell to its source. Nico said, "Despite what Leviticus said in the Old Testament, I always believed pigs are clean animals."

"They can be if the farmer mucks their pens properly," the sergeant replied, "We haven't reached the farm yet, and I've already decided to tell my wife never again to buy pork."

A portico of stone columns and a sagging wood-shingled roof spanned the front of the old farmhouse. Nico stood on the path a safe distance back, fearing the roof might collapse at any time. The sergeant knocked on the door and called to Nardo. "This is official business. Open the door."

Nardo pulled the door open and stepped out under the portico. His mouth was smeared with grease, as though he had not washed or wiped it since his last meal. He was shirtless, and his unkempt hair was as greasy as his mouth.

"We are investigating a murder," the sergeant said forcefully with the intent of unsettling the pig farmer. "A man was kept here ..."

Before the sergeant could finish his sentence, Nardo blurted, "I had no choice. They made me keep him here."

He displayed the gash on the side of his head. "See, he hit me. He would've killed me. They made me keep him in the barn. But I know nothing about a murder. They took him away in my wagon. He was alive when they took him." His words flowed like a waterfall.

"Who kept him here?" the sergeant asked.

"My cousin."

"His name," the sergeant demanded.

"Bruno. His name is Bruno."

"His family name? What is his family name?"

"Palmieri or Parmerini. Maybe. Something like that. I'm not sure. He is not a close cousin. The only name he uses is Bruno. He only comes here when he wants something."

"Where can we find him?" Vittorio asked.

"In Milan. He lives in Milan. That's all I know. I don't know where in Milan."

"You said 'they.' How many were there?" Vittorio asked.

"There was a second man, but I never heard his name, and I never saw him before."

"Is that all? Just the two of them?"

"Yes, just the two."

"Your cousin, Bruno. What does he look like?"

"He's big. Wide shoulders and thick arms. One eye...it always looks like he's squinting."

"And the other man?"

"He's not as big. That's all I remember. I didn't see him much." After a slight pause, Nardo added, "Oh, and he wasn't messy. Bruno is always messy, but the other one wasn't. His tunic looked clean, like it was new."

Nico asked, "The man who was kept here, did they say why they were holding him?"

"No, they only said that someone would come to talk with him. But no one ever came."

"Where did they keep him?" Vittorio asked.

Nardo pointed to the barn. "There. They had him tied in one of the stalls."

"Show me," Vittorio demanded.

The farmer led the others to the stall. He was not bothered by the stench, but the others found their eyes beginning to tear. Squishing of the mud-shit mixture underfoot caused Nico to look down and grimace at seeing his shoes covered with the brown ooze. Now, Nico thought, I understand why soldiers who slog in mud every day wear boots. Maybe I will buy a pair when I return to Milan.

Despite the smell, Vittorio methodically searched the stall, looking for clues. He lifted the chain that had been used to secure Salvetti. One end was fastened to a wooden post. Caught in the links at the free end, Vittorio found threads that matched those of the cloth patch he had cut from Salvetti's tunic. Scanning the floor, he spotted an object almost buried in the ooze. The investigator reached down and recovered a white ceramic button with a red design identical to the one that the servant had said Salvetti received as a present from his wife. Vittorio carried the button to a nearby water trough, where he rinsed it and cleaned his hands. He held the disk up for Nico and the sergeant to see. "This confirms Salvetti was here. This is a button from his tunic."

Vittorio found a pitchfork standing in a pile of straw. He gently dragged the implement along the mud floor of the stall, hoping to uncover other evidence. After combing the entire area, he announced, "There is nothing else here."

Vittorio walked to where Nardo was standing and stood directly in front of him, their noses nearly touching. He asked, "What happened to the man who was chained here?"

"They took him away in a wagon. He was alive when they left here. I swear to the Holy Mother he was alive."

Nico and Vittorio thanked the sergeant for his help and turned to leave. "What about me?" Nardo asked.

The sergeant replied, "The army is responsible for investigating the crime; they are the ones who will decide your fate."

22

RETURN TO MILAN

Nico and Vittorio spent less time in Gaggiano than they expected, but regrettably the excursion produced little information. They had the given name of one of the killers, but they did not know how to find him, who hired him, nor the motive for the crime.

The gray sky and brown landscape devoid of people and animals further dampened their spirits and hindered conversation. Each man turned the events of the day over in his mind, searching for a clue they might have missed and pondering their next steps.

At one farm on the road to Milan, the sight of a young woman in a field pulled Nico's thoughts from the problem at hand. He recalled Bianca walking in a meadow near Siena. Momentarily closing his eyes made the image even more vivid. He pictured her in the same blue dress that she had worn when he was last with her in Siena. Her hair gleamed in the sunlight of his memory. How many days since they were together? How many more until he would see her again?

The appearance of the Milan city wall in the distance

dispelled Nico's reverie. "It is still early," he said to Vittorio. "Messer Avocino may still be in his office. If Bruno has committed crimes in the past, he may be known to the guardia, and Avocino may know where to find him."

"I suspect Bruno might be a common name in Milan," Vittorio said. "Still, the name is the only lead we have, and there is a chance that Avocino might know him." They dropped the horses at the stable and followed Corso Vercelli through the city gate into the walled city. From there, it was only a brief walk to Avocino's office. However, instead of taking the most direct route, Nico prevailed upon Vittorio to divert to a street where Nico had previously seen a shoemaker.

Looking through the small front window of the shoemaker's shop, Nico saw the old cobbler with a mallet in hand. They entered the shop where the skilled artisan was tacking a strip of embroidered fabric to wooden platforms to create fashionable clogs for one of his wealthy female patrons.

The old man looked up from his handiwork, puzzled to see two strangers. He had worked his trade in the same location since he had finished his apprenticeship and joined the guild more years past than he could remember. He knew everyone in the district because they all came to him for footwear.

"We had a mishap and need new shoes," Nico said.

The cobbler, already hunched by the burden of age, bent lower to view their problem. As soon as the odor reached his nostrils, he jumped back and turned away.

"Pig shit!" he exclaimed. "Until the angels took him, my brother had a farm with pigs. I will never forget that smell. The only thing that stinks more than pig shit is chicken shit. My brother had chickens too."

He inspected the two men, who were too startled by his remarks to respond. "You come here to ask me for shoes so you can walk in pig shit? A craftsman in my brotherhood worked for hours making the shoes you wear. That poor man would be in tears if he knew how you dishonored his craft. A piece of our soul is in every shoe we make, and you drag his soul through pig shit."

Vittorio sensed that the old man was about to eject them from his shop, so he intervened. "We were helping the guardia pursue a murderer. The trail led us to a pig farm."

Nico saw the wisdom in Vittorio's approach, so he added to the appeasement, "I have never been on a pig farm before, and never pursued a killer before, and I hope never to repeat either of those experiences."

Vittorio's strategy produced the desired result. "I hope you caught the bastard," the cobbler grunted. The shoemaker did not mention that his father had enjoyed a lengthy career as a member of the guardia before the Lord took him. The cobbler held in high regard all who helped the guardia.

From a workbench behind him, he took a square of leather and held it out to Nico. "Tanned from calf hide. Feel it. As soft as the bottom of a baby. I make shoes for you from this, and you will be walking through a cloud."

He grasped another piece and held it out to Vittorio. "Goat hide. No leather tougher than this. I put it underneath to protect the soft upper part." He smiled as he added, "Goat hide will last longer than me, maybe even longer than you."

The cobbler dipped a rag into a container of liquid on his workbench and handed it to Nico. "Here. This will clean some of the pig shit. Not all, but some."

When they had removed as much of the muck as possible, the shoemaker measured their feet. "Come back in two days," he said, then he returned his attention to the platform shoes he was working on when Nico and Vittorio had interrupted him.

Nico and Vittorio continued to Messer Avocino's office. At the top of the stairs on the upper level of the building, they could hear Avocino speaking with someone in his office at the far end of the corridor, so they waited by the stairs, hoping that the conference would end soon. The hallway channeled sound, allowing Nico to hear every word of the instructions being given by Avocino to his aide. Nico recalled that the first time he had come to Avocino's office to discuss the Salvetti abduction, the lawyer had also left his office door open, enabling anyone in the hallway to eavesdrop on his conversation. Nico vowed that if he ever had an office of his own, he would close the door when he consulted with clients.

Before long, the clerk emerged from Avocino's office and went across the hall to another office where three other men were working. From their dress and their actions, it appeared the two men preparing documents were notaries. Nico judged the third man to be another clerk.

Nico tapped on the open office door to get Avocino's attention. The lawyer looked up from the document he was reading and signaled for Nico and Vittorio to enter. "Come in. Be seated. I received a report that the body from Gaggiano was identified as Signor Salvetti, but I suspect you already know that since you are probably the ones who made the identification."

Nico would have acknowledged Avocino's assumption with a single word or a nod, but Vittorio, the always precise investigator, said, "We brought one of Salvetti's servants to the army camp. He is the one who identified the body."

"There is more," Nico added. "We have just returned from Gaggiano, where we learned that two men were involved in Salvetti's abduction and murder. One of them is named Bruno, and he lives in Milan. We thought that if Bruno had been in trouble in the past, you might know of him and how to find him."

"I do not recall ever prosecuting anyone named Bruno;

however, I only prosecute crimes in this district. If he had ever been apprehended in another district, I would not know of him, but there is someone who might. Do you know Bruno's surname?"

"The person we spoke with in Gaggiano was not sure of the surname. He thought it might be Palmieri or Parmerini."

Avocino shouted, "Alessandro!"

The same clerk who had left Avocino's office earlier poked his head into the room. Now Nico understood why Avocino kept his office door open: it saved him from having to walk across the hall. Nico thought, maybe someday there will be a way to call a person in another office without having to shout.

Avocino said to the clerk, "See if Sergeant Dellanetta is available to join us."

While they waited for the sergeant, Avocino said, "You said that two men were involved in the killing. Do you know the name of the second man?"

Nico shook his head. "No. Salvetti was kept at a farm owned by Bruno's cousin. The cousin is the one who told us about Bruno, but he does not know the name of the other man."

"What is happening to the cousin?" Avocino asked.

A somewhat cynical Vittorio answered, "Officials in Gaggiano said that the army would decide whether to charge him for being involved in the crime. The cousin is a pig farmer. His farm is the only source of pork for people in the town. Those in Gaggiano who enjoy pork might become unhappy if their only pork supplier is imprisoned. I suspect the food preferences of the people in town will influence whether the pig farmer is prosecuted."

A lanky man with a narrow face and pointy jaw appeared in the doorway. His hair was pulled back in a horsetail, and his chin held a hint of black stubble. Avocino motioned for him to enter and introduced him. "Sergeant Dellanetta oversees all criminal records in this district. The Office of the Podestà sends reports of all suspects and criminals to each district in the city. In this district, the reports are received by Sergeant Dellanetta."

Avocino turned to the sergeant. "A murder has been committed in Gaggiano by a man known as Bruno who lives here in Milan. His surname might be Palmieri or something similar. Do you recognize the name?"

"I have seen reports for someone called Bruno. I don't recall the surname," Dellanetta replied, then he bellowed, "Alessandro!"

Seconds later, the clerk dutifully appeared in the doorway. "In the cabinet behind my desk is a thick blue folio." Before the sergeant could give further instructions, Alessandro spun around and sped away through the hallway.

Alessandro returned with an overstuffed folio. Dellanetta removed three pages and spread them across Avocino's desk. "These three reports describe thefts in which a man called Bruno is a suspect." He picked up one of the reports and refer-ring to it said, "A victim in one of the crimes claimed he heard the name Bruno. His wife said she heard the name of a second man. She said his name sounded like 'Tonno,' but she was so frightened that her memory is not reliable. None of the victims saw the thieves because the crimes were committed at night. Since the guardia had nothing other than the name Bruno, it took no action. All three of these incidents in these reports were thefts. None involved violence, and certainly not murder."

"This case does," noted Vittorio. "Bruno's cousin has identi-fied him as one of the abductors of Signor Salito Salvetti, the head bookkeeper at the Medici bank, the man whose body was found at Gaggiano. Do the reports say where Bruno lives or how to find him?"

"No. Again, there was not enough information to identify him."

Nico said, "In Florence, criminals and thieves regularly frequent taverns and brothels. I assume that is so in Milan as well. Would it be possible for your men to ask patrons of these places if anyone knows him?"

The sergeant tried unsuccessfully to suppress a burst of laughter. "That approach might work in Florence, but here in Milan, thugs and lowlifes don't talk to members of the guardia."

Nico pressed, "What if your men don't wear uniforms? That way they would not be recognized as members of the guardia."

Out of respect for the naïve foreigner, the sergeant refrained from further laughter. "Thieves in this city know my officers better than they know their own mothers. My men could dress as nuns, and they would still be recognized. Thieves take pride in being able to identify anyone who might imprison them."

Nico tried one last time, "Would it be possible to ask the tavern owners?"

Dellanetta spread his palms in a dismissive gesture. "If it became known that a tavern owner cooperated with us, he would lose all of his patrons. Your ideas are excellent, but they would not succeed here in Milan. I wish I had some officers who are unknown to the criminals, but I do not."

Seeing Nico's disappointment, Dellanetta tried to be helpful, "What we can do is have our officers question criminals who are already in prison. Those in prison often reveal information in exchange for a simple favor. Prison food is not the best, as you might imagine. Two days past, a prisoner gave us the name of his cohort in exchange for a focaccia from a nearby trattoria. It does not take much incentive to loosen the tongue of a hungry man."

The sergeant, deep in thought, rubbed his chin before continuing. "I will do this because the captain said you openly shared information you had gathered. But understand, I can only do this unofficially. Salvetti's murder is now under the purview of the army. We cannot take official action."

Massimo was already at the guest house when Nico and Vittorio arrived after their meeting with Avocino. He had bathed, groomed his hair, and was wearing his finest tunic. He sat on a couch, sipping a glass of wine and grinning broadly.

"What are you so happy about?" Nico asked. "Did you have a roll with Portinari's maid?"

"Better than that, lawyer. The contessa invited us to dinner again tonight, and her sister Benedetta will be joining us. One of the servants assured me that the fair lady is not betrothed."

"Is that all you learned in the army, how to drink wine and chase women?" Nico quipped.

"Of course not; I also learned to gamble."

Nico attempted to inject discipline into the banter saying, "Just remember, you are a representative of the Florentine government."

But Massimo kept jesting. "Oh, I won't forget. I told you my newest discovery is that nothing impresses women more than diplomatic credentials."

Nico parried again. "Benedetta belongs to a noble family. Her father was a marchese. If you offend her, the Milanese nobility may cut away one of your most favored parts."

"Now you are getting my attention." Massimo laughed, took another sip of wine, then he turned serious. "Have you made any progress in resolving Salvetti's abduction?"

Nico and Vittorio took turns describing the identification of the body, their findings in Gaggiano, and the discussions with Messer Avocino. When they finished, Massimo asked, "What do you intend to do next?"

Vittorio replied, "I will continue interviewing people at the bank, but with different questions now that we know Salvetti was killed. Abductions and beatings are ways that criminals convince victims to settle gambling and other debts but killing does not serve that purpose. I need to give more attention to other motives.

"We must also search for the person named Bruno. He is responsible for Salvetti's murder, and we know he is somewhere in Milan. Sergeant Dellanetta said people in the taverns won't talk with the guardia officers, but I am not known here in Milan. I can visit taverns in the city to ask about Bruno. There is no reason people won't talk with me."

Massimo burst out laughing. "Never did anyone look more like a member of the guardia than you. If you go into a tavern, all the miscreants will disappear like rats leaving a sinking ship."

Vittorio didn't know whether to feel pleased or offended by Massimo's remark.

Massimo continued, "If there is anyone who can get information from lowlifes, it is me. Spending time in taverns is also a favorite pastime of soldiers. I can easily blend in with the drunks of Milan."

Nico laughed. "You've often said with pride that drinking, gambling, and chasing women rank high among your skills, so if you hadn't become a soldier, might you have become a hunted criminal?"

Massimo shrugged. He knew Nico's inference was made in jest, still, he felt compelled to defend his profession. "It's true that soldiers and criminals enjoy similar diversions but that does not mean our lives are the same." After reflecting for a moment, he said, "The florin and the denaro both carry images of Saint John and the lily, but no one would trade one coin for the other."

"A perfect comparison," Nico agreed, "because between those high and low value coins is the soldo. It can represent the mercenaries. Some people claim that mercenaries have value, whereas others regard them as having little worth."

Vittorio raised a hand to interrupt the banter. "Those analogies are entertaining but flawed because good men and bad men can be found in each group."

Nico raised an eyebrow. "Good men among criminals?"

"And also misdeeds by holy men," Vittorio replied. "Two years past I attended mass in Pisa on the feast of San Ranieri. When the service ended, a priest following close behind a well-dressed parishioner lifted the man's coin purse and dropped it into the poor box."

Massimo smiled. "Did you apprehend the priest?"

"Fortunately, it did not come to that. The priest saw me watching him, so he retrieved the coin purse and returned it to the owner who thought that he had dropped it. To show his appreciation for its return, the wealthy patron gave a generous donation to the church."

Nico said, "Still, you must have been conflicted."

"I was."

"Returning to the matter at hand," Massimo said. "I intend to devote my full energies tomorrow to sampling the beers available in the taverns of Milan...and seeking a thief named Bruno."

23

PRIVY COUNCIL CHANCERY, MILAN

Giorgio, a clerk at the Privy Council Chancery, stared at a note he picked from the stack of incoming correspondence. Confused by the wording, he asked his colleague, "Filippo, do you understand what this means? It asks, 'Is it permitted to release the body of Signor Salvetti to his family?'"

"Who sent the note?"

"A physician at the army camp. I don't know why he is asking the council for permission to dispose of a body. The military has procedures for disposing of remains."

"I don't understand either," replied Filippo, "but I'm glad that you found that notice instead of me. It makes no sense. I would ignore it." Giorgio took his friend's suggestion and placed the paper in the waste pile with other useless information sent to the council each day.

For the next two hours, while Giorgio went about his regular duties, he kept thinking about the discarded query. If it had come from a low-level bureaucrat, he would not be concerned, but surely the army physician had a reason for inquiring. Finally, curiosity got the better of him, and Giorgio rummaged through the trash basket and retrieved the note. "I am going to the army camp," he told Filippo. "I need to find the reason why this note was sent to the Chancery."

The army camp was three miles outside the city. It was a permanent encampment with soldiers living in buildings, not tents. The military unit numbered in the thousands, so the facility resembled a mid-sized town. A guard at the perimeter fence directed Giorgio to the medical building, where he found the physician who had sent the message.

"I am from the Privy Council," Giorgio announced. "You sent this note asking for the Council's permission to release the body of a Signor Salvetti. The army has procedures for handling the remains of its soldiers, so why are you asking the Council for permission?"

"The dead man was not in the army," the physician replied, "He was a foreigner whose body was recovered in Gaggiano. He was murdered. The officials sent the body here because the army has jurisdiction in murder cases."

A murdered foreigner. That raised Giorgio's anxiety.

"His name was Salito Salvetti. The Florentine diplomats who identified the body said that he was the head bookkeeper at the Medici bank."

A foreigner murdered. Foreign diplomats identified the body. Oh, shit, the stunned clerk thought. "Oh, shit," he said aloud. "You said foreign diplomats. Who were they?" Giorgio stammered.

"I don't recall their names. There were two of them, and they had a letter pressed with the Florentine seal. So, can I release the body?"

"I don't know. I'm just a clerk." Giorgio's face paled, and his breathing quickened. "This is not good. This is not good," he muttered, turned and strode away.

He did not hear the physician's final words, "The body is starting to decay."

The advantage of being a lowly clerk is that troublesome problems can be passed up the chain of command to a superior. Back at the chancery, Giorgio scoured the building looking for his immediate supervisor. Unable to find the uschiero, he went directly to the chancellor.

The chancellor was the fourth and youngest son of a silk merchant. At an early age, the child's tutor recognized that the boy had an uncanny ability to remember facts. Using a stack of cards with different drawings on one side, the tutor demonstrated the boy's memorization skill to a member of the Council of Justice by having the boy recall the pictures on an array of twenty cards placed face down. The boy passed the test by correctly recalling each image. That simple demonstration impressed the council member who set the young boy on a path of government service. Initially, the boy served as a clerk at the Council of Justice; gradually, he rose in status to become Chancellor of the Privy Council.

Every official report and record pertaining to foreigners came to the attention of the chancellor, who filed the details in his limitless memory. The chancellor was pouring through a new stack of documents when Giorgio filled his doorway.

"Excuse me, sir, but we have received a request that needs rapid attention."

The chancellor signaled for Giorgio to enter and held out his hand to accept the sheet that Giorgio was holding. "It is a peculiar request," he said after reading the note.

The chancellor closed his eyes, pressed a hand to his temple, and let his mind scan through recent reports. Salvetti,

Salvetti, he kept telling himself. Then finally, he said aloud, "Two recent reports mentioned the name Salvetti."

He summoned an aide and instructed him to retrieve the reports. Giorgio trembled as he recounted what the army physician had told him. "Salvetti was a foreigner, and two foreign diplomats identified his body," he explained.

The aide returned with two sheets and handed them to the chancellor, who read them aloud for the benefit of Giorgio and his supervisor, who had joined the meeting.

"This report was submitted by an official and physician in the town of Gaggiano."

A body was found in the Naviglio Grande at Gaggiano. A stone tied to the body kept it submerged for an extended period, making it difficult to tell how long it had been in the water. It appeared that a heavy object struck and fractured the skull.

Both of these factors are indicative of murder. Marks on the wrists suggest he was tied with rope. The body is clothed in a well-made silk tunic of an unusual style, suggesting that the person might be a foreigner.

The chancellor then read the second report, a perfunctory note from the guardia in Milan's Nuova district.

The wife of a Medici bank employee reported that her husband is missing. The missing person is named Salito Salvetti. At this time, there is no reason to suspect that he is a crime victim.

To Giorgio, the chancellor said, "You did well to gather information from the army physician; it builds the bridge between these two reports and points out serious discrepancies."

Both Giorgio and the supervisor looked puzzled. Neither of them noticed a discrepancy. The chancellor explained, "The guardia in Milan filed its missing person report days after the body was found in Gaggiano. Surely the victim's wife notified the guardia promptly, so why was the report delayed? The report from the Nuova district does not mention that the missing person was a foreigner, and neither report mentions any involvement of foreign diplomats. I am certain the Privy Council Secretary will want to explore these discrepancies. We cannot have foreign diplomats identifying bodies of murder victims before the guardia even knows there was a murder."

To his aide, the chancellor said, "Find the investigator who wrote the report. Find out what he, the prosecutor, and the magistrate of the Nuova district know about the foreign diplomats. And tell them to prepare to give accounts of their actions to the Secretary."

24

AT BIERPOSTO IN MILAN

A message delivered by one of Pagatore's thugs summoned Bruno and Tonio to Bierposto. At their last meeting at the tavern, a storyteller had drawn a raucous crowd that filled the establishment. This time there was no entertainer and only a few patrons. Tonio spotted Pagatore as soon as he stepped inside. Bruno followed Tonio to Pagatore's table. They pulled out chairs, preparing to sit, but Pagatore held up a hand, signaling them to remain standing. He flipped a coin onto the table to pay for his beer as he rose. He pointed toward the rear of the room and said to the two arrivals, "We need privacy where these fools can't overhear."

Pagatore led them through a corridor to a dingy storage room where the three could be alone. As soon as Tonio closed the door, Pagatore snarled, "That job turned to shit." He sat on a crate, the only seating in the room. The two thugs remained standing.

Bruno's hands clenched into fists, and his arms tensed, like a snake ready to strike. Pagatore anticipated the reaction. He slid the crate back out of Bruno's reach. "Hold your ass for a minute. The client agrees that the blame isn't all yours. You didn't know that someone else would go in Portinari's place."

Pagatore waited until Bruno's neck muscles relaxed before continuing. "But the murder...that was all your asinine doing. I told you the target was not to be harmed."

"He saw us. He could identify us," Bruno protested.

Pagatore waved away Bruno's objection. "He saw you because you are a moron. If you had a brain, you would have covered his eyes."

Again, Bruno's muscles tensed, but he did not lash out. Pagatore prided himself on knowing how much he could taunt the thief without suffering a reprisal.

Tonio, impatient with the bickering, said, "If your only purpose in calling us here is to hurl insults, then I'm leaving."

Pagatore looked directly at Tonio. "Your plea convinced the Intermediary that the cock-up was not your fault. He is willing to give you another chance. If I could find someone else to do this job, I would, but time is short, so I am stuck with both of you."

"We can take the bastard if you give us the right information," Bruno snapped.

"The client wants to put pressure on Portinari, but taking him now is too risky. He has a bodyguard, a Florentine soldier who follows him everywhere."

"A bodyguard? Only one bodyguard? One bodyguard is not a problem," Bruno boasted.

The more reasonable Tonio asked, "What does the client want us to do?"

"There is another way to get Portinari's attention. Portinari lives in a farmhouse outside the city. When he is at work, his wife and a maid are alone at the house. The two women have no protection. The client wants Portinari's wife taken, but the two women are together, so you will have to take both."

Bruno's face glowed with an evil grin. "I can already tell I'm going to like this job."

Pagatore pounded a fist down hard against the crate beside him and snarled, "You are not to hurt the women. You are not to harm them in any way. If anything happens to them, the client will hunt you down and feed your balls to wolves. The wife's father is rich. Rich enough to hire an army of mercenaries to carve you into tiny pieces if any harm comes to his daughter. Do you hear me?" Pagatore fixed his stare on Bruno.

Bruno gave a dismissive wave of his hand but said nothing.

Pagatore turned to address Tonio. "You are to take the women and leave this." He handed Tonio a sealed envelope addressed to Signor Portinari. "Leave this letter where Portinari must see it."

"What does it say?" Bruno asked.

"I don't know; I don't want to know, and neither do you." Then to Tonio, Pagatore said, "Keep that swine's filthy hands away from the letter and keep him from hurting the women."

He handed Tonio a single sheet. "This is a map to the farm-house where you can find the women. You are to keep them for two days and then release them."

Tonio raised an eyebrow. "Release them after two days?"

Pagatore repeated what the Intermediary had told him. "Two days will be enough for Portinari to agree with the client's demand. The wife is a respectable woman. Find a decent place for her. She cannot be kept in pig shit. Treating her poorly will invite retribution that none of us want."

Tonio wondered, does Pagatore think that merely abducting the woman will not draw retribution? "When must it be done?" he asked.

"Soon...today or tomorrow. The client is under pressure because you bungled the last job. If this job fails, it will be the last one I get from this client, and it will be my last job for you."

Tonio spoke his thoughts aloud. "We need to find a place..."

"A place where they will not wallow in pig shit," Pagatore finished Tonio's statement as he rose and moved toward the door. Before stepping into the corridor, he turned back and said, "In the tavern there is a braggart called Mouseface. I heard him talking about a retreat house near Monza that the Dominican monks use in summer. He said it is vacant at this time of year."

Bruno and Tonio followed Pagatore back to the tavern where a wimpish man was swilling beer and boring an unfortunate patron with one of his fabrications. Pagatore pointed. "That's him. That's Mouseface."

Bruno stepped behind the disinterested listener, grabbed him by his collar, and pulled him from his chair. "Go somewhere else. We have business to discuss," he ordered.

The two thugs slid into chairs, one on each side of Mouseface. Color drained from the little man's face and his right eye twitched. He started to reach for his beer but changed his mind and brought his hands close to his chest and away from Bruno.

"You spoke of a retreat house near Monza," Tonio declared.

Mouseface's eye twitched faster. He imagined that the two might have been sent by the father of a girl he had seduced in the old sanctuary.

"Tell us how to find it," Tonio commanded.

Mouseface realized that this was not about the girl; they just want to locate the retreat house. Relief let him take his first breath since the men appeared. Gradually, he found enough courage to speak. "It is on a hill overlooking the town."

Bruno grabbed Mouseface's wrist and twisted his arm. "How do we find it?" Bruno barked.

Mouseface described in detail the route from the center of Monza to the hilltop retreat house. The thugs seemed satisfied with the information Mouseface gave them, so he summoned the courage to take a badly needed gulp of beer, and that emboldened him to begin one of his far-fetched stories.

"I bedded three, no four, girls in that house. Being taken on a bed where monks say the rosary gets girls excited."

Bruno shoved Mouseface's chair, slamming it against the table and sending the glass of beer crashing to the floor. Without another word, Bruno and Tonio exited the tavern.

Bruno could already feel heat building in his loins. Even if he could not touch the wife, there was the maid. Surely the maid did not have a rich father, and the client would not give a shit about the maid. Portinari is probably poking her, he thought, so why not me? He preferred robust women with generously padded buttocks and big breasts. Age did not matter. In his experience, older women appreciated his advances more than younger ones. Older women were not adventurous on their own, but they were accepting of his unconventional practices. "Let's get them now," Bruno babbled.

Tonio let his glance drift down to pebbles scattered at the side of the road. His gaze shifted from stone to stone as he considered the issues needing attention before they could abduct the women. Was the retreat house well isolated from other dwellings? Could people in the town see activity at the hilltop retreat house? What food and supplies were needed to keep the women for two days? How would they transport the women from the farm to the retreat house? How could they hide their identities while keeping the women for two days? Would it even be possible to conceal their identities for two days?

25

MILAN

Nico and Vittorio were not yet awake when Massimo prepared for his day's activities. His first task would be escorting bank manager Portinari from his rented farmhouse to the Medici bank. He would spend the rest of the day visiting taverns throughout the city, trying to find someone who knew a thief named Bruno. To blend in with regular tavern goers, Massimo needed to dress as they did. The locals would not speak with him if he wore the uniform of a Florentine soldier.

The previous evening, Massimo had asked one of the house servants where he might get a disreputable tunic. He expected the servant would direct him to a church that cared for the indigent. Instead, the servant pulled from the trash a tunic that had been discarded by the palazzo's cook. The well-worn garment had a smattering of red stains on one sleeve.

"Yesterday the cook had an accident while he was making soup," the servant explained. "He was wearing an apron, but the sleeves of his tunic were not protected, and it is not possible to remove beet stains."

"Perfect," Massimo said. "The stains look like blood spatter. They will add to my persona."

The servant registered surprise that Massimo wanted to create a persona at all, much less one that would be improved by blood spatter, but he held his tongue.

Massimo spread the tunic to examine it carefully. "Does the cook have a twin? This garment is large enough to fit two people."

"The cook is Sicilian," the servant responded, as though being Sicilian adequately explained the cook's girth.

Massimo wondered how many Sicilians the servant had met to form his opinion because most Sicilians he knew were thin and wiry. Massimo took the garment, knowing that a cord sashed at his waist would keep the fabric from bulging excessively.

Hose were not an issue. Those worn by all men were similar, except for the fancy silk ones laced with gold strands favored by pretentious merchants.

Shoes were another matter. Massimo shared the practice of soldiers who regularly polished their boots to a mirror-like sheen. That discipline would not serve him well today. He considered the discarded shoes that Nico and Vittorio had worn in Gaggiano. Slogging through pig shit had made them shabby enough, but neither pair was large enough to fit his feet, duck feet his commanding officer had once labeled them. Massimo accepted the label proudly, knowing that many women believed the myth that the size of a man's feet corresponds to the size of another part of his anatomy. As many women—well, not an outrageous number of women—could testify, Massimo himself lent proof to the myth. Still, he had bathed in frigid rivers with enough other soldiers to know the predictor did not apply in all cases.

He had not yet taken time to polish the boots that he wore

on his journey from Florence to Milan. They were covered with road grime. No self-respecting soldier would wear boots in their condition, but it would not be unreasonable for a transient visitor to Milan to wear scuffed army boots, so he settled on those boots as his best option. Massimo mussed his hair, and he was ready to begin the day.

On rainy and cold mornings, he chose the most direct route from the guest house to the stable where he boarded the carriage that would take him to the Portinari farmhouse. When the weather was pleasant, he found it invigorating to walk a longer, more circuitous route at a rapid pace. In the army, physical exercise was part of his routine. This assignment as a commissioner did not afford him that opportunity, and he missed it. The morning walks were his only substitute.

The driver had already hitched horses to the carriage and was ready to depart when Massimo arrived at the stable. Massimo would have felt self-conscious riding inside the coach from the stable to the farmhouse. He preferred sitting outside next to the driver, and the driver welcomed his company.

From their previous conversations, the driver knew that Massimo was part of a team sent by officials in Florence to investigate the abduction of Salito Salvetti. He also knew that Massimo's purpose in accompanying Portinari was to protect the bank manager from suffering a similar fate. The driver knew little beyond that because Massimo shared as little information as possible. The driver might learn of Salvetti's murder, but if he did, it would not be from Massimo.

Massimo planned to visit taverns later in the day, asking total strangers if they knew someone named Bruno, so there was no harm in starting the day by asking the driver. The driver had been rambling on about how difficult it was to raise children. "My son, he spends all his time with his friends talking about girls," the driver lamented. "And the daughter is even more difficult. The wife thought the girl should learn music, and now the girl spends all her time playing the lyre."

Massimo took advantage of a brief lull in the driver's diatribe to squeeze in a question of his own. "Might you know anyone called Bruno?"

The unanticipated question froze the driver's mouth in an open position. When he recovered from the surprise, he responded, "Bruno? Is he a player in one of the horse games? The one where men ride around, striking a ball with a long stick?"

The amusing response made Massimo grin. "Bruno is a person, but he is not an athlete. He is a thief. I want to find him because he may be the one who abducted Signor Salvetti."

Now Massimo had the full attention of the driver. All thoughts of challenging children had vanished. "I don't know any thieves. Well, maybe I do, but if I do, I don't know it," the driver began. After a brief pause, he added, "If you want to find a thief, you should ask priests."

It was Massimo's turn to be surprised. "I don't picture thieves as churchgoers."

"That is so, but people who go to church ask priests to pray for family members who have gone astray. Every priest knows the names of all the sinners in his parish."

It wasn't a bad idea. Maybe Bruno had no concern for his black soul, but someone else might. If so, a priest might know a sinner called Bruno.

On previous mornings, Massimo went into the farmhouse to announce the arrival of the carriage. It was an unnecessary courtesy because the maid working in the kitchen could see them arrive through a window. Today, Massimo decided it would be best to wait outside. The driver and Signor Portinari might be oblivious to Massimo's strange dress, but Portinari's wife would surely notice his disheveled look and ask questions.

She was already worried about her husband's safety, so Massimo did not want to raise fresh fears by telling her that Signor Salvetti had been murdered and his killer was loose in Milan.

When Portinari appeared, Massimo opened the coach door and climbed inside after the bank manager. As usual, Portinari carried a stout leather case stuffed with important bank papers. He had settled into his seat and unlatched the clasp that secured the case when Massimo interrupted his routine. "Signor Salvetti has been killed... murdered," Massimo announced.

Portinari straightened and color drained from his face. His cracking voice said, "Are you certain? Does his wife know? Salvetti was a good man, a good friend."

"His body was identified yesterday by a servant from his house." Massimo withheld the gruesome details of the crime.

"Someone should have told me." Portinari leaned out of the carriage window and shouted to the driver, "Take us to Signor Salvetti's house."

"Are you sure that is a good idea?" Massimo asked. "This is a difficult time for his wife. She must be grief-stricken."

"All the more reason I need to go to her. Salito was more than just a bank employee. I am godfather to one of his children. I must do what I can to comfort Gherarda and the children."

When they reached the Salvetti house, Portinari dismissed the driver. To Massimo, he said, "Please deliver the terrible news to my assistant at the bank. I will stay here to help Gherarda make funeral arrangements."

Massimo walked to the bank to instruct Portinari's assistant; then he was ready to begin the hunt for Bruno. However, no taverns were open early in the morning. Their most devoted patrons were likely sleeping off the effects of the previous night's drinking in alleys across the city. Massimo did not hold great hope that the driver's suggestion of asking parish priests would yield any results, but at least priests were early risers, and churches were easy to find with their tall bell towers poking the sky. Massimo scanned the surrounding area and spotted the bell tower of San Sepolcro church only a short distance away. A handful of old women were attending mass when Massimo entered and took a seat in a pew at the rear of the nave. It had been years since Massimo attended a mass other than a funeral, but he quickly recalled the prayers and responses he had learned as a child.

When mass ended, the women remained in their seats, apparently feeling the need for additional purification. Massimo approached the priest. "May I have a word with you, Father?"

"Certainly, my son. Come with me to the sacristy, and we can talk while I remove my vestments."

Massimo did not waste words. "I am helping the guardia to locate a dangerous man, a thief, and a killer. He lives somewhere in Milan."

"And the place you chose to look for a thief and a killer is a church?" the puzzled priest responded. "The Testament tells us that Jesus absolved criminals and the wicked, but it was Jesus who sought those needing redemption. The wicked did not come into churches to petition His favor."

"I was led to believe that priests know all the sinners in their parish."

The priest laughed, "There is some truth in that. Who is it that you seek?"

"A thief named Bruno."

"There is one named Bruno in my flock. To discuss his sins would mean breaking the sanctity of the confessional, and that is something I cannot do. But I assure you, the Bruno who attends mass and takes the sacraments here is not the one you seek."

"I am a visitor unfamiliar with this city. I am here only to help apprehend this dangerous criminal. You must know your parish. Can you tell me where to look for someone who might know this Bruno?"

"I can offer nothing that you do not already know. Men like the one you seek have not only a single vice; they drink, gamble, and fornicate. You may be asking the wrong priest because there is little crime in this district. You may have better success asking Father John at San Bernardino alle Monache."

On his way to San Bernardino, Massimo spoke with priests at two other churches. Neither one knew anyone named Bruno. When Massimo reached San Bernardino, Father John had just returned from bringing communion to a bed-ridden parishioner. The priest ushered Massimo to the parish house, where he invited Massimo to share a morning meal. Since Massimo had already eaten a generous breakfast courtesy of the contessa's chef, he opted for a single piece of fruit while Father John topped his plate with a variety of breakfast fare.

Massimo asked Father John about Bruno as he had with the other priests. He expected the same unproductive response and was startled by Father John's answer. "I have heard about a thief called Bruno, although I cannot say he is one you seek." Massimo, pleased that his visits to churches might yield useful information, waited for the priest to elaborate.

"Nine months past, two of my parishioners, Antonio Missaglia and his wife, were awakened during the night by intruders. Antonio and his brothers are well-known armorers, so it is possible that the intruders were looking for weapons. If so, they were looking in the wrong place. The family has a workshop where they make and keep their weapons. Antonio had none in his home.

"The wife heard noises and awakened Antonio. The only heavy object in the bedroom was a statue of San Giorgio sitting on a bedside table. Antonio grabbed the statue and went to investigate. He encountered the intruders in the reception room. In the darkness, he saw only two shadowy figures. Antonio threw the statue and struck the head of one of the thieves. The injured one screamed, and the other cried, 'Bruno, what happened?' The one called Bruno moaned and told his companion they needed to leave.

"Antonio stayed awake for the rest of the night. When daylight came, he saw the invader's blood smeared on the Saint George statue. He reported the incident to the guardia, but they said there was nothing they could do because he could not identify the intruders."

"How did you learn all these details?"

"Antonio described the incident to parishioners at the next San Berardino Society meeting. He wanted everyone to know what happened so they could protect themselves and report any stranger in the neighborhood with a wound or cut on his face. Antonio recovered from the experience quickly, but his wife, the poor woman, still cannot cope. She suffers from terrible dreams and cannot sleep through the night."

"Did anyone else report a similar experience?"

"No, and I would know if it had happened again. The members of my flock care for each other. We are like a big family. That is why Antonio wanted everyone to know what happened."

Massimo left San Bernardino, disappointed that Father John could only confirm the existence of a thief named Bruno. It was mid-morning and taverns throughout the city were opening to serve laborers who preferred spending their noon-time breaks drinking rather than eating lunch. Most of the patrons were workers in local businesses who were unlikely to associate with thieves and criminals. Nonetheless, Massimo began visiting taverns and trying to engage the patrons in a discussion. At noontime, taverns drew small groups of coworkers, not isolated individuals. Members of those groups wanted to chat with each other; they did not welcome intrusions by strangers, so Massimo had no success gaining any information.

By mid-afternoon, the character of tavern patrons changed. Individuals gradually replaced the groups of employed laborers. Some were honest men who were out of work, but others were opportunists with few scruples who relied on minor crimes and petty thefts to make their way through life. In the military, Massimo developed a technique for recruiting rogues to serve as informants and spies. He decided that the same approach he had used in the military should also work in the taverns of Milan.

In the sixth tavern Massimo visited, a solitary individual sat at a table cradling a glass of beer in one hand and tracing figures on the dusty tabletop with his other hand. The man's clothes were old and unremarkable, but on his right hand was an elaborate gold ring inset with a red stone. For reasons Massimo did not understand, small-time thieves had a love for fancy jewelry.

Massimo approached the man and said, "You look like someone I knew in Bergamo. Have you ever lived in Bergamo?" Before the man could respond, Massimo pressed on. "Is your name Jacopo? Or maybe you have a brother named Jacopo?"

As Massimo expected, the man looked up and growled, "I am not Jacopo. I don't have a brother named Jacopo, and I have never been to Bergamo." Then he returned his focus to the dust-covered table.

To gain the man's interest, Massimo offered a compliment, "You have the same sharp eyes as his; that is why I mistook you for him." The next step in Massimo's approach had him dangle a hint of mystery, "I had to leave Bergamo, and I can't go back there." Massimo observed the mark softening, so he continued. "It's not easy being a stranger in Milan. I was excited to think I had found an old friend."

As Massimo turned to feign his departure, he added, "Your beer is almost gone. Let me get you a fresh one to make up for disturbing you." He called to the tavern keeper. "Bring my friend another beer," and spreading his hands apart, to show that it should be a large one. A compliment, a mystery, and a free beer. If that trilogy didn't soften the mark, nothing would.

"I am called Anguilla," the man said. "I once knew someone named Jacopo, but he was not from Bergamo. Why can't you go back to Bergamo?"

Massimo knew he had found his mark: a loner with a flashy gold ring who was willing to engage in conversation. Massimo slid back down into his chair and began his fabricated story.

"There is a rich bastard in Bergamo who thinks he owns the entire town and everyone in it. You know how these rich men are. One day I was in a tavern, much like this one. At the next table, the bastard's servants were complaining about him. I remember one of them saying that all the fancy dinners at the house were served on silver plates, and the guests ate with silver spoons.

"I came up with a plan to get that silver. It was a brilliant plan. I sneaked into the storage room near the kitchen and filled a bag with silver. Unfortunately, as I was leaving, a knife cut a hole in the sack. The knife slipped out and clattered to the floor. The cook heard the noise, so I got my ass out of there as fast as I could. I fled to Pavia, where I could sell the silver. I lived well in Pavia until all the silver was gone. There aren't many targets in Pavia, so that's why I came to Milan."

"Are you looking for work?" Anguilla asked.

"Yes, if it's the right kind of work. I'm looking for someone named Bruno. I was told he could help me. Do you know him?"

"Yes, I know him. I did a few jobs with him, but he's a reckless bastard. He takes too many chances."

"Do you know where he lives...where I can find him?"

"I don't know where he lives, but he hangs out in the Ticinese district. He works with a partner known as Tonio. I've never met Tonio, but people say he is smart and plans every move carefully. If that is true, I don't know why he works with Bruno."

Anguilla drained the last of the beer in his mug, rose, and said, "I have to piss." Massimo took advantage of Anguilla's absence to slip away. Finally, he had made progress: he learned the district that Bruno frequented and the name of his partner. The next day he would focus his efforts at taverns in the Ticinese district.

26

PRIVY COUNCIL SECRETARY, MILAN

Nico was at the Medici bank with Vittorio when Messer Avocino's clerk delivered a message ordering the Florentine diplomats to appear before the Secretary of the Privy Council. The
order and the clerk's appearance were completely unexpected.
"The note does not state a reason for requesting our appearance," Nico observed.

The clerk replied, "Council members never give reasons for
their actions, nor do they make requests. The letter is not a
request. You are ordered to appear. Messer Avocino has also
been ordered to appear."

"There is no time or date mentioned. When will the
hearing be held?"

"The council believes in swift action. When the councilors
order someone to appear, they mean immediately. I can escort
you to the hearing if you wish. Messer Avocino will meet us
there."

Nico assumed the Privy Council might have learned of
Salvetti's murder and wanted to take control of the situation.
Vittorio was meeting with the officers of the Medici bank, so

Nico decided that rather than interrupt Vittorio, he would go to the hearing by himself. He could fabricate an excuse for Vittorio's absence should it become necessary. Of greater concern was Nico's ignorance of Privy Council protocols, but he had no time to seek guidance nor to prepare before the hearing. He could only hope that the Privy Council Secretary would be as tolerant and open-minded as the district magistrate.

Messer Avocino, the guardia investigator, and the district magistrate were already seated around an ornate table in the opulent conference room of the Privy Council Secretary when Nico arrived. One wall of the room displayed the customary painting of Duke Sforza that adorned meeting rooms in all government buildings. However, this painting was the largest and most skillfully rendered of any Nico had seen. Another wall had windows looking out to a manicured courtyard with a central fountain where a life-sized marble Amphitrite, the wife of Poseidon, brought forth a gushing spray. Silk tapestries woven with gold accent threads covered the room's remaining walls.

Nico chose the empty chair next to Messer Avocino. Across the table, the investigator repeatedly dabbed at his forehead to stem a cascade of sweat. The meeting had not begun, yet his handkerchief was already saturated. The immediacy of the council summons had not given him a chance to change from his wrinkled uniform to a dress uniform. In contrast to the agitated investigator, the magistrate slumped in his chair with arms folded across his chest, and his eyes partially closed. He could not have looked more relaxed and disinterested.

Avocino leaned toward Nico and said in a hushed voice, "It is customary for hearings of this type to be conducted by the

Council Secretary, but he is away on personal business. In his absence, the charge falls to a delegate of the Ducal Court. Unfortunately, the member assigned today is a know-nothing, pompous ass. His name is Scotti, but as you will soon understand, to other members of the Ducal Court he is known as the Squirrel.

"Wealthy and influential men in the duchy get invited to serve as advisors to the duke. Scotti comes from a family with huge land holdings near Lake Maggiore. They are the largest timber supplier in the duchy; the family donated all the lumber for the framework of the Milan cathedral. The patriarch of the family is highly respected throughout the duchy. Two of his sons operate the family business, and rumor has it that he sent his third son as his representative on the Ducal Court just to get rid of the useless fool."

"I am struck by how everyone is reacting so differently to this inquiry," Nico said. "You appear to be unconcerned, apprehension is causing the investigator to melt, and the magistrate seems bored."

"We all have different roles; therefore, some of us are more accountable than others. The guardia is responsible for filing reports of all incidents involving foreigners. If the report sent to the council is flawed, the investigator will draw the blame." Avocino smiled as he said, "The magistrate followed the law, per the treaty that you uncovered. Since he did nothing wrong, he will not suffer the council's wrath."

"You too seem detached," Nico opined.

"I had a role in the matter, but I am not a decision-maker, so I will not be called to account."

"And me?" Nico asked.

"You ..." The entrance of the surrogate secretary interrupted Avocino's response.

He had close-set beady eyes and a narrow pointy face. His

lips were parted slightly, revealing rows of yellow teeth. He does look like a squirrel, Nico thought. Aside from his face, he was unremarkable, being of medium height and slight of build. What he lacked in physical stature, he attempted to compensate for in dress. A pearlescent border highlighted the embroidery on his snow-white tunic while silver buttons polished to a mirror sheen scattered their reflections across the room as he walked. Scotti strutted to a high-backed throne at the head of the table. The investigator and Messer Avocino rose in a show of respect, and Nico followed their lead. Only the magistrate remained seated.

The last person into the room was the secretary's aide who placed a folio on the table and spent several minutes explaining its contents to Scotti, who peppered the aide with a flurry of questions. After the aide answered the last question, Scotti instructed him to remain in the room in case Scotti needed additional assistance.

Nico could not see all the documents in the folio that the aide had provided, but he did see one sheet that listed the steps Scotti should follow to conduct the inquiry. Reading from the script, Scotti announced in a high-pitched voice befitting a small rodent, "The secretary is unavailable today. I am Councilor Scotti, and I will be conducting this hearing." He decided to target the investigator first. Glaring at the apprehensive officer, he waved a paper in the air and asked, "Are you the one who wrote this report about the missing banker?"

The investigator, unsure of whether to stand, rose to a half-standing position. Avocino saw the awkward, some might have said comical, stance and patted his hand on the table as a signal that the investigator should be seated.

In a weak voice, the officer answered, "Yes."

Scotti readied his verbal attack. "Your filing came after Salvetti's body was found. A filing made by officials in

Gaggiano stated that the body had been in the water for several days. I presume you submitted your report as soon as the widow declared that her husband was missing. Shall we summon the widow to learn why she did not notice for several days that her husband missing?"

"She did inform us as soon as her husband disappeared. That is when I filed the first report."

"The first report? Where is this first report?"

"It must have gotten lost."

"Are you accusing the Privy Council Chancery of losing documents? That is a serious charge."

All color had left the investigator's face, and his heart beat faster. "No, certainly not. I don't know where it was lost, but when I learned it was lost, I wrote another report. A second one. The one you are reading."

"How did you find out that the first report was missing?"

"Uh, someone must have told me."

"Who told you?"

"I don't remember."

"Have you written any other reports about this incident, reports about the progress being made to find the killer? We do not have any other reports. Perhaps those were lost too."

"I have not written any other reports, only the one. I mean, only the two."

"Is your investigation still underway?"

"I am not aware of any continuing investigation."

"You are not aware? It is your investigation. Surely if it were ongoing, you would be aware of it."

The investigator said nothing.

Scotti summoned a forceful tone. "Reports go missing. The lead investigator cannot recall how he learned that his report went missing. He doesn't know if the investigation is continuing. This is shameful. Even Venetians are not this incompetent.

Tell your captain that a team will be sent from the Council of Justice to correct his abysmal operation. Now go. I have heard enough of your pathetic excuses."

The investigator looked to Avocino for an indication of whether he should rise immediately and leave the chamber. Avocino gave a quick nod. Scotti waited until the investigator left the room before looking to Avocino and the magistrate. "Can either of you tell me how foreign diplomats became involved?"

Nico opened his mouth to answer, but he was silenced by Avocino placing a restraining hand on Nico's arm. Nico looked over at the lawyer, who gave a barely perceptible shake of his head as a cue for Nico to remain silent.

The magistrate sat up straight, unfolded his arms, and said, "I am the magistrate of the Porta Nuova district. I granted the Florentine diplomats permission to investigate the disappearance of their countryman in accordance with a treaty between the Duchy of Milan and the Republic of Florence."

"Treaty?" the puzzled Scotti repeated. The only treaties he knew of concerned trade arrangements, and he had only a limited understanding of those. But he was well-practiced in substituting arrogance when he lacked knowledge. In a condescending tone, he proclaimed, "Ministers negotiating trade pacts do not have the authority to concede privileges to foreigners." He did not know for sure that his statement was correct, but to him, it seemed plausible.

In a confident voice, the magistrate responded, "The treaty does not concern trade, and it was signed by Duke Sforza, not by a trade minister."

Avocino noticed the magistrate's lips curl up slightly in a hint of a smirk at seeing Scotti totally baffled. Avocino enjoyed watching the two men sparring as much as he enjoyed watching a game of netball. Fearing he might be humiliated,

Scotti looked to the aide for support, but the aide merely shrugged and held his hands palms up in surrender. The only treaty the aide knew of that might have been signed by the Duke was the Treaty of Lodi, but he wasn't sure whether that treaty was actually signed by Duke Sforza or by one of his representatives. In any case, he was fairly sure that the Lodi treaty did not grant foreigners the right to conduct investigations in the Duchy of Milan.

Seeing that Scotti was bewildered, the magistrate decided to end his confusion by providing facts. "Amendments to the Treaty of Lodi drafted ten years past, when the Kingdom of Naples joined the Italic League, granted to the signatory nations measures for the protection of their citizens."

Scotti beckoned for the aide to join him, and the two conferred for several minutes before the aide returned to his seat. Unable to press the magistrate on the relevance of the treaty, Scotti opted to issue a jurisdictional ruling. Scotti turned to Nico. "District magistrates do not have the authority to act on diplomatic matters; therefore, the permission granted by the district magistrate is invalid and vacated."

Scotti closed the folio before him thinking that the matter had been settled, but Nico had learned from Professor Beccaria, the University of Pavia law professor, that any ruling could be appealed to the Privy Council Tribunal. Nico wasn't sure whether it was proper to voice an objection to Scotti's decision, but he was determined to contest the ruling. He rose and announced, "The Florentine Republic places great value on the safety and security of its citizens. As we have just heard, the guardia is not pursuing the person who murdered Signor Salvetti. Since the ruling provides no mechanism for finding the murderer, I must appeal to the Privy Council Tribunal and ask that it grant Florentine investigators the freedom to search for the killer and to see that he is brought to justice so that no other Florentine citizens become his victims."

Scotti took Nico's retort as a personal affront. His face tightened into an angry snarl. "Who are you?" he growled.

"I am Messer Nico Argenti, an envoy of the Florentine Republic."

Scotti glared at Nico with a piercing stare and then stalked from the room without another word. Avocino, who found the whole proceeding amusing, placed a hand on Nico's shoulder. "This hearing is finished, my friend," he said. "The next move is yours if you do indeed intend to appeal Scotti's ruling."

Avocino rose to leave, and Nico followed. Before Nico reached the door, the aide approached him. "I am the principal notary of the Council Secretary. If the secretary had conducted this inquiry, I am confident he would have shared your interest in finding the perpetrator of the crime. In a previous inquiry similar to this, the secretary dispatched army officers to hunt the offender. I believe the secretary would have done the same this time."

"If I file an appeal, will the Privy Council tribunal be inclined to grant the Florentine envoy the freedom to continue the investigation?" Nico asked.

"Possibly. One can never be certain. If you wish, I can show you to the clerk who accepts petitions on behalf of the tribunal."

27

MONZA

"This is the first time we've been asked to snatch women," Bruno said through the devilish grin painted across his face. "Let's get them now."

"We should visit the retreat house first." Tonio cautioned.

"You heard Pagatore. The client wants them snatched now," Bruno protested.

"But what if there is no retreat house? What if Mouseface lied?" It took a while for Bruno to register the significance of Tonio's caution; then, as always, he reluctantly accepted Tonio's wisdom.

For five centuries, Monza was the chosen coronation site for kings and emperors. Despite its illustrious history and its proximity to Milan, neither Bruno nor Tonio had any knowledge of Monza. At a stable just outside Milan's Porta Nuova city gate, they hired a wagon with a bed large enough to hold two captives and obtained directions to the town from the stable owner. "Go along the canal, the Naviglio Martesana, until you see a road branching to the left. That road goes arrow straight to Monza. It was built by Roman legions, and they always built straight roads, even when they had to pass through swamps," the stable owner chuckled. "The valley is flat, so you will see the cathedral at Monza in the distance long before you arrive."

A half hour after leaving Milan, spires of the cathedral became visible, and a short time later, the foothills of the Alps appeared on the horizon. As they neared the town, the winding Lambro river snaked its way close to the road. The road took them to the central piazza fronting the centuries-old cathedral. Tonio said, "This cathedral is the starting point for the directions that Mouseface gave us. He said to follow the road that goes north."

"How in hell can we know which way is north? And how the hell did Mouseface know which way is north?" Bruno whined.

Tonio looked around. Four roads emanated from the central piazza. "The sun," Tonio responded. "When you look away from the sun at mid-day you are looking north." Tonio pointed, "So that must be the road."

A short distance outside the town, they reached the stone pillar that marked the turnoff Mouseface had indicated. Bruno pivoted the wagon onto the path that soon narrowed into a track suitable for horses but barely wide enough for the wagon. Tree branches slapped the side of the vehicle and forced the two riders to defend themselves from being hit by switches.

The path rose slowly from the valley floor and steepened as it neared the crest of the hill, where a stone building sat in the center of a clearing. "That rodent head was telling the truth for a change," said Bruno. "I thought this place was just another fantasy he pulled out of his ass."

Tonio climbed down and listened. Other than the breeze whistling through the pine trees, there was no sound. He could see the Monza cathedral in the distance, but no other structures were visible. He walked around the building. At its rear were a covered latrine and a woodpile. Tracks of small animals, possibly field mice, crisscrossed the dusting of snow covering the ground. Tonio rapped on the side of the latrine to drive off any animals that might be taking refuge inside, but none fled from his intentional disturbance. A lack of any odor told Tonio that the latrine had not been used recently, perhaps for months. All signs indicated that this isolated location was an ideal place to keep captives with little chance of their being discovered.

After walking around the building, Tonio approached the retreat house entrance. "It's locked," he called to Bruno, who had been watering the horse.

"I can take care of that," Bruno replied. From a nearby rock pile, he hefted a large stone, carried it to the entrance, and smashed it down onto the lock. "It's not locked now," he boasted.

Bruno pushed the door open and was enveloped by a cloud of soot and fetid air. "Shit! It smells like a monk died in there." He waved away the floating particles and stepped into the sparse interior. "It's colder than a virgin's tit in here. If we don't die of stink poisoning, we're going to freeze to death," he whined.

Tonio followed his irritable friend into the building and moved to the table at the center of the room. Surrounding the table were six straight-backed chairs. Only one, the abbot's chair, had a padded seat; the others had hard wood seats. There were no other furnishings in the room.

On one wall, a fireplace had pots and utensils stacked on its hearth. Tonio realized the fireplace was meant for cooking. It would struggle to heat the room. He crossed the room to a short hallway with three tiny rooms on each side. Each cell was barely large enough for a wood frame bed and a side table on which sat a washbasin and a water jug. Each bed held a straw-filled pad and a thin cotton blanket. The blankets were adequate for cool summer nights, but useless against the cold now funneling down from the high Alpine peaks.

Tonio returned to the main room carrying a bed pad under each arm. "We need to move the bedding into this room," he announced. "The fireplace cannot possibly heat the other rooms." He stacked the two thin pads on top of each other. "All we need are three beds because one of us must be awake at all times."

Bruno nodded his agreement, then asked, "Why did you pile two together?"

"The pads are thin, and the floor is cold," Tonio explained. Bruno accepted the explanation and followed Tonio to fetch the remaining bed pads.

Their last task before leaving the retreat house was to collect wood from the woodpile behind the building. They set logs and kindling in the firebox, ready to be lit upon their return. "Now we get the women," Bruno said as he grinned in anticipation.

28

THE PRIVY COUNCIL TRIBUNAL, MILAN

The Privy Council notary led Nico from the Secretary's conference room across a courtyard and into an adjacent building. The notary stopped in the entry and pointed to the far end of a corridor. "The filing clerk's office is at the end on the right. He has the forms for filing petitions with the Council Tribunal."

Nico walked the length of the corridor. When he reached the clerk's office, he paused in the doorway. He watched as the clerk wrote a few words, scrunched his nose in displeasure, scratched out the words he had just written, and tried again with different words. The scene reminded Nico of himself in years past when his tutors made him write essays. His thoughts never formed themselves well in their first outing.

The clerk scarcely looked up when Nico entered and asked about the forms needed to file a petition. From a shelf on the cabinet behind him, the clerk grabbed several sheets, handed them to Nico, and said indifferently, "These are the forms."

Generally, lawyers sent their couriers to obtain forms that the couriers took to their respective law offices to be filled out by lawyers. The couriers then returned the completed documents. The clerk became curious when Nico did not leave the office. Instead, he took the forms to a vacant desk and entered the required information himself. When he finished, he handed the papers back to the clerk.

"I will see that the scheduler gets them," the clerk said as he set the completed forms atop a pile of papers on his desk.

"Is the tribunal in session?" Nico asked.

"No cases are being heard today. The members are deliberating."

"Is the scheduler available?"

"Yes, but ..." Nico interrupted before the clerk could finish his statement.

"Then I suggest you bring this filing to the scheduler directly. A citizen of the Florentine Republic has been murdered, and the substitute Secretary provided no redress for the crime. His ruling contravenes a treaty to which the Duchy of Milan and the Republic of Florence are parties, and it leaves other Florentine citizens at the mercy of a savage killer. If this breach of the treaty is not rectified immediately, the Republic of Florence will be forced to safeguard its citizens by suspending its activities in the duchy. As you may know, Duke Sforza depends on the Medici bank to provide financing for the new hospital. It would not please Duke Sforza if that project were delayed, so I encourage you to stress the urgency of this matter to the scheduler."

Nico's mind flashed to a time when he was a youngster playing cards with the boys of his pallone team. Across from Nico sat the player who had mastered the skill of bluffing. He had no tells and consistently outfoxed others, even when he held only a random assortment of cards. His talent earned him the tag name Bluffo, a name that stayed with him into adulthood. Although Nico would never have Bluffo's skill, he did delight in making the clerk believe that he could influence activities of the Medici bank.

The clerk froze for a few moments, stunned by Nico's tirade. Never had anyone demanded that a petition receive the immediate attention of the Privy Council tribunal. The clerk was thankful that he was not the one who must bring the matter to a magistrate; he need only pass the petition to a registrar two years his senior, the scheduler. When the clerk regained his composure, he lifted Nico's filing document from the pile and scurried out of his office without another word.

Nico sat behind the vacant desk, folded his arms, leaned back, and waited for the clerk to return. Several minutes passed before the clerk returned. He was trailed by another man who announced, "I am the scheduler."

For an instant, Nico abided by the protocol that lawyers should remain seated when approached by clerks, but then quickly decided instead to heed his uncle Nunzio's guidance: never let status displace courtesy. He rose and introduced himself cordially, but formally, "I am Messer Nico Argenti, a commissioner and diplomat of the Republic of Florence."

"You believe your petition requires urgent consideration, Messer Argenti?" the scheduler asked.

"Yes," Nico replied. "One Florentine citizen has been abducted and murdered, and we fear others may be in similar danger until the killer is apprehended."

"Your timing is fortuitous. No tribunals have been scheduled for today, so a magistrate can be available to hear your petition in three hours," the scheduler responded. Nico deduced that the scheduler must have already consulted with one of the magistrates. Only a magistrate could have made a specific time commitment.

The schedular handed a card to Nico. "On this card is the name of the magistrate who will conduct the hearing and directions to the tribunal chamber where the hearing will be held. Be prompt. Magistrates do not tolerate delay."

Nico thanked the scheduler and the clerk for their prompt action. He left the clerk's office, wondering how best to prepare for his presentation to the tribunal.

Nico had the chance he wanted, an opportunity to plead his case; unfortunately, he had only three hours to prepare. Three hours would have been enough if the tribunal were in Florence, where Nico knew procedures and prior rulings, but precedents were different in Milan. Nico did not even know whom he would be facing as the opposition. Might the Privy Council Secretary send one of its lawyers to defend Scotti's ruling? Surely Scotti himself would not appear.

Nico needed help from someone who knew the laws and procedures of the Duchy. Professor Beccaria would have been a perfect resource; however, the professor had already returned to his duties at the University of Pavia. Messer Avocino was the only lawyer Nico knew in Milan. Might Avocino be willing to help his former adversary?

Nico hurried to Avocino's office, panting when he burst into the room. Surprised by his out-of-breath intruder, Avocino said, "I didn't expect to see you again so soon. Did you file a petition with the Council?"

"Yes. And that is why I am here. A magistrate has granted a hearing in three hours ... less than three hours."

"What kind of magic did you cast?" Avocino asked, "I submitted a filing two months past, and it is still not scheduled."

Nico managed a smile. "I drafted an appeal that accused the substitute Secretary of violating an international treaty and threatened retribution by the Republic of Florence if the Council did not take corrective action."

Avocino laughed. "You have *coglioni grande* my young friend to question a ruling from the office of the Privy Council Secretary. I am almost afraid to ask why you have come to see me."

"I need help from someone who knows the intricacies of the judicial system in the duchy."

"Unfamiliarity with our system has not muffled your tongue thus far. Why are you concerned now?"

Nico's shoulders slumped. "It was wrong of me to have challenged the Council Secretary. It was an impetuous act...a failing I need to eliminate."

"Don't criticize yourself unfairly. Exuberance motivates many young lawyers. My position as district prosecutor precludes me from assisting you, but the Magistrates Guild can give you the name of an available lawyer or notary."

Nico left Avocino's office pondering his options. As Avocino had suggested, he could ask the guild for a recommendation, but Nico doubted that any competent lawyer would be available immediately. Then he recalled Avocino suggesting that a notary might serve his purpose, and Nico knew of one quick-minded notary, or to be precise, a page who was studying to be a notary.

At the Florentine embassy, Nico sought out Ugo, the page who had befriended Vittorio during his confinement. Without preamble, Nico asked the youngster, "Are you familiar with the procedures followed at Privy Council Tribunals?"

Ugo froze momentarily, surprised by the unexpected question. "How could you know? Earlier this year, a lawyer working for the embassy pleaded a case before the Privy Council Tribunal. He had a great many documents, so many that he asked me to carry some of his folios; then in the council chamber I helped to organize the documents.

Watching him and the proceedings was fascinating, and enlightening."

An hour later, Nico and Ugo arrived early for the hearing. The tribunal chamber was vacant when they entered. Positioned in front of the raised platform where the magistrates would be seated were two tables, one for the prosecution and one for the defense.

Nico hesitated, unsure whether he was the prosecutor or defense in this proceeding. He had filed the petition, which intimated he was the prosecutor. On the other hand, the Secretary's ruling restrained a Florentine envoy, so one might argue he was defending the envoy. Nico knew the protocol in Florence, but this was Milan.

Ugo noticed Nico's indecision and said, "You may sit wherever you wish. In this hearing there will be no lawyers speaking in opposition. The magistrate will hear your plea, question you to discern the facts, and then render his decision."

"Interesting," Nico said. "In Florence, a lawyer would be present to advocate for the prior ruling, the one made by the substitute Secretary."

Nico chose to sit at the defense table, not based on any principle, but because it was closer to where he was standing. Ugo sat next to him. Nico spread out two pages of notes he had generated during the preceding hours. As he reviewed his notes with Ugo, a door at the front of the chamber opened. A clerk entered and announced the arrival of the magistrates.

Three men in judicial robes entered and took seats behind the judge's bench on the raised platform. Nico was surprised to see three magistrates. The scheduler had implied that a single magistrate would hear his petition. He looked to Ugo, who only shrugged. He had no explanation to offer. What neither man knew was that the three magistrates chose to participate because they were curious about the foreigner who was emboldened enough to challenge a ruling of the Secretary and then press for his petition to be heard immediately.

The senior magistrate, seated between his two colleagues, began, "Messer Argenti, the petition you filed does not name your client. Who is your client?"

"I represent the Republic of Florence," Nico replied.

"We understand that you are a Florentine diplomat, but my question is this: on whose behalf are you seeking redress in this specific instance?"

"May I have a moment to confer with my ... associate?"

"A moment. A brief moment," the magistrate responded, hiding his amusement that the young Florentine had not considered who had legal standing to appeal the Secretary's ruling.

Nico turned to Ugo, who speculated, "The Salvetti family?"

Nico considered Ugo's suggestion briefly; then dismissed it, saying, "It is true that the Salvetti family suffers, but their grief cannot be lessened by a ruling of this tribunal."

Ugo offered another possibility. "The Medici bank?"

"Much better. Thank you, Ugo."

Nico pivoted back to face the magistrates and announced, "Signor Piello Portinari."

Nico's response mystified the magistrates. None of them had ever heard of Piello Portinari. The senior magistrate asked, "Who is Signor Portinari, and how is he injured by the Secretary's ruling?"

"Signor Portinari is the manager of the Medici bank branch in Milan. The victim of the crime, Signor Salito Salvetti, was the head bookkeeper at the Medici bank. From interviews with bank employees, conversations with acquaintances of Signor Salvetti, and other evidence, it appears that Signor Salvetti's abduction and murder may be related to his responsibilities at the Medici bank. Other bank employees now fear that they, too, might become victims of the killer. Their fear makes it impossible for them to perform their duties effectively. Signor Portinari shares their fear. As a precaution, a guard accompanies him when he travels between his house and the bank. Signor Portinari cannot manage the bank properly when he and other employees are preoccupied with their own safety. This matter needs to be resolved quickly, and the Secretary's ruling made no provision for doing so."

The senior magistrate looked to those seated on either side of him. Both nodded their agreement that Signor Portinari had proper standing to question the ruling. The magistrate continued, "We have reviewed the report prepared by the notary who attended the hearing earlier today. His report confirms that the guardia is not pursuing those responsible for the crime, nor should they continue in that capacity. Signor Salvetti was a foreigner, as is Signor Portinari. All criminal matters involving foreigners are within the jurisdiction of the Privy Council, not district officials. We concur that the matter must be addressed; therefore, this tribunal orders that the army of the Duchy of Milan investigate the crime."

The magistrate glanced down at the document before him. "This petition requests permission for the Florentine envoy to help with the investigation. We have examined the cited clause in the treaty amendment and we find its wording to be vague.

"Nonetheless, the Duchy strives to accommodate its valued allies to the extent possible. Can you tell us, Messer Argenti, in what way the Florentine envoy might add to the progress of the investigation?"

"The Republic of Florence has the highest regard for the army of the Duchy of Milan. Its members have long demonstrated their abilities and courage on and off the battlefield. However, there are several reasons why the Florentine envoy is uniquely able to advance the investigation.

"First, the envoy is a trained investigator who found clues to the nature of Signor Salvetti's captivity when he examined the body. Subsequently, the body was buried as Signora Salvetti requested; consequently, no one else can examine the body to gain the information known by the envoy.

"The envoy then traveled to Gaggiano to view the site where Signor Salvetti was held prisoner. There, too, the envoy found relevant clues. The site is a working farm. It has not been preserved, so again no one else can gain firsthand knowledge of the conditions of Salvetti's captivity."

Nico paused to study the faces of the magistrates to gauge whether his arguments were convincing. Their expressions showed they followed Nico's arguments, but they were not persuaded. The senior magistrate broke the silence. "Is there anything else, Messer Argenti?"

"Yes. As I mentioned earlier, evidence suggests that the abduction could be related to activities of Signor Salvetti's employer, the Medici bank. The Florentine envoy has been interviewing bank officers to discover how outsiders gained access to private bank information and which project might be crucial enough that someone would resort to murder to deter the bank from continuing its activity.

"Bank officials are reluctant to disclose confidential records and client relationships to anyone. Understandably, the Medici bank would object to sharing private information with Milanese army officers. However, Florentine law requires that the bank cooperate with inquiries from authorized representatives of the Signoria, so the envoy is uniquely positioned to discover the motive for the crime. I respectfully request that he be permitted to continue with his investigation." Nico concluded by saying, "I await the tribunal's ruling," and reseated himself.

The magistrates conferred with each other for several

minutes. They spoke too softly for Nico to hear their words, but by observing their gestures and expressions, Nico judged that one of the men did not share the same position as his colleagues. Eventually, the lone man stopped speaking. Either he was persuaded by the others, or he decided that further objection was futile.

Upon reaching consensus, the senior magistrate announced, "There are two distinct issues to consider. One is the pursuit and prosecution of the person who committed the crimes of abduction and murder. The second separable issue is the discovery of the underlying motive for the crime.

"This tribunal finds that officers of the Milanese military are fully capable of apprehending the perpetrator of the crime. If the Florentine envoy has relevant information, it is in every-one's interest that he shares his knowledge with the military investigators. We see no advantage in having the envoy conduct an independent investigation. We believe that doing so could be detrimental. Therefore, this tribunal affirms the decision of the Secretary to revoke the envoy's investigatory permission.

"As to the other matter, uncovering the motive for the crime, this tribunal regards the questioning of Florentine citizens who are employees of the Medici bank to be totally within the purview of the Republic of Florence and its representatives. We concur that it is appropriate for Florentine authorities to extract information from bank employees. However, any citizens of the Duchy of Milan implicated during that questioning must be referred to the Milanese investigators. Florentine envoys are not authorized to interrogate any Milanese citizens."

The senior magistrate turned to address the clerk, "See that Messer Argenti receives a copy of this ruling." The three magistrates then rose in unison and exited the chamber.

Ugo looked up in anticipation of hearing Nico's comment on the ruling. Nico placed a hand on Ugo's shoulder. "I appreciate your assistance. Your suggestion to focus on the Medici bank was insightful. When you are ready to apply to the University of Pavia, I will be pleased to intercede with the acceptance committee on your behalf.

"The ruling is not the best possible outcome, not what I had hoped for, but it is well considered. It commits army investigators to pursue the killer, and it allows Vittorio to search for the crime's motive."

29

ROMAN RUINS, MILAN

Nico inhaled deeply as he exited the tribunal chamber and stepped outside into the cool afternoon air. His eyes were fixed straight ahead; he walked without thinking of his destination as though drawn by a distant force. Ugo followed Nico out of the building and came alongside the lawyer. For several minutes, neither man spoke. Ugo, although reluctant to disturb Nico's thoughts finally said, "People at the embassy are fearful of the Privy Council. It must have taken great courage for you to challenge the Council's ruling."

Ugo's words dispelled the tension that had gripped Nico all morning. Suddenly Nico felt lighter as though a weight had been lifted from his shoulders. He paused, turned toward the young page, and smiled. "Maybe more imprudence than courage, Ugo."

"Have you prosecuted many cases before similar tribunals in Florence?"

Nico's smile widened. He hesitated briefly while counting the days backward to his guild induction. "I've never appeared before any tribunal. I was inducted into the lawyers' guild only fifteen or sixteen days past."

Ugo's jaw dropped open in amazement that a new lawyer would dare confront the Privy Council. The two men walked in silence again for several minutes before Ugo asked, "Did you always want to become a lawyer? Perhaps your father was a lawyer?"

"When I was young, my time was split between studying and playing ball. My favorite game was maglio. Whenever I mentioned the games, my tutor would remind me that no one can earn his living by playing ball. Eventually I came to accept his wisdom and spent more time studying and less time on the ball field. My father was in the army, but he never influenced me to follow his course. It was my father who introduced me to Chancellor Scala while the Chancellor was a law student at the University of Florence. I was immediately impressed by his self-assurance. He was determined to become a lawyer. When classes were suspended at the university in Florence, Scala moved to Milan to complete his studies. While he was in Milan, he corresponded with father and I got to read his letters. The longer he studied the more enthusiastic he became about his chosen path. It was Scala's dedication to his career that convinced me to become a lawyer."

Buoyed by his victory–his partial victory–at the council tribunal, Nico felt the need for a respite from the pressure of the Salvetti murder investigation. The route from the ducal court to the Florentine embassy wove through an unfamiliar part of Milan. While passing a church he had not seen before with a name unknown to him, he paused, turned to Ugo, and announced, "I have been in your city for several days without making time to explore any of its wonders."

"Wonders?" Ugo echoed as a question.

"Unusual sites, historical monuments, treasures prized by

the Milanese people, something to give me a pleasant memory of the city."

Gesturing to the church beside them, Ugo asked, "Would you like to visit this church?" Seeing Nico stare into the distance, Ugo said, "Maybe a different church. Milan has many beautiful, historic churches."

Nico gave a dismissive wave with his hand. "Perhaps another time. Churches are everywhere. Florence has many wonderful churches as well. There must be sights that are unique to Milan, ones not found in Florence." Nico resisted laughing at his own foolish request. Ugo had never been to Florence, so he could not possibly know what sights Florence lacked.

The absurdity of Nico's statement was lost on Ugo, who replied, "We are not far from the Imperial Sector."

"The Imperial Sector?" Nico questioned.

"The Romans established a colony called Mediolanium, which later grew into the city of Milan. The area with the original Roman settlement, we call the Imperial Sector.

"The Roman buildings survived intact for a millennium until Emperor Frederick Barbarossa's troops punished the Milanese by burning the city. They destroyed many of the Roman buildings, but others have survived."

Nico rubbed his hands together in anticipation. "I would enjoy seeing those ancient buildings. There are remains of a Roman colony in Fiesole, a town near Florence, but not in Florence itself. The Romans never colonized Florence because the area where the city is built was a swamp in ancient times."

Ugo pointed to a street veering off at an angle. "This way." Then after they had walked a short distance, he said, "You can see the Roman Circus ahead on the left." Their path cut directly across the huge oval where Roman athletes competed in races. Nico stopped in the middle of the track and tried to imagine chariots thundering around the oval, cheered by a boisterous throng of onlookers.

After crossing the oval, they climbed an embankment. At the top, Ugo pointed to his right. "That ruin was once an emperor's palace. I forget the name of the emperor."

Nico swept his eyes across the complex. Awed by its size and distraught by its ruin, he said, "It must have been magnificent when it was new. What a shame that in thoughtless rage, men destroy these impressive creations. Maybe someday we will cease such wanton destruction."

From the ruins, they resumed their trek to the Florentine embassy. As they neared the palazzo, Ugo said, "Word travels quickly at the embassy. By now, everyone will know that I was with you. They will want to know the reason. What shall I tell them?"

"Tell them the truth," Nico said, then grinning he added, "Tell them you helped argue a petition before the Privy Council Tribunal."

Ugo's eyes widened. "I did not .... No one will believe I attended a council tribunal."

Nico's grin widened. "Next time, we will commission an artist to create sketches. Everyone would believe if you had drawings depicting you seated before the robed magistrates."

In a wavering voice, Ugo asked, "Next time? Will there be a next time?"

"No one can know the future, Ugo. Until then, if anyone doubts your story, show them this." Nico handed Ugo the card on which the scheduler had written the name of the magistrate and directions to the tribunal chamber. At the top of the card was the mark of the Privy Council. Ugo accepted the card, handling it carefully as he would a prized possession.

"Will you make a report to the ambassador?" Ugo asked.

"Perhaps later." Nico wished the ambassador had been

more welcoming rather than viewing the commission as an affront to his authority. The ambassador interacted with Milan's nobility every day. In those meetings, the ambassador might have overheard an offhand comment that could have been helpful. Nico vowed he would try to establish a cordial relationship with the ambassador when there were facts to share.

After parting from Ugo at the embassy, Nico decided to visit Messer Avocino to tell him the tribunal outcome. The guardia office was strangely quiet when Nico arrived. Many of the offices on the second level of the building were unoccupied. At the end of the hallway, Avocino sat alone in his office. His desk was clear except for a single sheet. Standing in the doorway, Nico asked, "Am I intruding?"

"No, not at all," Avocino replied. "Today has been unusually peaceful. The criminals must all be away on holiday. I fear we will pay for this solitude when they return."

Nico described the proceedings at the tribunal. When he mentioned that the magistrates had charged the army with investigating the abduction and murder, Avocino said, "The army's judicial unit has competent people. The Privy Council controls the unit's budget, so it acts quickly and aggressively whenever the council gives it a mandate."

"Will the army investigators be inclined to cooperate and share information with Signor Colombo?" Nico asked.

"The army tolerates the guardia, but they are not especially cooperative with outsiders. They expect the guardia to share information freely, while they share as little of their findings as possible." Avocino shrugged, "I have no basis for predicting how they will behave with a foreign investigator."

30

DINNER WITH THE CONTESSA, MILAN

From Avocino's office, Nico headed to the Palazzo Torelli guest house. After his busy and stressful day, he hoped to relax with a glass of wine by a warm fire. That possibility faded when he entered the guest house to find Massimo and Vittorio wearing spotless tunics freshly laundered by the contessa's servants.

Nico looked from one colleague to the other, then said, "I have never seen you both dressed so impeccably. The only reason Massimo combs his hair and dons a clean tunic is to impress a woman. Has he found one for you too, Vittorio?"

In his usual serious manner, Vittorio replied, "Contessa Maddalena has a visitor from Castile. She would like us to join them for dinner."

"I'm pleased to see that the Privy Council did not imprison you. Did you amaze them with your legal magic?" Massimo quipped.

"There is much to tell," Nico replied.

"Vittorio and I are eager to hear the details, but dinner is in one-quarter hour. You will dishonor the contessa if you go to dinner looking like you spent the day mucking stalls in a barn."

Nico groaned when he saw his reflection in the mirror hanging near the door. Massimo was correct; he needed to wash and change his clothes. "I had better save my story for later," he said.

A short time later, as the men walked from the guest house to the palazzo, Nico showed the others the package he carried. It was carefully wrapped in white paper and fastened with a red ribbon. "This is the book we talked about, our gift for the contessa."

"When did you find time to shop for books?" Vittorio asked.

"I didn't shop. I asked my cousin to buy the book in Florence. He sent it to Milan by an embassy courier."

Massimo stepped close to Nico and put an arm around Nico's shoulder. To Vittorio, he said, "Our lawyer has already learned how to use embassy couriers to deliver his personal packages. Law schools must teach courses on how to take advantage of government privileges. Soon he will have the couriers delivering love notes to his lady friend." Nico said nothing.

The contessa and her guest were viewing a portrait when the men entered the dining salon. When she heard the three Florentines enter, she turned to greet them. "Alonso, may I present Florentine diplomats Nico, Vittorio, and Massimo." The contessa gestured toward each man as she announced their names. "Signori, I am delighted that Alonso Enriquez, Count of Malgar and Admiral of Castile, will be joining us for dinner."

Vittorio spoke for the group. "*Es un honor conocerle.*"

Alonso's eyes widened. "I struggle with Italian, and you speak Castilian like a native. Surely you did not learn the language in Florence."

"I made frequent trips to Seville with my father when I was

a child. My father was a consul of the armorers' guild. He jour-
neyed to Seville to procure iron ore."

Nico and Massimo shared a look. Vittorio's revelation about
his youth came as a surprise. Both men realized how little they
knew about each other. They were barely together as a team
when Vittorio had been dispatched to Milan. Now they were
reunited, but their hectic pace allowed little time for casual
conversation.

The admiral said, "Ah, yes, mines in the Sierra Morena
mountains have supplied iron ore and other metals since
Roman times. Iron is crucial for us to make weapons used in
our struggles against the Moors, but I have often wondered if
the world might be better without iron. Without weapons there
could be no war."

"Before swords, men battled with wooden clubs," Massimo
said. Alonso acknowledged the truth in Massimo's statement
with a resigned shrug.

The contessa accepted Alonso's arm and let him escort
her to the dining table. Nico and Vittorio stepped aside,
allowing Massimo to accompany the contessa's sister
Benedetta. When Massimo offered his arm, she took it
eagerly.

After everyone was seated, Nico handed the package he had
been carrying to the contessa, saying, "This is for your daughter, Orsina." The contessa raised an eyebrow in surprise. "It is a
copy of Boccaccio's *Famous Women*. During our last dinner, you
mentioned that you wanted Orsina to learn about women of
great accomplishment whom she could view as role models.
We thought this book might help achieve that goal because it
cites one hundred of the most notable women throughout
history."

"What a thoughtful gesture. *Famous Women* can be an inspi-
ration for any young woman. I am sure Orsina will love it. But

where did you find it? The only copy I have ever seen was in the Ducal Library at Pavia."

"The printing machines in Venice are giving Boccaccio a resurgence in popularity," Nico replied.

"The Boccaccio you describe is very different from the one I know in Castile," Alonso said. "In my country, his most well-known work is *Il Corbaccio*."

"*Il Corbaccio* came from the mind of a bitter old man," said Benedetta indignantly. "It casts women as inferior, vile creatures; I could not even finish reading that awful story. Boccaccio wrote exquisite love poems in his youth. It is sad that the people of Castile do not know Boccaccio's tender, caring side." Benedetta sat back in her chair and folded her hands in her lap, fearing that her outburst might have insulted their guest.

"I cannot explain why Boccaccio's other works are unknown in Castile. I assure you that we Castilians are loving, romantic people. Perhaps when the newly printed books from Venice reach Castile, we will discover the younger Boccaccio."

Dinner began with servers bringing bowls of warm soup. "This is cream of chestnut soup," the contessa explained. "It is late in the year for chestnuts, but throughout this autumn, the weather was unusually warm, so the chestnut crop extended longer than normal."

Upon tasting the soup, Alonso exclaimed, "Delicious! This reminds me of home. One of our long-standing traditions is to have chestnut soup on All Saints Day."

When Benedetta finished her soup, she addressed Alonso. "My sister introduced you as the Admiral of Castile. I usually associate admirals with ships, but Milan is far from the sea."

Vittorio was delighted that Benedetta asked about the admiral's purpose in coming to Milan. He, too, was curious, but he thought it might be impertinent for him to raise the subject.

"Many men who held the title Admiral of Castile did spend

most of their time at sea. My grandfather led Castilian naval forces to victory against the Moors in the last great sea battle. However, in recent times the duties of the admiral have changed. I do oversee the merchant and naval fleets of the king-dom, but I also serve in other capacities at the pleasure of King Juan, and it is one of those roles that brings me to Milan.

"In Castile we have a breed of sheep called merino. Merino sheep have the softest fleece you can imagine. Wool merchants in Milan are eager to import merino fleece, and King Juan wants to be sure that all fleece exports are transported on Castilian ships. My mission in Milan is to make arrangements for shipments from our port city of Cadiz to Genoa."

"If the sea voyage is to Genoa, why are you in Milan rather than Genoa?" Vittorio asked.

"Milanese merchants are involved in all the negotiations: shipment by sea from Cadiz to Genoa, shipment by land from Genoa to Milan, and contracting for the price of the fleece itself."

Nico asked, "Has someone else come from Castile to nego-tiate the purchase contracts?"

"Yes, the king's trade minister. He will meet with Milanese wool merchants and a member of Duke Sforza's court."

Throughout the remainder of the meal, Nico pondered how the admiral's mission might affect Florence. The Florentine Republic had a large merchant fleet that sailed from Pisa to Africa, the Levant, and north as far as England. Nico wasn't aware of any trade between Florence and countries of the Iberian Peninsula, but international trade was not his expertise. He had not even known about the iron ore trade that Vittorio mentioned. He doubted that shipping between Castile and Genoa would be of consequence to Florence.

The fleece itself, however, was a different issue. Castile was much closer than England to Italian ports. Obtaining fleece from Castile could give Milanese merchants a cost advantage compared to Florentine merchants who relied on English wool. And if merino wool is as fine as Alonso implied, it could provide Milanese wool shops with a quality advantage as well. One of the regular patrons at cousin Donato's restaurant was a member of the Florentine wool guild. Nico decided the matter was worth pursuing when he returned home.

When dinner ended, Benedetta excused herself, to Massimo's disappointment, and the contessa led the men to the library where servants had set out candies and a lemon-flavored digestivo. Alonso had one glass of the potent liquid before bidding farewell to the Florentines and promising the contessa that he would see her again before he departed from Milan. The contessa sensed that her guests had business to discuss, private matters of the Florentine republic, so she too excused herself and escorted the admiral from the library.

Massimo refilled his glass, then settled into one of the thickly padded chairs. "I have slept in beds that were far less comfortable than this chair. Another glass or two of this soothing drink, and I might spend the night here."

Vittorio said, "Before sleep takes hold of us all, I am eager to hear about today's legal ruling. Every day has given us a different verdict, so tell us, Nico, what is the latest judicial order?"

"Today we received two rulings," Nico replied. "If you recall, I was summoned to a hearing, along with Messer Avocino, the district magistrate, and the guardia investigator, by order of the Privy Council Secretary. When we arrived at the secretary's office, we learned that he was unavailable and that a substitute would preside in his absence. The substitute was completely incompetent. He spent most of the time berating the investigator."

"I would have enjoyed seeing the investigator denounced,"

Vittorio scoffed.

"He then made a fool of himself as he tried to rebuke the wily magistrate. He ended the hearing by storming out of the chamber, but before he did so, he declared that we are no longer allowed to investigate the crime because district magistrates do not have the authority to grant permissions to foreigners. He did not allow me to plead our case, nor did he say who will search for Salvetti's murderer."

"So, if we continue the investigation, we all risk confinement in the embassy," Massimo surmised.

Vittorio smiled at Massimo, "You rescued me before; I'm sure you can rescue us again if necessary." Vittorio then turned to Nico, "You said there were two rulings. What was the second one?"

"A council notary who attended the hearing recognized the injustice and showed me where to file an appeal to the Privy Council Tribunal."

"An appeal could take weeks, or even longer," Vittorio lamented.

With pride in his voice, Nico replied, "That would be true, except I impressed on the tribunal scheduler the urgency of the matter. I threatened reprisals by the Republic of Florence if they did not act on the appeal immediately."

"For a lawyer, you have coglioni grande, the coglioni of a soldier," Massimo quipped.

"That is exactly what Avocino said when I told him about the appeal."

"How long is 'immediately' to Milanese bureaucrats?" Vittorio asked.

Nico smiled, "Three hours. I had exactly three hours to prepare a presentation to Milan's supreme tribunal."

Massimo raised his glass, "A tribute to you for having stayed awake in all your law school classes."

"I enlisted Ugo, the page at the embassy who is studying to become a notary. He helped me avoid the pitfalls in Milan's unique legal procedures."

"Ugo has a bright future," Vittorio said. "Every night, he brought treats to my room, although I think he did so because it gave him a chance to ask me endless questions about Florence."

Nico continued, "Before the hearing began, the three tribunal magistrates read the transcript of the secretarial hearing, and they had already taken steps to correct the failings of the incompetent substitute secretary. They charged the army's judiciary unit to find Salvetti's murderer."

"The army is sure to be more capable than the guardia," Vittorio said, nodding.

"The magistrates were attentive and sensitive to my plea, but they were unwilling to order army investigators to share information with us. They claimed that doing so would violate the sovereignty of the duchy; however, they did not prohibit the army from sharing information. They left the decision to the discretion of army investigators."

"That is reasonable," Massimo declared. "When I carried out military operations, I did not want courts or civilians telling me how I must behave. The army always wants to make its own decisions."

"I was most disappointed that the tribunal declined to restore the district magistrate's authorization for us to conduct our own independent investigation." Nico began laughing as he continued. "The tribunal said the document I cited in the original hearing was vague, and in truth, I agree with them. I was successful in convincing the district magistrate only because he had never seen the obscure document. The tribunal ruled that it is improper for foreigners to question Milanese citizens in an official capacity."

"But they can't prevent us from asking questions unofficially," Massimo opined. "Several people in the taverns I visited have met or heard of Bruno. One of them was able to give me the name of his associate Tonio. I believe that in one of the taverns, I will find a person who knows how to find the two men. Tomorrow I will be visiting taverns in the Ticinese district."

Nico and Vittorio nodded to show they shared Massimo's optimism. Nico looked to Vittorio and asked, "Has any useful information come from the bank employees?"

Vittorio gritted his teeth in disappointment at his slow progress. "I will continue interrogating bank employees until I learn which of them disclosed information about Portinari's meeting with the architect. One of them is guilty, and I will find the culprit. However, it is highly unlikely that the person who disclosed information would have been told the motive for the abduction.

"Everything I have learned affirms that neither Salvetti nor Portinari had personal issues of any consequence, so my attention is on other possibilities." Vittorio turned to Nico. "While I search for the informer, you could delve into the bank's new business opportunities. It is possible that the abduction was initiated by a competitor to put pressure on the Medici bank."

"Portinari may be reluctant to talk about the new projects," Massimo said. "He gave me the impression that competitors will bid on the projects, so the Medici bank is keeping details of its proposals close."

"They have no choice but to reveal the details," Nico said. "The Medici bank is a Florentine company. Our investigation proceeds with the full authority of the Signoria. I'll begin by getting a list of the bank's projects from Signor Portinari in the morning."

31

MONZA

On the way to the Portinari farmhouse, Bruno and Tonio stopped at a market to buy food and items they would need during their stay at the retreat house. The side road leading to the Portinari farm angled off from the same arrow-straight Roman road that connected Milan with Monza.

As Tonio anticipated, rows of grapevines surrounded the farmhouse, making it impossible for them to remain hidden during their approach. Bruno drove the wagon between two rows of vines, and the men bent low to stay out of view. If the women saw anything, it would only be a horse moving through the vineyard. Bruno stopped the wagon near the house and peered between vine plants. There was no indication from the house that the women had seen their approach.

The most challenging part of the abduction would be subduing the women without letting them see the faces of their captors. Tonio was confident that if the women were able to identify Bruno, he would kill them, as he had killed Salvetti.

Tonio intended to use distractions to hide his identity during the abduction, although he admitted to himself that his plan was risky. He donned the turban-like cappuccio that he had purchased at a shop in Monza and positioned its dangling endpiece to cover his right eye and cheek. As he approached the house, he carried a silvered jewelry box and held it prominently in front of him.

Bruno knocked on the door and then stepped to the side, out of view. The knock elicited no response. Bruno repeated the action, this time pounding hard enough for the door to shudder on its hinges. Moments later, the maid pulled the door open. As Tonio hoped, her eyes went immediately to the shiny jewelry box. She hardly noticed the man carrying the item.

"I am to deliver this to Signora Portinari."

"I will take it to her."

"No, I must deliver it. There is a message," Tonio said emphatically.

The maid turned and beckoned Tonio to follow her into the house. When her back was turned, Bruno sprang from his hiding place. He wrapped one arm around the maid, pinning her arms against her sides. She tried to scream but was thwarted by Bruno thrusting a cloth into her open mouth.

Tonio took a rope that had been looped at his waist and used it to tie the maid's hands. She protested with the only means available to her: she kicked back like a horse and landed several strikes on Bruno's shins. The pain only made him retort, "You are a feisty bitch, aren't you?"

Tonio wrapped a strip of cloth around her head to cover her eyes, then he used a second rope to bind her ankles. She could no longer kick, but she squirmed incessantly until Bruno dropped a loop of rope over her head and drew it tight into a choker leash. He yanked the leash, to prevent her from resisting, and then applied additional pressure to force her to follow him to the wagon. He slapped the immobilized woman hard on the buttocks before pushing her into the wagon bed.

With the maid secured, both men entered the house to search for Signora Portinari. Moving toward the rear of the house, they passed through the reception salon and into the large room that served as the kitchen and eating area. There they found the woman standing at a table with her head bent down and her wet hair dripping into a metal basin, waiting for the maid to return and finish washing her hair. As they had done to her maid, the men tied and blindfolded Signora Portinari. Bruno took the signora outside while Tonio gathered heavy blankets from the bedroom and four bottles of Nebbiolo wine from Signor Portinari's stock.

Tonio secured the women's choker leashes to a stake on the wagon bed and adjusted the tension to inflict only minor discomfort as long as they remained motionless. In a rare display of praise, Bruno said to Tonio, "Your scheme worked. Taking the women was as easy as taking the banker, and neither of them looked upon our faces." With a smirk, he added, "Although wearing the cappuccio and carrying that jewelry box, you looked like one of those kings who brought stuff to Jesus."

Blankets hid the women from view as the wagon passed through Monza. At the retreat house, Bruno tended to the horse while Tonio lowered the women from the cart.

"I am going to remove the gags from your mouths. There is no one around here. If you scream, no one will hear," said Tonio.

Instead of screaming, the women reassured each other that they were unharmed thus far. They dared not admit that they might be destined for the same fate as Salvetti. Tonio slackened the ropes around their ankles so they could walk by taking small steps, and he led them inside.

Bruno lit the fire and pulled the shutters closed over the two small windows, leaving only the dim orange of the flames to light the room. Tonio turned to put his back toward the fire and his face in shadow, then he removed the blindfolds. "You will be held for two days, and then you will be released."

"Is that what you told Salvetti?" the Signora asked indignantly.

"Who is Salvetti?" Tonio wondered.

"The banker. The one you killed," she replied.

"He was a risk," Tonio explained, "because he could identify us. If you are not foolish, you will not be harmed."

Signora Portinari faced Tonio defiantly and asked, "Is it ransom that you want? My father can pay. Let me send a message to him."

"It is not about a ransom."

"What is it then? You plan to hold us for two days and then release us? That makes no sense."

Tonio agreed. It made no sense to him either, but he always found it best not to question a client's motives. "I do not know the reason, but it must make sense to someone."

Signora Portinari realized she was making no progress with her questions, so she changed the subject. "It is cold," she said.

Bruno rubbed his codpiece and leered. "I have something that can make you warm."

Bruno's comment silenced the two women. Tonio pulled two chairs away from the table and moved them closer to the fire. Standing behind the women, and with a tight grip on the choker leashes, he guided them to the chairs.

Bruno opened a bottle of Signor Portinari's Nebbiolo wine and took a draw directly from the bottle. "This stuff sure beats the swill they serve at the worthless taverns in Milan."

He positioned the padded abbot's chair where he could sit and assess the maid. She had the plain face of a simple country girl. Plain is good, Bruno told himself, although not as good as ugly. Ugly women were always agreeable; plain women often needed inducement. She was young, past her teen years for sure, but not by much. Bruno preferred experienced and compliant older women, but he never dismissed the challenge of conquering a young maiden. Her loose-fitting dress kept him from appraising her breasts. I'll test their size and shape later when I unwrap her, he thought.

Bruno's eyelids drooped further with every slug of wine. When the bottle was half drained, he was asleep and remained in that state for hours until his own belch awakened him. He pushed himself up from the chair and strode, unsteadily, to where Tonio was feeding wood to the fire. "Have our guests been behaving?" Bruno asked.

"The Signora said she has to urinate," Tonio answered.

"So do I. I'll take her," Bruno said gleefully. He grabbed Signora Portinari's choker leash and jerked her out of the seat. "The latrine is outside. Let's go."

"Wait!" Tonio called. "It is still light out. Her eyes must be covered." While wrapping a cloth across her eyes, Tonio cautioned her, "Do not try to remove this. Remember what became of the banker. You do not want to look upon our faces." Next, he began untying one of her hands.

"What are you doing?" Bruno growled.

Tonio only glared at his colleague. When Bruno and the Signora were gone, the maid said, "How could you let her go with him? He is an animal."

"He won't touch her. He was warned that if he harms her, her father will send an army for vengeance."

"And me?" the maid asked in a trembling voice.

"You have no benefactor but I will try to keep him from you."

Tears welled in the maid's eyes. Tonio took a handkerchief from his pocket and placed it in her hand. She looked up but saw only his silhouette outlined by firelight.

Signora Portinari strode back into the room defiantly and returned to the chair where she had been sitting. Both of her hands were tied, and one of her cheeks was red. Bruno followed a step behind, keeping tension on the choker as though he were restraining a disobedient dog. He crossed the room to the warmth of the fire and snatched the half-full bottle of wine as he passed the table. Even in the dim firelight, Tonio thought he detected a reddening of Bruno's cheek as well. Neither Bruno nor Signora Portinari spoke of the incident.

The retreat house was too far from town to hear the cathedral bells announcing the hours, so Tonio relied on his growling stomach as his mealtime scheduler. When Tonio opened the sack of food he had purchased in Monza, the rustling sound aroused Bruno from his wine stupor. He muttered, "Let the maid do it. She must know how to cook."

Tonio eyed the maid who nodded her willingness to oblige. He placed the sack on the fireplace hearth and beckoned for the maid to join him. As he untied her hands, he warned, "Do not turn around. If you see his face, you will not leave here alive."

After dinner, Bruno opened a second bottle of wine and settled in the abbot's chair, staring at the dancing flames. It was a behavior that Tonio had seen before. Bruno could sit for hours in a trance, not speaking nor moving. Tonio made sure the women, who were now sleeping, were covered with the heavy blankets. Then he took advantage of the situation by stretching out on the bed alongside the two women. He closed his eyes, thanking the gods that tomorrow would be the last day; the women would be free by nightfall.

32

MEDICI BANK, MILAN

Piello Portinari had documents spread across his desk when Nico entered the bank manager's office. Alerted by the knock on his door, Portinari set down the folder he had been reading and signaled for Nico to be seated in the chair facing the desk. "Everyone at the bank is distraught over Salvetti's death. It is a tragedy. He was a respected colleague and a good friend." Portinari looked tired. With an unsteady hand, he gestured to the papers before him and added, "But business must continue. How may I help you?"

Nico answered, "As Signor Colombo told you, we believe the abduction may be related to one of the projects that the bank is financing or considering. Identifying the project could help us to discover the motive for Salvetti's abduction and murder."

Portinari shrugged. "The Medici bank has greater resources than others doing business in the Duchy of Milan; consequently, we receive loan solicitations from nearly every project in the duchy that desires financing."

"Do you respond to all the requests?" Nico asked.

"No, not at all. The board of directors in Florence sets limitations on the funds available to each bank branch. This branch in Milan consistently produces high profits, so the directors grant us a generous allocation. But that is not enough for us to bid on every project needing financing. We analyze every request and generally select those that promise to be most profitable."

"You said that 'generally' you select the most profitable projects. Are there exceptions?"

"Sometimes," Portinari managed a chuckle as he explained, "As an example, the Lord of Castell'Arquato sought funding to enlarge his castle. The lord's income is meager, so there is a risk that he will never be able to repay the loan. However, the lord is Duke Sforza's brother, so we arranged the loan. That is one case where we made an exception. As a foreign bank, it is a good policy for us to give favorable treatment to the duke and his relatives."

Nico nodded. "For conspirators to sanction an abduction, and ultimately a murder, the project of interest must involve a large amount of money and hold the promise of substantial profit. And most likely, the funding request was issued recently. Are there any projects that meet those criteria?"

"Let me think," Portinari said. He brought his hands together as though in prayer, closed his eyes, and bent forward until his forehead rested against his palms. Moments later, he opened his eyes and sat up straight. "Four projects come to mind. One is Duke Sforza's personal undertaking, the hospital for the poor. It is not a new project, but recently the duke decided to expand the building to double its originally planned size. The expansion will require twice the initially allocated funding."

"Is the proposed expansion attracting the interest of other banks?"

"Oh, yes. Because the hospital has the duke's support, several banks see it as an inroad to future opportunities in the duchy. Proposals came from other banks in Florence and even one bank in Rome. I don't recall their names, but my aide can provide you with them."

"What are the other major projects?" Nico prodded.

"Two are related. Although Milan is far from the Adriatic, it has access to Adriatic seaports through canals that connect to the Po River. The Po crosses the Italian peninsula and empties into the sea near Venice. Now that Milan and Venice are at peace, Milanese merchants are eager to establish trade with Venice so they can gain access to markets in the Levant and Asia as well as those of Venice itself.

"One of the projects seeks to enlarge the canals so they can accommodate more massive barges. The ducal ministry responsible for roads, bridges, and waterways is the sponsor of that venture. One month past, the ministry announced its intent to expand the canals, and engineers are now doing design work. The design will be completed within a month; at that time, the ministry will request proposals from banks to fund the construction. The Medici bank regards the canal expansion as highly profitable and low risk. I have already received approval from the bank directors to submit a proposal.

"The related project is being formulated by the Ministry of Trade. Their goal is to foster trade with Venice by making loans available to Milanese merchants. The ministry will use funds obtained from banks to make loans to merchants."

Nico's brow furrowed. "Why don't the merchants get loans directly from the banks?"

"It would be risky for Milanese merchants to establish business relationships with traders hundreds of miles distant in Venice. Banks, including the Medici bank, are reluctant to lend money for such risky ventures, but the Ministry of Trade is willing to accept that risk to achieve its goal of expanded trade with Venice. This arrangement insulates banks because the ministry will incur the losses of any projects that fail. This project is in its infancy because the ministry has not yet decided which imports and exports it wishes to promote."

"Do you know which of your competitors are interested in the project?" Nico asked.

"The project is so new that I do not know the intentions of other banks. We endeavor to keep Medici bank plans secret, and our competitors do the same." In a sarcastic tone, Portinari added, "Embassy people are the ones who spend time at parties and fancy dinners. Those are the occasions when low-level bureaucrats try to sound important by leaking confidential information. The embassy is always rife with tidbits, some real, others merely rumor. If you want to operate on hearsay, speak with the Florentine ambassador."

Portinari's suggestion reminded Nico that rumors had given birth to the Florentine Security Commission. Those same rumors were responsible for his being in Milan. Still, he wanted his actions to be driven by facts rather than by rumors. He pondered the projects that Portinari mentioned, wondering which of them might lead someone to contrive plots of abduction and murder. Then Nico remembered Portinari had said there were four projects. "What is the fourth project?" he asked.

"It is the only sizeable project not sponsored by a ducal authority," Portinari replied. "It is an idea of the *universitas mercatorum mediolanensium*. As he mouthed the Latin phrase, his lips curled up in a thin smile in anticipation of Nico's response.

Nico's jaw dropped. "What is the ..."

Portinari completed Nico's question. "The *universitas mercatorum mediolanensium* is an organization of wholesale wool merchants. It is like the wool guild in Florence, but there is an important difference between the two organizations. In Florence, guild members are free to conduct their businesses as they see fit; whereas, in Milan, the merchants' organization has rules of conduct that all members must follow. The *mercatorum* has learned of a breed of sheep in Castile claimed to have very high-quality fleece."

"Merino sheep," Nico declared.

Portinari's eyes widened. "You know of merino sheep?"

"Last evening, I was introduced to Signor Alonso Enríquez. He is representing the Crown of Castile in discussions of shipping arrangements with Milanese merchants."

"Then you may know more about this project than I."

"I know only that Signor Enríquez believes merino wool is superior to English wool, and that it is less costly to ship fleece to Milan from Castile than from England. He implied that negotiations are moving swiftly."

"Yes, they are. My staff are working diligently to prepare a funding proposal."

"I imagine other banks are doing so as well," Nico speculated.

"Again, I do not have an insight into our competitors' operations, but your assumption is reasonable."

Nico considered the four projects Portinari described as he went from the manager's office to the room where Vittorio was interviewing bank employees. The hospital project was an unlikely contender because the Medici bank was already financing the initial construction work. Any competitor who saw the hospital project as crucial would have acted when Duke Sforza first announced his intention to build the hospital.

Trade with Venice promised to be the most lucrative of the

four projects, but it was only a concept. It was too soon for competing banks to guess the Medici bank's strategy. That left two possibilities: canal expansion and merino wool.

Nico took one step into the meeting room and paused, unsure whether his presence would interrupt the interview in progress. Vittorio eyed Nico and pointed to a chair near the room's entrance. Nico moved silently to the designated spot.

The man seated across the table from Vittorio had slumped forward until his chin rested on his chest. "Sit up! Look at me!" Vittorio bellowed.

When the man raised his head, Nico recognized him as one of the records clerks. "You said Giulia caused the problem. Who is Giulia and what is the problem?" Vittorio demanded.

"Giulia is my wife," the man whimpered.

Vittorio pounded his fist onto the table and barked, "You are not helping yourself. Tell me something useful."

Nico found the interaction fascinating. He had never seen how intense Vittorio became when interrogating a suspect.

"We are married for only one month, not even one month, and now she is gone. She returned to her father," the man replied.

Vittorio was impatient, but he waited, sensing that the distressed clerk would continue without further encouragement. A moment later, the story unfolded. "Her father demanded that I return the dowry, but I can't. I spent it."

"You spent it," Vittorio echoed.

"I bought things for the house, and things that Giulia wanted. Clothes for her... and jewelry. Giulia likes to wear jewelry."

"A sad story, but how does it connect to the bank?" Vittorio pressed.

"A man approached me when I was walking home from the bank. He said his patron would pay for information about

Signor Portinari. He pushed a paper into my hand, and he was gone. I read the paper when I got home. It was a list of questions: Is Signor Portinari married? Does he have any children? They were all simple questions. I saw no harm in answering them. The next day the man came again, and I returned the sheet to him with answers to the questions. In return, he gave me a pouch, and inside were two florins."

"Continue. What happened next?" Vittorio urged.

"He said that his patron wanted to speak with Signor Portinari, but they could not meet at the bank. He said it had to be a private meeting away from the bank, and if I could tell him where to meet Signor Portinari, I would earn enough to pay back the dowry."

"Did you tell him that Signor Portinari would be meeting with the architect?" The clerk nodded. "Tell me about the man. What is his name? Describe him."

"He did not tell me his name." Recalling the man's image sent the clerk into an involuntary shiver. "He has bulging eyes and a hooked nose...and he has a bad limp. When he walks, his whole body shakes from side to side."

"How did he find out that you had to pay back a dowry?"

"I don't know how. All he asked was that I tell him when Signor Portinari would be alone. It seemed a harmless request, and if I told him, my debt would be paid. He never said why he wanted the information." The clerk lowered his head into his hands and whimpered.

For a long minute, Vittorio said nothing, then he ordered, "Get out of here."

Nico watched the sniveling clerk push himself up from the chair and stumble toward the door. "One last question," Vittorio called. "On your wedding night, was your wife a virgin?"

The man's face flushed. "No," he answered in a barely audible voice.

Nico moved to the table and sat next to Vittorio. "Congratulations. You seem to have found the culprit," Nico said, then added, "But isn't it strange that someone knew about the dowry?"

Vittorio laughed, "For a lawyer, you're very observant. My next interview will be with the clerk's father-in-law. I am confident he can lead us to the Intermediary."

"There is one thing I don't understand. Why did you ask if his wife was a virgin?" Nico asked.

Before Vittorio could reply, a shadow spreading across the table caught his attention. Both men turned to see the doorway filled by a Milanese army officer who entered without hesitation and demanded, "Which of you is Signor Colombo?"

Vittorio stood and announced, "I am Vittorio Colombo."

"I am Captain Osvaldo Ghetti of the Milanese Army judiciary unit. I have been assigned to investigate the murder of Signor Salito Salvetti. I understand that you examined his body, and you viewed the crime scene."

Vittorio nodded and motioned for Captain Ghetti to be seated. Nico introduced himself; then he and Vittorio joined the captain at the table. As soon as he was seated, Ghetti asked, "What did you discover?"

Vittorio considered how much information to share. No matter how much he provided, he expected to get nothing in return. Rivalries kept investigators from aiding even respected colleagues; certainly this officer would not share facts with a stranger. Vittorio began with facts already known to the captain. "I viewed Signor Salvetti's body, and I examined the sites where he was abducted, held captive, and put into the canal. I do not know where he was murdered."

Ghetti was accustomed to dealing with guardia investigators who gave away little without prodding, so he was not surprised that Vittorio revealed no useful information. He rephrased his question, "What did you observe when you visited the site?"

This time, Vittorio was more forthcoming. "He was held at a pig farm. The farm owner said that two men brought Salvetti to the farm. One man is named Bruno, and he lives somewhere in Milan. He is the farmer's cousin. The farmer did not recognize the second man. In the barn where Salvetti had been held, there were fibers and a distinctive button torn from his tunic."

Ghetti nodded, pleased with Vittorio's answer. He followed with a series of questions about the farm, the canal site, and the condition of the body. Finally, when Ghetti exhausted his prepared list of items, he said, "Is there anything else you can tell me that might help my investigation?"

Vittorio debated telling the captain the name of Bruno's accomplice. He knew that having the name could help the army's investigation. Still, he did not want to admit that Massimo was questioning people in taverns in violation of the tribunal's ruling. He chose his words carefully. "Recently, we learned that Bruno's associate might be named Tonio. Someone, I don't recall who, reported hearing the two names linked together."

Ghetti stroked his chin as he processed Vittorio's statement. He recognized the ambiguity in Vittorio's words because he had used similar ploys himself. Rather than press the Florentine for a source, Ghetti said, with a hint of sarcasm, "Even though you cannot recall where you heard the name, having the name of the second offender is helpful." Then in a normal voice, he continued, "When thugs are not causing trouble, they spend more time in taverns than anywhere else. I will send my team to question tavern owners; one of them is sure to know Bruno and Tonio."

Nico said, "Sergeant Dellanetta said that tavern owners won't talk to the guardia."

The captain smiled, "Dellanetta is a good man, but he is merely a member of the guardia. Tavern owners may not talk with his people, but they will talk to my mine." He turned to Vittorio and said, "I trust you will tell me if your interviews with the bank employees yield anything useful."

"Certainly. How can I contact you?" Vittorio asked.

"I will contact you," Ghetti stated curtly.

Vittorio said, "If I am not at the bank, you may find me at the guest house at the palazzo of Contessa Maddalena del Carretto."

Ghetti rose to leave. With a smug smile, he replied, "Yes, I know."

33

THE TICENESE DISTRICT, MILAN

Tavern regulars rarely spoke with strangers, even if the stranger was willing to buy a round. That reluctance hampered Massimo's search for Bruno and Tonio. The previous day, Massimo had found a derelict who was short on coin and thirsty enough to accept a mug of beer on a stranger's tab. As the beer flowed, the man's tongue loosened. He took a long draw from his third mug and slurred, "Yuh, I seen those two in here. Bruno's a vicious bastard. He started a fight with somebody, so the barkeep threw his ass out into the street."

"When was that?" Massimo asked.

The man wiped beer dribbling from his chin and said, "A couple days past."

"Does Bruno come here often?" Massimo asked.

"He's not here much. He drinks at a fancy place in the Ticinese when he has enough coin."

That tidbit helped Massimo to narrow his search. To orient himself to the Ticinese district, Massimo walked the main street of the neighborhood, the Via Ticinese, from the center of the city to the nearest city gate. At each intersection, he scanned the side streets looking for taverns, spotting six by the time he reached the city gate. He also observed that shops on the eastern part of the district were less reputable than those to the west. He guessed Bruno might fit better in a seedy tavern, so he began his search in the eastern sector. Standing beside the Ticinese city gate, he peered into a narrow side street. Midway along the road, a faded sign displayed *La Donna Cordiale*, the friendly lady. Initially, Massimo thought the sign marked a bordello. Only the drawing of a foam-topped beer mug on the door kept him from bypassing the establishment.

Upon entering, Massimo noted the only patrons were two men sitting at a table in the rear of the room. They were engaged in animated conversation, so Massimo doubted that they would welcome interference from a stranger. He was about to leave when a plump older woman who was standing at the bar called in his direction, "Welcome, stranger." The woman's kindly face reminded Massimo of his aunt Teresa.

She filled a mug and set it on the bar in front of Massimo. "The first glass for every newcomer comes with my compliments."

"You must be the friendly lady." As soon as the words escaped his lips, Massimo realized how frivolous they were. The only thing worse he could have said was that she looked like his elderly aunt Teresa. He sipped his beer and contemplated how to restore his dignity. Before a fitting recovery came to mind, the woman asked, "Are you a butcher?"

Massimo was taken aback by her question until he looked down at himself. He held up the stained tunic sleeve and opted to follow her conversational lead. "Beet soup," he said. "Impossible to remove. I ruined this perfectly fine tunic." He hoped she wouldn't pursue the topic. Although he relished good food, he knew little about cooking.

"Ah, I thought it was blood. Where are you from, stranger?" she asked.

Relieved that she had changed the subject, Massimo chose the name of a city he had visited. "I was a cook in Pavia until the restaurant owner's son returned from Rome. Now he is the cook, and I need a job. A friend in Pavia said Milan is expanding rapidly. He said there is always work in this city.

"My friend said I should find a man named Bruno." Massimo laughed. "He didn't say where I might find Bruno, only that Bruno likes to drink beer. I have been going from one tavern to another looking for him."

The woman's expression turned serious. She asked, "Your friend in Pavia, is he an honest man?"

Massimo feigned surprise. "He's not a close friend, but I believe him to be honest."

"There is one called Bruno who comes here occasionally. I've heard him called a thief, and he has never denied it. He almost seems proud of that label."

"My intent is not to judge him," Massimo replied. "I only seek his help to find work. Is there any special time of day when thirst brings him here?"

"His appearance doesn't depend on time. When he is short of coin, he takes pleasure in our cheap local beer, and he is as likely to show at noon as when we are about to close. When his pouch is filled with silver, he fancies the expensive imported beer at Bierposto."

"Bierposto?" echoed Massimo.

"A tavern on the other side of Via Ticinese where everything is expensive. Bruno has not set foot in here recently, so he must be dropping his silver at Bierposto."

Massimo enjoyed a second beer and chatting with the woman. After finishing the second beer, he headed to Bierposto. Before entering the upscale tavern, he peered in through the window. Old men hunched over beer mugs occupied three tables. Long moments passed before one of the old-timers lifted his glass and took a sip. The men's conversation flowed as slowly as their beer. Stepping inside, Massimo saw a teenaged boy sweeping the raised platform where entertainers performed in the evenings. No one was at the bar, but as Massimo approached, he spotted a man and a woman busily working in a room behind the bar. When the man glimpsed Massimo, he wiped his hands, came out of the room, and stood behind the bar. Gunter knew all his regular patrons and many who frequented his tavern only occasionally. He was reasonably sure he had never met Massimo. "I am Gunter. What can I get for you?"

"Beer," Massimo replied.

"Doppelbock?" Gunter asked. Massimo's silence and bewildered expression told Gunter that he needed to explain. "Doppelbock is a dark beer from Saxony. It is the favorite here at Bierposto."

Massimo nodded. Gunter filled a large mug and set it before Massimo, who took a long draw. Massimo's face brightened. "Ah, I understand why this is a favorite. It doesn't taste like flowers."

Gunter smiled, pleased that Massimo appreciated the house's specialty. With obvious pride, he explained, "Doppelbock is brewed when the temperatures in Saxony are cool. And it is brewed from grains. Local beers here are brewed from... almost anything.

"As you can see, afternoons are not a busy time at Bierposto. A musician from Naples will perform in the evening. His bawdy songs are popular with our patrons. Whenever he performs, every table is filled."

Massimo took another sip of beer, then said casually, "I am

looking for someone named Bruno. Maybe the music will draw him."

Massimo noted a flash of recognition in Gunter's eyes at the mention of Bruno's name. Before he could ask, Gunter said, "Bruno hasn't been here for several days, and he's never shown an interest in music. But there is someone who might help you find him. The last time Bruno was here, he was talking with Mouseface, so Mouseface might know how to find him."

"Mouseface?" Massimo echoed incredulously.

Gunter laughed. "That is what everyone calls him, and I'm ashamed to say I don't know his given name."

"Might Mouseface be here this evening?"

"He is often here in the evening, but today he's not in Milan. However, I'm certain he'll be here tomorrow morning."

Puzzled, Massimo asked, "He greets his mornings in a tavern? This doppelbock is an excellent beer, but not a typical breakfast fare."

"Tomorrow morning, my wife"—Gunter gestured to the back room where Maria was working busily— "will make crema pasticchi, a cream-filled pastry. Mouseface never misses Maria's pasticchi."

Massimo had time for only one beer before he had to escort Signor Portinari from the bank. He drained the mug, assured Gunter that he would return, and set out for the Medici bank. The carriage stood ready in a clearing near the bank when he arrived. He chatted with the driver until Portinari appeared. Under his arm was a thick document folio. On the ride to the farmhouse, Portinari was more talkative than usual. He informed Massimo that Vittorio had uncovered the traitor who had disclosed information that resulted in Salvetti's murder.

When the carriage stopped near the farmhouse, Massimo climbed out and extended a hand to help the banker. As Portinari moved toward the house, Massimo's focus shifted to the open door beyond. Something was wrong. Instinctively Massimo reached in vain for the sword that was always at his side when he was an active soldier. "Wait!" he cried out as he ran toward the house.

Massimo's outburst froze the startled banker in mid-step. "The door!" Massimo shouted as he streaked past Portinari. Seeing the open door, Portinari shared Massimo's fear. He dropped the document folio. Papers flew from the folder and swirled in his wake as Portinari dashed to the house screaming, "Stefana! Stefana!"

Massimo stopped inside the entrance and listened for any movement. Hearing none, he advanced straight ahead and waved Portinari to the corridor that led to the bedrooms. When Massimo reached the empty kitchen, he peered out through a window and scanned the vineyard, looking for any sign that the women might be in the vineyard. With that hope dashed, he turned just as Portinari entered the kitchen.

"They are not in the bedrooms," Portinari said in a high-pitched voice driven by his rising panic.

Massimo's eyes locked onto a folded paper placed in the center of the otherwise clear table. He read the words, "For Signor Portinari" before handing the note to the banker who unfolded the sheet and read the message aloud.

"You will receive instructions. Follow them, and your wife will be returned. Talk with the guardia, and you will not see her again."

Portinari fell to his knees, sobbing. Attracted by the commotion, the carriage driver moved cautiously to the house, fearful of what he might find inside. He made his way to the kitchen and stopped in the doorway. Massimo called, "Come here. Help me lift him." The two men eased Portinari to his feet and maneuvered him outside to the carriage. "Take us back to the bank," Massimo ordered.

On the ride into the city, Portinari muttered incoherently. "It is my fault. I should never have taken her from Florence. Why did I agree to live in that isolated farmhouse?"

Massimo mulled over the fate of the two women. Portinari's wife had value to the abductors, but the maid had none. There was no blood in the house, and the maid had been taken along with Stefana. Both women must be alive, at least for now, Massimo reasoned.

At the bank, Massimo jumped from the carriage. "Wait here," he called to the driver as he dashed inside to fetch Nico and Vittorio. A minute later, the three Florentines streamed out of the bank and climbed into the carriage. Massimo instructed the driver, "Take us to Palazzo Torelli."

On the way, Massimo explained to Vittorio and Nico what had happened at the farmhouse and read the note left by the abductors. Hearing the threat again brought Portinari to tears.

Massimo and Vittorio guided Portinari into the guest house and settled him on a couch. The nearly incoherent bank manager struggled to find words. "I'll do anything. Whatever they want. Anything. I must have her back safely. I can't let anything happen to her. Why did they take her? What do they want?"

To Vittorio, Nico said, "This confirms your belief that Salvetti's abduction was connected to bank business."

Vittorio, furious with himself, stormed across the room, then turned and faced his colleagues. "It is my fault she was taken. Massimo guarded Signor Portinari. The thugs couldn't get to him, so they took his wife. I should have realized that this would happen."

"You couldn't have known..." Nico began, but he stopped abruptly when Vittorio's expression showed that the investigator didn't want to hear any excuses for his failure.

Vittorio moved to where Portinari was seated. He stood

directly in front of the hapless banker, looked down at him and said, "You have my word; no harm will come to her. We will find her."

Nico, Massimo, and Vittorio sat together around the table discussing how to make good on Vittorio's promise that Stefana would be unharmed. "The note says not to involve the guardia, but I think we should tell Captain Ghetti and trust that he will be discreet," Nico said. Silence filled the room while Vittorio and Massimo considered Nico's suggestion. Sensing that Vittorio needed convincing, Nico added, "When you described how you learned Tonio's name, the captain knew you were withholding information; yet he did not press the issue. I believe he can be trusted."

Vittorio nodded. "Your instinct was correct when you said we should engage with Messer Avocino. He provided the information that let us find Salvetti, so I'm willing to trust your intuition regarding Captain Ghetti. He seemed like an honorable person, and one who's inclined to act, unlike that useless guardia investigator."

Pleased to have Vittorio's support, Nico said, "In the morning, I'll go to the army camp to inform the captain." Next, Nico voiced the discouraging fact that they all were thinking. "There's no way to tell where the women are being held. They took Salvetti out of Milan. If they do the same with the women, they could be anywhere."

Massimo brightened. "If she was abducted by the same men who took Salvetti, I might have a lead. Today I was told about a person called Mouseface who may know where to find Bruno. The Bierposto tavern serves breakfast pastries made by the tavern owner's wife. Apparently, Mouseface never misses a morning when she makes her special cream-filled pastries. She'll be making them tomorrow, so I plan to be at the tavern to question him."

"Portinari needs to be at the bank in the morning because the men who have Stefana may try to contact him with their demands. Can you visit the tavern before escorting Portinari to the bank?" Vittorio asked.

"Yes, I can do that since Portinari will be staying here at the guest house tonight."

Vittorio thought about his options. He was eager to discover the motive for Salvetti's murder, but Stefana's situation was dire. "I will join you at the tavern," he said.

34

BIERPOSTO, MILAN

Like their patrons, taverns have personalities. Some are somber establishments where the troubled share their woes and commiserate with other hapless men. Others are boisterous venues that attract happy revelers. Most draw their biggest crowds in the evenings. At Bierposto, Massimo and Vittorio found the tavern filled at breakfast time with cheerful diners enjoying Maria's delicious pastries.

Gunter recognized Massimo from his visit the previous afternoon. Gradually, he made his way through a throng of patrons to where Massimo was surveying the crowd. Pointing to a table near the middle of the room where a lone patron munched on a cream-filled pastry, Gunter said, "That is Mouse-face. He is the one who may know where Bruno can be found."

"You did not exaggerate," Massimo said. "The pastries certainly are popular with the morning crowd. We look forward to tasting them, if this hungry crowd doesn't devour all of them. We'll be sitting with Mouseface. Bring pastries for us and one more for him."

Massimo and Vittorio pulled chairs close on either side of

Mouseface, who pivoted left and then right, puzzling over why the two strangers chose his table and why they squeezed in near him. Massimo wore a tunic from the days when he was attached to his army unit. He had removed the military insignias, but the tunic's official-looking style made Mouseface anxious. When Maria brought pastries to the Florentines, Vittorio looked up, flashed a broad smile, and said, "Please bring another for our friend." She returned quickly with another plate. Vittorio and Massimo enjoyed the delicacies without speaking. They ate slowly, and Mouseface matched their pace. By the time they finished eating, many of the other patrons had already departed.

The two Florentines angled their chairs to face Mouseface. Massimo said, "Two days past, you had a long conversation with Bruno." When Mouseface turned his head to face the stranger who was speaking, Vittorio leaned in behind Mouseface, close enough for Mouseface to feel warm breath on the back of his neck. In a menacing tone, Vittorio said, "We know you spoke with him, so don't try to deny it."

"He came to me," Mouseface sputtered. "He and Tonio."

"What did he want?" Vittorio asked.

Without turning to face the questioner, Mouseface replied, "They wanted a quiet place away from the city where they could be alone for several days without being disturbed. Someone, I don't know who, told him that I knew of such a place."

"A place to keep the abducted women?" Massimo taunted.

Startled, Mouseface slid his chair away from the table and stammered, "They never said anything about abductions. I swear it." Vittorio slammed the chair forward, pinning Mouseface against the table.

"Are you telling us you weren't curious what they wanted the place for?" Massimo asked.

"I'm not foolish enough to question Bruno, and if I did ask, he wouldn't have told me."

Now it was Vittorio who pushed Mouseface away from the table so both Florentines could face him. "What did you tell him?" Vittorio demanded.

"I told him about the retreat house near Monza. Monks use it in the summer, but it's vacant at this time of year. That made Bruno happy. He said it was exactly what they needed."

The Florentines each grasped one of Mouseface's arms and pulled him to a standing position. "You're going to take us there," Massimo commanded.

The cold morning air condensed Nico's breath into a fine mist. He kept a brisk pace to ward off the chill during his hour-long trek to the military camp. Outside the city walls, smoke spiraled into the chalky sky from chimneys of the dwellings he passed, and only the crunch of gravel underfoot broke the early morning silence. One final bend in the road and Camp Giorgi came into view. Lines of soldiers moving in different directions trotted past each other. In the distance, cavalry units in ceremonial dress were assembling in an open field. Nico recalled that the one time he had visited a Florentine army encampment, the few soldiers who were milling about strolled casually between buildings. The Florentine camp had lacked the vibrancy of this Milanese garrison. Had something happened overnight to precipitate this level of activity at the Milanese base, or is today a holiday in the duchy, Nico wondered.

Nico presented himself at the guard post. "I am Messer Nico Argenti to see Captain Ghetti." He had his letter of introduction at the ready, but the soldier did not request identification.

The guard said, "As you can see, all units are engaged in exercises, so no one may enter without an escort. I will send a messenger to ask if the captain is available. If he can meet with you, his aide will come to collect you."

Curious about the activity, Nico asked, "Is the camp always this busy or is today special?"

"Another dignitary is visiting," the soldier replied. "I think he is a Bohemian duke. Bohemia has so many dukes that I can't remember which one is scheduled for today."

Nico flashed a sympathetic smile, although, in truth, he knew nothing of Bohemian nobility. He watched the messenger scurry from the guard station; then he shifted his gaze to the horses performing intricate drills on the parade ground. "Those demonstrations are sure to impress whichever duke is today's honored guest." The guard beamed an appreciative smile.

Soon, a voice behind Nico announced, "I am Corporal Petrucci. I can take you to Captain Ghetti." Nico turned to face a soldier about his own age, wearing a snow-white dress uniform with gleaming silver buttons. His boots and leather scabbard shone mirror-like.

The corporal led Nico directly across the exercise yard toward a row of low buildings. He did not alter his pace as lines of soldier brushed past, heading in various directions. Nico followed closely behind the corporal to avoid being swept up in the flow. At the first building, Petrucci announced, "This is the office of the commandant." They passed two other buildings before the corporal turned and said, "This is the office of the judicial unit. Captain Ghetti's office is in this building."

Inside, men sat at clusters of desks spaced throughout a large open area. Along one wall, a fireplace pumped heat into the room. The opposite wall consisted of a row of small offices.

Some offices were open to the central room; others were
screened for privacy by canvas curtains. Petrucci approached
one of the curtains and pushed it aside, allowing Nico to enter.
He announced, "Captain, this is Messer Argenti."

The captain looked up expectantly. Nico took Ghetti's
expression and his silence as a cue that the captain wanted him
to speak, so he began, "Signor Portinari's wife has been abducted." The statement made Ghetti's neck muscles tighten. Nico
continued, "Signor Leoni escorted Portinari home from the
bank yesterday. When they arrived at the farmhouse, the
women were gone."

"Women?" Ghetti echoed.

"Portinari's wife and their maid."

Ghetti asked, "Signor Leoni, is he one of your colleagues?"

"Yes, he is a member of the Florentine security commission.
Previously, he was a Florentine army officer." Ghetti raised an
eyebrow upon hearing that Massimo had been a soldier.

"There was a note," Nico continued. "It said that Portinari
will be contacted with instructions, what he must do for his
wife to be released. The note said that Portinari must not
contact the guardia."

"The note warned against contacting the guardia, yet you
come to me. A wise decision, but you should have come sooner." Ghetti said. "Every hour exposes the women to greater
danger."

"You are investigating Salvetti's murder. We believe the
same people who committed Salvetti's murder also abducted
the women and that both incidents are related to financial dealings of the Medici bank."

"A reasonable assumption," Ghetti agreed.

Nico paused for a moment, then said, "This is a delicate
situation. The people responsible must not learn that I came to
you."

Ghetti nodded and leaned back in his chair. "Where is the note? I need to see it."

"Signor Portinari has it. He is at the bank."

"You said that Signor Leoni is Portinari's escort. I assume his role is to safeguard the bank manager." Nico nodded. Restating the truth, Ghetti said, "Unfortunately, that didn't have the outcome you expected. The criminals could not take Portinari, so they took his wife instead. Is Signor Leoni also at the bank? I wish to speak to him."

"Signor Leoni will be at the bank later. He is no longer escorting Signor Portinari. We are concerned that Signor Leoni's presence would deter the criminals from contacting Signor Portinari."

"I understand," Ghetti said; then he looked to Corporal Petrucci. "Find Davini and Gelmo. Tell them this is a hawk mission, and Signor Portinari is the nut. Then fetch our mounts and bring one for Signor Argenti as well. We are going to the Medici bank." Petrucci turned smartly and left the office.

The captain's order made no sense to Nico. "A hawk mission? Portinari is the nut?" he echoed.

Even without seeing Nico's puzzled expression, Ghetti knew his instructions needed explaining. "A member of my team devised the colorful analogy. Hawks circle high above, unseen by their prey, until they swoop down and strike without warning. Like hawks, Davini and Gelmo are highly skilled at surveilling without being seen."

Despite being fanciful, Nico found that part of the analogy surprisingly appropriate. "And the nut? Did you say Signor Portinari is the nut?"

"Just as hawks seek out rodents, rodents seek nuts, so it can be said that by catching rodents, hawks are protecting the nuts." Ghetti smiled. "Yes, that analogy takes more imagination, but again, it is efficient. With only a few words, Davini and

Gelmo will understand precisely what is expected of them. Now, while I prepare to leave, wait outside for Corporal Petrucci to return with the horses."

Portinari was sitting in his office staring straight ahead when the men arrived. Nico broke the trance by announcing, "Signor Portinari, this is Captain Ghetti of the Milanese Army judicial unit."

Portinari tensed and glared at Nico. "The note warns against contacting the guardia. Surely that warning is meant to include all authorities. By involving the military, you put Stefana in greater danger." Portinari found his feelings shifting from worry to anger.

"We have experience dealing with these situations," the captain explained. "You are justified in being concerned, but understand that only three of my most trusted men know the situation. I assure you, the criminals will not learn that we are involved." Ghetti did not tell Portinari that two of his men were hawks who would keep watch on him. "May I see the note?"

Ghetti took the paper from Portinari's outstretched hand. He studied the salutation; then he took a blank sheet from Portinari's desk and penned the identical words: *to Signor Portinari.* "What do you see?" he asked the others.

Nico and Portinari examined the two sheets; then they looked up at Ghetti. "The words are the same," Portinari responded.

"Look again, carefully," the captain said. His slight grin showed that he enjoyed seeing them struggle to notice what he had seen immediately.

"The letters are shaped slightly differently, especially the letter S," Nico said hesitantly, not sure whether his answer was the correct one.

"Exactly," Ghetti declared. "Every school child in Milan learns to form his letters the same way I form mine. Duke Sforza does not form his letters like mine because he spent his childhood in the south, and southerners pen their letters like the Greeks. The person who wrote this message forms his letters as you do. This message was penned by a Florentine."

Was it possible that a Florentine was implicated in the abductions and in Salvetti's murder? Who in Florence would benefit? A rival bank, perhaps?

Before the men could speculate on the possibilities, Vittorio and Massimo appeared in the doorway. Not wanting to give Portinari false hope, Vittorio said, "Nico, Captain, may I speak with you both outside?" In the bank anteroom, he and Massimo recounted their conversation at the tavern with Mouseface, who stood silently nearby.

When Massimo and Vittorio finished speaking, Ghetti faced Mouseface. "You can lead us to the retreat house?"

Mouseface merely nodded. Ghetti dispatched the corporal to requisition additional horses from the nearest stable. The men filed into the street to wait for Petrucci's return. Nico looked for the two hawks but saw no one, so he assumed they were not yet in position. Ghetti stepped to the middle of the roadway, raised his arm above his head, and rotated it in a circular motion. From the corner of his eye, Nico glimpsed a man step out of an alley between two buildings. The hawk wore a gray tunic and gray hose that matched the color of the building's stone façade.

Nico turned in the opposite direction in time to see the second hawk, dressed in a laborer's smock, come out of a tanner's shop. Gesturing to Mouseface, the captain told his men, "This person believes he can show us where the women are being held. Remain here with Signor Portinari and be extra vigilant in case this is a ruse to lure us away." Moments later, Corporal Petrucci returned with horses, and the men departed for Monza.

35

MONZA

Corporal Petrucci was familiar with the road between Milan and Monza, so he led the column. Behind him, Captain Ghetti rode alongside Massimo. The captain used the opportunity to ask Vittorio about his observations at the farmhouse where the abduction had occurred. Next in line was Mouseface. His equestrian skill surprised everyone. There was more to the little man than a rodent-like face and a penchant for cream-filled sweets.

Nico and Massimo followed. Their pairing let Massimo relate to Nico the encounter with Mouseface at Bierposto. "When we arrived," Massimo began, "Gunter, the tavern owner, pointed to the table where Mouseface was gobbling a pastry; however, I can't fault him for that. Vittorio and I sampled the pastries too, and we agree they are exceptional. He didn't deny our accusation that he had told Bruno about the retreat house. On the contrary, he spoke freely after Vittorio scared him until he almost shit. Vittorio has a knack for doing that."

"Did he say who told Bruno about him?" Nico asked.

"He claimed he didn't know. Vittorio and I did not have

much time to question him. Perhaps with some pressure his memory might improve, but the tavern owner said that Mouseface boasts about his exploits, real and imaginary, to anyone who will listen."

"So, he may have told many people about his hideaway," Nico opined.

"Probably. He certainly delighted in telling us that he took women there. No doubt he enjoyed impressing others with his stories as well. Still, if we have a chance to question him further, we might learn the names of people he talked with recently."

"Did Bruno say why he was interested in the retreat house?"

"According to Mouseface, Bruno only said that he wanted a place he could stay for several days without being disturbed. He claims Bruno told him nothing about the women."

At Piazza del Duomo in the center of Monza, the riders switched positions. Ghetti moved Mouseface to the front, where he could lead the others out of town on a side road. Any doubts about Mouseface knowing the route to the retreat house faded when he paused at a nearly invisible turnoff and declared confidently, "This path is steep and narrow, so we should form a single line. The house is at the top of the hill."

Captain Ghetti moved in behind the leader, so he would be able to prevent Mouseface from fleeing or alerting occupants of the building when they drew close. The riders fell silent, and the column advanced slowly up the path. When they neared the hilltop, Ghetti glimpsed a stone structure beyond a stand of pine trees. He motioned for the others to stop and said in a low voice, "We go on foot from here." After they dismounted, he told Mouseface, "You remain here," and added firmly, "If you are not here when we return, I will send an entire cavalry unit to hunt for you. And when they find you, you will pray for the devil to rescue you from them." Mouseface stepped back, wanting to distance himself from Ghetti's threat.

The other men climbed to the edge of the clearing at the top of the hill, where Ghetti held up a hand to pause their advance and said, "From here, we can see only one doorway. We need to know if there are any others." He sent Vittorio around the left side of the building and Massimo to the right side. When Vittorio returned, he reported, "There are windows at the rear, but no doors on the left or at the rear."

Massimo said, "There are no exits on the far side, but there is a wagon. No horses; just a wagon. Someone who came in the wagon must have left on horseback."

Vittorio said, "We believe two men did the abductions, but they were paid by others, so we cannot know how many are in the building."

Ghetti and Petrucci drew their short swords. They bent below window height as they approached the entrance. Massimo and Vittorio followed. Each of them had taken a fallen tree branch to serve as a club.

When Ghetti reached the entrance, he raised the door latch slowly, and exhaled in relief that the door was not locked. He swung the door open and all five men rushed inside.

In the dim light, they saw the maid pressed against the table at the center of the room. Rope bound her hands, and a gag filled her mouth. Her skirt had been pushed up to her waist. Bruno stood behind her with his hose down around his ankles and one hand gripping the maid's hair.

Alerted by the sound of the intruders, Bruno instinctively turned toward the sound. He froze at the sight of the two soldiers brandishing swords. Ghetti sprinted ahead and struck Bruno's face with the flat of his blade. The powerful blow sent Bruno staggering backward. As he fell, Bruno's cheek caught the tip of Ghetti's sword. Blood streamed from the laceration.

Massimo grabbed the thug as he fell and hurled him across the room. Bruno's head struck the stone wall. Dazed by the impact, he slumped to the floor.

Freed from Bruno's grip, the maid sunk to her knees. As soon as Nico removed her gag, she began sobbing. He untied her hands and helped her to a chair. Vittorio scanned the room and found Stefana gagged and tied to a chair in the corner of the room. Vittorio went to her and loosened the rope binding her hands. Instantly, she ripped the gag from her mouth, untied her feet, and rushed to the maid who was sitting bent forward and sobbing. Nico stepped away to give the women space.

While Massimo watched Bruno, the two Milanese soldiers with their swords at the ready advanced into the corridor to check the bedrooms. They moved as a pair from room to room. When they returned, Ghetti looked at the mattresses on the floor. He said, "The other rooms are empty and cold. They must have slept here where it is warmer."

Massimo pulled a chair away from the table and set it against a wall out of the maid's field of view. He lifted Bruno from the floor and dropped the semi-conscious thug onto the seat. Ghetti pressed the tip of his sword against Bruno's throat with enough pressure for Bruno to realize that any abrupt movement might be fatal. "Where is your partner?" Ghetti demanded.

Information gained during his conversations at the taverns let Massimo deduce that this thug was Bruno, the one often described as uncivilized. He moved alongside the captain and said, "I believe that this one is Bruno and the missing one is Tonio."

Bruno had yet to regain his senses. His only response to Ghetti's questions was incoherent muttering. Vittorio took a bottle of wine from the table, grabbed Bruno's hair, pulled his head back, and doused him with the cool red liquid. Bruno coughed, spit, and twisted from side-to-side. Ghetti reduced the pressure on his blade, but not before Bruno's spasm pressed his flesh into the blade's sharp edge, resulting in a thin line of blood across Bruno's neck. He blinked rapidly, then opened his eyes to see the intense glares of the men facing him. "Where is Tonio?" Ghetti barked.

Bruno eyed at the captain but said nothing. Ghetti pressed the tip of his blade against Bruno's chin. "My patience is limited. Where is Tonio?" the captain repeated.

"At the market in Monza," Bruno spit out the words.

Ghetti turned to Petrucci. "Corporal, get the horses out of sight, so Tonio will not see them when he returns."

Petrucci bolted out the door and across the clearing to the path where Mouseface waited with the horses. "Help me move them," he demanded. With Mouseface's assistance, Petrucci led the animals to the far side of the building where they could not be seen by Tonio when he returned.

Ghetti continued his interrogation. "You murdered Salvetti," he declared. Bruno's only response was his lips turning upward into an evil grin. "We have proof that you abducted him and killed him. You abducted and abused these women. Tell me who paid you to do it. Who paid you to kill Salvetti and abduct the women?"

After a meaningful silence, the captain said, "You will go to prison peacefully, or you will be made to suffer. Your fate depends on whether you answer my questions. Now, who paid you?"

When Bruno refused to answer, Ghetti gestured toward Vittorio and Massimo. "The one you killed, the banker, was a Florentine. These men are Florentine. Would you prefer that I give you to them? Do you want to feel their vengeance?"

In a conciliatory tone, Bruno said, "Pagatore." Then in a firm defiant voice he said, "There are jobs that the rich scum of

Milan are too cowardly to do themselves. Pagatore pays us to do the deeds for them."

"Where can I find this Pagatore?"

"I do not know, and your blade cannot cut deep enough for me to say different. Pagatore comes to us; we do not go to him."

As Ghetti opened his mouth to speak, Bruno anticipated the question and said, "He finds us in taverns. Me and others. It takes many of us to satisfy the wishes of Milan's corrupt elite. We take risks for a few silver coins while the rich bastards remain hidden, protected from any suffering."

Nico noted that Stefana had calmed the maid. He moved next to the captain and suggested, "It would be best for the women to leave this place. We can take them back to Milan."

Ghetti nodded. "I will want to speak with them later, but there is no reason for them to remain here now."

"It is not safe for them to return to the farmhouse, and we cannot tell Signor Portinari that the women have been rescued," Vittorio asserted. Everyone stared at him while they tried to puzzle out his reasoning. He explained, "If the conspirators learn that the women are free, they will realize that their plot has been foiled, and they won't try to contact Signor Portinari." He looked to the captain. "By keeping the women hidden, your men, the ones you called the hawks, will have a chance to apprehend the person who brings instructions to Signor Portinari."

"But why can't Portinari be told that the women have been rescued?" Nico asked.

"He would want to go to his wife, and the conspirators might be watching him," Vittorio replied. "I know he is in pain, but secrecy is the only way to be sure the conspirators don't discover that the women have been found."

Ghetti nodded. "Signor Portinari will suffer by not knowing that his wife has been rescued, but your plan has merit. For his sake, let's hope the conspirators contact him soon." Ghetti turned to Nico, "Take the women to Santa Marta convent. The sisters will be able to care for them, and the women can remain there out of sight."

"I'll prepare the wagon," Massimo said. He took blankets from the makeshift beds and went outside to harness a horse. Minutes later, he returned and said to Nico, "The wagon is ready."

Nico and Stefana helped the maid to the wagon. After the maid was settled, Stefana climbed into the wagon bed beside her, and Nico joined Massimo.

Massimo took the reins and headed the cart down the hill toward Monza. They proceeded slowly to keep the wagon from jarring as they moved down the hill on the uneven path. When they reached the basilica in the center of Monza, they turned south in the direction of Milan.

Neither Nico nor Massimo noticed the man across the piazza who stared at them as they rode past. The women huddled together in the wagon bed did not see the man either, but Tonio recognized them. He watched them until they disappeared from view on the road to Milan, debating whether he should return to the retreat house or follow the wagon to Milan. There was nothing he could do to help Bruno. Ultimately, he decided it was time for the two men to separate, so he chose a safer option: he headed away from Milan, east toward the town of Bergamo.

For two centuries, the sisters of Santa Marta convent had sheltered women in distress. Massimo and Nico guided Stefana and the maid into the vestibule where a young nun greeted them. "These women need sanctuary," Massimo said. It was a familiar plea, one that the nun had heard often, but usually it was made by a troubled woman. The nun was taken aback by two men seeking sanctuary for two women.

The nun ushered the women to a bench, then said, "I will get the Reverend Mother."

After the nun left the room, Massimo pulled Nico aside and spoke softly, "Signor Portinari will be leaving the bank soon. Even though Captain Ghetti's hawks have been watching him, I prefer to have my own eyes on him. If you agree, I will follow Signor Portinari and leave the women with you."

Nico nodded his assent and followed Massimo to the door where he could speak without being overheard. "Remember, Signor Portinari cannot know that his wife has been freed."

Rather than join the contessa for dinner where they would need to explain Portinari's presence, the Florentines took their evening meal in the guest house. Worry over Stefana kept Portinari from eating. He pleaded with God: "I'll do anything to keep her safe. Please let me see her again. When will they tell me what I must do?" Shivers punctuated each utterance. Massimo kept the banker's wine glass filled and encouraged him to drink.

Portinari's pain distressed the Florentines, all the more because they knew that Stefana was being cared for by the sisters at Santa Marta convent. Captain Ghetti had posted two guards at the convent; neither they nor the sisters knew the names of the women in their charge. "Anonymity is an effective safeguard," Ghetti had declared.

The three Florentines fought the urge to tell Portinari that his wife was safe. They knew that if he learned Stefana's whereabouts, he would rush to her, take her from the convent, and whisk her to a refuge, most likely her father's vineyard in Tuscany. Those actions would surely alert the conspirators, and any hope of catching them would be lost.

After dinner, Massimo transitioned Portinari's drink from wine to potent grappa. The banker repeatedly sipped without thinking until his speech slurred and his eyelids drooped. Portinari's words came slowly, "I didn't sleep last night. Tonight again, I will spend the hours in prayer." He rose from the table and shuffled to his room.

"Poor *tizio*," Vittorio said as his gaze followed the distraught banker.

"We cannot let this continue," Nico said. "Worry is crushing him." Nico looked to the others to gauge their feelings.

"The people behind the abduction must want this to end quickly," Massimo said. "I will follow Portinari tomorrow. If he isn't contacted by the end of the day, then I agree we should tell him that his wife is safe."

Vittorio nodded his agreement. He stood, strode to the fireplace and back to the table. "If Portinari is not contacted tomorrow, there may be another way to find the conspirators. The bank clerk who was paid for information that led to Salvetti's abduction was desperate for money. Someone approached him and offered to cover his debt in exchange for information."

Nico looked puzzled. "How did the person know about the debt?" he asked.

"That's where the situation gets interesting... and complicated," Vittorio replied. "The clerk's wife left him shortly after they were married, so her father demanded that the dowry be returned."

"I'd be damned if I'd repay a dowry," Massimo declared.

"They might have had a marriage contract," Nico said. "Dowries are often an item in marriage agreements." Massimo gave a dismissive shrug.

"The clerk couldn't return the money because he spent it buying jewelry and other gifts for his wife," Vittorio explained.

"Let me guess," Massimo said, smiling. "She took the jewelry with her."

Vittorio laughed. "Even the devil could not deceive you, Massimo. Indeed, she did take the jewelry." Vittorio refilled his wine glass and then continued, "I'm sure the marriage was a fraud and that the bank clerk was not her first victim."

"Is that why you questioned whether the bride was a virgin?" Nico asked.

"Yes. Her having been deflowered by another man does not prove her a criminal, but it does fit the puzzle: if the failed marriage was a scheme concocted by her and her father, then the clerk was yet one more in a line of men she seduced."

"Do you believe she is responsible for Salvetti's abduction and murder?" Nico asked.

"No, not directly," Vittorio replied. "But I am confident that the two crimes are related somehow, and tomorrow I intend to find the connection between them."

36

THE JUDICIAL CHANCERY, MILAN

The following morning, Nico set out to learn more about the two major projects being pursued by the Medici bank: the canal expansion and the importation of merino wool. For no particular reason, he chose to start with the canal project. Nico was unfamiliar with the structure of the duchy government, so he needed to find someone who could tell him who administered the project.

Had the Florentine ambassador been more cooperative, he would have sought assistance from the embassy. After all, an essential role of the embassy was connecting Florentine officials and businessmen with Milanese ministers and administrators. Instead, Nico decided to seek help from Chancellor Scala's friend, Piero Tollino.

Snow flakes danced in the air as Nico walked from the contessa's guest house to the judicial chancery. The workday had barely begun when Nico entered the chancery lobby, and already notaries had their heads buried in documents as clerks busily shuttled folios from one desk to another. He stood in the doorway of the large central workroom, observing the activity and wondering how much paper passed through the hands of those workers in a year. He watched Tollino across the room give directions to a notary.

Tollino soon caught sight of Nico and smiled as he ushered his Florentine acquaintance to the conference room. "I visited with Maddalena yesterday, and she told me how delighted she is to have you and your colleagues as her guests. She especially enjoys the dinner conversation when she gets to hear about your activities. She said that she couldn't recall the last time there was as much exciting news at Palazzo Torelli. And her sister Benedetta thinks Massimo is charming... but perhaps I shouldn't have mentioned that to you."

"The contessa has graciously opened her home to us. She treats us like members of her family. We will never be able to repay her kindness." Nico laughed as he said, "As for Massimo, he does not need any encouragement, so I will not mention Benedetta's comment to him."

Shifting the conversation slightly, Tollino said, "I have heard from other sources that your activities have been largely successful."

"You deserve a measure of credit for our successes. You introduced me to Professor Beccaria, and his advice was instrumental in securing the release of Signor Colombo."

Tollino smiled broadly. "The successes I had in mind were your encounters with the Privy Council Secretary and the Council Tribunal. Many lawyers in Milan try their best to avoid those venues."

Modesty drove Nico's gaze lower. He said, "The verdicts were compromises, not outright victories.".

"You should consider it a victory that you survived without an adverse judgment or censure. The council has a well-earned reputation for being harsh." Tollino continued, "I was sorry to hear that your countryman, the banker, was murdered. Has his killer been found?"

Nico regretted that he could not tell Tollino about Bruno's capture, but if that information became known widely, it could compromise the plan to apprehend the conspirators. Nico said, "We have learned that there were two abductors; one is named Bruno. The council tribunal charged the army with investigating the murder, and Captain Ghetti of the Judicial Unit is leading the effort. He and his team are pursuing the matter vigorously, so we are hopeful that he will catch the killers soon."

Tollino nodded and asked, "What brings you here today?"

"We believe that Signor Salvetti's murder was related to Medici bank business. The bank is working on a financing proposal for the canal expansion project, and a rival bank may want to remove the Medici bank from the competition. I would like to know which other banks have shown interest in the canal project."

Tollino replied, "I am aware of the canal expansion, but I have no detailed knowledge of the project. Expenditures for programs such as canals are the purview of the Financial Chancery."

Tollino summoned a messenger and dispatched him with instructions to get the name of the person administering the canal project. "The Financial Chancery is not far," Tollino said to Nico. "The messenger will return shortly." While they waited, Tollino quizzed Nico about life in Florence following the death of Cosimo de Medici.

"There was a brief struggle for power among the wealthy elite, but supporters of Cosimo's son Piero are now firmly in control of the Signoria," Nico explained. "As you know, Piero is not well. Some say he is already grooming his son Lorenzo to succeed him."

"Governments alternate between periods of stability and times of turmoil," Tollino said. "We in Milan are fortunate that Duke Sforza has brought peace and stability to the duchy for the past decade."

The messenger returned and handed a note to Tollino. He unfolded the paper, read it, and frowned. "This is not good news. The administrator responsible for administering canal projects rarely shares information with others. Some say he fears that disclosing information might somehow reveal his incompetence."

"Is he incompetent?" Nico asked, startled by Tollino's comment.

"I don't believe so. I suspect insecurity is the cause of his fear," Tollino replied. Nico stayed silent, unsure how to respond. Moments later, Tollino's face brightened. "The Ducal Engineer, Bertola da Novate, is the designer of the canals. He will have met with any potential financiers to describe his plans for the expansion. If you approach him properly, he might reveal the names of the interested banks."

"You said, 'approach him properly.' What does that mean?" Nico asked.

Tollino explained, "As a lawyer, you are concerned with facts and evidence. The men you associate with, investigators and magistrates, live in that same world. Others, artists, for example, live in a different realm. Theirs is the world of imagination and creativity."

Tollino's words made Nico recall when his artist friend, Sandro Botticelli, pointed out differences between mediocre and exceptional paintings. Sandro saw qualities in paintings that Nico had never noticed.

Tollino said, "Engineers straddle both worlds. They deal with facts, such as the laws of physics, and they use creativity to innovate. Signor da Novate will be more open to sharing factual information with you if he sees that you appreciate his creativity." Nico nodded as he absorbed Tollino's advice. "Show him that you appreciate his accomplishments," Tollino added.

Tollino' suggestion made Nico think of Bianca. She also straddled two worlds. She was an artist who not only created beautiful dress designs of her own, she could look at another designer's creations and tell whether a particular design element was a simple embellishment or the beginning of a new fashion trend. She was also a business woman who supervised the work of girls in her employ and labored to satisfy her customers. Nico recognized and appreciated both of her abilities.

Nico said, "I understand. I will do that." Tollino gave Nico directions to da Novate's office and wished him success.

37

DUCAL ENGINEER'S OFFICE, MILAN

Nico climbed to Signor da Novate's office on the second level of a building not far from Duke Sforza's castle. The office door was propped open by a small wooden model of a trebuchet sitting on the floor. Nico stopped at the threshold and scanned other models that were scattered around the room's periphery. He looked from one model to the next, bemused that he had no notion what purpose some of the devices served. They proved Tollino's claim that engineer Novate dwelt in a realm of innovation foreign to Nico's own experiences.

At the center of the room, three men studied a drawing spread across a worktable. One of them had gray hair and gray stubble at his chin. Nico guessed him to be Signor da Novate. A fourth man carrying an armful of rolled drawings paused as he passed Nico and asked, "May I help you?"

"I am Messer Nico Argenti. I wish to speak with Signor da Novate."

Nico held out his official letter of introduction. The man scanned it without taking it from Nico's outstretched hand. "I will convey your request to the maestro," he said, before proceeding to a pigeonhole cabinet where he filed the documents he had been carrying. He crossed the room to the worktable, made a brief statement–he was too far away for Nico to hear his words–and then continued with his duties. Da Novate's eyes darkened as if a shadow had brushed his face, suggesting that he did not welcome interruptions. He glanced in Nico's direction, then returned his attention to instructing his associates. To pass the time while he waited, Nico examined the drawings covering the wall near him. The papers had yellowed with age, and their edges were cracked and curled. The finely inked lines had not degraded, so the original words and symbols were perfectly legible, but Nico could discern only some of the changes that had been added in chalk and faded over time.

One set of drawings depicted a canal with each numbered sheet representing a section of the whole. Nico found other sketches, those of machines, more intriguing, in part because deducing their purpose presented a challenge. Studying one drawing, he wondered whether the machine might be related to canals. The answer came from a voice behind him. "That is a dredge."

Nico whirled around to see the scowling face of Signor da Novate. The engineer had strong, chiseled features. He wore a meticulously tailored pale blue tunic of high-quality silk. Nico pointed to an item on the drawing and said, "This must be the barge." Then sliding his finger to target a different item, he said, "and this must be the scoop." He paused a moment before adding, "But I don't understand how it works. What makes it move?"

Nico turned back to the engineer, whose scowl had vanished. "That sketch shows only part of the dredge," Da Novate explained. He pointed to a different drawing. "The barge connects to this wheel," he tapped his finger on the paper, "which is turned by a horse or an ox."

As Tollino had predicted, da Novate's demeanor softened upon seeing Nico's interest in his work. Pressing that advantage, Nico asked, "Is this your design?"

"It is one of my earliest, done while I was a student at Padua. My professor agreed that the design is sound, but he judged it to be too complex. 'Simplification is the supreme elegance' was his motto." Da Novate's reverie lasted only a moment before he turned away from the drawing. "My assistant said you carry the credentials of a Florentine envoy. Did the embassy send you?"

The previous evening, Massimo had offered Nico advice. "Stretch the truth if you must," Massimo had said. Nico found Massimo's words amusing since he had witnessed how easily Massimo could stretch the truth. Still, Nico accepted the advice and had fabricated a pretense to explain his purpose in visiting the engineer

"Thank you for speaking with me, Signor da Novate. I am not with the embassy. I am a representative of the Florentine Signoria. My mission is to examine the practices of Florentine banks operating in the duchy to make certain that they operate with integrity and in compliance with Florentine laws."

Nico decided to take a risk by speculating. "The reason for calling upon you is that I understand two Florentine banks are interested in financing the canal expansion project."

"That is so," da Novate replied. "I have presented the project plan to officers of the Medici and Strozzi banks."

"Have those banks already submitted their competitive proposals?" The engineer raised an eyebrow. "Competitive proposals? No, they are not in competition. The canal expansion is a major undertaking. No single bank would be able to finance the entire project. The Baldesi bank in Venice has also expressed interest in providing funding. The canal project will require the participation of all three banks."

"Why is the project so expensive?" Nico asked.

"People think canals are made simply by digging big ditches. That would be so if the ground were perfectly flat and the soil soft, but look around. The world has hills and giant boulders. This project will extend the Martesana canal to reach the Adda River. The route goes through an area with numerous hills. The canal grade must be precise, and locks will be needed to control the water flow. Nothing of this complexity has ever been done before." Da Novate guided Nico to a mechanical model sitting atop a side table. "This is a replica of the locks that will be used in the new sections. The design is a major improvement over the existing locks because a single person can operate the gates," the engineer said proudly. He demonstrated by depressing a lever that swung open the model gate.

Nico found the discussion to be mildly interesting, but it was not relevant to his purpose. He already had the information that he needed: the project needed funding from all three banks, so none had reason to dissuade the Medici bank from bidding on the project. Nico took the first opportunity to thank the engineer for his hospitality politely and excused himself.

Nico met Massimo for lunch at a trattoria. The contessa's chef had prepared an ample breakfast for the men only a few hours earlier, so neither man was especially hungry. A simple midday meal would suffice. The trattoria owner welcomed the two patrons and guided them to a table. "My crusty bread and hearty beet soup are the best to make you forget the cold outside." Both men nodded their approval. The owner rubbed his hands together and headed to the kitchen.

"I took your advice," Nico said with a guilty smile. "I stretched the truth by telling Signor da Novate that I was sent by the Signoria to look for improper business practices by the Florentine banks."

Massimo's outburst of laughter attracted the attention of other patrons. "That is more than a slight distortion of the truth; it is an outright fabrication." Nico reddened with embarrassment. Massimo jested, "Continue honing your skill until you can tell falsehoods without realizing you are doing so. Then you will be worthy of being an army officer. As I recall, your father was an army officer. You may have inherited a talent for deception from him. He would be proud of you. I am proud of you."

Conversation stopped briefly when a server appeared carrying two bowls of steaming beet soup. Nico inhaled the earthy aroma of beets and herbs he could not identify. He took advantage of the server's interruption to shift the discussion. "Signor da Novate was surprisingly forthcoming. Without my asking, he mentioned the names of the three banks that are interested in funding the canal expansion project."

"He is an engineer; he may not appreciate how fiercely businesses compete with each other," Massimo ventured.

"He said the banks are not competing with each other. The project is a massive undertaking that needs funding from all three banks. It is unlikely that the abductions and the pressure on the Medici bank are related to the canal project."

"Eliminating one possibility is progress. Portinari told you about two promising candidates. What is the other one?" Massimo asked.

"The importation of merino wool from Castile," Nico replied.

Massimo sighed and said, "Merchants have been importing wool forever. In years past, they bought wool in France and the

Netherlands. Now merchants buy their fleece in England. That transition was inconsequential, so why would anyone care if they start obtaining wool from Castile? The whole business seems mundane; hardly a reason for killing."

"I share your sentiment, but Signor Tollino gave me the name of a wool merchant who is a major proponent of the project. He is one of those who met with Signor Enriquez, the Admiral of Castile. I want to be thorough, so I intend to call upon the merchant later to get his perspective. Would you like to join me?"

"As much as I enjoy your company," Massimo quipped, "I am going to continue watching Signor Portinari."

"Do you lack faith in the 'hawks' assigned by Captain Ghetti?"

"They are soldiers, so I give them the benefit of trust. Still, I place the most trust in my own eyes."

Nico and Massimo went their separate ways after lunch. Nico headed to a palazzo where members of the wholesale wool merchants' organization meet to discuss matters of mutual interest. He was received in the lobby by a man who called himself a steward of the organization. "Is Signor Martino della Torre available?" Nico asked.

The self-important steward replied in a dismissive tone, "Signor della Torre keeps a busy schedule. If you give me your name, I will try to arrange an appointment."

Once again, Nico was thankful for the coaching Massimo gave him. "I am Messer Nico Argenti. I represent the Republic of Florence regarding the Medici bank financing of fleece imports from Castile." With a flourish, Nico flashed his letter of introduction, but he did not hand it to the steward; he merely waved it in the air. "It will be in Signor della Torre's interest to meet with me if he wishes his project to proceed swiftly."

The steward was momentarily speechless, awed by Nico's words and credentials. "Wait here. I will see if the Signor can be interrupted." A minute later, the steward returned and announced, "Signor della Torre has consented to meet with you." Then he conducted Nico to an anteroom where Signor della Torre sat before a table spread with tarot cards. Della Torre rose to welcome his visitor. "My wife enjoys the tarot, but I do not get the sense of it," the merchant said as he brushed the cards aside. "I was told that you represent the government of Florence. I am curious what interest the Florentine government has in business dealings between Milan and Castile."

"The Medici bank is an independent entity, but it is also a pillar of the Florentine economy. For that reason, the Florentine Signoria needs assurances that the bank operates prudently and does not undertake excessive risk or invest in questionable ventures." Not wanting to arouse the merchant's hostility, Nico continued, "Be assured that these reviews of banking practice are routine and in no way imply any inappropriate behavior by the Medici bank or its clients."

The merchant gestured for Nico to take a seat near him and asked, "How can I assist your inquiry?"

Nico leaned back, relieved that della Torre's demeanor was agreeable, unlike the officious steward. He chose to approach the merchant with the same pretense he had used with the engineer. "I understand that three banks have shown interest in financing the business venture with Castile."

Della Torre looked puzzled. "If that is so, then your sources have an insight that I lack."

Nico realized his ploy had failed. He struggled to think about how he should reply if the merchant asked for the names of the three banks. Although Nico did not see her,

Goddess Fortuna must have smiled at him, because he was spared that indignity. Instead of asking for names, della Torre said, "We have discussed terms only with the Medici bank. Some of our members suggested that we approach the Bank of San Giorgio in Genoa, but we have not. The proposal from the Medici bank satisfies all our needs. Our organization wishes to cultivate a long-term relationship with the Medici bank. We see no advantage in pitting one bank against another."

Nico recovered, saying, "Clearly then, my source is mistaken." He shifted his focus. "You emphasized the desire for long-term relationships, so you must have high confidence that the venture will be profitable."

Della Torre rose from his seat, crossed the room, and extracted a hank of fleece from a cabinet. He returned to the couch and handed the fleece to Nico. "Have you ever felt anything so soft? Everyone in the wool business is amazed when they first touch merino wool, but even you, a layman, must appreciate its richness. Fabric made from merino wool is not scratchy like cloth from English wool. We have negotiated exclusive rights to merino wool with representatives of the King of Castile. So yes, we expect this to be a profitable long-term relationship."

"My understanding is that Castilian ships will carry the fleece from Castile to the port of Genoa. Is that so?" Nico asked.

"Your source got that fact correct. Our Genovese friends are not pleased with that arrangement. The wanted Genovese ships to transport the fleece, but we had no alternative. The Kingdom of Castile was adamant on that condition."

The merchant smiled as he watched Nico fingering the fleece. "The shipping arrangements are of little consequence to us. Castile is not far from Genoa, so shipping costs will be small, certainly much smaller than the cost of bringing wool from England." Della Torre's words echoed the claims made by Admiral Enriquez.

"When do you expect shipments to begin?" Nico asked.

"Representatives of the kingdom have already approved the agreement, and wool producers in Castile have warehouses filled with fleece ready for shipment. The directors of our organization meet tomorrow to give their approval. Merino fleece should start arriving in Milan within weeks."

Nico's spirit sank. In neither of the projects cited by Portinari was there a hint that another bank had reason to subvert the involvement of the Medici bank. He decided to ask della Torre directly about potential detractors. "Are there any who oppose the project?"

The merchant stiffened, startled by the unexpected question. "No," he said slowly as he thought about the prospect. "All of our merchants are in favor, and the Ducal Council supports the project. Sheep ranchers in Castile and the Crown of Castile will benefit. The Genovese will carry the fleece overland from their port to Milan. There is more demand for wool than the English can provide so they will not be harmed." He shook his head. "I cannot think of anyone who would have reason to oppose the project."

A cold wind lashed Nico as he exited the palazzo. He pulled his cloak tight and headed back toward the guest house. Alone with his thoughts, he struggled to understand why he had failed to uncover a motive for the abductions. Portinari had cited four projects that could have drawn competitors. Nico had examined the two most likely candidates and found no competition. Had he not probed deeply enough? Or was there another motive for the crimes?

38

NEAR THE MEDICI BANK, MILAN

Massimo had followed Portinari from the Palazzo Torelli guest house to the Medici bank in the morning, anticipating that the conspirators might contact the banker. He felt they would act quickly, but the morning passed without incident. Late in the day, Massimo again positioned himself to watch Portinari as he returned to the palazzo. Massimo saw men leave the bank at the end of their workday while he waited for Portinari, who would be the last to leave the bank. Massimo could not see Captain Ghetti's hawks, but he knew they were ready to react if anyone approached Portinari as he left the building. Massimo assumed the hawks were stationed near the bank, so he took a position a fair distance from the bank along the route that Portinari would walk to reach the guest house. Other than the departing bank employees and a young boy amusing himself with a ball, the street was empty.

Portinari emerged from the bank, tested the door to be sure it locked behind him, and headed along the street toward the narrow alley where Massimo hid. As Portinari approached the boy, the youngster ran to the banker, pressed a paper into his hand, turned, and ran. Massimo saw the hawks spring from cover and chase the fleeing child.

The youth's path took him directly toward Massimo. When the boy came near, Massimo stepped from his hiding place, reached his arm across the boy's chest, and lifted the urchin into the air. The boy's legs kept pumping before he realized that he was motionless. Finally, he went limp and looked up at the man who was holding him. By then, the hawks, Davini and Gelmo, were standing alongside Massimo.

Massimo set the boy down and released him while Gelmo gripped the youngster's collar to prevent him from running away. Portinari had stopped walking as soon as the note was delivered. When he regained his composure, he looked ahead and saw, in the distance, the boy, Massimo, and two other men. He walked toward the group, and when he reached them, he handed the paper to Massimo.

Massimo introduced the hawks to Portinari and then read the message aloud. "If you want your wife returned, withdraw the proposal to finance wool purchases from Castile." Massimo put an arm around Portinari's shoulders. "You can ignore this ultimatum. Captain Ghetti has already rescued Stefana. She and your maid are now at Santa Marta convent."

Disbelief in Portinari's eyes gave way to hope. "Is she unharmed?" he stammered. "Are they both unharmed?"

Massimo assured him that the women were safe. Gelmo said, "I will take you to your wife at the convent."

After the two men departed, Massimo and Davini turned their attention to the boy. The shabbily dressed urchin looked down, his head bent forward and his shoulders hunched. He had never been close to an army officer, and now one held him with a powerful grip. "Who gave you this note?" Davini asked. The boy replied so softly that neither man could hear him.

Massimo bent down. He lifted the youngster's chin so he

could look the boy in the eye and repeated Davini's question. "Who gave you this note?"

"A man." The boy held out a two denari coin. "He gave me this. He said I should give the note to the man who locked the door at the bank."

"Can you describe the man? What did he look like?"

"He was just a man. He didn't look special." Tears welled up in the boy's eyes. He hesitated and then said, "There was one thing. When he gave me the coin, I saw one of his fingers was too short."

"Too short," Massimo echoed.

"Yes. His middle finger. The end of it was missing."

Following Massimo's lead, Davini dropped to one knee and asked, "Where did the man give the note to you?"

"At a trattoria near where I live."

"Which trattoria? What is the name of the trattoria?" Massimo asked.

"I don't know the name. It has a blue sign with a bird."

"I know the place. It is Trattoria Angelo in the Porta Romana district," Davini said.

The youth looked sheepishly at Davini and asked, "Did I do something wrong? Are you going to take my coin?"

"You did nothing wrong. You may keep the coin." Davini reached into his pocket and withdrew a five denari coin. "And here is another coin as a reward for helping with an army investigation. You can go." The boy pocketed both coins and scampered away.

Davini led Massimo through the city to the Porta Romana district. On a short side street, an aging blue sign hung above the entrance of a small shop. Lettered across the sign was the single word 'Angelo' and above was a drawing of a nondescript bird.

It was too early for dinner, so the men were not surprised to find no customers inside when they entered. The only occupant was a middle-aged woman wearing a white apron and carrying a stack of soup bowls. She set the bowls on a nearby table and turned to greet the men. "Dinner will be in one hour. Delicious vegetable soup."

Massimo looked through a doorway into the kitchen area where a man was chopping vegetables. He said to the woman, "We would like to speak with Angelo."

She said indifferently, "You can find him at the cemetery in Brolo," then she burst out in hearty laughter and explained, "Angelo was my husband's father. He owned the trattoria until he died more than twenty years past. In his honor, we keep his name. Everyone in the neighborhood knows Trattoria Angelo. You may speak with my husband, Lucio, if you wish."

"Perhaps you can help us," Davini said. "We are looking for a man, one of your customers. The only description we have of him is that one of his fingers is deformed. The tip of his middle finger is missing."

Recognition flashed in the woman's eyes. "I know him. His name is Pagatore...at least that's what he is called. He is here often. Always he comes alone and keeps to himself."

"Pagatore," Massimo repeated. He turned to Davini and said, "That's the name Bruno mentioned," then to the woman, he asked, "Do you know where we can find Pagatore?"

"He lives above the clothing shop at the end of the street. Has he done something wrong?"

"We need to ask him some questions," Davini replied.

They thanked the woman and walked to the clothing shop. Inside, a cheerful older man greeted them. "I have some excellent silk tunics in the newest styles."

Not wanting to waste time in banter, Davini asked directly, "Does a man named Pagatore live in this building?"

The man nodded his head vigorously. "Yes. He has the apartment on the third level."

Massimo fingered the collar of a light green tunic hanging on a rack. "Maybe later," he said to the owner as he and Davini left the shop.

They climbed to the third level and listened at the door but heard no sound from within the apartment. "Pagatore! Open the door!" Davini shouted.

They listened again. This time they heard footsteps briefly and then again silence. Davini drove his shoulder into the door, splintering the frame and sending him crashing into the room. Massimo rushed in after him. Across the room, Pagatore leaned against a wall with his arms folded over his chest. Davini bristled, "Why didn't you open the door?"

Pagatore flashed a self-satisfied grin. "I never open the door to anyone who stands on the landing screaming at me. You might have been a drunk or a thief." He scanned Davini from head to foot. "Maybe you are a thief. Just because you're wearing a uniform doesn't prove anything. You could have bought the tunic in the clothing shop below."

The veins in Davini's neck bulged. His voice rose in volume and pitch. "Stop the shit, Pagatore. We know you paid to have the bank clerk killed and the women abducted. Bruno gave us your name."

Still trying his best to irritate the soldier, Pagatore said, "I never told him to kill anyone. He is a barbaric fool. He can't blame the killing on me."

Massimo crossed the room, grabbed Pagatore's tunic, dragged the paymaster to a chair, and shoved him down into it. "Bruno is in custody, and the women are free," Massimo snapped. He held out the paper given to Portinari. "This is the note you paid the boy to deliver to the bank manager. The scheme to pressure the Medici bank is finished."

"Is it?" Pagatore asked defiantly. "I am just a courier. I don't kill people, and I don't care about the business of the Medici bank. All I do is deliver messages, the same as the boy who gave you that note."

"No, you are not like the boy," Davini growled. "He does not comprehend the meaning of the note. I doubt that he can even read. But you understand when you pay to have people abducted. Abduction is a crime, and abduction of foreigners will draw the attention of the Privy Council."

"Ah, the Privy Council," Pagatore scoffed. "Which members of the council? Some of them are among my best customers. They are always in need of people to do the unseemly deeds they cannot do for themselves. Let me get my book, and I can read their names to you." Pagatore glared at the soldier defiantly. "Do you think any of them are going to prosecute me?" Pagatore spit on the floor.

Davini fell silent while he thought about his options. He could bring Pagatore to the army base for questioning. Interrogations of uncooperative suspects were known to last for days, while the culprit was given little chance to sleep and only moldy bread to eat. Some of Davini's compatriots resorted to violence to loosen a culprit's tongue, but he did not subscribe to that brutality.

Massimo stepped forward and offered another approach to Davini. "The victims of his crimes are Florentine citizens, and I am an envoy of the Florentine government. I could take him to Florence and put him on trial there. I doubt that any Florentine magistrates are in his book."

Davini threw his hands into the air and stepped back. "Yes, that solution is acceptable. Take him away." Davini turned and began to leave. Massimo pulled Pagatore up from the chair and shoved him toward the door.

"You can't do this," Pagatore shouted. "I'm a citizen of Milan.

You can't take me to Florence." Massimo and Davini ignored the protest. One more push sent Pagatore out of the apartment and onto the stairway landing. "Stop, stop!" His tone had shifted from protest to pleading. "What do you want to know? I'll tell you."

Massimo slammed Pagatore against the wall. "Who paid you to arrange the abductions and to deliver the note to the bank manager?"

With Massimo's hand pressed against his chest, Pagatore struggled to speak, barely managing to say, "He calls himself the Intermediary."

"Where can we find this Intermediary?" Massimo barked.

"I don't know. I swear, I don't know. He comes to the trattoria when he has a job for me. That is the only time I see him."

"Describe him. What does he look like?" Massimo continued.

"He's thin. He has bulging eyes and a hooked nose. Something's wrong with his legs because he shakes when he walks. Every time I've seen him, he was wearing a dark gray tunic."

Massimo looked to Davini, who said, "I don't know of anyone who fits that description, but I can have the podestà circulate the description among the guardia in Milan."

Massimo released his hold on Pagatore and said to Davini. "It's a long ride back to Florence, and I'd rather not have this low-life's company on the journey. I trust the duchy can find a way to dispense a fitting punishment for him."

Davini dragged Pagatore back into the apartment. "The book you mentioned. The one with the names of your clients. Where is it? Perhaps you are unaware, but Duke Sforza is eager to eliminate corruption in his government. When he sees the names in your book, your council member clients will be worrying about their own asses. They won't be concerned about saving yours."

39

BASILICA SANT'AMBROGIO, MILAN

An old priest hunched over his broom as he cleared leaves from under the portico at the Basilica of Sant'Ambrogio. He swept in short strokes with barely enough force to propel the leaves. "May I help you, Father?" Vittorio said as he reached for the broom that the priest gratefully relinquished. The old one moved aside and watched Vittorio make short work of the task. "Bless you, my son. The Lord will remember your act of kindness." When Vittorio did not turn to leave, the priest's lips curled up in a knowing smile. He said, "You are here for a purpose. How may I help you?"

The Medici bank clerk had told Vittorio the name of the woman he had married and the name of the church where they were married. Before confronting the woman and her father, who had demanded that the dowry be returned, Vittorio wanted evidence that the marriage was a fraud. He said, "A woman named Giulia Nardelli was married recently in this basilica. Would it be possible for me to see the marriage record?"

The priest's eyes narrowed as he processed the unusual

request. Marriage records were not private but rarely did anyone ask to see them. "Come with me," he said without emotion and led Vittorio to an office at the rear of the church. He scanned boxes filling the shelves of a cabinet. "Ah, this one," he said as he removed one of the boxes and placed it on a table. "These are the records of marriages, baptisms, and deaths for the past three years." He gestured for Vittorio to come closer. "My eyesight is not good. You may search for the record you seek. The most recent ones are in front."

Vittorio thumbed through the papers until he found a sheet that listed Giulia Nardelli as the wife and the bank clerk as the husband. He removed the page from the box to view it carefully. Alongside the notation Sacrament of Matrimony was the date given to Vittorio by the clerk. Vittorio read aloud the barely legible signature of the priest who performed the ceremony. "Friar S. Possini. Is Friar Possini a priest in this parish?"

"I do not know a Friar Possini," the priest replied.

Vittorio carried the paper to a window to avail himself of brighter light. Squinting, he said, "Rossini. It could be Friar Rossini."

The priest clapped his hands together triumphantly. "Yes, there is a Friar, but he is not here at Sant'Ambrogio."

"Is it unusual for a priest who is not of this parish to officiate a wedding at the basilica?" Vittorio asked.

"No, not at all. The friar could be a friend or relative of the husband or wife."

"There is a notation on the sheet," Vittorio said. "The word is 'oratory.'"

"The oratory is a small chapel separate from the basilica. Small weddings and baptisms are held there. Many couples prefer to be married in the chapel's intimate surroundings. I can show you if you wish," the priest offered.

Vittorio was more interested in the friar's whereabouts.

"Where can I find Friar Rossini? Do you know his parish?" he asked.

"I have never met him, but I have heard that he serves the Lord by praying with the sick at hospitals. Others like him bring the word of God to children at orphanages. Those monks have no parishes." The priest bowed his head and crossed himself. "Facing constant misery and suffering as they do requires great devotion and deep faith." He returned his eyes to Vittorio and said, "To find Friar Rossini, you would have to ask at the hospitals."

Vittorio nodded to acknowledge his understanding, but he felt discouraged because it might take considerable time to find the monk. He returned the paper to the box. Then he casually thumbed through the other records. His eyes widened upon seeing another record dated six months earlier that also listed Giulia Nardelli as the wife. He scanned the page incredulously. It bore the same signature, Friar S. Rossini, but the name of the husband was different.

Vittorio pulled the record from the box and read it aloud. The priest's jaw dropped open. He crossed himself and blurted, "Madonna, Holy Mother of God."

"Could this marriage have been annulled?" Vittorio asked.

"No. No. Annulments are granted only under the most extreme circumstances. If the marriage had been annulled, I would know it. There has never been an annulment at Sant'Ambrogio."

Vittorio read the husband's name. "Do you know him? Is he a member of this parish?"

"No, he is not one of our parishioners." The priest paused, then opened his eyes wide. "There is a well-respected family in Milan with that name. The patriarch is an official of the guild of stonemasons. The guild has been very generous with donations to the church." His brow furrowed as he added, "It is a large family."

Vittorio returned his attention to the box and continued searching through the records. Slowly he moved back in time: ten months, one year. At sixteen months, the name Giulia Nardelli again looked up at him. He pulled that card and read it. The priest slumped. Vittorio caught the old man before he fell to the floor and guided him to a chair. Vittorio read the signature, S. Rossini. "This is terrible," the priest moaned. "How could Friar Rossini commit such a sin? He could be excommunicated."

Vittorio read the name of the husband. With a flash of recognition, the priest said, "Yes, he is one of our parishioners. He makes candles. All the candles in the basilica come from his shop. He became the owner when his father died a few years past." The priest watched anxiously while Vittorio looked through the remaining records, but further searching revealed no additional sheets with the name Giulia Nardelli.

Vittorio debated whether to search for the friar before approaching Giulia Nardelli. Although there were only two or three hospitals in Milan, monasteries and convents also ministered to the sick. If Friar Rossini also visited those clinics, finding the monk could require a prolonged hunt. Vittorio's investigative instincts told him it is always better to get as much information as possible before confronting a suspect, so he opted for a compromise: he would inquire at the three hospitals. If those queries proved fruitless, then he would turn his attention to the woman.

As he walked from the basilica to Ca'Grande, Milan's largest hospital, Vittorio reviewed his experience at the basilica. The three marriage records fueled his suspicion that Giulia Nardelli engaged in fraud. She seduced men who could pay to avoid a scandal. Her father endowed each union with a substantial dowry; then, she convinced her gullible husband to spend the sum on lavish gifts for her. After the money was gone, she abandoned her husband and fled with the gifts. Her father claimed that his daughter had been wronged and demanded that the dowry be repaid. The husbands acceded to the extortion to avoid being painted with accusations of infidelity or impotence. Giulia's choice of the bank clerk as a target did not fit the scam's usual pattern. Unlike her other 'husbands,' the bank clerk was not wealthy enough to repay the dowry after buying lavish gifts for his bride. The clerk had been selected for a different purpose, and Friar Rossini might know that purpose.

A nun greeted Vittorio when he entered Ca'Grande hospital. In response to his question about Friar Rossini, the nun said, "He comes here for two days every week. Yesterday he spent the entire day praying and giving comfort to those in the ward. His words lift the spirits of the most unfortunate who have no hope. If anyone deserves sainthood, it is Friar Rossini."

"Do you know where I might find the friar today?" Vittorio asked.

"Today, he is visiting the Ambrosian monastery. Friar Rossini is not an Ambrosian, but he visits sick children being cared for at the monastery. Yesterday he showed me rosary beads that he planned to give to a young girl at the monastery."

The nun gave Vittorio directions to the Ambrosian monastery. It was a fair distance outside the city, so Vittorio thanked the nun and rushed out into the street, hoping he could reach the infirmary before Friar Rossini departed. As Vittorio passed through the city gate, a farm wagon came up behind him. The driver had sold his goods at the city market and was returning to his farm. Vittorio called to the driver. "The Ambrosian monastery. Might you be going near there?" The driver slowed the wagon and motioned for Vittorio to climb aboard.

When he reached the monastery, a monk led Vittorio to the room where Friar Rossini was talking with a bedridden girl. They were engaged in a conversation that made the girl's smile overpower her sad eyes. Vittorio stopped outside the room, not wanting to intrude on their privacy. "Friar Rossini will be out soon," the monk said. "The girl needs her rest."

Vittorio waited in the corridor until the friar appeared; then he said, "Friar, I wish to speak with you about Giulia Nardelli." Upon hearing the woman's name, the monk stiffened, and a vein in his neck pulsed rapidly. "Let us speak outside," Rossini replied.

They walked to a garden–just a dirt patch at this time of year–behind the monastery. Vittorio introduced himself as a Florentine envoy who was investigating irregularities at the Medici bank. "Records at Sant'Ambrogio basilica show that you married Signora Nardelli to a clerk at the Medici bank. The records also show that you extended the Sacrament of Holy Matrimony to the Nardelli woman three times. I cannot imagine what would make a servant of God commit such a sacrilege."

The friar's face turned ashen. He sat on a stone bench, looked up at Vittorio, and spoke with difficulty. "Giulia lives with Domenico, my brother. All his life, since he was a young boy, trouble found Domenico. He always chose fraud and deception over honest work. And now he has ensnared Giulia in his latest scheme."

"And you?" Vittorio questioned.

"Yes, me too." Rossini's voice sputtered, and his words came slowly. "Guilia is not Domenico's daughter; she is my daughter. When I was a young priest, there was a woman in my parish who..." He paused to reflect. "I lost my way to the temptation of the flesh. Giulia lived with her mother until three years past when her mother died. Domenico said he would provide for

Giulia. I knew his generosity would have a price, but I had no choice but to agree; she could not survive on her own."

"So, your solution was to desecrate the Sacrament of Matrimony and make your own daughter into a bigamist?" Vittorio responded harshly.

"I did not. I could not do such a thing."

"I saw the records," Vittorio protested.

"They are just pieces of paper, and yes, I am guilty of signing those papers. But I did not celebrate the sacrament. I performed the ceremonies in Latin, so none of those present could understand. I gave a blessing and asked God's forgiveness, but I did not marry them." His body shifted in discomfort at his own rationalization.

The friar's words baffled Vittorio even further. Is it better that you send your daughter to live in sin, Vittorio wondered, but he said nothing and waited for Rossini to continue. "I never thought anyone would ever see the records. No one ever looks at old records. I did it for Giulia. *Mea culpa.*" After a long silence, Rossini met Vittorio's eyes and asked, "What will happen now?"

Vittorio answered in a stiff voice. "That is between you, Giulia, and God, but if she were my daughter, I wouldn't want her to be a criminal and a fornicator. My interest is in finding someone called the Intermediary, and I believe your brother can lead me to him." Vittorio turned to go, leaving the friar with his conscience.

From the Ambrosian monastery, Vittorio returned to the city and headed directly to the address that Friar Rossini had given him for Giulia's father–whom he now knew to be her uncle. The apartment was on the second level above a butcher shop in a shabby section of the city. Vittorio pounded on the door until it opened just enough for a seedy, unshaven face to peer out. "Domenico?" Vittorio growled.

"What?" the face snarled.

Vittorio shouldered the door open with a force that drove Domenico stumbling backward into the room. Vittorio charged in and grabbed the plump man by the collar. "Are you the guardia?" Domenico grunted.

Ignoring the question, Vittorio demanded, "Tell me about the Intermediary!"

Realizing that Vittorio's vehemence was not directed at him, Domenico's muscles relaxed, and he answered plainly. "He found me. He had heard about Giulia and wanted her to seduce a man who worked at the Medici bank. He said he would pay if she could put the clerk in debt."

"Where can I find the Intermediary?" Vittorio pressed.

"If he finds out..." Vittorio twisted Domenico's collar tightly, choking off his response and turning his face white.

"Where can I find him?" Vittorio repeated. He loosened his grip enough for Domenico to respond.

"I only met him twice. Both times he sent messages for me to meet him at a tavern, *Il Cuculo Verde*, The Green Cuckoo." Vittorio lifted Domenico into the air, shook him, and then threw him against a wall. "Knowing the meeting place tells me nothing. I want to find him now."

Domenico slid to the floor and made no attempt to rise. "After our meeting, I watched him leave. He crossed the street and walked only a short distance. There is a problem with his leg, so it is hard for him to walk. He entered a building... Let me think. There was a shop..." Another pause. "The shop sold metal things, mugs, and utensils. He must live above that shop."

Vittorio stepped back, put clenched hands on his hips, and snarled, "Never again include Giulia in your demented crimes. If you do, I will see that you rot in prison until you meet the devil." He turned and stormed out of the apartment.

Outside, he pondered his next move. Ideally, he should

inform Captain Ghetti before taking any action, but that would mean traveling to Camp Giorgi. He dismissed that possibility because he was eager to apprehend the Intermediary, and going to the army camp would take time. He chose a different option, stopping at Palazzo Torelli to get directions to *Il Cucolo Verde* from the contessa's servants.

Nico looked up from his notebook when Vittorio entered the palazzo guest house and said cheerfully, "I had a successful morning with the canal engineer and the wool merchant." Nico stopped speaking abruptly upon noticing Vittorio's excited state.

"I know how to find the Intermediary," Vittorio announced. "And I believe he is the key to finding who is behind the abductions and Salvetti's murder."

Nico suggested, "We should inform Captain Ghetti."

"Later. I want to catch the bastard before he can flee." Vittorio turned to leave, and Nico rose to follow him.

The directions given to Vittorio brought them across the city to Palazzo Marliani, a large and easily recognized landmark. At the next intersection, they turned right and walked until they spotted *Il Cucolo Verde*. Vittorio stopped in front of the tavern and surveyed the storefronts opposite: a butcher, a jeweler, and a metalware shop. Nico caught sight of a sign in the jewelry store window, Alpine Garnets. He was about to comment when Vittorio pointed to the metalware shop and said, "He lives above that shop."

The building had three levels with enough space to accommodate at least two apartments on each of the upper levels. The storekeeper eyed the two men approaching his shop. The door was open only a crack when he began his pitch. "We have an excellent assortment of copper items. All are of the finest quality. They are sure to please you or a favorite person." He gestured toward the disk on the wall behind him. "This plaque won the coveted artist award at the guild fair in Cremona. Look at the exquisite detail."

Vittorio gave the briefest glance at the engraved copper plate before returning his attention to the shopkeeper. "Perhaps another time," he said. "We are looking for a man called the Intermediary. He lives in this building."

"I don't know the tenants," the store owner replied. "They come and go. Most don't stay long."

Nico explained, "He has a hooked nose and has difficulty walking."

"I may have seen someone like that, but I can't say his name. Maybe one of the other tenants can help you." As they turned to leave the shop, he called after them, "All the copper items are on sale. You won't find better prices anywhere."

They climbed the stairs, and when they reached the second level, Vittorio declared, "I'll knock on doors until he answers or until someone tells us where to find him."

They paused at the nearest apartment door and heard the sound of a young child within. Vittorio rapped on the door, and moments later, a woman's voice called through the closed door. "Who is there?"

"We are looking for a man with a hooked nose who has difficulty walking," Vittorio replied.

The woman responded tersely, "Upstairs."

At the top level, a man's voice came from one of the apartments. Nico pressed his ear to the door. "He is singing," Nico announced. Both men agreed the occupant was not likely to be the Intermediary.

Vittorio listened at the second apartment, then shook his head and said, "Nothing." With his confidence building that this must be the Intermediary's apartment, he banged loudly on the door but drew no response. Vittorio turned sideways, preparing to shoulder the door open.

Nico raised his hand, stepped forward, and thumbed the latch. It popped up, and the door swung inward. A smell like sour cheese assaulted Nico before he set foot into the single room apartment. A quick survey showed the austere room was unoccupied.

Vittorio entered, walked directly to the wardrobe cabinet, and pulled its doors open. "Empty," he said, as much to himself as to Nico. In a corner of the room, a soiled tunic lay on the floor. "He's gone," Vittorio said more forcefully.

Nico heard a scratching sound near his feet. He looked down to see a mouse scurrying past with a bit of paper in its mouth. Other torn pieces of paper were scattered across the floor. Nico gathered the scraps and spread them on a table. "These are from a letter," Nico declared.

Vittorio joined Nico, and the two men arranged the scraps to read the writing. The mouse had taken most of the pieces to use as nesting material, so the men had only a few remaining fragments. The word *bank* appeared on one piece, and another held the word *next*. The largest piece showed two words, *leave Milan*. A scrap from the left edge of the page had the letters *Maur*. "It could be a name. Possibly the Intermediary's name is Maurizio," Nico speculated.

Vittorio lifted one piece to examine it closely. "This is from the bottom of the page," he said. "The letters must be the sender's initials. The first letter is definitely an *S,* and the second letter appears to be an *R.*

Nico peered over Vittorio's shoulder. Recalling Captain Ghetti's observations, he declared, "The sender is a Florentine!" Seeing Vittorio's surprise, Nico flashed a knowing smile and said, "Florentines and Milanese style their letters differently. A Florentine penned this letter S."

Both men dropped to their knees and inspected the floor, hoping to find more writing. Finally, after finding no additional scraps of paper, Vittorio stood and exclaimed, "Damn! I wanted to catch the bastard, but all we have are a few bits of paper."

Nico's brow furrowed and he was silent for several minutes; then he exclaimed. "Florence! Wool!" Vittorio's eyes narrowed as he tried to process Nico's outburst. "Florentine wool businesses are the ones that will suffer if Milan has access to superior Castilian wool. The Intermediary must have been sent by the owner of a woolen mill in Florence," Nico explained

Vittorio nodded then scowled. "But it appears that the Intermediary has fled Milan. He has escaped."

Nico ran a hand through his hair. "There may be nothing else we can do in Milan, but we are not finished. We still need to find the Intermediary ... Maurizio, if that's his name, and the S.R. person."

"In Florence?" Vittorio questioned.

"Yes, in Florence," Nico answered.

Vittorio's expression showed his skepticism. "The crimes were committed in Milan. How can charges be brought in Florence?"

Nico grinned. "The law can be flexible. I am certain we will find a way to prosecute S.R. in Florence."

Vittorio put a hand on Nico's shoulder. He said nothing but thought, this young lawyer has grown his confidence during our brief time in Milan.

The men exited the apartment and descended to the street where Nico pointed to the sign in the nearby jewelry store window and asked, "Are you familiar with garnets?" He entered the store trailed by Vittorio. A display counter held an array of rings and bracelets adorned with brilliant deep red garnets. Nico examined the gemstones and asked, "Are the stones from Milan?"

The proud store owner replied, "Not from the city, of course, but yes, they were mined in the Duchy of Milan. In the north. The foothills of the Alps." He held up a bracelet ringed with stones for Nico to view.

"It is elegant," Nico mused, "but too fanciful for Bianca."

The shopkeeper's eyes brightened. "Ah, wait one moment," he said. Then he walked to the rear of the shop, reached into a case, and returned with a teardrop-cut garnet suspended on a thin gold chain. He held the necklace aloft to let the light dance on the stone's finely cut facets.

"The artist swears this is an exact copy of the one that Duke Sforza's daughter wore at her betrothal to the Duke of Calabria." Upon seeing Vittorio roll his eyes, the store owner admitted, "Artists sometimes exaggerate, but you must agree it is a lovely creation." Nico left the shop with a distinctly Milanese gift for his special lady.

40

DAYS LATER IN FLORENCE

Signor Mozzi and Chancellor Scala sat at a desk pouring over a document when Nico entered Mozzi's office. Mozzi waved Nico to a conference table while he continued his discussion with Scala. Nico walked across the plush carpet and sank into a thickly padded armchair. He folded his hands in his lap, not wanting to mar the shiny finish of the oak tabletop. The elegant furnishings in Mozzi's office surpassed even those of the Signoria's meeting room.

Portraits of historical figures in ornate gold frames lined opposite walls. Nico recognized only two: Cosimo de Medici and Leonardo Bruni. Using his artist friend Sandro's criteria for judging paintings, Nico judged the artwork to be originals created by masters, not copies made by fledgling apprentices. Across the room, a silver drink service, goblets, and a pitcher rested on an oak sideboard that matched the conference table patina.

Minutes later, Vittorio strode into the room and sat beside Nico. In contrast to the plain clothes he wore in Milan, Vittorio had donned a tasteful tunic embroidered at the collar and cuffs.

Nico peeked at his own unsophisticated garb and felt uneasy until he observed that Scala and Mozzi wore plain tunics, not unlike his own.

"Have you had any new thoughts since leaving Milan?" Nico asked.

Vittorio shook his head. "No. I still believe our assumption is correct that the instigator is someone in the woolen business with the initials S.R. My next step will be to search the *tassa dei traffichi*, the commercial tax records, to find the names of people with those initials."

"The tax records are stored in the chancery annex," Nico said. "Chancellor Scala can arrange for you to view them."

Nico was about to mention his plan to speak with wool guild consul Spinelli when Mozzi and Scala came to the table. "Shall we wait for Signor Leoni?" Mozzi asked.

"He was delayed in Pavia," Nico replied.

"Pavia?" Mozzi echoed quizzically.

"He stopped to visit a friend," Nico explained.

"Ah," Mozzi said, flashing a knowing smile. "Then let us begin. We... Scala, Corsini, and I... read your dispatches. We are pleased there is no longer a threat in Milan, and the Signoria will be happy to learn that their newly formed Florentine Security Commission has proven successful. However, before we meet with the Signoria, we would like to hear details of what transpired in Milan and the basis for your belief that a Florentine is responsible for the crimes."

For the next hour, Nico and Vittorio recounted their exploits with frequent interruptions by Scala and Mozzi seeking clarifications. Neither man mentioned their frosty relationship with the Florentine ambassador. When they finished their account, Mozzi said, "The positive relationship you fostered with the Milanese army and the district prosecutor may serve our republic well in the future. I will see that a letter is sent to Contessa Maddalena del Carretto expressing the Signoria's gratitude for her hospitality."

Mozzi paused to punctuate the end of the Milanese phase of the investigation; then he asked, "How will you continue pursuing the perpetrator in Florence?"

Vittorio described his plan to search the tax records, to which Scala responded by writing a note directing the chancery notaries to grant Vittorio access to the chancery annex records. Nico then told of his intention to meet with Signor Tommaso Spinelli. Mozzi sat up straight. "A good choice," he said. "Tommaso knows the full extent of the woolen business. If there are scoundrels, Tommaso can point you to them."

Nico had planned to go directly from Mozzi's office to Palazzo Spinelli, but instead he made a detour to change into more stylish clothes. Dress was never a consideration at the university; however, as a lawyer and member of an official Florentine commission, he needed to show respect for Spinelli's elite status. Nico realized that he would be violating another social norm by calling upon an upper-class gentleman without an appointment. He decided that the urgency of catching a killer gave him latitude.

Nico had no sooner pulled on the bell-rope at Palazzo Spinelli than the door swung open, and a stern-faced steward glared at him. Nico's clean, stylish tunic proved its worth because the servant did not dismiss him as a solicitor or direct him to the rear delivery entrance. The servant remained silent, waiting for Nico to state his purpose. "Messer Nico Argenti to see Signor Tommaso Spinelli on business of the Signoria."

"The master is engaged," came the frosty response, tempered only by, "You may wait if you wish."

Without knowing how long he might have to wait, Nico followed the servant to an anteroom. Tommaso Spinelli was among the wealthiest men in Florence, yet the anteroom décor was modest. A lone painting of a battlefield scene hung on one wall. Nico could not tell whether it depicted a historic battle or a confrontation between imaginary foes. Details rendered in the scene kept Nico occupied until two men engaged in spirited conversation came from the palazzo interior and passed the anteroom doorway. Their exchange faded when they exited to the street. Behind them, a third man, older, with thinning gray hair and a shuffling gait, entered the room. "I am Tommaso Spinelli," he said in a strong voice that belied his age. Nico began to rise in deference to his host, who motioned for Nico to remain seated. "What business of the Signoria brings you here?" Spinelli asked.

Nico told Spinelli of the murders and abductions in Milan. He gave a brief summary of the evidence that led him to believe that the person responsible was a Florentine with the initials S.R. "Dozens of shops in Florence take part in the woolen business," Spinelli began. "Some do only dyeing, others carding, and still others weaving. Most of them are small shops, too small to be involved in the crimes you described. I know the owners of all the large shops; they are honest, respectable men, and none have the initials S.R." Nico slumped, discouragement evident in his eyes.

Spinelli added, "You should consider the merchants who export wool cloth to Rome, Naples, Sicily, and as far as the Levant. I am not close with the merchants, but I can say there is one, only one, whose family name begins with the letter R." Nico brightened for an instant until Spinelli added, "Guido Rondelli. Guido is like me, an old man. He owns the company, but his two sons make the day-to-day decisions. Them, I do not know."

Nico raced from Palazzo Spinelli to the chancery annex. A harried notary recognized Nico and directed him to the room where Vittorio was sifting through tax records. Upon seeing Nico, Vittorio said, "I found three men in the wool trade with the initials S.R. They all must have small shops because their tax assessments were modest, so they do not have the resources to finance a series of crimes in Milan."

"Rondelli!" Nico exclaimed.

A dubious Vittorio responded, "The records do not list anyone with a wool business named Rondelli."

"Signor Rondelli is not a shop owner; he is a merchant who sells Florentine wool in other countries."

Vittorio asked a clerk for the tax records of merchants and quickly located a sizeable assessment under the name Guido Rondelli. "Guido is the owner; his two sons manage the operation," Nico explained.

"Birth records will tell the names of the sons," Vittorio said and beckoned for a clerk.

A pimply-faced clerk listened to Vittorio's request and said, "You are correct that the names are in the birth records, but I can tell you that Signor Rondelli's sons are named Stefano and Paolo."

"You know them?" Nico asked.

"Only their names. If you would like to know more, Galetto may be able to help." The clerk pointed across the room to the senior notary, whom Nico had met on a previous visit to the annex.

After introducing Vittorio, Nico said, "Galetto, we are investigating a crime and seeking information about Stefano Rondelli. He is a wool merchant and son of Guido Rondelli. The clerk said you might know him,"

Galetto's face darkened as he said, "Chancellor Scala mentioned that you were investigating the murder in Milan. Stefano Rondelli has never been accused of a crime; however, I have heard him spoken of in harsh words by other merchants. Some refuse to do business with him. They say he lacks his father's integrity."

"Who might know the details of his questionable dealings?" Vittorio asked.

"He rarely discusses his business matters with other men," Galetto said. He paused only briefly, then added, "Stefano is a woman chaser who preys on vulnerable women, courts them until he tires of their company, then discards them and moves on to his next conquest. His last prize was a peasant woman named Clodia. Her father was killed in a tannery accident, leaving the poor girl with no means of support. Her pretty face and large breasts attracted Stefano like a lodestone. He dressed her in fancy clothes and exhibited her like a trophy until the Venetian ambassador's reception last week, where Stefano found a new object and cast Clodia aside like the others before her."

"Her testimony could be important. Where can we find her?" Nico asked.

"That I cannot say. She lives along the river in the tannery district." Galetto replied and returned to sorting documents.

Massimo was approaching the chancery annex just as Nico and Vittorio were leaving. "Chancellor Scala said I might find you here," Massimo said.

"I trust your time in Pavia was enjoyable," Nico quipped.

Flashing a grin of delight, Massimo replied, "Out of respect for the lady, I will say only that I quenched a deep desire."

After Nico told what they had learned from the chancery notary, Vittorio said, "We are going to question the woman Clodia."

Massimo laughed. "No sane woman will open her door to two strange men."

"This is Florence," Vittorio retorted. "I am a member of the guardia. She will have no choice but to open her door."

Massimo shook his head. "You can force your way into her house, but unless you plan to beat her, she won't speak freely."

"What do you propose?" Nico asked.

"A woman. Send a woman to speak with her." Massimo waited a moment for them to consider his suggestion before adding, "A woman accompanied by one charming man."

"Interrogating people is serious work. Police work. And women are not competent to do policing," Vittorio said stiffly.

"Might the charming man you have in mind be a soldier?" Nico asked. Before Massimo could answer, Nico added, "And where would we find a suitable woman?"

Massimo looked directly at Nico. "From what I know of your sister, she would be perfect. She is intelligent and compassionate, as you yourself have said."

At the mention of Alessa, Nico opened his mouth to protest, then held his words. Massimo might have an ulterior motive for spending time with Alessa, but his idea had promise. Alessa had a gift for drawing people out. She could play the role of a concerned and jilted woman. And Massimo did have a talent for charming women. It took persuasion by Nico and Massimo before Vittorio finally agreed.

41

THE TANNERY DISTRICT, FLORENCE

Via dei Malcontente extended away from the city center to a district along the Arno River, where tanneries and mills spewed out offensive odors. There were no tall palazzos, only a few shops, and the simple homes of Florentine peasants. Massimo, the handsome, broad-shouldered soldier, and Alessa, the dark-skinned woman with chocolate eyes, neared a row of dingy cottages. Nico and Vittorio trailed far behind, resigned to watch from a distance. Massimo glanced at Alessa, "Are you comfortable doing this?"

"No one is better able to understand her abuse than me," Alessa replied.

At one cottage, a heavyset woman was plucking feathers from a chicken carcass. Massimo approached her and asked, "Scuse, Signora, can you tell us which house belongs to Clodia?"

"The poor girl. Always I see her, she has tears. Her father died. A rich bastard made promises." She spat on the ground. "Now the bastard sent her away." The woman pointed to a structure that others might have called a hovel. "There. She lives there."

A fair-haired woman with long blonde curls answered Alessa's knock by cracking the door enough to reveal her puffy eyes and tear tracks. Alessa held out a basket filled with food items from the Uccello and said, "These are for you."

The girl looked down at the basket, then back up at Alessa. "Don't be afraid; I just want to talk with you," Alessa said with a small smile.

The girl slid the door open until she spotted Massimo. Alessa said, "I know your fear. As a girl, I was taken from my family, so I know your pain." She glanced at Massimo. "He is a friend. We brought these to help ease your pain."

Clodia cautiously opened the door enough for Alessa to enter, followed by Massimo. Alessa set the basket on a table and embraced the tense woman. Massimo remained a distance away. Clodia wore a thin cotton dress frayed at the collar and sleeves. Alessa saw no sign of any costly gifts or fancy clothes that Clodia must have worn when she was Stefano's companion. Massimo walked across the sparsely furnished room past two sleeping alcoves to the fireplace. Above it hung bunches of turnips and onions, and a bin on the floor held potatoes. A nearby shelf held a crock of animal fat and a bowl of beans. Massimo took a dish and knife from the shelf, returned to the table, and removed the foodstuff from the basket: cured meat, bread, cheese, almond milk, pear preserves, and eggs. He cut wedges of cheese and meat and a thick slice of bread, which he spread with the preserves. Clodia yielded to the temptation. She took a bite from the cheese wedge, then clasped it in both hands close to her breast.

"Stefano is a weasel," Alessa said. "No woman should suffer for men like him."

Clodia sank down onto a chair and tears welled in her eyes.

"He said he cared for me. He bought me things and took me places. But I should have known. I did not fit with his people. They talked of things, things I did not understand. Look at me; I am nothing."

"You are not nothing," Alessa countered. "You are a good person. Stefano is wicked. He is a criminal."

Clodia stiffened upon hearing the accusation. In a soft voice, Massimo asked, "Did he ever mention Milan?"

"Milan?" Clodia echoed.

"Stefano is responsible for a serious crime in Milan," Massimo replied.

Clodia spoke slowly as she strove to remember details of her time with Stefano. "Once, we were going to a celebration at his guild. He had the driver take the carriage to a place where he could meet a man named Maurizio." The name registered instantly with Massimo as the person Nico believed to be the Intermediary. "Stefano told Maurizio to go to Milan. Something about the wool business." Massimo prodded her to recall the location where the meeting with Maurizio took place, but then backed away from the two women when he saw that his questions were upsetting Clodia.

Alessa gave Clodia time to calm herself, then she asked, "Do you recall what Stefano wanted Maurizio to do in Milan?"

"He said something in Milan could hurt his business. He gave Maurizio the name of a man who could fix the problem."

"Do you remember the man's name, the one who could fix the problem?

Clodia rubbed her hands together as she tried to recall the name. A few moments later she shook her head and said, "No."

Massimo opened his mouth to speak, but Alessa raised a hand, signaling him to hold his thought. "Think again," she said. "It's important."

Clodia closed her eyes. A minute later, she opened them and said, "Pagatore."

Massimo poured apple juice into a cup and handed it to Clodia. He pulled a chair close and sat facing her. In a soft voice, he said, "Pagatore murdered a man and abducted two women. Stefano hired the killer. He is responsible and needs to pay for those crimes. You need to tell a magistrate what you told us."

The color drained from Clodia's face. She began shaking her head. "No! I cannot do that! I cannot face Stefano."

Alessa put an arm around Clodia's shoulders and clasped her hands. Massimo explained, "You will not face Stefano. He will not see you. That is not how trials are conducted. A prosecutor will submit an accusation to the court. If the accusation is accepted, the prosecutor brings witnesses before the magistrates. Testimony is done in secret, so there can be no reprisals. Only the prosecutor and the magistrates will know what is said. Stefano will not learn the names of the witnesses nor what was said to the magistrates."

Clodia stopped shaking her head, but she said nothing.

Alessa leaned close to Clodia and said, "Stefano mistreated you. He is a cruel person. The women in Milan were defenseless. They were taken from their home, and the man who was murdered had a wife and young son. Stefano must pay for these crimes, and he must not be allowed to bring suffering to others. My brother will be the prosecutor at this trial. He will make sure you are protected."

They spoke at length with Alessa and Massimo continuing to reassure Clodia that her identity would be protected. Finally, Clodia agreed to testify. She provided additional information to Massimo and Alessa. When they finished discussing Stefano, Alessa said, "The death of your father and the rejection by

Stefano are terrible things, but you have a whole life ahead of you. Have you thought about what you will do?"

Clodia shook her head roughly. "I have no skills. For women like me, there are only two choices, a convent or a bordello."

"No, those are not the only choices," Alessa insisted. "There are kind families who need servants and nannies. I will return tomorrow with another basket, and we can discuss your future."

Nico and Vittorio listened to Massimo and Alessa describe the information they had obtained from Clodia.

Vittorio beamed. "Excellent. She confirmed the name Maurizio and she told us where to find him."

Nico said, "Her testimony alone would not be persuasive, but hers in combination with Maurizio's should be convincing."

Vittorio and Nico headed to the San Giovanni district to confront Maurizio. Clodia recalled that Stefano had met with Maurizio outside a furrier shop not far from the San Luca convent. Nico knew that area because he passed the convent whenever he visited the Chancery archives. Vittorio saw the shop first. "There," he said, and pointed to a three-level stone building with a shop at street level and apartments on the upper levels.

"Yes, I know Maurizio," the shopkeeper replied when questioned by Vittorio. "His space is above my shop."

Nico and Vittorio climbed to the second level landing and stood outside the apartment. Nico was reminded of their failed attempt to capture the Intermediary in Milan: the Intermediary had already fled the city, leaving a mouse as the apartment's only remaining occupant. Although he could hear no sound from within, Nico hoped this attempt to apprehend Maurizio would be successful.

Using his authority as a Florentine investigator, Vittorio did not knock. He shouldered the door open and stepped into the apartment. The hook-nosed Intermediary, sitting at a desk across the room, turned to face the intruder. His face showed resignation, not surprise. "Investigator Colombo, I expected you would find me eventually, but you needn't have charged in like a bull. I would have answered if you had knocked."

"You are an accomplice to the crimes of abduction and murder," Vittorio bristled.

Maurizio remained seated and laughed. "I carried a message from Florence to Milan. How does that make me an accomplice? I was merely a messenger. When couriers deliver messages, do you accuse them of being criminals?"

Anger built in Vittorio's voice, "If you think this a game, you are mistaken. You did more than carry a message; you hired the killers."

Maurizio smirked. "The crimes you speak of were in Milan. Did the Milanese guardia send you? Do they intend to bring charges in Milan?"

Vittorio, unsure of the legal situation, looked to Nico, who said, "The Florentine Security Commission has the authority to bring charges in Florence for crimes committed in Milan."

"The commission for what?" the Intermediary asked, his bravado fading.

"The Florentine Security Commission was established by the Signoria expressly to deal with these situations. You can be prosecuted here in Florence." For the first time, the Intermediary looked worried. Nico stood rigidly straight with his arms folded across his chest and added, "There is only one way you can help yourself. Stefano Rondelli is ultimately responsible for the crimes. If you testify against Signor Rondelli, the prosecutor will grant you leniency."

"How can you say what the prosecutor will do?"

"Because I am the prosecutor," Nico replied with conviction.

"Then tell me, signor prosecutor, what you mean by leniency."

"Rondelli initiated the conspiracy that caused the death of a Medici bank employee and the abduction of the bank manager's wife. Rondelli must be made to pay for those crimes. Say what you know about him and no charges will be brought against you."

Vittorio pulled Nico aside. "You are willing to let him go free, to avoid paying for his part in the crimes?"

"Without his testimony, there would only be Clodia's word alone against an established Florentine businessman and that would not be enough to convince a magistrate of Rondelli's guilt. I am not happy with letting Maurizio escape punishment for his part, but it is a necessary compromise."

Vittorio growled to show his displeasure, then nodded to express his understanding. Maurizio stood and smiled thinly. "I will tell what I know."

42

TRIAL PREPARATION AND DAY 1

Criminal cases were heard by tribunals under the auspices of
The Eight of Guard. It was midday on a Friday when Nico
made an official filing to inform the Eight's clerk of his intent to
accuse Signor Stefano Rondelli of high crimes. Generally, all
initial filings were sent to a low-level tribunal. Senior magistrates heard only cases of major significance. However, the case
against Stefano Rondelli was exceptional because his crime–his
alleged crime–was not committed in Florence. Low-level
tribunals had no precedents or experience dealing with crimes
committed outside the republic. For that reason, Signor
Corsini, First Chair of the Eight, selected three senior magistrates as the tribunal to decide the case. Late in the day, Nico
received notification that he was to appear before the tribunal
on Monday morning to deliver his accusation.

Nico spent the following two days writing the accusation
and preparing witnesses. He opted to meet with the witnesses
first so he would know the exact content of their testimony
when he wrote the accusation.

As an investigator, Vittorio had testified in many criminal

cases, so he needed no coaching. Nico met individually with Piello Portinari, Maurizio Vannucci, and Clodia Pucci. He told each what the magistrates would expect of them, and he cautioned them to relate only facts and not speculations. Nico scrupulously avoided scripting statements for them to recite. He recalled a warning frequently repeated by his favorite criminal law professor, "Witnesses must deliver their understanding of the facts, not a story devised by their lawyer."

Signor Portinari had returned to Florence specifically to testify at the trial. Portinari took advantage of his time in Florence to meet with bank officials regarding bank business. In deference to Portinari's status, Nico agreed to meet with him in a Medici bank conference room. Nico opted to meet with Maurizio in a well-appointed Chancery conference room because the small office assigned to the Florentine Security Commission might belie the commission's authority. Massimo and two other soldiers were standing in the corridor when Maurizio exited the conference room at the end of his interview. Maurizio stiffened. "What is this? You said I would not be charged with a crime."

Nico stepped between Maurizio and the soldiers. "You will not be charged. These men will escort you to an army camp where you can stay until you deliver your testimony." Maurizio opened his mouth to protest, but Nico interrupted his objection. "It is for your protection. When Rondelli learns that charges have been filed against him, he might deduce that you would be called as a witness. As you know, Rondelli does not hesitate to employ killers to do his bidding." Maurizio nodded his understanding.

"Shall I arrange protection for the other witnesses, Clodia and Signor Portinari?" Massimo asked.

"That should not be necessary," Nico replied. "Signor Portinari and his wife are staying at his father-in-law's vineyard in

Chianti. He travels in a carriage between the vineyard and the Medici bank offices in Florence. That should afford him ample protection. Signor Rondelli will have no reason to suspect that Clodia will be a witness."

To avoid overwhelming Clodia, Nico met with her in the commission's austere office. Nico said, "The magistrates are not enemies; they just want to learn what happened. Tell the magistrates what you saw and heard when Stefano met with Maurizio. The magistrates will be on a platform some distance from where you will be standing, so speak loudly enough for them to hear you."

"Will they ask questions?"

"They might. Answer their questions if you can. If you don't understand a question or if you are unsure what to say, look toward me and I will help you." Clodia practiced her testimony, repeating it several times until she and Nico felt confident that she could deliver a coherent message to the tribunal.

On Sunday morning, Nico attended mass with his family. Then he spent the remainder of the day preparing his accusation. Formal accusations set forth the charges against the accused and they detailed the steps taken by the accused in committing the crime. They were crucial because no other charges could be added during the trial, and witnesses could only testify to support charges that were included in the accusation. An entire course at the university was devoted to preparing accusations for a range of civil and criminal matters. Nico spent Sunday afternoon reviewing the copious notes he had taken during that course, but they were of little help because the cases considered in class were simple crimes such as theft and assault. The case against Rondelli was far more complex. Nico

wrote a first attempt and then revised it until it was almost
illegible. His fourth attempt finally resulted in a document that
pleased him.

Trial day 1

On Monday morning, Nico walked alone, deep in thought,
from Casa Argenti to the courtroom where a lone notary sat
waiting for the magistrates and the accuser. Accusations were
always made in private to protect the identity of witnesses, so
there were no spectators in the gallery. Nico gave his name to
the notary, confirmed that he was the accuser, and took a seat.
Several minutes later, a side door opened, three magistrates
filed in and took positions on the raised platform at the front of
the room.

As soon as they were seated, a gray-haired magistrate whom
Nico did not recognize announced, "Under the authority of the
Eight of Guard, this tribunal is convened to hear an accusation
by Messer Nico Argenti representing the Republic of Florence.
Messer Argenti, you may begin."

Nico stood and read his prepared accusation:

Before you, Honorable Defenders of Justice, on behalf of the
Republic of Florence, I enter this accusation against Signor
Stefano Rondelli, a citizen and resident of the parish of San
Cristofano of Florence. From trustworthy sources, it has been
learned that Stefano Rondelli acted to obstruct the business
of the Medici bank in Milan, and through that act instigated
the abduction and murder of an honorable and respected
Florentine citizen and the abduction, confinement, and
maltreatment of two innocent women.

Stefano Rondelli, having learned that the wool guild in the Duchy of Milan intended to import high-quality fleece from the Kingdom of Castile, determined that such arrangement could adversely affect the operation and profitability of his wool merchandising business. To prevent this arrangement from being consummated, Stefano Rondelli conspired to prevent the Medici bank branch in Milan from financing the business arrangement.

To carry out this crime, Stefano Rondelli dispatched a courier to Milan to engage the services of a criminal agent known to Stefano Rondelli and to convey instructions for abducting, intimidating, and threatening the manager of the Medici bank in Milan. Those actions resulted in the abduction and murder of the head bookkeeper of the Medici bank, Signor Salito Salvetti, a respected citizen of the Republic of Florence. Subsequent actions following from Stefano Rondelli's instructions resulted in the abduction of Signora Portinari, the wife of the bank manager, and her maid.

After Nico finished reading the accusation, he remained standing while the magistrates spoke with each other. Minutes later, the gray-haired magistrate asked, "You have witnesses prepared to testify?"

"Yes, witnesses and a sworn statement."

"Sworn statement?"

"The abductions and murder occurred in Milan. An official in Milan has information pertinent to this case. He cannot travel to Florence, so he has provided a statement sworn before a magistrate in Milan."

The magistrate stroked his chin. "But sworn statements do not allow for questioning of the maker by this tribunal."

Nico responded quickly. "I understand that admitting

sworn statements is unusual , but I ask the tribunal's indul-
gence in the interest of justice."

The magistrate turned to his colleagues. They conversed
briefly; then he said, "The statement may be introduced, but we
reserve judgment on whether it will be accepted as evidence.
We will hear testimony from the witnesses tomorrow. Provide a
copy of the accusation to the recording notary."

The magistrate turned to the notary. "Have Signor Stefano
Rondelli informed that he has been accused of crimes and
provide him with a copy of the accusation. Inform him that he
has five days in which to appear before this tribunal to present
his defense. This tribunal will reconvene tomorrow."

Nico waited for the magistrates to exit before he left the
courtroom and walked the short distance to the Uccello. It was
too early for lunch, and Mondays were the least busy days of
the week, so the restaurant was empty of patrons when Nico
entered. Donato beckoned Nico to a table at the rear of the
room. "You look tired, cousin, and it is yet early in the day. The
lawyer business must be demanding." Donato poured a glass of
bright yellow liquid and held it out to Nico. "This potion will
restore your spirit, my special mixture of grappa and lemon
juice. Now sit and tell me what weighs on you."

Nico sighed as he lowered himself into a chair. "As Caesar
once said, 'the die is cast.' I presented the accusation against
Rondelli to the tribunal. The magistrates asked no questions.
They wish to hear testimony from the witnesses tomorrow."

Donato looked perplexed. "You are ready, and the witnesses
are prepared, so what troubles you, cousin?"

"What if the witnesses are not well prepared? This is my
first prosecution as a member of the Florentine lawyers' guild.
If I have forgotten something, I will forever feel myself a fool."

Donato place a reassuring hand on Nico's shoulder. "This is
not your first appearance before a tribunal. You held forth

before the Privy Council in Milan. Your training at Bologna has prepared you well to practice here in Florence. I am confident you will perform admirably."

"Thank you for your kind words. I wish that I shared your confidence."

Donato laughed. "Drink the remainder of the lemon-grappa and your confidence will return."

43

TRIAL DAY 2

When Alessa entered the kitchen, Nico sat at the dining table staring into space and ignoring the half-eaten breakfast roll on a plate in front of him. "Your aura is less bright than usual. You are troubled," Alessa observed, as she placed a crock of raspberry preserves on the table.

Her words drew him back to the present. "I'm just thinking about the trial. Trying to guess what questions the magistrates might raise, so I'll be ready to give cogent answers."

Alessa moved closer and looked down at him. "Your eyes are red. Did you not sleep last night?"

Nico smiled thinly to acknowledge her concern. "One unknown disturbed my rest. I can't guess what Signor Rondelli will say in his defense. I don't believe he will plead guilty to the charge, but if he does not, how will he defend his actions?"

"Will he be offering his defense today?" Alessa asked.

"No, he will be given a transcript of today's proceedings, including the witness statements; then he will have several days to prepare and present his defense."

"So, you need not worry about his defense today. Push that

worry to tomorrow," Alessa said as she bent and kissed him on the forehead.

Nico spread raspberry preserves on the half-eaten breakfast roll and changed the subject. "Thank you for agreeing to conduct Clodia from her home to the courtroom. She did well composing her testimony in the practice session, but having you accompany her to court will give her confidence."

Courtrooms for criminal cases were located in the Palazzo del Podestà. Adjacent to the courtrooms were several interrogation and interview rooms. During trials, those rooms held witnesses whose identities were being protected while they awaited their turn to testify. Two of the five witnesses Nico intended to call, Clodia and Maurizio, were sequestered in interview rooms. The three remaining witnesses, Signor Portinari, Vittorio, and Signor Matteo da Vigo, a consul of the Florentine wool guild, sat in the gallery. Neither they nor Nico felt that their identities needed to be hidden. Signor Portinari requested that he be allowed to testify first, so he could attend a meeting being held at the Medici bank. Nico acceded to Portinari's request, even though the case might have unfolded more coherently if Portinari had been the second to speak.

The session began with the senior magistrate declaring, "The tribunal hearing accusations against Signor Stefano Rondelli is in order." He turned to face Nico and said, "Messer Argenti, you may begin."

Nico straightened his tunic and ran a hand through his hair to smooth any errant strands. He rose, stood tall, and made eye contact with every magistrate before speaking. He had repeatedly practiced the opening words for this, his first appearance before a Florentine tribunal. "Honorable magistrates, you will hear from five accusers and be presented with two sworn statements to demonstrate that the defendant, Signor Stefano Rondelli, initiated a conspiracy to disrupt the operation of the Medici bank and that the consequences of his actions make him an abettor to the crimes of abduction, involuntary confinement, maltreatment, and murder. The first witness, Signor Piello Portinari, is the Medici bank branch manager in the Duchy of Milan. He will describe the nature of the bank business targeted by the defendant."

Nico signaled to Portinari, who moved from the gallery to the witness box. "Signor Portinari, describe the financing arrangement between the Medici bank and the Milanese wool guild."

Portinari explained that the guild requested financing to enable the importing of merino wool from Castile. When Portinari finished, Nico said, "When the financing proposal was being created, the bank, and you personally, experienced a series of reprehensible events. Describe those events to the tribunal."

Portinari recounted the abduction of Signor Salvetti and concluded by saying, "He was an excellent employee and a personal friend." Next, Portinari detailed his wife's abduction. He paused several times when the memory of her ordeal made it difficult for him to speak.

Nico said, "Tell the court how those terrible incidents are connected to the business arrangement between the bank and the wool guild."

After describing the events, Portinari said, "This message that was left for me when my wife was taken."

He gave the note to Nico, who read it aloud. "You will receive instructions. Follow them, and your wife will be returned. Talk with the guardia, and you will not see her again."

The words brought forth gasps from the magistrates. When they quieted, Portinari continued, "A messenger delivered this message to me the following day."

He passed the second paper to Nico, who read, "If you want your wife returned, withdraw the proposal to finance wool purchases from Castile."

The notary delivered both notes to the magistrates. Each one stiffened in turn as he viewed the notes. One magistrate asked, "Has your wife recovered from that terrible experience?"

"I'm not sure she will ever recover. She is afraid to be left alone. Every time she hears a noise she stiffens with fear."

When there were no further questions, Nico dismissed Portinari who scurried from the witness box and out of the courtroom, hoping that he would never have to recall the painful memory again.

Nico called his next witness. Addressing the magistrates, he said, "This witness is a consul of the Florentine wool finishers guild. He will tell why Castilian fleece is critically important."

The rotund consul walked to the witness box and smiled at the magistrates. After being introduced by Nico, he began speaking, "Our members serve customers in France, the Levant, Austria, Saxony... everywhere. Our success depends on delivering the finest quality finished wool cloth, and to do that, we must begin with the finest raw cloth. Merino sheep have the softest, most luxurious fleece, which results in the softest, most luxurious wool cloth. Our members prefer to obtain raw cloth from Florentine weavers." He spread his hands, palms up. "They are our brothers in commerce, but we will be forced to buy from Milanese mills if those are the only source of merino cloth."

Puzzled by the consul's statement, one magistrate asked, "Why are your members unable to obtain merino wool from Florentine weavers?"

"Merino sheep are bred only in Castile. We understand that the organization of wholesale wool merchants in Milan has entered into an exclusive arrangement with the Kingdom of Castile, so merino fleece will not be available to Florentine weavers."

The magistrates listened with rapt attention as the threat to the Florentine wool industry became apparent. Nico smiled inwardly, pleased by the magistrate's keen interest. He turned to the witness and said, "Tell the magistrates what impact will this arrangement have on Florentine wool merchants like Signor Rondelli."

The guild consul shrugged, as if to suggest that the answer should be obvious. "Merino wool is of higher quality than the English wool processed by shops in Florence, and the cost of shipping merino fleece from Castile to Milan is much less than the cost of shipping English fleece to Florence. Signor Rondelli and other Florentine wool merchants will be at a serious financial disadvantage."

The magistrates buzzed with clipped conversations. Nico waited until the conversations faded before continuing. Then, having put the motivation in perspective, Nico turned to the crimes themselves. "The next witness is a distinguished investigator of the Florentine Guardia and member of the Florentine Security Commission, Signor Vittorio Colombo."

Vittorio, who had considerable experience testifying at trials, strode confidently to the witness stand. He needed no prompting. He began by describing the wanton murder of the bank accountant. His report of the abduction and confinement of Signora Portinari and her maid, in greater detail than Portinari's account, stunned the magistrates. Several remarked to the men beside them as Vittorio was speaking. Vittorio refrained from mentioning the sordid details of Signora Portinari's ordeal, but his reticence prompted a stream of questions from the magistrates, questions they hesitated to ask Portinari. Was she mistreated? How long had she been held captive? Where was she held? How was she rescued?

In response to the last question, Vittorio gave full credit to the Milanese army. "The women were freed by soldiers led by Captain Osvaldo Ghetti of the Milanese Army. The person responsible for killing Signor Salvetti is now in prison; his accomplice remains a fugitive. Men under Captain Ghetti's command also apprehended the agent who hired the killer."

As Nico and Vittorio had pre-arranged, Vittorio stopped speaking at that point, and Nico rose to address the magistrates. He held out a document. "This is a sworn statement taken in Milan that summarizes the confession of the person who killed Signor Salvetti and abducted Signora Portinari."

The senior magistrate waved his hand and said, "You may read the statement."

Nico began,

"On the twenty-fourth of November, Signor Pasquino Pagatore was taken into custody by officers of the Judicial Unit of the Army of the Duchy of Milan. He has admitted that a person known to him as the Intermediary paid him to retain the services of men to prevent the Medici bank from financing the purchase of merino wool. We have obtained written instructions given to Pagatore by the Intermediary. The instructions state that the men tasked with the job must stop at nothing to prevent the financing. The men contracted by Signor Pagatore abducted and murdered Signor Salvetti, a citizen of the Republic of Florence. Subsequently, they abducted Signora Portinari, a citizen of the Republic of Florence, and her maid, Signorina Arcimboldo, a citizen of the Duchy of Milan.

"The statement bears the signature of Milanese Army Captain Osvaldo Ghetti. Below is a declaration that the above statement was sworn under oath. The declaration is signed and marked with the seal of a district magistrate of the Duchy of Milan."

Nico handed the document to the court notary and announced, "The remaining two witnesses will be testifying in secret." Vittorio and the wool guild consul rose and exited the courtroom. At Nico's request, the notary conducted the Intermediary into the courtroom.

Maurizio wore a smug expression as he sauntered to the witness stand, confident that his willingness to testify was saving him from prosecution. Nico glared at Maurizio as a warning for him to exercise restraint. Then, he introduced the witness, saying, "This witness is Signor Maurizio Vannucci, also known to his associates in Milan as the Intermediary. He was dispatched to Milan by the defendant and told to instruct Signor Pagatore to abduct Signor Portinari."

The senior magistrate signaled Maurizio to begin. "The defendant, Signor Rondelli, sent me to Milan to deliver two messages. The first message told Signor Pagatore to have the bank manager abducted. The second message was for the bank manager after he was abducted. It demanded that the bank stop funding the merino wool purchase."

The brevity of the Intermediary's testimony left the magistrates with many questions. One magistrate, baffled by the narrative, asked, "Do I understand correctly, you delivered a message that instructed someone to commit a crime?"

"I am a courier. I transport messages and items as requested by my clients. I do not pass judgments on their business," Maurizio answered crisply.

"Did the message to Signor Pagatore say that he was to stop at nothing?"

"I do not recall the exact wording of the message, but that was the essence."

"You were told by the defendant to take whatever steps were necessary to prevent the Medici bank from funding the purchase of merino wool. Is that correct?"

"Yes, Signor Rondelli would accept no excuses. He insisted that the bank be stopped from funding the wool purchase." The magistrate looked to Nico for an indication that Maurizio would be prosecuted for his role in the crimes. Nico remained stone-faced. Maurizio caught the look and almost smiled, confident that he had been granted immunity.

Another magistrate asked, "Why did the defendant select you to deliver the messages?"

In a flippant tone, Maurizio replied, "I do not know his thoughts. You will have to ask him for his reasons."

The magistrate continued, "Did the defendant give you Signor Pagatore's name? Did he tell you how to find Signor Pagatore?"

"Yes, Signor Rondelli gave me Pagatore's name and told me how to find him."

"When the abduction of Signor Portinari failed, who decided to abduct his wife?"

"I don't recall. It may have been the men hired by Signor Pagatore, or perhaps Pagatore himself," Maurizio lied. He knew the magistrates would never learn that it was he who had decided to target Signora Portinari. There were no further questions, so Maurizio was dismissed. He left the room with the same smug expression as when he entered.

Next, Nico called Clodia Pucci. He escorted her to the witness box, gave her a minute to adjust to then tense situation, then asked her to describe the meeting she had witnessed between the defendant and Signor Vannucci. Clodia gripped the witness stand with both hands to steady herself. She began tentatively. "Stefano was taking me to a celebration at his guild. On the way, he told the carriage driver to take us to Via del Giardino because he had to speak with someone. When we arrived, Signor Vannucci joined us. I learned his name because Stefano said his name when he sent the driver to fetch him. We remained seated in the carriage, and when Signor Vannucci appeared, he stood outside while the men talked. Stefano said, 'They cannot be allowed to bring that damn fleece from Castile. It could ruin me. The funding must be stopped.' Those were his exact words. Stefano handed an envelope to Signor Vannucci, who nodded and said he would leave for Milan in the morning." Her short testimony had quickened her breathing, and she trembled, but her words were persuasive. There were now two witnesses accusing Stefano Rondelli.

The magistrates, sensing her distress, asked only two questions. "Was that the only time you met Signor Vannucci?"

"Yes."

"What is your relationship with Signor Rondelli?"

She looked down and said softly, "I was his inamorata, but that is ended."

Nico waited until the notary escorted Clodia from the chamber, then he stood and addressed the magistrates. "Witnesses have described the crimes committed in Milan and testified that the defendant instigated those crimes. Therefore, I ask that you find the defendant, Stefano Rondelli, guilty of all charges detailed in the accusation."

The senior magistrate instructed the notary, "See that a transcript of these proceedings is delivered to the defendant by the end of the day." Then he declared, "This trial is in recess."

Nico exited the courtroom through the side door and went to the interview room to meet with Clodia and Alessa.

Nico smiled. "Yes, I am pleased. Maurizio Vannucci gave reasonable answers to the questions, although he could have been more deferential to the court." Nico looked directly at Clodia. "You were excellent. The question about your relationship with Stefano was unexpected, but you answered it perfectly."

"The magistrate said that Stefano will receive a transcript. Will my name be mentioned? Will Stefano learn that I testified against him?" Clodia asked, her voice trembling with concern.

"No, he will not learn your name. Witness secrecy is important. Notaries are skilled in writing transcripts to preserve the anonymity of witnesses," Nico replied.

The three exited the Palazzo del Podestà and walked along Borgo dei Greci. The fresh air outside was welcome after sitting in the stuffy courtroom. Nico did not even pull his cloak closed. When they reached Piazza Santa Croce, Nico stopped in surprise to see the two women turn right and head toward the river. Seeing his perplexed expression, Alessa announced proudly, "We are going to Armando's silk shop. Clodia works there helping the women who operate the looms."

Armando, a friend whom Nico called by his childhood tag name Bluffo, owned a business that made silk cloth. Several women worked at his shop, operating spindles and looms. "Alessa introduced me to Armando," Clodia said. "I started working there yesterday."

"Bluffo is a good person. He will treat you well. Give him my regards," Nico said as he turned left toward the Uccello.

44

TRIAL DEFENSE

"Why must I be here? I'm paying you to represent me," Rondelli complained.

Messer Tomasso Deti ran a hand through his silver hair and grimaced. It may have been a mistake to accept this client, he thought. Deti was regarded as one of the most capable criminal defense lawyers in Florence. His legal practice centered on representing men charged with violent crimes from assault to murder. He found this case intriguing because Rondelli was not charged with committing a violent act himself; rather, he was accused of inciting others to violence.

Florentine law was derived from Roman law, which assumed that every man was responsible for his own actions. Under Roman law, a man who commits a violent act bears the entire guilt. Over time, laws had been broadened to allow guilt to be shared among complicit parties. That interpetation gained acceptance and became embodied in Florentine statutes. Deti intended to argue that the broad statutes were not relevant in the case against Rondelli.

Appearance of the magistrates spared Deti from his client's persistent grumbling. As soon as the magistrates took their positions on the raised platform, the senior magistrate announced, "This tribunal is in order. Messer Deti, are you representing the defendant, Signor Stefano Rondelli?"

Deti stood. "Yes, with your permission, I will represent Signor Rondelli."

"Have you received a copy of the accusation and a transcript of the witness testimonies?"

"Yes, I have."

"Signor Rondelli, do you accept Messer Tomasso Deti as your legal representative in this matter?"

Deti bent down and said to his client, "Stand when addressing the tribunal."

Rondelli rose and said, "Yes, I am paying Signor Deti to be my lawyer."

The magistrate asked, "Signor Rondelli, you have seen the accusations against you. How do you plead?"

Rondelli looked toward his lawyer and then back toward the magistrates. "Not guilty."

The senior magistrate declared, "Messer Deti, you may begin the defense."

Deti rose. "Honorable magistrates, the accusation alleges several crimes were committed. Let us consider them in turn. First, the accusation claims that Signor Rondelli sought to obstruct the business of the Medici bank. Use of the term 'obstruct' implies an illegal act, but that contention is not supported by the sworn statement, which states that the intent was to 'prevent' the Medici bank from financing the wool purchase. There are many perfectly legal ways that the Medici bank might have been prevented from completing a funding arrangement. As an example, another bank might have been encouraged to underbid the Medici bank proposal. Prevention does not equate to obstruction. Moreover, the accusation states that the obstruction was to be carried out by abducting the bank manager, an event that never happened."

Rondelli smiled. His lawyer was earning his substantial fee.

Deti continued, "The formal accusation and witness testimonies cite abductions and the murder of a bank employee. Signor Rondelli and I share the views expressed by the witnesses that those acts were reprehensible. When one man encourages another to commit a crime, both men share the guilt. However, none of the witnesses testified that Signor Rondelli directly instigated crimes of abduction, confinement, or murder. Signor Rondelli neither told anyone to commit those crimes, nor did he encourage anyone to commit those crimes. The men who committed the terrible crimes did so of their own volition. I ask that Signor Rondelli be acquitted."

Deti returned to his seat. Stefano leaned back and folded his arms across his chest, satisfied with the points made by his lawyer.

The senior magistrate asked his associates if they had any questions for Messer Deti. Hearing none, he announced, "This tribunal is adjourned for deliberation." The magistrates filed out of the chamber.

The magistrates adjourned to a nearby conference room, where they removed their judicial robes and enjoyed light refreshments before beginning their deliberation. They were eager to discuss the case while the facts were fresh in their memories. They had copies of the formal accusation and a transcript of witness statements. Each man also had his own notes taken during Messer Deti's presentation.

The three men selected to serve as magistrates all had extensive experience in criminal law. All three came from prominent families respected for their long service to the Republic. Orlando Buselli, the senior magistrate, not only had the most magisterial experience; he was also the oldest of the three. He was the first Florentine to earn a law degree at the University of Pavia. Matteo da Seano was a shy man with a small private law practice. He had served several times as a consul of the lawyers' guild. Jacopo Tafi, the youngest of the three, held doctorates in both civil and canon law. He had a modest private practice and taught law at the University of Florence.

Orlando began the discussion by asking, "Does it trouble anyone that this case pertains to crimes committed outside the Republic?"

"I have no problem judging this case," Matteo began. "All cases heard by the Mercanzia court involve disputes between merchants. Most of those disputes involve ships and cargoes in foreign ports, so there is precedent for Florentine tribunals to adjudge crimes and civil actions that occur outside the Republic."

Jacopo nodded and said, "The Signoria created the Florentine Security Commission specifically to deal with threats originating in other jurisdictions. In my view, it follows that tribunals in Florence have the responsibility to act on the Commission's findings."

"Are we agreed that this tribunal has the authority and duty to render a judgment in this case?" Orlando asked. The others nodded. "Then let us begin by considering the prosecution's case."

"The statements made in the accusation were well supported by witness testimony," Jacopo said. "The first witnesses summarized the importance of the Castilian wool.

Signors Portinari and Colombo described the crimes, and the final witnesses testified to Signor Rondelli's guilt."

Matteo nodded. "I agree, Jacopo. As a new lawyer without an experienced associate, Argenti presented a well-structured case."

Orlando asked, "Should we admit the sworn statement as evidence?"

Matteo replied, "It was clearly identified in the transcript as a sworn statement, not a witness statement, and Deti didn't object to its being included as evidence. Also, the statement provided background and corroboration for Signor Vannucci's testimony, but it didn't introduce any new allegations. I see no reason for the statement to be excluded from consideration."

The three magistrates concurred with Matteo's view. No other issues were raised concerning the prosecution case, so Orlando asked for comments about the defense presentation. He began by providing his own observation. "Deti effectively demonstrated that means could be taken to dissuade the Medici bank without necessarily resorting to illegal measures."

"I agree; Deti refuted that point," Jacopo said. "I was surprised that Deti didn't counter the testimony that his client wanted to have the bank manager abducted. Deti merely dismissed that issue by saying that the abduction did not happen. While that is true, I am left believing that Rondelli was certainly willing to instigate a crime."

Matteo said, "Deti didn't dispute that the other crimes did happen, the abduction and murder of the bank employee and the abduction of the two women. He claimed only that Rondelli didn't explicitly authorize or instruct anyone to commit those crimes. But Rondelli did send Vannucci to Milan to hire men and order them to 'stop at nothing' to prevent the Medici bank from financing the wool purchase."

Orlando declared, "The question before us is whether

Rondelli's apparent willingness to sanction one crime plus his instructions to 'stop at nothing' constitute grounds to find him guilty of the other crimes." Matteo and Jacopo nodded. "To answer that question, each of us needs to review relevant precedents and scholarly opinions. I propose that we reconvene in two days to render our verdict."

45

VERDICT

Striding through the corridor toward the commission office, Massimo caught sight of Vittorio. Inside the office, the investigator stood facing a wall arrayed with note cards. Each card contained a single piece of information reported to the chancery by Florentine envoys and embassies. On a table near Vittorio were variously colored yarns. Massimo watched as Vittorio pulled a blue strand from the pile, fastened it to one of the note cards, then stretched it to attach its other end to a second notecard. "Both of these items relate to unusual activities in Austria," Vittorio said aloud to no one other than himself.

The overcast sky let little light enter through the room's small windows, so Massimo almost missed seeing Nico, who was sitting quietly in a dimly lit corner. Massimo slid a chair beside Nico, sat, and placed a hand on the lawyer's shoulder. "You should be happy. The trial went well, and soon you will be traveling to Siena to spend time with Bianca. The thought of spending time with a woman always raises my spirit. So, why do you look troubled?"

"I keep thinking about the trial and wondering whether I missed something... something that would have made the case more persuasive."

"All that was missing was testimony to show how Rondelli learned about the negotiations taking place between Milan and Castile, but finding Rondelli's source would have taken time. It would have meant delaying the trial." Massimo turned toward the investigator. "Vittorio, you have testified in many trials. Do you believe the trial should have been delayed until we discovered Rondelli's source?"

Vittorio finished placing a length of yellow yarn and then turned to face his colleagues. "No, it rarely matters how criminals get the information that leads them to commit their crimes. Their actions alone are sufficient to convict them. Your case was well prepared. I have seen many experienced lawyers who would not have done as well."

"It also troubles me that Maurizio will bear no responsibility for his actions," Nico said, "The magistrates seemed surprised that Maurizio was not being charged. Was I too lenient in waiving prosecution in exchange for his testimony?"

"You were more lenient than I would have been, but your decision was not without precedent," Vittorio replied. "Lawyers often bargain to get the cooperation of a key witness, and Maurizio's testimony against Rondelli was crucial. Rondelli and people like him are the ones who finance the criminals. Now that we know Maurizio's role, he may lead us to others like Rondelli."

Conversation stopped when a clerk entered the room and cleared his throat. "Chancellor Scala would like to see you in his office."

"All of us?" Vittorio asked.

"Yes."

~

Scala was standing facing a wall covered with notecards when the three commissioners entered his office, but his wall lacked the colorful yarns favored by Vittorio. He motioned for the men to be seated at his conference table. "The magistrates have reached a verdict in the Rondelli trial. They judged him guilty of instigating the abduction of the bank clerk and the two women. They decided that Rondelli's instruction for the criminals to 'stop at nothing' inspired the abductions even though he did not explicitly name the victims." Scala paused briefly before adding, "However, the three magistrates did not agree that his guilt should extend to the clerk's murder."

Scala scanned the men's faces to gauge their reaction. Only Vittorio responded by shaking his head to show his displeasure that Rondelli was not convicted of Salvetti's murder. Nico and Massimo watched Scala intently, waiting for him to report the punishment. "Rondelli was sentenced to a fine of three thousand florins and two years imprisonment."

Again, shaking his head, Vittorio said, "He'll probably appeal the sentence asking that a greater fine be substituted in place of prison time. All wealthy bastards do that. Our prisons hold only the unfortunate poor who cannot pay."

In a dispassionate tone, Scala said, "Our legal system does allow that course. While Rondelli won't be punished for the murder, you can take solace in knowing that the one who killed Signor Salvetti is imprisoned in Milan."

Scala leaned forward and placed both hands on the table. His eyes lit up as he spoke. "The Signoria is extremely pleased with the outcome of the Florentine Security Commission's first assignment. They received a letter from Signor Portinari in which he credited your actions for saving his wife. He said that were it not for your efforts, his wife might have met the same fate as Signor Salvetti."

Massimo interjected, "Captain Ghetti of the Milan army also deserves credit. He responded quickly to our request for assistance." Vittorio nodded his agreement.

"Did you receive any report about our activities from the Florentine ambassador?" Nico asked.

"No, I did not. And that is unlike the ambassador. He usually communicates in detail about everything happening in Milan, especially about events that displease him." Massimo winked at Nico, who returned the gesture with a quick grin.

Scala leaned back. "Another matter has surfaced that deserves your attention; however, since you have been away for many days, you may have personal matters that need tending. I propose that you deal with any personal issues and that we meet again in four days to discuss your next assignment. Is that agreeable?"

The three commissioners glanced quickly at each other before nodding in anticipation.

EPILOGUE

Siena

When Manzio and Dorena Cellini, Bianca's parents, heard that Nico would be visiting Siena, they invited him to dinner at their apartment. Dorena's butcher saved a shoulder roast from a wild boar he had butchered that morning. Dorena bought vegetables at the central market and bread from a nearby bakery. Manzio purchased wine at a nearby enoteca, and Bianca made dessert. Tradition held that Nico, as the honored guest, should not contribute, but Nico, like the Cellinis, eschewed social constraints. Before leaving Florence, he had stopped at the Uccello to secure a sack of Turkish figs to be served as a nibble before dinner.

Rather than heading directly to Dottore Cellini's apartment, Nico met Bianca at her loft. He wanted at least a brief time alone with the woman who filled his dreams. Bianca's face beamed as she pulled open the door and wrapped her arms around Nico. He pulled her close and kissed her full on the lips.

Her fragrance warmed him as their tongues danced together. For a long moment, the world did not exist.

Nico took a step back to burn the image of her lovely face into his memory anew. Bianca rested her head on his shoulder and said softly, in hardly more than a whisper, "I'm so glad you are safe. I was worried. You put only good news in your notes, so I can never tell if you are well or injured."

Nico returned her smile and replied. "I have no wounds. Later...after dinner...you can see for yourself." From the pocket in his tunic, Nico withdrew the necklace with the brilliant red stone and fastened it around her neck. "It is a garnet from the Alps north of Milan."

Bianca looked down, then holding Nico's hand, she led him to a mirror where she could view the stone. She squeezed his hand and kissed his cheek. "It's lovely."

Nico bent and kissed her neck. "It is more lovely because you are wearing it."

Bianca resisted the heat that flowed between them and said, "My parents are expecting us. I am eager to hear about your time in Milan, but my parents, too, wish to hear about your appointment to the new commission. We should go."

On their way out of the apartment, Bianca fetched the dessert she had made. As they crossed the central piazza and approached the dignified Gallo district, Nico said, "I would like to know what you have been doing while we were apart."

Bianca danced a few steps along the street and said in joyous tones, "Princess Isabella of Castile wore the dress I made for her at her thirteenth birthday celebration. Isabella's mother, the queen consort of Castile and Leòn, sent a letter to thank and compliment me for the gift. She said that her daughter looked charming wearing my creation. Word spread quickly among women who attended the celebration, and now I am overwhelmed with requests from them to make dresses for their daughters. I have had to hire two more girls to help with the sewing. One request is from the wife of Piero de Medici. She wants a dress made for their daughter, Nanina. I will be going to Florence next week to meet with the girl and her mother to learn their preferences for styles and colors."

Nico brightened at the prospect of seeing Bianca again the following week. Now that I am a practicing lawyer with an appointment to a Florentine commission, he thought, it may be time to talk about our future. Next week, he said to himself.

When they reached Via della Fonte, they climbed to Dottore Cellini's apartment on the second level above the pharmacy. Manzio opened the door, embraced his daughter and then Nico. Nico kissed Bianca's mother, Dorena, on both cheeks and handed her the bag he carried. "Ah, figs," she said excitedly. "The last time I tasted figs was in Naples. They are not available at the market here in Siena."

She took Nico by the hand and led him into a modest sitting room furnished with a cluster of cushioned chairs. An arrangement of three books between matching glass figurines displayed on a side table caught Nico's eye. Manzio moved beside Nico and rested his hand on Nico's shoulder. He said with pride, "They are copies of the Tortula texts written in Salerno two hundred years past. They were the first treatises on women's illnesses and are still the standard of practice today. That set was presented to me when I left my teaching position at the university's medical school." He motioned toward the seating area. "Come, let's have some wine."

As Manzio filled their wine glasses, he said, "Bianca told us that since you last visited with us, you were inducted into the lawyers' guild, appointed to a government commission, and sent on assignment to Milan. I passed through Milan once on my way from Paris to Salerno. My time in the city was brief and unremarkable. I suspect that your time in Milan was more eventful. We are eager to hear about your journey if you are free to share the information."

Nico began by describing the abductions of two Florentine citizens and the murder of one. His accounting of the hunt for the perpetrators held the Cellinis spellbound. Nico's pulse quickened as he told of his appearances as a prosecutor before a district magistrate and a representative of the Milanese Privy Council. "Pursuing killers must be dangerous. Weren't you afraid?" Dorena asked.

Nico took a sip of wine before replying. "My fellow commissioners are skilled in dealing with dangerous criminals. One of them, Massimo, is a decorated soldier, and the other, Vittorio, is an experienced investigator, so I never considered myself in danger. This was our first assignment, so it took time for us to learn how to work together and trust each other. By the time we returned from Milan, we complemented each other well."

Bianca said, "Perhaps I can meet your colleagues next week when I am in Florence." Nico gave a slight nod that only admitted the possibility of a meeting. He didn't know whether Massimo and Vittorio had already made plans for their time, and he wasn't sure that he wanted Bianca exposed to the handsome soldier.

Nico continued the story by telling how evidence gathered in Milan led them to a conspirator in Florence. He finished by recounting the trial of Stefano Rondelli. "I called witnesses who detailed the crimes and their motivation, and two accusers who implicated Signor Rondelli as the person who instigated the crimes. The witness testimony was strong, but I didn't know how the defense would approach the case, so I was unsure of the outcome. I wasn't allowed to be present during the defense, but I learned afterward that the defense tried to prove that Rondelli didn't directly instigate the crimes."

Nico paused until Bianca gave him a friendly poke and said, "Don't keep us in suspense. What was the verdict?"

"The magistrates found Signor Rondelli guilty of inciting the abductions, but they did not find him guilty of murder. They levied a fine of three thousand florins and sentenced him to a two year prison term."

Manzio shrugged. "It seems a small price to compensate for the loss of a life."

"True," Nico agreed, "but that is not the only punishment that he will suffer. The Medici bank was furious at being the target of his exploit. They vowed that no Florentine bank will deal with the Rondelli merchant company until Stefano Rondelli is removed. It is now his father, Guido Rondelli, who must deal with his wayward son."

While Nico spoke, Dorena had been gazing at her daughter's necklace. After Nico finished speaking, Bianca smiled and touched a finger to the necklace. "It's a garnet," she said. "Nico brought it from Milan."

Dorena moved to take a closer look. "It's beautiful!" she exclaimed; then began laughing. "I noticed it the moment you came into the apartment. I was wondering when you were going to mention it." She turned to her husband. "Thanks to Nico, Milan is now a safe destination, so we should spend our next holiday there. I could use some new jewelry."

ABOUT THE AUTHOR

Ken Tentarelli is a frequent visitor to Italy. In travels from the Alps to the southern coast of Sicily he developed a love for its history and its people. He has studied Italian culture and language in Rome and Perugia. At home he has taught courses in Italian history spanning time from the Etruscans to the Renaissance. When not traveling Ken and his wife live in New Hampshire.

∽

What was life like at a Renaissance university?

Sign up for our newsletter at http://KenTentarelli.com/nicos-story and download -free- *Nico's path through the University of Bologna* in his own words.

ALSO BY KEN TENTARELLI

The Laureate: Mystery in Renaissance Italy

(Nico Argenti book 1)

Nico Argenti returns from the university to find Florence, his beloved city, gripped by power hungry aristocrats. He is drawn into the turmoil and must uncover the conspirators and thwart their hired assassin before it is too late.

The Advisor: Intrigue in Tuscany

(Nico Argenti book 2)

Nico Argenti uses his legal training to help a small mountain town outwit a vindictive knight who has little respect for the law. He travels to Lucca to locate documents from the papal archives then to Chianti to interview displaced refugees before confronting the rogue knight.

Made in United States
North Haven, CT
10 July 2023

38789815R00203